'The feeling [illegible] subterranean, images rising to the surface to be caught by the sun. The sound of voices — distant then near. The sound of one voice, in its own key, singing the dream into daylight. This is Kunal Basu. Listen to him' Jeanette Winterson

'At a historical level, the novel occurs along the trail of opium. At a personal level it happens in the lives of many people in many lands . . . spiritually the novel happens at the level of desire, in all its multifarious manifestations' *Oxford Times*

'Basu spins a complex, captivating tale, weaving in dreams and visions in a manner reminiscent of Gabriel Garcia Marquez or Salman Rushdie. The historical backdrop is dazzlingly evoked. This is not a straightforward historical novel, though: the chronology of Hiran's experiences is uncertain, so let go of your linear outlook and get swept away' *www.ivenus.com*

'Basu has found a fresh angle . . . The blend of personal discovery and political revolt is handled with authority' *Independent on Sunday*

'Basu has a gift for conjuring up scenes' *South China Morning Post*

'Basu's White Calcutta of the late 19th century is as real as the Daniells at Victoria Memorial. Similarly, you can almost walk through Basu's Black Calcutta — the brothels of Boubazaar, the narrow winding alleys — the smell of the frying jalebis, the sweet, putrefying garbage in the gutters and the jasmine garlands the baboos take to their women. Basu's writing remains luminous through the journey' *The Statesman*

'Just one whiff is enough. You don't have to be an opium addict to savour the slow burning languor of the sticky-sweet saga of the opium trade that Kunal Basu places before you. There is nothing timid about Basu's intentions. He has opium in his blood' *India Today Magazine*

'This is a story of many journeys, real and metaphysical. The reader is seized by a fascinated restlessness. The list of books at the end of the novel suggests to the reader the bedrock of concrete historical material over which Basu weaves his winding tale, crowded with vividly imagined moments, strange encounters, fleeting conversations and lovingly chosen detail' *The Telegraph* (Calcutta)

'In *The Opium Clerk*, Basu has bravely explored virgin ground. The novel leads us through a labyrinth of mysteries and perplexities, which was indeed the once thriving colonial underworld' *The Times of India*

'This novel marks a major turning point for a comprehensive human archetype capable of absorbing into the fiction mode the complexity and uniqueness of the expatriate experience' *Deccan Herald*

Kunal Basu was born in Calcutta but has spent much of his adult life in the USA and Canada where he taught at McGill University. He currently teaches at Oxford University's Templeton College. *The Opium Clerk* is his first novel.

The Opium Clerk

Kunal Basu

PHOENIX

For Chabi and Sunil Kumar Basu

A PHOENIX PAPERBACK

First published in Great Britain in 2001
by Weidenfeld & Nicolson
A Phoenix House Book
This paperback edition published in 2002
by Phoenix,
an imprint of Orion Books Ltd,
Orion House, 5 Upper St Martin's Lane,
London WC2H 9EA

A CIP catalogue record for this book
is available from the British Library.

ISBN 0 75381 339 4

Printed and bound in Great Britain by
The Guernsey Press Co. Ltd, Guernsey, C.I.

All is clouded by desire . . . as fire by smoke, as a mirror by dust, as the unborn by its mother.

Krishna in *The Bhagavad Gita*

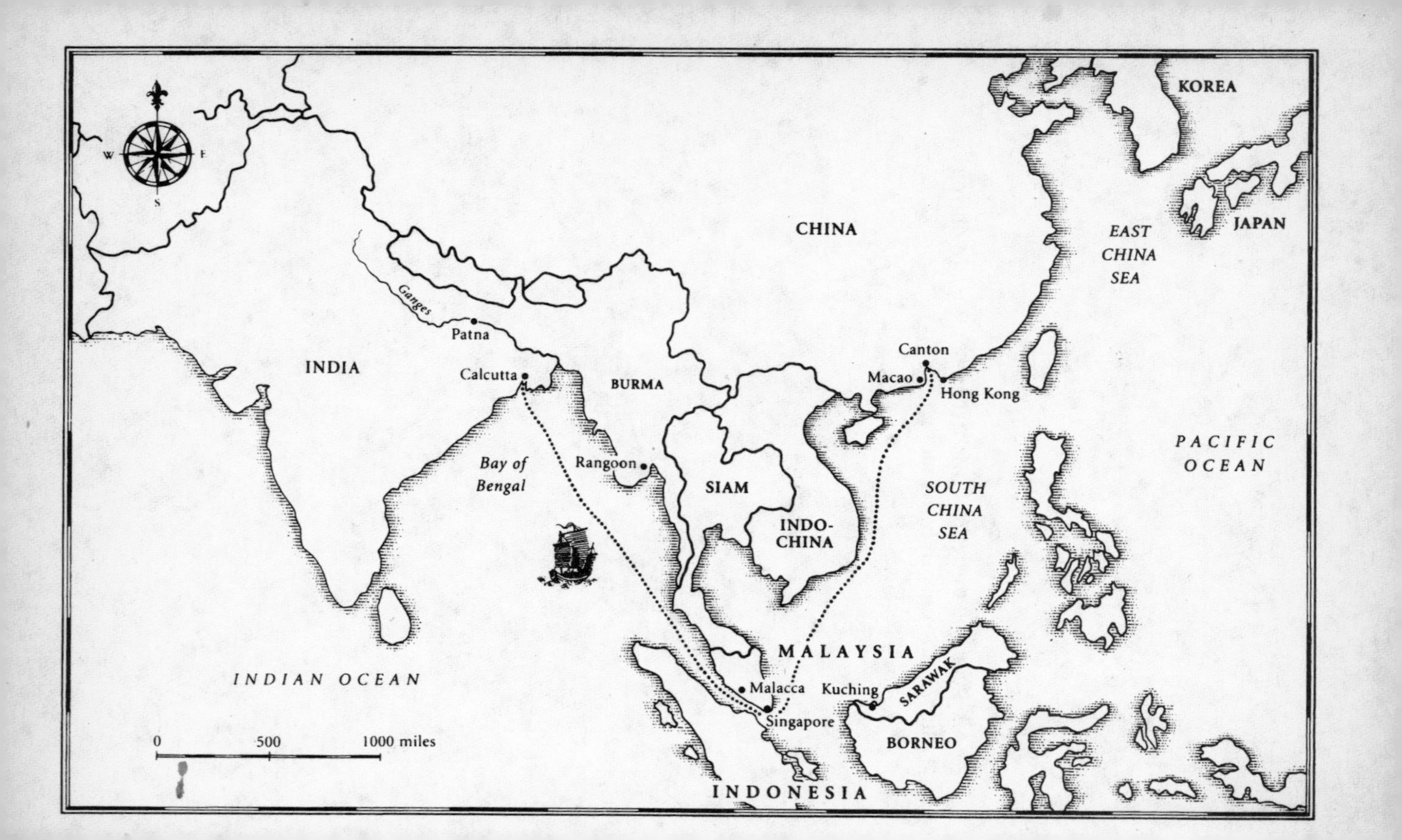
W
E
S
KOREA
JAPAN
CHINA
EAST
CHINA
SEA
INDIA
Ganges
Patna
Calcutta
BURMA
Canton
Macao
Hong Kong
PACIFIC
OCEAN
Bay of
Bengal
Rangoon
SIAM
INDO-
CHINA
SOUTH
CHINA
SEA
MALAYSIA
INDIAN OCEAN
Malacca
Kuching
SARAWAK
Singapore
BORNEO
INDONESIA
0
500
1000 miles

Calcutta

His Life-line was shorter at birth. Palms side by side, he could see both lines clearly. The one on the left hand – wrought by birth – dipped gracefully below the index finger. Shrouded by undergrowth, it skirted the arc of Venus without a care, then, just above the wrist, tapered out into a small island. A period of delicacy . . . he worried. A sudden fatigue?

The one on the right – wrought by action – was less precipitous. He took comfort in its unbroken passage – neither too red nor too pale, too broad nor too thin – crossing bumps on a flat Plain of Mars, it circled the thumb easily. He had to turn his hand over to find its end.

Why was the line on the right longer? he would muse. A life extended for its own reasons? For quite a while it remained the only mystery in an open journey through fate, engaging his mind as a breeze engages the sails. What, he'd ask himself, had lengthened his years, and why?

In appearance, his hands were remarkable: a rare example of the Exaggerated Conic, with small and delicate fingers pointed like young lotus leaves, skin smooth and clear, lines muted in reverence. To these hands belong a field of dreams. In them one finds the Line of Intuition – the third eye, *La Croix Mystique* – indicating a love of the occult. And, unmistakably, the mark of the Ring of Solomon, distinguishing the true instinctive from the sensual, the inspired from the egotist, the noble from the impostor.

'Most desirable, but useless,' his teacher would sigh till the young lotus leaves turned moist. He had known other pupils with such palms: heavenly errors – children of benevolence and melancholy, devotion and curiosity. One needed only to look into the palm of a beggar to see their fate. Some would start well, weather a poison wind, then succumb later to a life of bitter solitude. Others would offer the most inspired poetry, yet the world would invariably cast them as failures. Some, by a strange confluence, might manage to hold the reins of power. Even so, their dreams would come to nothing. A few, and the teacher had known some in his time, chose the delicious fantasy of suicide.

A weak beginning and end, with a solid middle. Now in his thirties there was nothing to trouble him – a quiet sail between one receding monsoon and another approaching – a solitary Conic returning home from his desk at the Auction House each day to his mother. It was in the Auction House, at his window facing the river, that he'd stop to inspect his palms, hold them out to the fading light. Here, among other signs, he saw an affinity of opposites – Saturn and the Moon – that usually corresponded to the bearer's unsightly appearance. He knew himself to be the exception to that rule, not by virtue of a correcting mark or a salutary mount, but by the providence of his name.

He was rarely reminded of Patna, the city of his birth. For one thing, his mother was not keen on reminiscence. Her memories were those of distress – of losing one and gaining another. It made it difficult for her to remember a happier time, when she had minded a small household with a small but assured income. Her husband was a priest, or a priest's apprentice rather, and neither of them was in a hurry. From their relative comfort, Saraladebi and Jyotirmoy dreamt of greater comforts, longed for a few extras such as a yearly visit by the marvellous steam loco to her father's house in Calcutta. She had planned to give birth to her child, her first, in the small attic on the roof of their house there in Jaanbazaar, tended by her mother's favourite nurse. Jyotirmoy had readily agreed to the arrangement. A successful priest needed a son. He was more anxious than she about the birth.

This was the time of the Mutiny, and travel at such a time seemed unreasonably hazardous. The sepoys would ignore her, she thought, but what if they trained their weapons on the white engine-driver? For Jyotirmoy, even his wife's bearing was a target, of looters and lustful men. Coffrees, lower castes, Mussalmans, Mistizos, half-n-halfs. 'They'll go after the engine-wallah first,' he said. 'Then rob the other passengers.'

They decided to err on the side of prudence, remain in Patna till the child was born. There'd be other occasions.

If she had cared, Saraladebi could have remembered those last four months before her son was born as a period of unusual calm, of blissful routine. Each morning, Jyotirmoy left for his patron's home, his absences and returns bringing them closer to each other than ever before. She could have remembered the hours they spent discussing a name for their son, their roles for once curiously reversed – she the devout, and he the everyday heretic. Nothing short of the trinity would do for her son.

'Well, how about Asurs?' he'd quip.

'Name my son after a headless monster!'

'But remember, the Gods come looking for demons to tame, not pious women!' Didn't she want to invite divine visits? But the fact was, Saraladebi didn't care if the devil rode his chariot over their home, as long as her son had an auspicious name.

As Saraladebi and Jyotirmoy locked themselves together, the Mutiny drew closer. Its cannons and howls could no longer be drowned by the gentle gush of the Ganga's current. Fires appeared behind the gnarl of trees that surrounded their small home. But they had no real cause for fear as Jyotirmoy left in the morning for his patron's house. They knew that before long they would board the marvellous steam loco. As the devil came riding his chariot, Jyotirmoy was in the middle of the Parade Grounds making his way back home with a cradle of offerings. The British soldiers leading the charge at dawn against rioting sepoys might have attempted to swerve, might have overlooked a solitary brahmin lost in thought. But the hoofs had done their damage in no time. Jyotirmoy's dying thoughts were, as always, on the one who lived inside the womb.

Hiranyagarbha, they called him, the Golden Embryo, his name chosen by Jyotirmoy's senior priest. And, although he rarely had occasion now to think of Patna, it had given him his name. He was born on the very day of his father's death – 14 June 1857. *Panic Sunday.* A posthumous child born in a year of calamity.

'What does it mean?' Saraladebi asked in a hushed tone, covered from head to toe in widow's white. The senior priest started quoting from the *Rig Veda.* 'In verse seven, He seems to appear after the waters. In verse nine, the waters appear from Him. In His belly, the golden seed lies like an egg. A seed of fire is placed in the womb – it is the embryo that impregnates the ocean.'

'Which God is he?'

'He is the Unknown God.'

In a few years he had become Hiran, Hiroo, Hiranbaboo to friends and fellow clerks at the Auction House. Only the senior priest in his letters to Saraladebi stuck to the original. The priest was also the first to examine the boy's palm. It was he who first saw the Exaggerated Conic. To Saraladebi, since then suspicious of her trinity, he was simply Hira – the glittering diamond.

Even after six years at the Auction House, Hiran frequently lost his way. The Auction House sat on a gentle curve of the Strand, with the river as its neighbour. From its vantage, it kept watch on two significant points of reference – the Kidderpore docks two miles downstream, and the pontoon bridge just round the corner. Another river flowed through its chambers, disgorging people like great shoals of fish, and a tide of paper, files, trays, stacks floated from one room to another. To Hiran, paper was the source of all confusion. Every room in the east wing had its share, jostling among desks and cabinets, each recipient intent on leaving his own mark: writers, clerks, assistants, baboos. It changed form frequently: emerging from an envelope bearing unfamiliar stamps, it might make the round of the tables, then disappear into a file that held more of its kind. Turning dark corridors on a chaprasi's head, it went up a flight or two to yet another sun-filled room facing the river. Here it would gracefully age – soot-black ink turning to rust – until the day of judgement arrived. Then, it would be rescued, a mad search scattering clouds of dead insects, riding back once again through dark corridors to shine on someone's desk as on its first day, fawned over by delighted eyes, back to clinch a point or two. Frequently, its reappearance marked something significant: a settlement or cancellation, a discharge, even a sentence of death.

A calmer river flowed through the west wing. Here the

European department heads had their offices. Only the very best made it here, arriving in envelopes with grand insignias. The air was cooler, allowing the ink and paper fragrance to linger.

To Hiran, the entire Auction House seemed like a giant machine devouring its daily ration of paper – reading, marking, stacking, losing and recovering at regular intervals. Anonymity cast a spell over them all; every chamber, file, tray and cabinet, every head stooped over its desk appeared to be one and the same. He often had trouble finding his room again after a stroll by the river during tiffin-break.

In the beginning, Saraladebi had shown resolve. She had decided to apprentice her Hira to Jyotirmoy's senior. She saw a little boy memorizing scriptures, a little priest with his sacred thread, running barefoot to the temple of a wealthy patron. The senior priest had reasoned with her. 'The boy must grow in a natural way, among his own kind.' He had pointed out the dangers faced by widows living alone with their infants, and urged her repeatedly to return to her father's home in Calcutta. By then she had come to her own conclusion anyway: her Hira was not a natural priest. She'd spend hours looking into his eyes wondering where his mind was. He was not gifted in memory – the rote of learning slokas tired him. The priest had tried an early dose of grammar: the precision of Sanskrit failing to impress. But he was not boisterous, rather withdrawn, sweet in his shyness. An unusually large forehead gave an indication of piety quite irrespective of early failure.

In resignation, Saraladebi came back to Calcutta, to live in her father's home in Jaanbazaar, with her boy of seven. A returning widow. She had asked for, and received, the least – the attic on the roof, her old quarters. Here, she would spend a life of moderation, conjure visions of Hira's future, tread the predictable road of a Hindoo widow under the benign gaze of a distant queen.

*

For Hiran the move to Calcutta was fortunate. First, the residue of his mother's priesthood ambitions took him to the tole – the religious school – in Ahiritola. Saraladebi had confided in her youngest and most sympathetic brother, railing in part against her destiny and expressing suspicion at the senior priest's motives in turning away Hiran. She doubted his sincerity, his hasty judgement on Hira's future. She felt robbed. 'Who can replace a dead father?' Mahim had comforted her and carried Hiran on his broad shoulders to the steps of the tole. He had put him down and smiled. 'This is where others have brought you. You may enter, if you wish.' It was Hiran's earliest memory of his uncle.

Hiran took an instant liking to his teacher. A tall man with sharp eyes, he spoke in a sing-song way, and appeared not the least ruffled by the cacophony of young voices that filled his modest home. On his first day, Hiran was given a clay bowl for periodic ablutions, a mat of raw cotton, several palm-leaves, and strict instructions on hygiene. Unused to friends, Hiran would frequently drop his eyes before the other boys or look away when speaking. Before long they would mimic his rustic tongue, breaking into an uproar when their teacher stopped to correct his *s*'s. Didn't he know the difference? The soft *s*, like a hiss; *sh* – the granular; and the unlikeliest of them all – *sm*. Saraswati – the Goddess of learning; Shiva – the God of destruction; and S(*m*)asti – the Goddess of fertility.

To Hiran, they were all the hissing kind. His studies reminded him of earlier bouts with the senior priest in Patna: Grammar and Rhetoric, Metaphysics and Astronomy, Law and Logic. Only the *Panchatantra* was different. Listening to the teacher's sonorous voice reading stories from the five tantras, his mind grasped a vital link between fable and song. He liked them all. The story of the jackal and the hermit, the cobra and the crow, the heron and the crab, the lion and the hare, the bug and the flea, the story of the potter, of the merchant and his young wife, of the four learned fools. Riding back on Mahim's shoulders, he recited them for his uncle just as he had heard them. Often, he'd begin with his favourite: the story of *Uddhata*, the singing donkey.

'In a town there lived a donkey that belonged to a washerman. During the day he carried the washerman's loads, at night he wandered the fields. One night he met a jackal, and together they broke the fence of a farmer's garden. While the jackal gorged on poultry, *Uddhata* ate the cucumbers. Stomachs full, they began discussing their lives. Looking up at the full moon and a beautiful cloudless sky, the donkey felt like singing. He asked the jackal, "Tell me, which raga shall I sing?" . . .' From his perch, Hiran saw a field of black heads as Mahim wound his way through crowded alleys. They passed afternoon markets selling cucumber and poultry, fish, crab, and sides of freshly slaughtered lamb. Hiran would forget his story in the face of the wonder of wonders – a horse-drawn tram: shrill hooting, crack of whips, blind-folded animals. While they waited, stuck in a crowd before a temple or caught in a marriage procession, Hiran's mind would lose its haul of Grammar and Rhetoric, Metaphysics and Astronomy, Law and Logic.

On Sundays the regime was different. They rose early. Hiran would sit cross-legged on a cotton mat on their roof before Saraladebi's watchful eyes memorizing his prayers. The *Gayatri* first, of course:

tat savitur vareniam
bhargo devasya dhgmahi
dhiyo yo nah pracodayat

Let our prayers begin under the glorious sun, may his light enter our minds . . . His voice would grow tired and halting, losing the subtle cadence the teacher had struggled to instill. From slokas to simple poetry, his voice emitted less than melodious cuckoos. At last, it would be time for his uncle Mahim to wake. He would call across the terrace to his nephew, 'What does the donkey sing this morning?'

*

Strolling by the river at tiffin-break, Hiran's mind races back to the cucumber field. '"My friend," said the jackal, "you have come to steal and you'll only be asking for trouble if you sing. Besides, your singing isn't all that pleasant. If you wake the farmer, he'll come and beat us." When the donkey heard this he said, "My dear, you're a wild animal, you wouldn't appreciate the value of music. According to *Bharatamuni*, music consists of seven notes, three scales, twenty-one modulations, forty-nine rhythms, and three speeds. Ragas and raginis must be sung at the proper time, and in season." Then, the sleeping farmer heard the donkey braying. Running to the field with a stick, he struck without mercy. He hung a heavy wooden board around the donkey's neck. So, wherever *Uddhata* went, people knew he was nothing but a rotten thief.

'*He who has neither common sense, nor listens to his friend, is sure to be punished.*'

His uncle had offered a different moral: 'He who sings under the autumn moon will triumph over heartless enemies.'

There was something besides stories that drew Hiran's attention from his studies. Sitting before the teacher each morning memorizing slokas, he watched a steady procession enter and leave the room: men, old and bearded, women with heads covered, pompous baboos in gold-framed glasses, baniyas in conical hats, villagers with big toes blackened by mud. They would bow before the teacher – the younger ones touching his feet – and sit across from him on a mat of raw cotton. Then, they would spread out their palms. With furtive glances, Hiran followed his teacher's gaze. He'd hear the breath of the visitor quicken – sense a meek surrender overcome even the proudest kneeling before his teacher hands outstretched. Sometimes it would take a long time, his teacher turning the palms over as if searching for missing treasure. A frown sent the visitor into a serious of nervous coughs. Finally, when the sing-song voice broke the silence, there were sighs of relief as if the worst was over.

The teacher told stories to his visitors. With some he would patiently explain, others he reassured, or dismissed with a few words. Visitors had their stories too, amazing Hiran by their sudden confessions – a thief admitted his theft, a weeping widow her adventure, a father confessed to feigning disease, a son to plotting against his father.

Each morning he heard their stories. He saw a lying king, a brave servant, a pious wife, weak fathers, barren couples, passionate lovers. And to each story he found an apt moral. As his admiration for his teacher grew, Hiran saw in him the greatest gift – of discerning a true story from a field of simple lines. He was struck by the mystery of the palm. And began colouring the tale of the ox, the crab, the fowl, and the serpent with their human complements, unknown to his uncle.

It was then that he started paying attention. Gradually, the palm revealed itself. The fleshy mounts at the base of the fingers turned into heavenly abodes: Jupiter, Saturn, Mars, Apollo, Venus, Mercury, and the Moon. Each finger displayed three unique worlds within the narrow scope of three phalanxes. Besides key lines, he learned the value of influence lines, sister lines, forked heads, hearts, islands, grilles, and stars. True acknowledgement of the thumb came soon after. From his seat in the corner it took him longer to diagnose nails. He learned to imagine the hands, sense their strength without laying a finger. He could gauge almost anything from dark shadows cast on bare walls, except the amount left under a silver betel-nut cracker by the window.

Mostly, the palm appeared before his eye like the pattern of silken thread woven by Saraladebi on milk-white cotton. The image would draw him forward and he'd begin to see. In this he was bold, he liked to leap, sensed the music of the palms. He read them as stories – without a plan, allowing them to absorb him in their own way. At nine, after barely two years at the tole, he made his first prediction. Sitting by the teacher on the morning of *Janmastami*, he held up his own palms before his eyes, and in a rustic tongue mixing up his *s*'s, he said, 'A long life ended by a wound to the heart.' His teacher looked up from a book of slokas and smiled.

The other boys were amazed by Hiran's gift. They thrust their palms, sweaty after a game of catch, or snotty, red from warm ablutions or sticky with jilipi, and sat solemnly before him. He would begin with a simple pattern, then go deeper. Some waited patiently till the end. Others goaded him: 'When will I get married?' 'How rich will I be?' 'Will my grandmother live or die?' 'When will the teacher finish with me?' Those happy with his answers offered bits of jilipi, or brought a brand new English pen from home the next day. Some offered to write his essays, or to do his calculations. Once he received a mohor – a gold coin – with the mark of the Emperor on its face for predicting that a boy would have a younger brother soon. Sometimes the sessions would end in fights: he'd see a liar's hand, or a cheat's. In small radiant palms he would detect illnesses beyond cure. Staring at Raju – scion of the Rajahs of Shobhabazaar – he spelt out a conclusion: a bastard. With a bloody mouth he tried describing the boy's mount of Mercury. His teacher rescued him. Applying lime-paste over a scraped lip, he corrected his pupil. The mount wasn't everything. One needed to trace the forks that flowed down the rolling meadows. Hiran's aggressor could well have been a somnambulist instead.

That afternoon his uncle was told to take him home. His lessons at the tole were over. They should find other pursuits for him. 'Such as?' Mahim was curious. Perhaps he could learn to write plays for the Emerald Theatre, or sing devotional kirtans with kirtaniyas. The teacher explained with his usual kindness: the boy was a dreamer.

Riding back on his uncle's shoulders, Hiran forgot the blows to his face. Nor did he suffer at the thought of leaving the tole. His thoughts, if any, dwelt on his uncle's amused face. He seemed genuinely pleased at Hiran's talent and made no fuss about the untimely end of his priestly career. Making their leisurely way through crowded alleys, Mahim had held up his own palms against a falling light. 'What do you see, Hiroo?'

He had seen a shoal of dark heads swimming in a golden current.

Next, it was the turn of the mission school. 'You'll return to gaze upon my corpse!' Saraladebi cried. Her eyes had grown accustomed to the comings and goings of Kestans, Keranees, and Kintalis living in Jaanbazaar. She was no longer amazed to see alien forms on neighbouring rooftops, or pass them in the narrow lanes. Half-castes – with blue eyes and nails blackened by low-caste blood, half-sahibs, the children of drunken sailors, or of officers and their coolie women. Many were the sons of whores. These are the ones, she said, whose children flock to the mission school to learn *The Bible* and become disciples of Jisu, while their women dress in funny skirts and foolish topis. And what would they teach him? 'He'll learn to be an engine-wallah, a tailor measuring up dirty memsahibs, he'll become a cobbler . . . yes, a brahmin's son will polish the hide of dead cows!'

'He will learn to read and write English.'

'And what good will that do him?'

'For one thing, he could become a clerk at the law court. Or an assistant in a big company. A lot better than staring at palms for four annas on the pavement before Madan Mohon Jiu's temple.'

He heard his uncle laugh, and recite a poem he couldn't follow. Then, he looked at Hiran and winked. 'Maybe he'll learn to write like Byron.'

'Byron?'

*

On days when Hiran returned from the tole with a bruised lip, Saraladebi would complain about her son taking after his uncle. 'He'll turn out a good-for-nothing, just like you!' She accused Mahim of straying from his own kind: a brahmin's son eating beef, dressing up like a white monkey, spending his days with those who cared more for English than the scriptures, and nights God knew where. She would gesture with her eyes towards the north-east, where Boubazaar merged into Kenderdine's Lane, where nights were known to be lively.

His uncle would laugh at the exaggeration but at first Hiran believed her. On their walk to the tole they never stopped at the many temples on their way. Besides that, he knew very little of Mahim's life. In fact, in the first two years of their acquaintance, his uncle had kept him at a distance, given little in return for his *Panchatantra.* An attentive listener, Mahim could enter a story at will, surprising Hiran with clever twists and turns: 'Imagine now, a silent village at night, the farmer snoring in peace. A daring gang of bandits arrive at the fencing and plan a murderous attack. Only birds and animals are roused by their whispers. Each, in its own way, sounds an alarm . . . the farm-rat, the pregnant cow, the fowl, the cunning jackal. In his dream, the farmer hears them all. He sleeps all the more soundly. Familiar noises fail to wake him. The donkey, meanwhile, stares at yet another full moon in a cloudless sky, and in self-pity begins to sing the *Malhar.* The farmer is instantly awakened. Fearing an attack on his cucumbers, he rushes out to his field just in time. He raises an alarm that wakes the whole village.'

To illustrate, his uncle sang the *Malhar*, and Hiran had willingly discarded the rumours that tinged Saraladebi's tirades.

Mahim's attitude changed from the moment Hiran enrolled at the mission school. He opened, just for Hiran, the tall glass windows of his quarters that warded off the other residents of their house. On his first day in his uncle's study, Hiran saw books – stacked in piles, opened and marked, rising and falling with snores by the pillow. He saw shirts with fine fronts and cuffs tousled over armrests of chairs, Scottish tweeds, navy blue serge, cord coats and matching waistcoats. Still unschooled, he failed to detect the scent of a smouldering Java cheroot. He knew his uncle was a student at the Presidency College. Rumour had him preparing to leave on a long journey – across the seas to his favourite England.

A white plaster bust stood on Mahim's desk: a man with curly hair and a girlish face. Mahim had smiled at Hiran, then in a voice still blunt with sleep recited the full ten verses of *Love's Last Adieu.*

For the next four years he became a student at his uncle's tole. The mission school was to be a mere diversion. He started by gazing at books he couldn't read, books with strange titles and strange names – Bacon, Hume, Paine, Bentham, Voltaire – copies of the *Calcutta Gazette*, and the *Calcutta Chronicle*, with his uncle's long hand in their margins. Even before learning the alphabet, he could recite names in the portrait gallery – David Hare, William Carey, Gerasim Lebedeff, Henry Louis Vivian Derozio. Returning from school, he would tackle Mahim as he bent over a thick volume. 'How can you be sure of the non-existence of God?' 'Can man's free will triumph over nature?' 'Will education alone free a superstitious mind?' 'Is it necessary to worship cows to be a good Hindoo?' He'd pick up the smouldering cheroot as he waited for Mahim to answer, draw it close to his nostrils, making a face. Sometimes Mahim had harsh words for him – pointing out errors on his spelling sheet. Or, he would open pages from Murray's grammar, ask Hiran to explain passages underlined in red.

Every evening Saraladebi made him bathe, to rinse away the evil spell of the mission school and its assorted Eurasians. And so, with every splash of the bucket, DaCostas, Vincents, Seals, Hormusjis, Ezras, and Paladians flowed down the drain-pipes to the open sewers of Jaanbazaar. Yet all the while her favourite heretic sat across the terrace injecting a more lethal poison. She seemed powerless to protect her Hira.

'If a man will begin with certainties, he shall end in doubt,' his uncle recited from Bacon, then read aloud passages from *The Age of Reason*, ending the evening with Danton: 'Truth, truth in all her rugged harshness!' But his uncle's glass cases held not simply the alien but a familiar Iswarchandra, Hemchandra, Bankimchandra, Nabinchandra. Climbing on the mahogany cabinet, Hiran found the two in embrace – both still unintelligible. Staring at the painting of a boy on the wall, barely older than himself, dressed in gold and frippery, he was reminded of Mahim's praise: 'Derozio is the greatest of them all.' Hiran learned how the half-Portuguese trouble-maker, poet, and leader of Young Bengal had died of cholera at twenty-two, not far from their home in Jaanbazaar.

The best lessons happened not in his uncle's study, but at the theatre. On these days, Mahim would discard his ash-stained aachkans, whipping up a storm of orders that sent servants scurrying to steam, iron, brush, polish, restore the glory of fine outfitters – the likes of Ramsay Wakefield, Cuthbertson and Harper, even the native Girish Chunder Dey & Co. Hiran saw his uncle in a variety of hats – Ellwood's black silk terai being his favourite. Then, they would ride a hired ticca-gari to Beadon Street, Chourangi, or Jorasanko. The circus was their excuse to Saraladebi, and although they frequently passed the waterproof pavilion on Amherst Street, the 'Great Monster' failed to entice.

Hiran saw his first play, *The Enchanted Tree*, at The Emerald – Calcutta's most famous theatre. He enjoyed the intermissions best. Ginger ale straight from Belfast, and hot buns made from American flour served by the Great Eastern Hotel. In the darkness of the theatre he saw faces writhing in laughter or leering – the actresses, he was told, were whores from their very own Jaanbazaar.

Then, there was The Corinthian Theatre – a favourite of the British officers. Hiran sat with Mahim in the special section marked for natives and cheered the visiting English comedians, laughed at the foibles of 'The Bengalee Baboo'. Afterwards, they had to search for their hired ticca-gari in a forest of elegant phaetons.

It was more exciting at The Star – the newest of the halls – which opened with *L'Elisir d'Amore* on Duke of Connaught's Day, with Mahim and Hiran jostling for seats.

On the way home, they had to pass Boubazaar's infamous alleys teeming with brothels. Usually, Mahim would steal the show, flapping his hands at an invisible enemy. He would astonish Hiran by denouncing the evils of caste. He would rail too against the practice of burning widows. 'Just like the Middle Ages!' The polygamous weren't spared either as Mahim spoke of the shame of the Hindoos. 'Men marrying brides as young as their daughters!' His uncle showed no such disgust for the English. 'No, not the English, Hiroo. It's only brainless baboos who stand between us and a glorious future.'

In the course of the year, as they rode their ticca-gari back in the middle of the night, Hiran began to revel in their arguments. In their walks through the vice-lined streets of Boubazaar, it didn't occur to him to press Mahim for personal details, except to ask, 'Is it true that you've taken beef?' Once again, his uncle had laughed and, unknown to Hiran, borrowed from Derozio: 'I am not a greater monster than most people!'

His mother's ritual – seeking blessings from numerous residents of their house before every test of merit – supplied the only bond with other members of the family who shared the Jaanbazaar house. In part, this was because Saraladebi was worried about the influence Hiran's cousins would have on his young rustic mind. She was conscious too of the taboos surrounding a posthumous child. 'The boy is inauspicious,' she heard murmured in the corridors. Mother and son hid themselves on the roof of the teeming house, with no neighbour but Mahim – himself hiding among books in his quarters. Hiran knew that they were poor in a once affluent family which had grown rich acting as an agent to the East India Company. Now, the ancestral pot was riddled with holes, feeding a great variety of dependants and a remarkable stable of idle servants. Every Saturday, stooped over her embroidery, Saraladebi would try to distract Hiran from his latest book borrowed from Mahim's library. She'd remind him quietly of her savings. It was a way of signalling approaching adulthood, of telling him that in a short while their livelihood would become *his* concern. Bitterness over her fate would sometimes intrude. She was resentful of Jyotirmoy's patron in Patna. They had plenty of tears for her after her husband's death, few items of compensation. She would smile remembering their departing gift – a brass vessel shaped as an urn. Scattering Jyotirmoy's ashes over the Ganga, the senior priest had let it slip through his fingers. He had promised to bring her another. Saraladebi had gently refused: 'Pray God never sends me more ashes.'

Hiran learned to detect her anxiety. He too knew the exact count of gold bangles, tiaras, necklaces and rings in their safe, and the exchange offered by pawnshops in Boubazaar. It would be hard, they knew, for mother and son to last the years left before his uncle's vision of a company salary came true. Yet thoughts on savings, gold bangles and diamond rings could not keep him occupied for long, he was anxious to return to his stories.

He was indifferent to the friendly gestures of the Brothers at the mission school. In the beginning he was asked to visit the Baptist Church at Lalbazaar on Sunday mornings to sing hymns with other boys from Hindoo households. Hiran was praised for his recitation and encouraged to inaugurate school functions with readings from the Bible. There were offers to join the Debating Society. Despite his quiet aloofness, the Brothers encouraged him to talk about the burning issues of the day, such as, should widows be allowed to remarry? Boys at the school made fun of the proximity of his home to Boubazaar and his ignorance of nautch girls. From the roof, they'd bet, he could pry into the intimacy of baijees from Lucknow, hill-sluts from Nepal, insatiable Coffreesses, pink and yellow Chinese. They sang bawdy songs that made his thirteen-year-old cheeks blush.

A Parsee boy, whose father dealt in salt, betel, and tobacco, took him to Cossitola – the fashionable shopping district for

Europeans. Walking nervously along the pavement, he saw shops selling everything imaginable: jewellery, crystal lamps, cricket bats and tennis rackets. Christmas cards hung over silver chains at Newman & Co., ice-water pitchers made from white metal reflected the sun. They passed Mr Pinchback's shop with its pictures and gilt frames, and toys that could be wound with a key like a clock – ballerinas turning circles inside a glass jar, squeaking white mice, butterflies. In one afternoon, Hiran saw his first photograph, his first piano, chandeliers, and, as he would later recall, blue and white trade porcelain from China.

They stopped for Signor Peliti's famous creation on their way back – chocolate buns shaped like the dome of Saint Peter's. This, and the theatre, was the beginning of secrecy – the beginning of his care in protecting his mother from her son's unpardonable sins, such as gorging himself from a foreigner's hand. He was less discreet over the trip to Ballygunge Maidan on a Sunday with his Parsee friend to watch the pigeon shoot. They had travelled – he for the first time – in a horse-drawn tram, spending extra for a cushioned seat. But the massacre turned his stomach. Dismayed, he watched the baskets emptied before a group of well-dressed Europeans, shut his ears with both palms as shots and cries filled the air.

The clash between the two worlds – the righteous mission school and his irreverent uncle – left him stranded. It was a strange result, as if the two balanced each other out exactly. Contrary to Saraladebi's fears, Hiran remained uninfected, casting his lot neither with priests, nor rebels. In the end he learned to recite the *Gayatri* without a flaw and, much to his mother's surprise, returned from school with a gold medal for elocution.

Later, Hiran would remember a trickle of blood by the nostrils that had escaped his attention the night he and his uncle returned from their only visit to the circus. It was a quiet walk uninterrupted by arguments. Silence made them alert to voices that seemed to grow out of raindrops. Without umbrellas, as usual, their faces glowed. In the friendly darkness, they stepped easily over puddles, avoiding rickshaws in the narrow lanes. Yet they were never far from light, or voices.

Unknown to themselves their pace had slowed. Hiran sensed a strange calm. Mahim had withdrawn too. He seemed to be brooding, as if intent on an exceptional puzzle. From time to time they'd hear a flutter – steps running down long corridors inside dark, shapeless houses. Hiran heard strains of music, was reminded of baijees from Lucknow. For a while he searched for hill-sluts and Coffreesses among the forms lining the doorways. He was tempted to stop, ask Mahim if it was true . . . that the women were really serpents from *Panchatantra* – poor things whose loves had been so shattered that none could draw them out from the ant-hills.

He saw men enter and leave the houses. From their gait he knew some to be visitors to his old teacher's home, recognized a swagger, a cough. Then, Hiran saw him – the man without a face. Stepping out of a passage, he blocked their way, making his uncle frown. He was lean, slightly drooping, swaying gently in the slanted rain. Like other creatures – except for the face: a shining moon surrounded by dark clouds, like a palm without lines. Hiran saw its flattened mounts, where the forehead, nose, mouth, and temples should have been. He was instantly reminded of his teacher . . . *such men are rare; in them one sees God's error or intention.* But somehow, the lean frame seemed to hold a deeper story. And he was blocking their path – a narrow gravel road circling the houses – forcing them to step back into a doorway cushioned with sarees.

In those few moments, Hiran saw a frightened urge. Pushing close, the man examined Mahim, then Hiran, searching for someone in a frenzy revealed only by a jerking shoulder blade and gurgles that came from somewhere inside the shock of grey hair. He seemed close to discovery, yet resigned to failure. If he had had eyes there would have been tears in them. A raw pair of lips twitched – pauses followed by a flicker of hope in what could have been large troubled eyes. Between sobs he was confirming his own suspicion, blaming the rains for an evening of fruitless search.

The meeting left its shadow. Hiran had heard of the dangers stalking honest souls forced to live among the rotten in the alleys of Boubazaar. He knew of thieves, of kidnappers who sold young boys to ships' captains, the undergrowth that had filled his mother with foreboding at the thought of moving back to Calcutta. In his thirteen years, Hiran had had his fair share of scares in a house with its resident ghosts and murderers. But he had learnt to take them in his stride. The *Panchatantra* had helped – he had grown up accepting the evil along with the good.

Hiran wondered about the agony on the unmarked face. What had he lost? A son . . . a brother . . . a friend? *Only the unknown ocean may return a lost ring, an eclipse reveal the sun.* He recalled his teacher again. *He leaves no signs on the one eternally unborn.*

Like an evil omen, that evening walk through Boubazaar signalled a crisis. Waking up next morning he heard Saraladebi's sobs. Hiran began searching his mind for dates, for his mother was given to grieving on selected anniversaries – the day of her widowhood, and that of her marriage. In her mind the union reminded of the parting, just as Hiran's birth evoked two departures – one from her womb, the other from her modest home in Patna. On these days she would lament her return to Jaanbazaar, to a house that no longer offered paternal affection.

'You've lost a second father,' she told him between sobs. Annada, her elderly maid, motioned Hiran aside. As he drank his morning's glass of milk, she told him of their bankruptcy. With typical composure, Annada described the sudden misfortune that had befallen each household under their roof, as well as the stable of servants. Hiran's grandfather's trust had been robbed by a cunning uncle – one most generous in handing out gifts during the annual pujas. With his arrest, their house had been mortgaged.

That evening, he went to the pawnshop with his mother. Taking out a bracelet from her purse she told Hiran that the *real* loser was his bride to be, the one she would have welcomed with her love and all her gold. It was still a distant loss, incapable at first of disturbing Hiran's routine: classes at the mission school, struggles on Sunday mornings over slokas, and delicious evenings spent with Mahim. Discussions with his mother on Saturdays took longer. Mother and son weighed their options – to sell now or wait – searching for ways to reduce their modest needs. Naturally, Saraladebi would not countenance cutting down on the supply of goat's milk required to nurture her growing Hira, or consider eliminating the annual feast for brahmins. Monthly trips to Kalighat took their toll of savings with the rent of a palanquin to shield her from the leers of the lower castes. Their diet, strictly vegetarian, left no room for further economy, although Hiran would begin to suspect a link between his mother's failing health and their need to economize.

Of course, the servants disappeared. First the Behari doorkeepers with their majestic whiskers, then the young boys who spent more time playing in the courtyard than sweeping and cleaning. The stable-hands too sought work elsewhere as there were few horses left. Suddenly the house seemed larger. Footsteps echoed in long corridors. Despite being at the heart of the city, a stone's throw from the notorious Boubazaar, it felt like a retreat. With less dripping laundry, the balconies showed more sky. And the house fell silent – no shouts for service, no scurrying feet and loud curses from resting servants.

Only Mahim's quarters seemed unaffected. The tall windows remained open, ready as always to expel the smoke of smouldering cheroots. There was no end to books and newspapers; a new Remington typewriter appeared, and bottles of scent, which were then lavishly sprayed on a delighted Hiran. But Hiran noticed a difference: Mahim was restless. Twice in the course of the summer he disappeared. 'He has gone to Hajipur,' Annada informed Hiran, 'to sell his share of the ancestral land.' With that he would be free to buy his passage on the steamer from Chandpal Ghaut to England. Hiran sensed an imminent parting. His uncle dwelt more on the future than on the past, seemed wistful: 'I shall return and find you an Editor, no less than Derozio, teaching these stupids a lesson!' 'Stupids', of course, included all Mahim's rivals and irritants such as the lone servant who had forgotten to polish his boots.

Mahim had been the favourite son of his father. Like the other relatives, the vast number of offshoots that populated the house, Mahim too had suffered at the bankruptcy. But his father had favoured him with more – a piece of land beyond the reach of Hiran's cunning uncle. Hiran's young ears learned to detect the sound of envy in the daily outpouring of household gossip. But it was an envy mixed with admiration – for the college-educated young man who spoke his mind with ease. Mahim, his poorer relatives felt, would be their saviour. Perhaps on his return from England, they would all grace a mansion closer to the river, near the Europeans. Despite everything, they believed he would mature into their dead patriarch, returning horses to their stables, and doormen to their post. He was expected to return from England a perfect baboo.

Later, Hiran learned from Annada how his uncle's hopes had been dashed. He had indeed gone to Hajipur to claim his rightful inheritance. But he had failed. No one knew what it was that made the District Magistrate suspicious and refuse permission to sell the land. Mahim had pleaded in impeccable English, but the officer had taken no notice. Mahim returned to Jaanbazaar on a rickshaw, exuding the smell of vomit.

Next morning there was no gossip, just the silence that comes with a known disaster. Mahim's tall windows were shut. Hiran circled their roof with a copy of Macaulay's *Minute* under his arm. He was eager to see Mahim, sensed just the spark that would light fireworks in his uncle, leading to a day that could well end with supper at the popular Hotel d'Europe. For a while Hiran was distracted by flying kites – a friendly rooftop rivalry between Muslim and Hindoo boys. His mind, fleeting between

Macaulay and the whizzing kites, left the roof travelling west towards the river where steeples blended with dark smoke from a steamer.

He searched for his mother that evening, knocking on closed doors in empty passages. She seemed to have gone visiting, although no one recalled seeing her leave. The absence of his second glass of goat's milk rang a warning bell. There were no servants to summon for help. It occurred to him to look in his uncle's study. Through the tall windows he saw her – sitting on the bed beside his reclining uncle, dabbing his forehead with a cloth soaked in eau-de-cologne. A smile, reserved usually for Hiran, replaced her habitual frown. He heard his mother speaking softly, with long pauses between the words. The aanchal had slipped from her head showing her luxuriant black hair. Hiran heard her laughter, felt a stream of tiny waves on the Belgian glass. For a brief moment, he saw Saraladebi as she must have looked when he was still in her womb.

He was surprised to see his uncle lying like a small child. He seemed to have surrendered willingly, basking in a warmth greater than the comfort of his books. Mahim was replying to Saraladebi – playfully, as if the two were recounting an old tale. Hiran saw them too as they must have been – brother and sister. He felt his uncle had escaped his misfortune with the help of an unlikely partner.

Next Saturday, as they again went over their finances, Saraladebi did not make her usual count of jewellery. She made it seem normal, as if the bangles, tiaras, necklaces, and rings had never existed. As if they had never had more to count on than the very small pension that came every now and then from Jyotirmoy's senior priest in Patna. In one stroke she eliminated the nonessentials – feasts for brahmins, offerings at her favourite temple, even the goat's milk, saying that Hiran's young bones were finally grown. Then she looked him in the eye and said, 'It's time for you, Hira, to make use of what you have learned.' It did not take him long to realize what 'use' she had in mind. From now on, Hiran would have to take the place of his father and earn a living for the two of them.

Hiran understood. In that fleeting glance between brother and sister, he had sensed – for the first time – the notion of everlasting reward. Despite misgivings, his mother had decided to be his uncle's saviour. And so, he bade farewell to the Brothers at the mission school, his mind seeking comfort once again in the *Panchatantra* – the tales he had learned as a child at the tole.

Hiran left Jaanbazaar and travelled by foot to the river. Arriving at ten each morning at the law court, he sat patiently on a stool of bricks under a black umbrella. Saraladebi had insisted on the umbrella, to shelter him from the fierce midday sun. Hiran's cousin, one who lived in his separate quarters at their Jaanbazaar house, had offered to help him. He was a mochtar – a clerk at the law court – and introduced Hiran to a team of letter-writers. Sitting outside the court, Hiran would use the English he had learned at the mission school to write petitions on behalf of the illiterate. It was really up to him, his cousin explained. There was no shortage of cases, no shortage of foolish villagers coming to Calcutta to seek the help of the law. Hiran could easily earn a living by properly recording their complaints. He had only one caution. 'Avoid brahmins. They pay with blessings!'

Hiran was bored by his work. Mostly he heard tales of ill fortune, of bankruptcy, theft, even murder. He had to spend an hour listening, then condense a prayer into one page. His clients marvelled that so much could be contained in such a short space. Some even doubted his honesty, requiring a second opinion from a more experienced writer. Sometimes a petitioner would take him to be the judge and beg him to seize the *real culprit.*

He spent six hours every day sitting outside the court, except for Sunday. Sunday still called for his usual routine – reciting slokas before a watchful Saraladebi. But after a while his mother ceased to pay attention, or to correct him if necessary. In her eyes he had become a keranee – a clerk – one who dealt with paper rather than the sandalwood and marigold of prayer. Hiran too began to feel disappointed, longed to barge into Mahim's study, to engage in questions of life and death, like, *Should India be free like England?* Once or twice he went to The Star by himself to see a play. But the evenings failed to revive him. Something was missing. He couldn't bring himself to taste a hot bun, or a ginger ale. The return through Boubazaar too seemed routine without the benefit of a good argument with his uncle.

One day at the court he met his teacher from the tole, recognizing the lean and drooping frame. He seemed surprised to see his pupil, asked where Hiran had learnt his English. Then he squinted at the Exaggerated Conic and sighed, 'Bless you, my son, a day will come when you'll move into the shade.' He left without paying.

To pass the time, Hiran was tempted to examine the palms that held out his fees. As he wrote, he would take the measure of his clients, gauging skill, inclination and taste. He'd see villainy in the palm of a blind man, signs of sudden death in an inheritor, or the unmistakable mark of insanity on the palm of a newly married groom. Try as he might, he felt unable to separate the palm from the petition of the bearer. Once he refused payment from an old man, for he had seen on his palm a cross on the line of Apollo, indicating failure.

As much as Hiran resented the untimely end to his schooling, the routine of daily work gradually restored a healthy balance. He discovered another world, learned to value the ordinary. Then, just as he had grown used to sitting under his black umbrella, he was offered a place in the shade.

Of all his friends from the mission school, only the Parsee boy remained. Still protective of her Hira, Saraladebi had forbidden him to visit the house. But he would wait for Hiran before the clock-maker Yasoufali's shop on Radha Bazaar. They travelled by tram to the kennels to watch hunting hounds being led into the jungle. They passed taverns and punch-houses on Flag Street for a glimpse of boisterous sailors, or discussed the latest feat of Signor Peliti – a wedding cake shaped like the Eiffel Tower. One day he took Hiran to see his uncle, an officer in an English firm. Between sips of tea from a fine china cup, Mr Kavasji enquired about Mahim whom he knew from his correspondence in the *Calcutta Gazette*. Then he asked, 'How do you tell the difference between a petition and an appeal?'

'Only by the confidence of the writer, Sir.'

He was asked to present himself to the Superintendent at the Auction House.

The dark chamber reminded Hiran of the theatre. The Superintendent paced like an actor before a giant mahogany desk. His face was truly pink, unlike the painted ones at The Star or The Emerald. And he spoke not to Hiran but to his report from the mission school and his certificate for elocution.

'Name an English poet of your liking.'

Instantly Hiran thought of Derozio, but he checked himself at the last moment. 'George Gordon, the sixth Lord Byron, Sir.'

He was placed as a clerk – a proper keranee – at a salary befitting his knowledge of English. The employment record bearing his full signature – Hiranyagarbha Chakraborti – left the table to join a tide passing over a desk or two, riding on the heads of chaprasis and displacing others before settling down, finally, in a remote corner of the Auction House.

On his first day of work at the Auction House he met Vincent D'Cruz. Hiran was looking for his desk, Vinny for Penny Blacks. He saw a short, boyish figure, dressed like a Black Christian, a red velvet cap on his head, and a silver cross dancing on his dark neck. He came up to Hiran and slapped him on the shoulder.

'Hiranyagarbha! Jewel of jewels! If you come across any good stamps, keep them only for me. The Queen in black is my speciality.' Then, with a whirl of curses, Vinny walked the bewildered Hiran along the dark corridors of his new employment.

By the end of tiffin-break, Hiran had mastered the east wing where the native employees sat, rows of clerks dozing in glass compartments. Vinny saluted each one as they passed.

'Crocodiles in loin-cloth,' he hissed at Hiran.

They halted before an impressive portico that marked the end of the east and the entrance to the west wing. Between the two stretched an expanse of green, as wide as an ocean. Above the portico hung a giant portrait, above that a silver plaque engraved with a silver hammer. Vinny joined his palms in reverence.

'Lord Kydd. The founder of the Auction House. The real hammer is kept in the Deputy Superintendent's office in the west wing.'

'The west wing?' Hiran wondered, looking across the lawn to the windows opposite.

'Only to be entered by permission, jewel. That's where the

British officers have their desks. Bangle Brown, Blinkey Brown, Muckraputty Brown.' Vinny pointed to each window in turn. 'That one's the Deputy Superintendent's. The Military Brahmin.'

'Military Brahmin?'

'Vegetarian, and non-veg, and sometimes fasts for months.' Back through the dark corridors of the east wing they went, Vinny waving a hand at each section head and his assistant, all gentoos, native clerks looking half-respectable in European clothes. 'And each a college boy, my jewel,' Vinny said. As he stopped to collect the English Queen, he would introduce Hiran: 'Look what they've sent us – a golden boy to cover our mud!'

From desks piled high with files, the gentoos examined Hiran, polishing eye-glasses as if inspecting a letter from an unknown sender. They seemed to know more of him than he of them. But the mystery of the link between Kavasji the Parsee, and Hiran – a brahmin boy from Jaanbazaar – hung like smoke in every room they passed. Someone asked for his father's name, another mentioned distant relatives, one claimed to be a neighbour. Some ignored Vinny's triumphant announcement altogether. 'They're nothing,' Vinny said, lighting up his Pall Mall. In one leap he landed at the base of the handsome wooden staircase and led Hiran to his office, to his desk facing the river.

Was he a gentoo then, a Bengalee in European clothes? Hiran wondered, suddenly conscious of his ill-fitting jacket, a parting gift from Mahim, and his recently tailored serge trousers. As she marked his forehead with a dot of sandalwood, Saraladebi had sighed. This was more painful than the mission school, more painful even than his secret visits to the theatre that she was perfectly aware of through her reliable Annada, more traumatic than the thought of her Hira sitting under the sun on a stool made from bricks. A brahmin's son turned into a mere clerk.

The ledger-writers and clerks who sat in the Records Department were all BAs. Vinny rattled off a list of colleges.

He and Hiran were both 'degreeless'. Vinny had enrolled at the Anglo-Indian School with the dream of becoming a harbour master. He came from a family of ledger-writers, but his fingers dared to grapple with more powerful forms such as a ship's capstan. Things had gone well for a while: he had learned to read maps, become familiar with the sandbars on the Hoogley, and then disaster had struck in the form of nautical geometry. 'The degree business was too much!' he explained, making Hiran laugh with 'Set topsail, stay trysail, cut staysail, hold . . .' delivered in gruff Scots. Vinny would have struggled on, despite the fails, had it not been for the Great Cyclone. Over two days in October, when the wind tore up the Esplanade moorings, setting adrift, wrecking, and stranding everything from men-of-war to native dinghies, his yearning for the sea had dried to a trickle. From the window of his family's rented house in Kidderpore he had seen church steeples buckle, roofs lift off, heard topgallants cracking like carrots. The cyclone had sobered him. He became a keranee like his brother.

Back in the fold, Vinny had become a master of intrigue. His knack for map reading gave him a true explorer's eye: he could spot a defaulting peasant, from curt 'Good mornings' predict the mood of the west wing, discover a treasure of gossip in a heap of dry paper. His short and bouncy frame found its way into extraordinary gatherings. In just a week, Hiran saw evidence of Vinny's powers. As the two returned from tiffin-break, Vinny pointed at British officers smoking cheroots on the lawn which divided the two wings. 'They are sleepy after last night,' Vinny said, smacking his lips.

Hiran was curious, pressed Vinny to go on. The end of an annual trading season, Vinny explained, was always marked with a masquerade held at the Superintendent's mansion. This one had gone on from two in the afternoon to four in the morning. Oysters on crushed ice, roast lamb, pies, chicken curry, soups, imported cheese and marmalade, tarts, a plum-duff set ablaze in brandy, claret, Napier Johnston's Scotch whisky, and champagne. Hiran's vegetarian tongue started to water. 'Ate like pigs.' From his hiding place behind a pillar, Vinny had seen men fight mock duels with Madras firecrackers. He saw wealthy merchants, ships' captains and pirates, memsahibs, but no filthy Jack-tars. 'No, Sir.' He had seen a few natives: Gullam Hussein, Ram Dollal Dey, Dorabjee Byramjee – all ship owners – and Mr Kavasji, whispering to the ladies over the billiards table. And the women . . . delicate hands, shapely ears, blue eyes and black lashes, tall erect figures, golden hair, and breasts . . . 'mango breasts, pineapple breasts, custard-apple breasts, orange breasts'.

Vinny had seen the Deputy Superintendent playing the piano, eyes on the keyboard. As he closed the lid of the piano, he spotted Vinny behind the pillar and winked.

'Mr Scott?' Hiran tried.

'No, my jewel. The *Deputy* Superintendent – Mr Jonathan Crabbe.'

As they walked by the Strand, Hiran asked Vinny how much of his account was true. 'Do you always dream such fantastic dreams?' Wheeling his bicycle beside Hiran, Vinny shot back, 'May my head go bald if I've lied!'

Hiran sat at a confluence of incoming and outgoing streams. The tide of paper arrived at his desk regularly. He would hold an envelope against the light in his fingertips, judge its enclosure, then carefully peel along the edges to save the stamps. A quick glance told him where a letter belonged – in which file, on which chaprasi's head, which chamber and section.

Names fascinated Hiran in the beginning. He would stare at a bold set of alphabets: Canton, Buxar, Patna, Hong Kong, Gaya, Kuching, Kumsingmoon. Some letters arrived in canvas bags smelling of the sea, others in brown paper with the crown printed on top. He sorted them into piles: petitions, reports, explanations, excuses, advice, complaints. Casual ones – greetings, travelogues – he saved too, in his 'Miscellaneous' file. Most were concerned with serious matters: 'It is advisable that what is sold should be of the quality best adapted for the markets for which it is intended as experience may point out. That if it be sold pure, it should be declared pure, and that if it be in any way altered or compounded with other substances, the alteration should be known and declared at the time of the sales, and that the weight and nature of the material used for the envelope should also be declared.' He was impressed by an honest tone. There were vain denials . . . 'The difference in profit, supposing it were probable, is not only inconsequential, but neither our duty to our employees, nor our regard to our countrymen would have permitted our making the desired consignments under our knowledge of the present adulterated state of the article.' As a former letter-writer he marvelled at the openness and had no trouble believing in the purity of the 'article'. Then, a list of recommendations . . . 'I would urge an increase of four annas per seer throughout the province of Behar.' And, 'The London market is capable at present of taking off from 60 to 100 chests annually, and I beg to seek your favour in the extension of the sale.'

The more intriguing ones usually began with a story: 'I beg to trouble you with a seizure which was made and brought to me yesterday by Mudaree, a merchant, and Fakeera, his servant, from a European, I believe a Frenchman. He brought it from the house of Peter Brilliard, a cook and a butler, from Dinapur. I beg leave to call your attention to a very cunning method made use of to carry off the article by packing it in jars with pieces of salted meat on the top to make it appear as a jar of provision. This man, Peter Brilliard, has long practised smuggling and has hitherto evaded detection. I now beg leave to solicit the severest punishment which the regulations admit of may be put in force against him.' In this instance, he was impressed, although the writing, he knew, would not stand his uncle's scrutiny. The reply, also flowing through Hiran's ledger, was impeccable . . . 'Under the circumstances, I am convinced that you will have no objections to issuing such orders to your police officers as you may judge necessary for the purpose of protecting the interests of Her Majesty's Government.'

For a long while he wondered what lay beneath the paper.

What did the stream of letters stand for? Whose purity did they seek to protect from unscrupulous adulterers? Whose theft called for harsh penalties? In exchange for which 'article' did the Auction House and its inhabitants receive their keep? What, he wondered, brought so many, and of such immense variety together, what attracted Jardine and Matheson, Dent & Co., the Messagerie Maritime, Austrian Lloyd, American Russell, German Hansa, even the Chinese with their unpronounceable names? For a good while Hiran chased the ghost behind the paper.

He had taken it at first for some kind of medicine. The tone of exchange suggested an object of universal value. Gold? The price was too low. It seemed to attract those with a flair for writing. His cousin, the law clerk, had thrown a hint: 'So you have exchanged ink for mud.' Even from Vinny he had heard that word. All that paper for mud? Hiran was certain it stood for something better than the dark refuse of the Ganga.

Then his Parsee friend added to his confusion: 'You must tell me what it tastes like, Hiran. My uncle says it's all you get in heaven! God's Own Medicine!'

He hesitated to ask Vinny. Beside the fear of ridicule, he sensed a breach of trust. Nobody at the Auction House referred to the precious article by name. Instead, he heard one metaphor after another: black-gold, poison, green-ash, gum, yen, and mritasanjibanee – that which wakes a dead man.

He thought of asking his superior, but Hiran was still nervous of approaching the portly Nabinbaboo. Dressed in the finery of a distinguished patron, he looked immaculate in white dhoti and an aachkan with a tiny watch-pocket. In winter a northern shawl stood guard against the river's breeze. A fine pencil moustache and an even finer line of gold from his eyeglass lent detail to a noble face. There were other signs of high birth: an impassive set of eyes meant for governance, deliberate mannerisms, and perhaps most important of all – a retreat into books rather than gossip during tiffin-breaks. Thick volumes lay on Nabinbaboo's desk, full of strange pictures: grotesque skeletons, rows of skulls, a variety of organs, Adam and Eve without their leaves. The contrast filled Hiran with curiosity. From his desk facing the window he would look sideways just as Nabinbaboo's hand went inside his drawer. There was more: small glass bottles filled with white translucent drops, like raw sugar. Once in a while Nabinbaboo, during tiffin-break, would have a visitor. His deep voice would command attention as he turned pages pointing out parts of the human body, like ugly remains from a butcher's knife. Hiran did not yet have the courage to ask what it was that enthralled Nabinbaboo's visitors, why they seemed grateful as they left with a bottle or two from his desk. He was too consumed by one mystery to be fully aware of another. A few times he came close, but decided to wait. The 'mud' remained illusive.

It was the end of the south-west monsoon. The river was full, with ships facing the city from Chandpal Ghaut all the way down to Kidderpore. Hiran and Vinny took their usual walk by the Strand, down to the slender jetty where gulls returned with their catches. Vinny was silent. They stopped to feed the birds, scattering crumbs past the reach of flying beaks, gazing at their own shadows cast by the sun on the giant sails.

There was the *Eugenia*, easy and smart. Sensitive to every yard of canvas, every touch of braces, tacks, and sheets; she was fast yet dry, lively yet stiff – swam like a duck, steered like a fish. There was the showy *Anaconda*, built at Blackwall docks in London, under the eye of a fiery Irishman. Like a yacht, not a curve, a line, or an angle betrayed the motto of balance. The teak and mahogany woodwork on deck and below had been carved by the finest cabinet-makers; brass rails and binnacles shone in the sun. Her sails carried the fragrance of tea from the south China shore. Then there was the famous *Seringapatnam*, built of English oak and Malabar teak, Tippoo Sahib, scimitar in hand, gracing the figurehead. The *Shahjehan*, the *Hoogley*, the *Malabar* – rusty East Indiamen, replicas of seventeenth-century galleons – carrying mail to Rangoon. And there were others with unpronounceable names: *Macquarie, Holmsdale, Thermopylae, Coulnakyle.*

A slaver, the *Nightingale*, captured off the Brazilian coast and auctioned as a prize, lay next to the *Witch of the Waves* with its Salem witch riding a broomstick at the prow. On the other boats, they saw Chinese dragons, cupids, nymphs, a rampant lion, and on the Moorish *Almadia*, a half-length naked man painted dark chocolate.

Nemesis, the man-of-war, was moored farthest from shore. The Chinese sailors called it 'the devil ship'. She was fitted with four eighteen-pounders on each side, two pivot guns and a Long Tom amidships. Her deck was painted red to hide the traces of blood.

They saw ghost-ships, ships that carried horses from Australia, fresh coconut from the Nicobar, fresh tobacco leaves from Borneo, ocean tramps searching for cargo, and convict boats with barred hatchways and red-coated sentries.

Dhows, Arab ships from Jeddah and Muscat, with square sterns and quarter galleries, were moored together above the Hastings pier, waiting for the north-east monsoon to give them a fair wind home.

They heard the evening prayer and saw kneeling forms.

Frigates, brigs, men-of-war, sloops, clippers, steamers, schooners, junks, yachts. Hiran heard Vinny speak, raising his voice above the gulls. Used to jokes, he expected a light-hearted diversion, but Vinny was serious. To become a harbour master one needed to know everything about ships, from their making to all the stories of their living and dead inhabitants. Only once did he show his usual self, as he described an arriving *Sylph*, its cabin windows decorated with feminine garments of the most intimate kind.

Like an approaching cloud, they saw the last ships of the season return. 'These are ours,' Vinny said. 'Back with silver for our mud.'

'Tell me about the mud. Where does it come from?'

'It grows on trees, jewel.' Vinny laughed, then asked, 'You

mean, you don't know? Didn't Nabinbaboo tell you?' Then he gave the truth to a credulous Hiran: 'It's opium. Afim, as you call it. Ya-pien to the Chinese. What else do you want to know?'

He had hoped for something else and the anticlimax left him brooding. He had anticipated something fit for display in expensive shops, like chiming clocks, or pearls.

Hiran was no stranger to opium – he could see the local opium shop from his window in Jaanbazaar, and the daily queues. It was good for old men, he had heard, made them sleep easily at night. Housemaids needed opium too – to soothe their aching bones after a day's hard work. He had seen their own Annada waiting before the opium shop, knew of her nightly dose of afim. It merited neither the veneration of Ayurveda's traditional healing herbs, nor the notoriety of alcohol. The dull brown cakes wrapped in leaves commanded no respect. As he lay on his bed in the morning, he had heard Annada describe a sleepless night, when afim had worked wonders on her bones, but played mischief with her mind. He had heard muffled laughter, caught a phrase or two . . . 'the fish caught me in its mouth . . . inside, I could hardly keep my saree on with the heat'. He had tried imagining Annada inside a fish without her much-darned saree, her hair strewn all over like streaking mud.

He remembered one afternoon at the tole when two young men had entered his teacher's room carrying a bundle draped in cloth which they dropped on the floor. Hiran heard moans coming from it, saw a pair of outstretched palms. Even before his teacher, he saw the vicious fork on the Head-line: one end stopping short of the Heart, the other running towards Luna, indicating the kind of great affection that calls for the sacrifice of all things, eventually bringing ruin. His teacher had smiled at the men. 'It's afim that rules his fate, not his palm.'

Despite Vinny's claim, it was hard to imagine that the whole enterprise, the desks, the paper, and a flotilla of ships, served only to provide simple comfort for Annada's aching bones.

He rehearsed the question in his mind as he waited for his

superior. How valuable is the substance of our trade? Nabinbaboo removed his glasses, stared at Hiran for a moment, then took a volume from his drawer and began to read in his deep voice: 'Without opium, the healing art would not exist. It resists poison and venomous bites, cures chronic headache, vertigo, deafness, epilepsy, apoplexy, dimness of sight, loss of voice, asthma, coughs of all kind, spitting of blood, tightness of breath, colic, the iliac poison, jaundice, hardness of the spleen, stones, urinary complaints, fevers, dropsies, leprosy, the troubles to which women are subject, melancholy and pestilences.'

For the next hour, Hiran, like a student at the mission school, returned with his teacher to the very beginning. At the end, Nabinbaboo told Hiran of an opportunity that had come up, by a rare coincidence, a mission that would take Hiran back to Patna, to visit their mud in its native soil. 'You'll be an apprentice for a short while at the opium factory, learning our trade from the beginning to the end. It will be your chance to observe the *papaver somniferum*.'

Saraladebi cried when Hiran told her he was going back to Patna. Sitting on the roof, surrounded by pots of dyeing thread, she asked him all the usual questions. Had he rung the bell at Madan Mohon Jiu's temple on his way to the Auction House, remembered to bring back a supply of Ganga-water for her daily puja? Had Annada's lunch left him hungry?

When he told her of his trip, she sat silently for a while, then cried like a new widow. Tears of memory. He had expected her to be anxious, shower a thousand warnings, even pretend a sudden illness to stop him. But he hadn't known the pain of birth and death borne by the same tears; he couldn't have known that in fact she was happy – whispering to her dead husband that her Hira was finally ready to visit the land of his ancestors.

Of course, happiness did not eliminate panic. 'You must promise never to set foot within a mile of those cursed Parade Grounds.' And, 'Who'll go with you, look after your belongings, cook . . .' She woke Annada from her afim sleep to ask the price of English wool. She insisted that he wear a new sweater to protect his young lungs from the Ganga. 'You'll see the river . . . it's young and wild, not like your tiny stream in Calcutta.' Annada calmed her with a lie. 'Your Hira will stay with sadhus. Maybe they'll find him a bride!'

Vinny had his own share of advice. Hiran, he said, wouldn't be alone at the factory. The Deputy Superintendent, Mr Crabbe, and his new wife would be visiting the plantations for an inspection. Hiran's Parsee friend's uncle, Mr Kavasji, would go along with them as their guide. 'They are training you to become a spy, jewel – showing you the men behind the letters.' Before Hiran could decide whether Vinny was joking or not, he was warned of serious dangers – thieves who posed as customs men robbing gullible villagers. Hiran decided to dress in the jacket Mahim had left him.

Only Nabinbaboo appeared calm. 'We want you to return a farmer, a collector, and a chemist rolled into one.' He explained to Hiran the key virtues of a senior clerk: a knack for sorting out lies from errors, and a feel for the pulse – like a play's director. 'You must know how a peasant measures land for his opium crop and how agents settle his rent. Watch Mr Eliot, the man in charge of the factory in Patna, pace the Examining Hall sniffing out the tainted opium from the pure. You must know everything.' Vinny laughed. 'Didn't I say they want to make a spy of you!' Then he smacked his lips. 'You'll throw Kavasji out of his office, like his fellow merchants threw out his father.' He folded his palms . . . 'Hiranyagarbha – Maharajah of Jaanbazaar!'

Sitting by Hiran's desk, Vinny showed him a letter. It had come from Lark's Bay, Macao, and carried a strange stamp. A harbour showed on one side of the postcard, ringed with flags of different colours. European homes stood by a tall pagoda. Vinny's portrait was drawn in water colour on the other side. It was signed Jacque Heurtebise. 'I sat for him on the quarter-deck at Kidderpore,' Vinny said proudly, adjusting his cap to the angle in the portrait. Captain Jacque, he explained, was no ordinary man. He had carried everything – coolies to the Americas, mutinous Hussars, a whole hatchful of dead lascars rotting from cholera. He had a true sailor's voice hailing a distant maintop. He gave orders in Hindoostani, and could make a ship do everything but talk! 'Captain Jacque is my friend,' Vinny said.

'He could steal twice from you and make you feel grateful.' Nabinbaboo, who had been listening silently from his desk, blew his remark over Vinny's cap. 'Tell him how your Jacque was caught smuggling, a good fifty cases of Malwa opium from the Portuguese of Goa.' Nabinbaboo described how Captain Jacque had set the barber to make a clean sweep of his hair, attached a pigtail through his cap and borrowed a huge pair of tea-stone spectacles, to disguise himself as a Chinese. He had fooled his buyers all right, returning with 132,000 Spanish dollars. 'Oh yes! He is a master all right – of practical jokes.' 'He is a human tiger,' Vinny muttered.

Had Vinny ever visited Macao? Hiran asked. Vinny nodded. 'That's where we are from. It's my Patna.' Then, he gave Nabinbaboo an angry look. 'Things will change, my jewel. You'll be the owner of the mud, and Captain Jacque will carry it away on his wings.'

'And where will *you* be, Vinny?'

'I'll be near you, your own blackie-white boy,' he said, taking off for the Strand.

Hiran couldn't remember how it started, who had raised the alarm. A siren howled through the rooms of the east wing, the paper tide stopped, letters remained half-opened, chaprasis dropped their files, Penny Blacks floated in bowls over silent desks. 'Another opium war!' Vinny's voice rang over the siren. Even Nabinbaboo seemed surprised. Putting his glass bottles carefully aside, he led Hiran out into the portico. They were among the first to arrive. There were hushed murmurs, frowns, and rumours. Mr Scott had choked to death over lunch, the Viceroy had been assassinated in a duel, the sepoys were revolting, the city was flowing with the blood of rioters!

A bugle-horn ordered them on to the lawn, to line up in single file, stop pushing, be quiet, and hold their hands forward in full view. Mr Scott and the Deputy Superintendent, Mr Crabbe, sat under the shade of a Gulmohor tree, with a team of baton-swinging policemen standing guard nearby. The air seemed still.

Mr Scott, a shy smile on his face, looked away as Mr Crabbe called them out one by one. He looked at hands – palms facing, then turned down – frowning through his pince-nez. Hiran was amazed. What was he looking for? Mr Crabbe seemed irritable, shooting orders under his breath. Sometimes he appeared close to a discovery, peering into the nails stretched out before him. 'He'll find Kavasji's blood on my hands!' Vinny laughed. Hiran saw a calm Nabinbaboo spread out elegant fingers gleaming under a blue sapphire. His eyes stared coldly back at Mr Crabbe. Vinny was next. A guard snatched off his cap. Hiran felt the hot breath on his neck of the next in line.

His own turn came and passed. Later, Vinny said Mr Crabbe had spent more time inspecting Hiran's broad forehead than his hands. Mr Scott had whispered into Mr Crabbe's ear then rose to leave, escorting his Deputy back to the west wing before he could begin another round of palm-gazing.

As they went back to their desks, Hiran sensed a changed mood. By then, the mystery had been solved. As the tide resumed slowly, someone pointed up at the portrait that hung below the hammer in the portico. They saw Lord Kydd, his face crudely painted over – top hat, clay pipe, yellow buttons on his frock coat, and a smile like a clown. 'Poor thing!' Vinny said. 'He never smiled when he was alive.'

The incident distracted Hiran from the journey he had to make. Lord Kydd left him with dreams of faces – some scarred by a brush, others painted over unlikely objects. Sleeping fretfully in the train on the way to Patna he saw the roaring snout of the engine, like a black moon, hiding behind the smoke – a cross between Mr Scott and a smiling Lord Kydd. Layers of flesh glowed in the midday sun. Grey eyes danced under a whistle. The engine called out through its open mouth, chattered like Vinny, drawled comfortably over the dark plains of the Ganga. Turning on his side Hiran heard it speak in verses, reminding him of a man on whose shoulders he had sat but whose face he couldn't remember. Only once was he completely awake, as they crossed over a bridge on a quiet river. Sweating in new wool he tried to make out its shadowed contours – like a line of hooded serpents along the bank. He saw the morning light up a red earth, a rough shadow tottering over hillocks, a faceless engine picking its way through a field of boulders.

His father's senior priest met him at the station. Overcome by fears, Saraladebi had written ahead, begging him to look after her Hira and his gentle stomach which was likely to suffer from the diet of sadhus. The senior priest took Hiran to his lodgings at the Natives' Resthouse of the opium factory where he would be an apprentice to Mr Eliot, the man in charge. He deposited his belongings, then they walked to the nearby Ganga. Hiran found him withdrawn, kind but aloof. He asked if Hiran knew what had become of their ancestral home – the hut with the small courtyard he had heard his mother speak of. He promised to take Hiran to see it after his business at the factory.

The Ganga was different in Patna. It seemed to bend frequently, like smoke from the steam loco. Electric blue eddies clashed against marble faces, gorges appeared from nowhere setting up a line of surf. It was a young river.

For the next few days as he walked through halls filled with men, Hiran thought of the loco and the river. He stood for hours inside the Boiling room, with bare-chested men bent over rows of vats. High ceilings let the steam rise, to hang like icicles from the slatted roof. The swirl of water, voices, and a dim light made it seem like an inferno. In the Drying room dark mounds lay like rows of marbles. He saw men stepping gingerly over narrow pathways, balancing dark, crude lumps on their shoulders, like the dung-carriers in Boubazaar's alleys. From the back of the tunnel he heard singing voices – boys testing dark balls with thin strands of kash. They shone like pearls under the beam's shadow, still glistening from moisture. The Balling room was more to his liking – with a clearly defined flow like the Auction House. Men sat on the floor before palettes full of herbs, added spice, rounded crude pyramids into perfect spheres – oily but dry, viscous but hard. He saw palms holding up the balls, suspending them in the air to test their roundness. He saw giant scales hung from the Examining Hall ceiling, boys from the Drying room carrying lumps from one table to the next, running under sharp orders, silence replacing singing. The Stacking room intrigued him most. He saw wooden shelves from floor to ceiling with opium balls lined along them like books in a giant bookcase, men climbing ladders to reach the shelves. Hiran saw men above him – dark as opium – floating in the air like actors on stage. A steady commentary filled the rooms: *solubility, alkaloids, concentrate, yield.* It reminded Hiran of Nabinbaboo.

Mr Eliot called him to his chamber. 'Why must the balls be rolled to such a small size?' he asked.

'Their bulk must be broken, Sir.'

'And why is that necessary?'

'Because they need to travel far, and to avoid detection,' Hiran answered. Next morning Hiran left the factory for the fields.

At first sight they appeared sad: an army with eyes downcast. White buds over frothy black soil, under a clear blue sky – the contrast shocked Hiran. He heard the deep voice of Nabinbaboo: 'The botanical family is large, twenty-eight genera, two hundred and fifty species; the bush poppy and tree poppy, Californian, Welsh, and blue poppies, the tulip poppy, the opium poppy. Their colour ranges from white to red. Never yellow or green.' Hiran remembered an afternoon at the Auction House, thick volumes spread over his desk. 'The Sumerians knew it six thousand years ago, drew its picture on ideograms, called it the plant of joy,' Nabinbaboo read. 'At first it was the monopoly of priests, then God got wind of its powers . . . Ceres, the Roman Goddess of fertility, also known as Demeter in Greece, was said to partake of its juice to forget her pain – *ad oblivionem doloris.* Soon, Helen – daughter of Zeus – was pouring it into the wine of her guests till . . . *they didn't shed a tear even though their mother or father were dead, even though a brother or a beloved son had been killed before their eyes . . .*' Nabinbaboo paused, then went on:

'The Romans got it from their Greek slaves, gave Somnus –

the God of sleep – a bunch of poppies and an opium horn. Later Venetian merchants began taking an interest.

'Each had it in their own way. Turks ate the fetid, brackish cakes flavoured with nutmeg, cardamom, cinnamon, and saffron. Persians drank it with wine. Egyptians dissolved it in delicate balms. From kings it passed to soldiers – and those who deal in pain. In one giant leap the Arabs took it over the Caucasian mountains and into Asia.

'In 1516 it was on the pen of Barbossa the Portuguese. He was amazed by the cargoes of mud travelling from Arab dhows to Chinese junks. The Chinese ate it too – in fish cakes sprinkled with vinegar. It didn't take the Malays long to acquire the taste, and Sarawak and Borneo became regular ports of call.

'But the marriage of the east and the west, the European conquest of the Americas, brought opium to the pipe's bowl. There was no stopping it then. No matter how much Tsar Romanoff tortured and exiled smokers, or Charles I and Murad IV opposed it, or Emperor Tsung Cheng, the Son of Heaven, issued his famous edicts, it had come to reside in the alveoli, the cup-shaped air cells of the lungs, from where it raced through the blood in just a simple breath or two.

'Even if the plant could have lived without man, the reverse was not imaginable. Initially it was thought only as harmful as wine, if infinitely more pleasurable. It became the bearer of ultimate sleep, doctors seized it with glee; murder and suicide were its twin gifts. It rode with Hannibal in his ring, resided in delicious sherbets consumed by Hindoo sattees as they climbed their husband's pyres, and, of course, in the intestine of Robert Clive – the victor of Plassey.'

Nabinbaboo paused. 'It wasn't long before the first alkaloid appeared in a Swiss lab under the Alps. Morphine and its twin brother, the hypodermic needle. And, by the time fear had risen over its sting, a stronger sibling was on its way – *heroisch*.'

Hiran knew that buds would swell with sap, become erect, point towards the sky. Shed the greenish-grey and burst into flowers – crushed and crinkled like ballerinas in chiffon – then dance in the breeze. Petals would fall, and pods await a peasant's three-pointed blade. Its white blood would coagulate under the sun into a gummy mass, ten days would give enough to fill ships, keep the tide moving in their Auction House.

It must have waited many thousands of years for man, he thought, sitting on his haunches at the top of a hillock. That was when he saw her, the woman, head hanging low like a sad poppy. This must be Mr Crabbe's new wife, Lilian, he thought, accompanying her husband on an inspection of the opium fields.

Mr Crabbe wore a blue silk shirt. Lilian, under a lace parasol, was tinged with the same blue. Her gloved hand held up a wounded pod. Behind her, an elegant Mr Kavasji, in priest's black, offered a cup of blue and white china. Together, they floated like a small cloud over the field, stood still with the breeze, then moved.

He saw them again – calling on Mr Eliot, dressed for a garden party. Hiran saw her auburn ringlets peeking out from behind the white canvas of a budgerow. Mr Crabbe was whispering in her ear, pointing her binoculars at the shore. He wondered what she saw.

He had seen the river bloom in his last days in Patna. Late for the flooding season, it had swollen overnight, devouring the white kash. It happened every tenth year, the senior priest explained: glaciers melting in the Himalayas. Hiran saw little islands with patches of orchard disappear under the rushing waves. 'Gone to feed the fish, just as your father fed the grass.' They had turned away from the river now, and were entering the Parade Grounds. He felt the finger-comb soft under his bare feet. The elderly man slowed him down, dragging his feet, eyes downcast as if searching for Jyotirmoy's blood. He looked at Hiran a few times, expecting questions. But Hiran was silent.

The priest led him to a small clearing where a hut and stable stood. There were children playing with stone pebbles in the courtyard, a kneeling form fanning a clay fire. Hiran sat on a cotton mat, quickly noted the sharp smell of manure blended with incense. He watched the priest's wife light the evening lamp. The elderly man smiled weakly, then handed him their monthly allowance. 'Ask your mother . . .'

'You should've launched a complaint. Mr Eliot would've thrown the scoundrel off your land!' Vinny said when Hiran explained. 'All along you thought he was sending money out of kindness, when it was just a measly rent!' Hiran tried explaining to Vinny the difference between the donkey stealing cucumbers, and a king robbing a poor brahmin. But Vinny wasn't listening. 'What you don't give wisely, others will force from your hand, and you'll end up like Kavasji's father with a bullet between your eyes.'

What would he say to his mother? That it was time to cancel the debt of memory and land? Hand over his dead ancestors to the care of the priest's wife?

Opening the solitary envelope on his desk, Hiran found an invitation from Mr Kavasji to join him in his west wing office. Warm and welcoming, he seemed every bit the friendly uncle. 'I hear you studied Sanskrit. Why did you stop? Didn't your father apprentice you as a priest?' He seemed curious, asked him when, how his father had died. Hiran hesitated, feeling the soft grass of Patna's Parade Grounds still under his feet. 'He was trampled, Sir, by horses . . .' After a moment's silence, Mr Kavasji cleared his throat. 'Listen, Hiran, I'd like you to help a friend of mine, a dear friend. Mr Crabbe . . . you know. He's a great admirer of India, engaged in translating ancient tales for English readers. He needs a bit of help, and if you agree he'd be quite willing to bear charges for you to visit his house every Sunday for a few hours.' He wrote out the address in a careful hand and thanked Hiran for agreeing.

Looking back, Hiran knew his hasty acceptance of Mr Kavasji's proposal was prompted by a wish to return to the world of stories, his only link with the realm of unknowns. But he also knew others would see it differently.

Vinny was perplexed at first. He was silent as they walked back along the Strand after their tiffin-break, stopping to gaze at the pontoon bridge that swayed over the river. 'It's all Scott's doing. He wants you to keep an eye on number fifteen, report on Mr Crabbe's shady deals.' 'Like what? And why would he choose a clerk from the Auction House, not a gardener or cook?' 'Because your evidence counts for more.' Vinny was smug. Then, he was breathless. 'It's Kavasji – the owl in a suit! He wants you to keep his friend engaged while he shares the nest with Lilian.'

'Kavasji and Mrs Crabbe?'

'You mean you didn't know? He learned a lesson from his father.' Vinny smacked his lips and told the story. Kavasji senior had been a fool – a merchant prince who owned a fleet of forty plying between Calcutta and Canton, even sent mangoes to Queen Victoria from his private orchard. No one saw him in the same pair of shoes twice and his women wore English bodices, high-heeled shoes, stockings, and English coats. But he was flawed nevertheless. Went bankrupt after a suspicious deal in opium fell through with the British Superintendent of Trade in Canton before the opium war of 1838. Other merchants had hedged their bets, but not foolish Kavasji. He shot himself in his Mandeville Gardens villa in Calcutta. The son came to work at the Auction House after his father's body had been offered to the birds, and the furniture to the auctioneers on Little Russell Street.

'Junior is no man's fool. He's a taker not a giver,' Vinny concluded with a well-designed sense of intrigue.

Once again, Saraladebi received this latest development with calm. Once again she saw her vision – her very own Hira charming his disciples with slokas. It didn't seem to matter that his tole would be in a European mansion. 'Remember, Rajah Nabakrishna Deb of Shobhabazaar was Lord Clive's private tutor.' She had heard too of famous pundits who taught Sanskrit to British officers at Fort William College. Hiran didn't mention the 'charges' to his mother, lest she should view his duty in less than noble terms.

He was duly forewarned: to refuse food, even water; to relieve himself in the fields before entering the mansion; to sit on the floor on his raw cotton mat; never to laugh, or betray emotion; never to touch a dog. He was advised to leave should his pupil appear drunk, to refuse gifts, and to avoid the company of low-caste servants. He should hold his breath till vapours of forbidden flesh passed by. He should never, *never* swallow the saliva of hunger.

He violated the edicts twice on his first day, partly as a result of the darkness at the Crabbes' house, number 15 Alipore Road, which reminded him of the Boiling room at their Patna factory. A curious vapour, invisible, tinged each object with its own aura. The light was similar too – a feeble yet well-plotted drift over edges of crystal. Before Hiran's eyes could adjust, he heard the opening score, the soft strings of an esraj. He sat down on one of the dark chairs. The sudden change – from a hot and bustling tram to a dark and perfumed interior – cast a spell. He saw a short and familiar Annada, her large breasts bursting through a much-darned saree, offering him his glass of goat's milk. It even tasted the same. Hiran felt her eyes on him as the sweet crust melted under his tongue.

He heard a lady calling, and the distant response of her maid. Occasionally, he heard even breathing, as in deep sleep.

The most arresting thing in the dark room was Mr Crabbe himself. He sat by the window on a teak recliner, the apex of a well-appointed beam highlighting the economy of folds on a red camel jacket, the wide pyjamas tied with silken strings, and red slippers with toes curled like a ram's horn. He had come in just as the esraj stopped, motioned Hiran to sit, then opened a gold-trimmed book and started reading. It seemed like a familiar exercise, performed at a slow pace, open to gentle interruption. His tone took on the nature of light – disciplined but quiet. From time to time he would look up and smile. A pause at the end of each passage seemed to invite approval. To Hiran, still overwhelmed, the reading appeared as pre-ordained as the lines of an actor, requiring neither interruption nor approval.

'The king sacrificed his riches to appease the Gods. But his young son, Nachiketas, a mere boy, saw futility in earthly offerings – cows that were too old to give milk, too weak to even graze or drink. *To whom will you give me, father?* he asked once, twice, and three times. His father answered in a rage . . . *I shall give you unto death.* And so, Nachiketas was sent to *Yama*, the God of Death.

'*Yama*, touched by the boy's piety, offered him three boons . . . *Name them, and they shall be yours.*' The familiar dialogue continued:

Nachiketas:	May my father's wrath abate, may he welcome me back into his fold.
Death:	And he shall.
Nachiketas:	Reveal the sacred fire that leads one to Heaven.
Death:	It lies in your heart, search.
Nachiketas:	When a man dies, some say *he is* and some say *he is not.* Teach me the truth.
Death:	Ask for sons and grandsons who will live a hundred years; for cattle, for elephants, for horses, for gold. Ask for the earth's empire and to live as long as you choose. I can give thee powers . . . these heavenly maidens, these chariots, this music . . . I shall bestow upon you, serve you. But ask me not, Nachiketas, to reveal the secret of death.

The man with the face of death stopped. He rose and opened the curtains, then came up close till Hiran could see the fine veins on his face. 'Shall I read one more from the *Upanishads*,' he asked, in a voice dripping with kindness, 'or would you rather join us for tea?'

Just then, Hiran caught sight of the empty glass of goat's milk on the arm of his chair, and his rolled-up cotton mat, and hastened to leave.

At his next visit there were more readings – from gold-trimmed books filled by a sloping hand. He was surprised by the stories, gradually learning his own role in the play and mastering the art of gentle interruption. They would wrestle over obscure passages, at times reversing the natural order: Mr Crabbe reciting in Sanskrit, and Hiran writing in longhand in

English. They began invariably with goat's milk, and the esraj. Then they launched into stories written on palm leaves by a fine quill. Hesitating at first, Hiran grew used to the taste of cheroots and managed later to disguise the sharp aroma under a generous layer of paan. The rest was easy too: counting the gold coins wrapped inside a soft chamois bag on his way home.

In the beginning, Hiran chose to engage simply with the text, ignoring the stories. Mr Crabbe would try to draw him into the realm of the characters.

'Why must crows and owls fight?'

'Because their king – Garuda – was busy serving Lord Vishnu. Without a master, subjects have little to do but quarrel.'

Mr Crabbe smiled, then asked, 'Could not one of them become the master?'

'Can a hunter become a brahmin, a barber a sadhu? It is possible only through an agreement, Sir.'

'What sort of agreement?'

'That one – once transformed from servant to master – shall never return to his previous form. This the owl finds difficult, and the crow impossible.'

'Tell me then, Hiranbaboo, why doesn't one destroy the other?'

'Because they must survive for the jackal to live by their blood.'

Once he came in drenched with rain, having misjudged the dark clouds over the river. As he hesitated by the doorway, he heard a different kind of music. There was more than one player, each encouraging the other, running merrily around a courtyard like infants. Footsteps echoed over the wooden floor, mixed with applause and banging doors; the empty staircase was strewn with coloured paper. A restless voice was trying to drown the musicians, capture the drone; there were squeaks, then laughter. The maid vanished into a dark corridor, much to Hiran's disappointment. The servants had adjusted to his habits – learned to leave the crust on his milk, add an extra spoon of sugar to his tea, feign surprise at his refusal then insist till he accepted a second cup – and called him pundit. He knew the cook and the doorman of number 15. The peon came regularly to the Auction House to run Mr Crabbe's personal errands. But his favourite among the servants was the maid. He would see her approaching from the corner of his eye, knew the sound of her bangles setting down the glass before she wiped the rim with her aanchal.

He went in and found Mr Crabbe sitting by the window. The esraj lay across his lap, but its strings were silent. A light seemed to rise from his grey pupils, filling the room with his will. He seemed, as usual, quiet, but his gaze was hard as it had been that day on the lawn of the Auction House. Hiran remembered Mr Crabbe staring at his palms, felt a pair of eyes on his forehead.

Once he had offered to read but Mr Crabbe had raised his hand: 'Aren't we all like Nachiketas, asking for useless boons?' Seeing Hiran's surprise, he continued, 'Go on, tell me, what would *you* have asked for?' Vinny's words flashed through his mind . . . *He is a Military Brahmin . . . both vegetarian, and non-veg, and sometimes fasts for months.* What did he have in mind? What did he want him to say? The boons that would satisfy a failed brahmin priest and a British officer had to be different, didn't they? Suddenly, Hiran felt tense.

To most of them at the Auction House, Mr Crabbe was the real *Yama*, the bearer of boons and death. Vinny would supply the latest story of Crabbe's power, like the infamous 'rice ordeal': Mr Eliot of Patna, they all knew, was an honest and just officer. He was known to be 'soft', accused of laxity and indulgence when it came to the natives in the factory. Happiest with numbers, his reports pleased the hearts of Hiran and the others in the east wing, arriving on the dot each month. He was a 'true officer', Nabinbaboo said, indispensable, the man who knew his opium better than anybody else.

On one of Mr Crabbe's visits to the Patna factory, he had found a whole tray missing while doing the count in the

Stacking room with Mr Eliot. Within moments, Mr Eliot had traced the missing lumps in an absent line of his ledger. Both sat brooding, then Mr Crabbe had taken over. First, he rounded up the five suspects from the watch-and-ward guard and wrote down their names in a gold-trimmed diary. Then, he set out on his hunt, a tour of the city through back alleys reeking of ganja and the stale love of brothel women. Armed with two sepoys, he strode to the Ganga where sadhus lit their fires, each like a funeral pyre with a single naked cremator. He selected one, a tantric, more mischievous than the others. Mr Crabbe had spoken into his ear and handed him a silver Akbar rupee.

Next morning everyone assembled before the soot-black sheds. The five suspects stood in a circle around a makeshift shrine with the tantric hovering close by. A frowning Mr Eliot sat on his straight-backed chair, face half-turned away.

'Why did he need a tantric?'

'Wait, jewel.'

'Surely Mr Eliot wouldn't have allowed any cruelty to his men.' Hiran frowned, unable to follow the story.

'Ssh . . .' Vinny hushed him.

At Mr Crabbe's nod, the tantric went into a terrifying wail, raising both arms towards the sky. Holding up a brass platter, he displayed small mounds of white rice, soaked and patted into five small pyramids. The tantric lurched towards the five accused, parted their jaws with one hand and fed each his share of the rice. He ordered them to chew, as hard as their last meal, then spit it all out on a green banana leaf. 'From the culprit's mouth the rice will come forth, not like milk, but dry as mortar.'

'That's unfair!' Hiran protested. 'The guilty *as well* as the innocent would spit dry. Saliva was bound to retract in fear.'

'The rice stuck to their lips and wriggling tongues. Mr Crabbe had them all arrested, bound hand and feet, and carried away like dead fish.'

Nabinbaboo feigned indifference when Hiran told him the story. Yet from his eyes behind gold-rimmed glasses, Hiran knew he cared. Cared enough to ask regularly if he had received his 'charges', gave casual advice: 'Remember, your employer is simply your employer.'

The rice ordeal intrigued Hiran. Somehow, the two images – Mr Crabbe among the budding poppy with his wife, and whispering to a tantric – seemed to belong in two different tales, each with its own cast of gods and animals. He had given Vinny that half-believing look.

'Call me a dung-eating pimp if I've lied!'

'Call me a leper! May my limbs rot, my tongue . . .' Interrupting his own story, Vinny unwrapped yet another secret: 'She's a Yenshee-baby, a real jolly-popper.'

Hiran was amazed. 'Lilian? You mean, she takes afim in her sherbets?'

'More than that, my jewel.' He proceeded to present his case. 'She has it in pills, in her tea, beer, lodnum . . . you name it. Now the snake Kavasji is her headcook, and number fifteen their pleasure-den!' Reading Hiran's mind, he went on, 'Oh yes! he knows . . . the house is too hot to hold him now!'

Hiran knew she was sickly. He had heard servant talk of tooth-aches, cramps, a swollen leg, colic, and slow fever. Sundays were her day of rest and he saw her rarely at number 15. But the deep, even breathing lasted throughout the morning, hung over the walls like a backdrop to the fluttering esraj and Mr Crabbe's readings. Hiran knew she was there. From time to time, Mr Crabbe would look up from his book, as if expecting something, but his face would remain impassive.

Hiran imagined her tone, examined murmurs laced with unknown words, conversations that seemed near yet diffused like uneven light. Was she really a 'hop-head', dreaming of fishes and drowning, like their Annada?

A tide had risen at the Auction House, silence replaced murmurs. A storm was about to break, they knew. Around

Kidderpore docks, busy birds made the most of the quiet between storms. Small black-headed gulls flew between the masts. Bigger ones, greyish-brown, swooped over the no-man's-land between the piers engrossed by the mystery of wet sand.

The *Cassandra*, back from Canton with a cargo of missionaries, lay in the moorings. Sailors from Chittagong stood on pilings bending sails, balanced over narrow bridges. Their headman – the sareng – called out orders from the spar-deck. Used to the choppy sea, they swayed at his call, held on to the ropes as if expecting the mast to rise and fall. The branch pilot in his seat under an umbrella looked bored, lighting up cigarette after cigarette in quick succession.

The captains would turn up around noon, each with his Indian servant. They looked bored too, and burnt from the sun. Some stayed long enough to check the cannons, to have musket-balls greased and counted. Around the branch pilot's desk, laughter rose above the sareng's call. At times the talk turned serious.

Leadsmen waiting to take charge of incoming and outgoing ships had set up surface nets – large bags tied to spars and held in the water by menials. The catch usually consisted of shrimps, swarming at the water's surface, bumalo, pomfret, and silver fish used as bait. Sometimes a sailor would holler in excitement at a river snake caught in the nets. They would rush down the masts or break away from scrubbing gullies, and chatter over the yellow and black creature, lifting it up by its tail. Captains usually took notice too, especially with rare marine fauna, strange-coloured shells, or sea-spiders. Men were instructed to soak these in spirits and keep them in glass jars till a junior officer found time to take a batch over to the Calcutta Museum.

Floating on a chalk-white river, far from the shore, fishermen dropped their nets and lay still.

Only the Auction House seemed to be in a frenzy. A grim Nabinbaboo read aloud the Royal Commission's six-point charter to Hiran and Vinny, the most important point first: 'Whether the growth of the poppy and manufacture and sale of opium in British India should be prohibited, except for medicinal purposes, and whether such prohibition could be extended to the Native States.' They knew of the arrival of the Commission's officers, a handful of Englishmen and the Maharajah of Darbhanga, raising the tempo to a fever pitch, investigating the sale of opium. They were after witnesses – officers, clerks, peasants, even addicts. Like the monsoon, their attention shifted course without warning – London to Calcutta, Patna, Benares, native states of Rajputana and Gujrat, even to Burma. To the gentoos in the east wing, used to a different tide, the flow of 'witnesses' appeared incongruous.

The 'mud' was valuable, no one argued with that. Second only to salt as a source of Government revenue. The prize of several wars, the trade had been won by the British from the Dutch and the Nawabs. Even the Emperor of China, Hiran knew, had agreed to its sale after losing his own war with the British. Everyone at the Auction House was proud of their 'mud', the uncrowned king of opium, far superior to the black and hard from Aden, or the other varieties from Surat and Persia which smelt of dirt and filth.

'The threat is from England,' Nabinbaboo explained. 'It's the Quakers, drawn to the souls of Chinamen, not their pockets.' These were the men behind the Commission, petitioning Westminster to put an end to a 'barbarous trade in a heinous drug'. The Commission was here to rule on the future of their Auction House.

'But without our mud what are the ships good for? Will they burn the ships too?' Vinny was shocked.

'Wait!' Nabinbaboo raised his palm, tinged blue by the sapphire. 'Where will the Englishmen and the Maharajah find their witnesses? Where will they find the addicts? All witnesses will be hand-picked by our Superintendent and his Deputy and paraded over the lawn!'

'So, in the end they'll only find clean hands!' Vinny laughed, then thumped on Hiran's desk. 'Didn't I tell you, it's like a play at The Emerald Theatre!'

'Listen to what our friends have to say.' Nabinbaboo drew a sheaf of paper from his desk. 'Here's Lord Salisbury, Sir George Campbell . . . even the Viceroy himself.' Once again he read to a rapt Hiran and Vinny: ' "The drug, opium that is, is no more harmful than alcoholic stimulants used by Western nations . . . the opium sot has a decided advantage over the drunkard, not being noisy, quarrelsome, and often dangerous as the other is." This is from *The Times*: "Casual pipes can be smoked without harm, and the smoker can give up the drug at any moment he wishes to." Listen to Mr Birdwood . . . "We are as free to introduce opium to China and to raise a revenue from it in India, as to export our cotton, wool and iron manufactures to France." Here's Samuel Laing . . . "The Chinese, whose greatest deficiency is in the imaginative faculties, resorts to that which stimulates the imagination and makes his sluggish brain see visions and dream dreams." '

'Isn't that true?' Vinny seemed confused. 'Why would we send it to China if they didn't want it?' Nabinbaboo nodded his head, went on reading: 'China wants our opium, our traders and merchants are ready to supply it.'

'But it's good for us.' Pulling out yet another page from Nabinbaboo's sheaf, Vinny read: 'If the Chinese must be poisoned, we would rather they were poisoned for the benefit of our Indian subjects than for the benefit of any other exchequer.'

'If it's just a game, why pretend? Why account for every chest, fill up ledgers?' Vinny brooded on their way home.

Hiran was tempted to tell him the story of the king and the proud warrior.

'One day the King called his favourite warrior, and said: "I want you to prepare a funeral." "For whom shall I arrange this grand cremation?" the warrior asked. "For you, my dear General. Inform all the ministers of my kingdom. Let them bring gifts for the dead – gold, sandalwood, and cattle. Let your wives go into mourning; hand over the reins of your horse to your favourite son. Then, choose three brahmins to conduct your last rites. Remember, all citizens must assemble at the square, all business must cease for the hour." "And how shall I die, my Lord?" "Death, dear General, shall arrive at the appointed hour."

'The warrior knew the King was playing a trick on him. Yet, he went about preparing the grounds, advising his son, saying farewell to his wives.

'Everyone knew the wise King would never stoop to murder. Yet, they went solemnly about the funeral. The warrior's wives wept real tears, his son took charge of his horse, the priests arrived, and a great pyre of sandalwood was built at the capital's square.

'Then, at high noon, the King appeared. First, he surveyed the arrangements, and motioned to the priests to begin chanting. For a whole hour he sat on his throne in silence facing the kneeling warrior. The crowd pulsed; the warrior's family wailed. Then the King asked his General to take his place on the sandalwood pyre. Lighting a strand of kash he stepped into the circle. Walking around the warrior seven times, he made as if to light the pyre . . .'

'Stop!' Vinny screamed. 'I thought you said it was a trick.'

'It was. Unknown to the warrior, the King had had the sandalwood replaced with stones.'

He was tempted to say more, draw a clever link between knowing and pretending. For once he understood Nabinbaboo perfectly. Hiran had no trouble seeing the Royal Commission's part in this simple tale.

The maid received him in the usual room, served his goat's milk and gave him a note in Mr Crabbe's sloping hand. His pupil asked to be excused from 'lessons' that day, and invited Hiran to a Hindoo puja that would be held next week at the home of an acquaintance. He would not be alone, he was assured, much less a stranger to the host, who was none other than Nabinbaboo.

Hiran remembered Mr Crabbe staring at Nabinbaboo's palms, and Nabinbaboo staring back with the ease of well-rehearsed actors. The invitation intrigued him. Did Nabinbaboo know of it? What was the bond between Mr Crabbe and Nabinbaboo?

His mochtar cousin who knew Nabinbaboo's family added to the intrigue: 'Your Nabinbaboo is the loser of the lot . . . squandering fortunes, sinking the family's name. Whoever heard of an aristocrat going to work in an office like a lowly clerk? He's a good-for-nothing, no match for his brothers. The eldest is the owner of a stable, the second a patron of the arts, the third . . .' Rumours claimed the brothers wanted to get rid of him. He had been passed off to the Auction House to protect the family's considerable fortunes. A rare illness made him keep a low profile, had him obsessed with homeopathy. One of the head clerks told Hiran of Nabinbaboo's *real* identity. 'He's a spy for his merchant brothers, sniffing the breeze, taking a hefty cut from smuggled opium.'

It was difficult to imagine Nabinbaboo as a 'black sheep', or a cunning thief. Despite occasional banter, he seemed genuinely concerned at Vinny's chronically ailing stomach, spent hours going over his symptoms, tracing the intestine in his books, writing every week in his patient's diary: vomiting, hiccups, palpitation, a bitter taste, burning bowels, green mucus with stool, retching, flatulence. He asked a red-faced Vinny if he was calm or restless at night, if his extremities felt numb, if his breath felt cold. He asked him to come back and report on the colour of his urine. It wasn't unusual to find Nabinbaboo and Vinny together, their backs to the river, the patient sitting with his tongue hanging out.

Sometimes Nabinbaboo read aloud from one of his books: 'Diarrhoea is generally a symptom, or is developed in connection with some other disease. It may at times be looked upon as a dangerous, even an alarming sign, and again as a precursor of returning health. It is both a favourable and an unfavourable indication.' Vinny was dumbfounded. 'Is it good or bad?' Frustrated at Nabinbaboo's frequent 'Hmm . . .'s, he pressed his case. 'Is it true I have to exchange my blood with a Chinaman?' Nabinbaboo returned to his books.

If anything, Nabinbaboo was to the east wing as Mr Scott was to the west – a master fisherman guiding errant shoals to the nets. Hiran rarely heard him raise his voice. The eyes behind his gold-rimmed glasses stared impassively. He did not seem capable of digression or risk, would rebuke Hiran if he showed undue haste in sorting the piles of letters.

Only once had he betrayed real surprise. A junior baboo, visiting from the Patna factory, had fainted beneath Lord Kydd's portrait. Nabinbaboo had slipped a white pellet under his tongue and fanned him with the end of his dhoti. The heat was blamed; the junior baboo had gone for a walk by the river during tiffin-break. Or perhaps it was the opium to which Beharis were known to be addicted; perhaps the long journey on the steam loco had tired him: his eyes were red from fatigue. Vinny, as usual, spurred on the speculations.

Hiran, however, quietly declared, 'It's the heart.'

Nabinbaboo looked up with a start. Hiran wasn't one to offer wild conjectures. Nabinbaboo's pointed brows showed surprise, and a desire for an explanation.

'It's the Hepatica . . . twisted and wavy, red near the Heart-line.' Hiran pointed to the limp palms, bloodless, with a blood-red health-line like a recent scar. The gentoos laughed, cracked jokes about Hiran's broad forehead. But Nabinbaboo was silent, still fanning with his dhoti.

A week later they heard the poor man had died in Patna of heart failure.

The incident hung over their desks, unspoken, tingeing their exchanges. They resisted a direct consultation, as if words would break the spell each had cast, but a bond formed between them.

'Hmm . . . I wish to take a day's holiday too.' Nabinbaboo

spoke of the puja at his ancestral home – a century-old celebration. Hiran watched him closely. Would he invite him now? An impassive voice spoke of traditions: customary feasts for brahmins followed by a gathering of Calcutta's best in the evening. Merchants and Maharajahs would be in attendance, the Viceroy himself had come in 1879, the Magistrate of Howrah visited every year, Secretaries and Aides-de-Camp were expected. After dinner there'd be a cultural event – a mix of East and West – sitar-players rubbing shoulders with amateur operetta. The evening, of course, would end with a feast for the beggars from neighbouring alleys.

'May I leave after tiffin-break . . . I've been invited to . . .' Hiran began.

'Yes.'

His mother was happy when Hiran told her of the invitation to the puja. Finally her Hira had found his own kind – men of respectable Hindoo families. She told him more about Nabinbaboo's family. They had been poor, poorer than Annada. The great-grandfather had gone to work as a steward in a rich trader's warehouse. A talent for numbers, and fierce loyalty had seen him rise above the others, but it was honesty that rewarded him most richly. Hidden in a consignment of zinc, he had found silver. Handing it over to the merchant, he received an oil-mill in return. After that advance, the family had risen rapidly – through trade and, as a handful of detractors claimed, usury and extortion in the name of the Company.

Even Annada had heard of the eight brothers – of their nautches, golden idols, and lavish courting of Europeans: 'Memsahibs dance in their courtyards like whores of Jaanbazaar!' 'Yes, yes . . .' Hiran waved her away, then imitated her tone: 'They light cheroots with ten-rupee notes, weigh their wives in gold then squander the gold among beggars!'

'Why don't you ask your friend to appoint you as priest in their family shrine? Then you wouldn't have to mix with that lot of half-castes,' Saraladebi said.

'You'll see how your friend treats you before the sahibs,' a hurt Annada put in. She knew more about kite-flying, pigeon-swirling baboos than Hiran, had lived long enough to remember the sins of their fathers and grandfathers. Saraladebi calmed her with a special paan smelling of sweet camphor.

Hiran kept the invitation to the puja a secret from Vinny.

On his way to Nabinbaboo's house, Hiran saw the city overrun by throngs of wretched beggars who had lost their homes in the year of floods. Alms changed hands, drums announced beggars, some dressed as dancers. One, made up as a European with the face of a dog, chased a bunch of urchins, curses streaming from his red-painted lips. The crowd egged him on, dropped coins in one bowl or another.

Nabinbaboo's house was near the tole where he had studied as a boy. He followed the road from memory. Temple bells had started to sound earlier than usual for the puja, drowning out the beggars. He was tempted to pay a visit to his old teacher, to consult him on the significance of a star he had spotted on the palm of the esraj player at number 15. He felt he could have erred spotting the star on so white a palm. Somehow it seemed to hold the answer to many of the mysteries at number 15.

When he arrived at Nabinbaboo's house, Hiran felt dizzy in the scent-sprayed doorway. Turbaned door-keepers ushered in a crowd of invitees to join the eight brothers in the marble-columned quadrangle. Hiran looked out at the garden through etched Venetian glass doors. He saw a peacock strut past an alabaster lion, stone infants clinging to their mothers, bashful maidens, and a pond with ducks.

Hiran recognized no one from the Auction House. At around eight the bells started, and the chants. Incense descended on them like a cloud from the upper level of the house where there was a shrine of deities, and the crowd fell silent. He could not see Nabinbaboo. He felt awkward, hoped to catch sight of a familiar face. Annada's words flashed through his mind – *You'll see how your friend treats you* – but Nabinbaboo didn't know he was there, did he? Why had Mr Crabbe asked him to come? Where was he hiding?

He was about to leave when the peon of number 15 spotted him and flashed a friendly smile. He led Hiran back up to the shrine, still buzzing with chants and rushing footsteps. He pointed at an open door and motioned Hiran to enter.

In the room sat Mr Crabbe on a red velvet settee beside a statue of a sea-horse. His face had taken on the colour of amber glass. Next to him Lilian examined a vase under the soft glow of a chandelier. Hiran heard the punkah, and the tinkle of glasses in the sudden silence.

Mr Crabbe motioned him to sit. Then he introduced Hiran to Nabinbaboo's brothers and their friends: 'Baboo Hiranyagarbha Chakraborti, my teacher of Sanskrit and the scriptures.' Lilian continued to gaze. One of the brothers with a certain resemblance to Nabinbaboo gave Hiran a courteous smile. 'Ah! A brahmin. Tell us, why must we have rains when the Goddess promises a safe harvest?'

'Was it a divine promise, or one made by pundits?' Someone cleared his throat.

'What would you prefer then, a famine or floods?'

'Beggars may sing as much as they want, is the government listening?'

'Why should anyone listen when the Goddess herself has turned a deaf ear?'

'You speak like a heretic . . .' There was good-natured laughter.

Mr Crabbe lit one of his cheroots, passed it on to Lilian. Hiran felt weak from the long walk and the effects of the incense.

'Who amongst us remembers . . .'

Before the speaker could finish, Mr Crabbe's voice interrupted from the settee. 'Let me tell you a story . . . a story from the *Panchatantra*, you know . . .

'Once there was a kind merchant given to charitable deeds. But fate was hostile and he lost his entire fortune. Gradually, his reputation diminished, and his friends left him one by one. Overwhelmed by grief he decided to starve to death.'

Hiran knew the story.

'In his sleep the merchant dreamt of a poor beggar who appeared before him and said, "I am your fortune, the sum of all your good deeds. Tomorrow I shall come to your home, just as you see me – a beggar praying for alms. Strike me on my head with a stick and I shall turn into gold. You'll be rich once again."

'The merchant woke early with a spinning head. He remembered his dream but blamed it on his rotten mood. Then he saw a beggar – the beggar of his dreams – appearing by his door. Delighted, he struck the beggar on the head and, just as promised, the beggar turned into a pile of gold.'

Laughter filled the room. The man with the face like Nabinbaboo clapped his hands. Was he going to tell them the rest of the story? Who was he mocking? Hiran frowned. Why had he chosen such a strange story? Wouldn't his listeners already know the ending . . . of the *other* merchant, the unscrupulous one, who had seen the spectacle from his window? He, of course, had drawn the wrong conclusion – waited for a beggar to come knocking on his door, a well-oiled stick at the ready. Faced at last with his prey, the cruel merchant struck mercilessly – like Mr Crabbe's men punishing defaulting peasants on their Auction House lawn. Blood, not gold, had smeared his palms.

'You must have told Mr Crabbe the story of death and the three wishes, have you?' Hiran felt Lilian's eyes on him. Her hands no longer held the vase. Hiran smiled weakly.

'Do you know what *my* wishes are?' Hiran shook his head. 'Why don't you tell him, Jonathan, before your witch goes flying off on her broomstick!' Hiran turned red, sensing a secret about to reveal itself. Mr Crabbe reached over the settee to whisper into Lilian's ear. In the shuffle of feet behind him, Hiran heard dancers – ankle-bells and the swish of their trains.

He excused himself before the dancing began, shaking Lilian's hand; she was busy with the magistrate's wife. But he lost his way in the passages. It was late and he knew Saraladebi would be anxious. He was worried about getting a ticca-gari at this hour, legs revolting at the prospect of another long walk. Following his ears rather than his eyes, he felt himself coming close to familiar voices. A short flight of steps brought him to the roof.

The damp air woke Hiran as if from a dream. From the ramparts he saw gas lamps lining the alleys below. Voices gathered like insects around the lamps, filling the lanes with their din. The breeze carried the sharp stench of burning wood.

From his vantage point on the roof, Hiran saw the beggars line up for their feast. He wondered if the dancers were there as well. Actors blended with beggars, sitting by the road with banana leaves stretched out, waiting for the doormen to bring over vats of rice. Hiran knew they were waiting for the priests to blow the conch-shells, announcing the end of the evening. Hiran waited too. He dozed off for a few minutes, and woke to a rapid volley of explosions. He saw the crowd stampede, heard a mixture of cries and moans rise up from the alleys like a cloud of gunpowder. More explosions followed. Hiran heard drums, and shrill calls for help. Breaking free he searched for the stairs. Panic clutched at his throat. He thought he heard Saraladebi scream, disappearing in a sea of mangled limbs: *Hira!* His head knocked against a stone column, bringing him to his senses with a thud of pain. The lights went out one by one, and darkness swallowed the pond and the marble statues. Then he saw Nabinbaboo in the full moon – his white aachkan flapping wildly – hurling bottles of soda-water down at the beggars below.

'Where were you, my jewel?' Vinny rushed in wearing a Chinese Hoppo's hat with a red button. 'Captain Jacque is here,' he said, 'but hiding from the Auction House. It's that Commission business.' Vinny had news, *pucca*-news: Captain Jacque had found him a bride, a real Portuguese . . . well, almost. The sister of a tanka girl who had nursed the Captain back to health after Hong Kong fever. She was fair-skinned, with long black hair, just a touch of slant in her black eyes from a Hakka grandmother, but without the snub nose. 'Marie, Marie . . .' He danced around Hiran's desk. 'And, you'll come with me to get her!'

Vinny was too excited to notice the empty desk facing Hiran – Nabinbaboo was yet to return from his holiday.

At the Auction House the tide had taken a different turn. The east wing buzzed with rumours: some even said Mr Scott was to be put on trial. The Royal Commission had heard some seven hundred witnesses, examined more than two thousand pages of testimony, appendices, reports, memoranda, and annexures. In the end the Maharajah and the Englishmen had acquitted Lord Kydd's hammer. But they had found startling irregularities in the course of their investigations – between chests received and traded, signatures, and debits to the Royal Treasury, empty files marked with fake labels at the east wing. Corruption was rampant in the Auction House, the Commission ruled. Some said that Mr Scott's nose was into everything, that he had grown richer than the Viceroy.

'Mr Scott is innocent. A fool, but innocent.' Vinny was quick with his theory. Distracted by Marie, he was still a keen observer of the tide. 'Your friends are the real culprits.' He looked at Hiran accusingly, demanded to know where Crabbe the Military Brahmin was hiding with the Parsee scarecrow. For a moment Hiran thought of telling him about the puja at Nabinbaboo's family home, but didn't. He worried for Nabinbaboo more than for himself.

'Why would Mr Crabbe set up the Superintendent . . .'

'Because he wants a share of the mud, a fat share. And your Kavasji is greedy too. Crabbe needs the money. Needs it for her . . . the sleepy memsahib.'

Later, at the Strand, Vinny went over the fantastic story with Hiran. Scott and Crabbe were enemies from the beginning, Vinny said – like the owl and the crow. The story went that Mr Scott had known his Deputy from when he was a boy in school. They were always together at the Auction House – inspecting, measuring, leaving early on Saturday mornings for a snipe-shoot – but it was the closeness of enemies, the intimacy of suspicion. The rumours had them both tainted by the mud – partners in a fraudulent enterprise. 'The Crabbes went with Kavasji to Patna to meet the old Nawab Mir Muneer's great-grandson. The little scoundrel helped the snake Kavasji smuggle out hundreds of chests right under Mr Eliot's nose. It was simple, my jewel. There's nothing these Mussalmans won't do for the taste of a white woman. The Crabbes wined and dined in the old Nawab's castle. They made Mr Eliot sign a fake release, sending off the smuggled opium to Mr Scott's personal account. Mr Eliot was too nervous to protest, he was scared of the Deputy, feared another *rice-ordeal.* Then, it was simple – the chests floated down on country-boats over the Ganga to the Sandheads.'

'But where's Mr Scott's hand in all this?'

Like a magician, Vinny pulled the rabbit out of the hat. 'Right here, my jewel . . . in your ledger, bearing your signature.' He described for an alarmed Hiran the forged letter that had flowed over his desk, ordering the transfer of five hundred chests of trade-opium to Mr Scott's personal account. 'Mr Crabbe told Blinkey to check the customs papers at Sandhead, and then, the loot was discovered. And Scott got the blame.'

Was Hiran a suspect too? Suddenly he remembered Nabin-baboo's early warning: 'Remember, a letter is not simply a letter, but the inner breath of the writer . . . a breath that hides as much as it reveals. A reader must cross the barrier of words and invade his thoughts.' Which of the two, he wondered, was the good merchant? Scott or Crabbe?

'What happened to the five hundred chests?'

'They were returned to Patna. Like an unwed bride to her father.'

Rumours flew about both wings. The Superintendent was to be put on trial, but it was Crabbe's doing, the gentoos whispered over tiffin-break. Mr Crabbe wasn't to be seen in the Auction House at all, and his house was empty during the day, like a haunted house. The gentoos pointed fingers across the lawn. Crabbe was not your ordinary British officer – those who came to India dreaming of mucking around for a few years before retiring home, rich, to live as country gentlemen. He had a taste for stories – vicious ones taught to him by a shadowy brahmin. Some relished the sleepy memsahib story. They saw her waxen bony face – yellow, shrunk over her cheekbones, eyes slanted like a Cheeny. 'Only her speech is English.' Mr Kavasji, of course, was consort to both – a clever hermaphrodite artful in his vengeance.

The room was dark as usual, but Hiran heard a different music: a moan, as if from drowning; saw Mr Crabbe's shadow hovering on the wall. He didn't notice the pile of books, nor his goat's milk. The house seemed empty. Hiran hesitated.

'Speak to me . . . Speak.'

'Where does it hurt?' he heard. 'Where, Lilian?'

A fit of coughing drowned his voice. Mr Crabbe was walking in a circle around the bed, his footsteps receding to the darkest corner. He heard Lilian's voice gasping over short stabs of breath.

Hiran sat on the tram. *You can't imagine the way she is . . .* The peon's words flashed through his mind. A recurring image – of a field of poppy – invaded the dark room at number 15.

He couldn't have known of the lace-maker with a baby across her lap – women of the Fens given to nature's tyrant laws, and the mercy of poppy. Even before the midwife had rubbed raw opium on her baby's gums, she had fed her colostrum rich in *Godfrey's* – poppy-tea smelling of brown sugar. 'Drops you are, darling!' She had rocked her to sleep with a half-penny of *Kendal's Black Drops*, fed three times to stop her wankle. Opium was her breast, the toy she left for her baby at the lodging house while she worked at the mill. Elsewhere, they crowded the druggist; there wasn't a home without its penny stick of pills. *Keeps women-folk quiet*, it was said, calmed wild horses before they went on sale, kept pigs and mad men from crying.

He couldn't have seen her then, among the legitimate and the illegitimate at the lodging house – a child of five nursing a child of two, while the nurse of seven kept an eye on her, in summers playing and sleeping in the dirt, in the winter before a hungry fire. She had learnt to mix it herself – drops with sugar and water, oatmeal and pap for infants. She saw older girls in back streets with lozenges, 'sleepy-beer' and sweetcakes, knew of the tincture used by whores to drug and rob their clients. It made the night sweet – and for some, like the nursery maid at the mill owner's house, too sweet: in a fit of jealous love she had had *a sup of laudanum*, and slept with her eyes open. She had grown up with tales of mothers ridding themselves of babies, of old women giving it to their husbands to quieten forever their pain, of doctors waking the dead with a mix of warm water and hair-oil. She was positively 'poison-proof', she'd brag, sitting with a pill between her teeth in church.

Years later, Hiran would remember Lilian telling him about the child of the Fens. She was luckier than the other girls, she would tell him, growing up in Lincolnshire, destined to live and die by the mill. Her mother had died early. After that, she had started on her rounds – as a maid in homes full of fine china and singing toys. She learned the custom of rich stately homes – they suited her, she started to dream of one of her own. Her fine, sad face drew more than coachmen and butlers. But she had spurned them all, coming to London to work in the home of a retired ship's captain. She heard new words, learned of faraway places, of powerful merchants. From maid she became governess, impressing all with her comely manners, and found her place among men and women she admired. There was one young man she met at a party, a strange one called Jonathan Crabbe. Like her, he wanted to fly, promised to carry her away on his powerful wings. Then, she became truly lucky, the stuff of gossip – the Fen girl who landed a Company man.

Her husband told her about the merry ladies and gentlemen she was about to meet in India. He told her of the bungalow that would be hers, beside a vast river, of the carriages and servants. She learned from him about the Auction House for Indian opium where her husband was a senior officer – more powerful than the mill owner of her town in the Fens. Wonderful! she had thought.

He was invited to tea on the balcony of number 15 after his lessons with Mr Crabbe. He saw Lilian and Mr Kavasji. She held a two-handled cup, round as a teapot, upon which hearts were impaled by Cupid's dart. She smiled at Hiran then turned to listen to Mr Kavasji. 'It was made for the English market, in the seventeen sixties. There would have been a tureen as well, with a European ceramic design like the German Künersberg.'

'Why don't they have Chinese designs?' Lilian asked Mr Kavasji. 'I'd love a *Fitzhugh* actually. You think that ape Jacque will be able to get me one?'

'Once I asked him to look for an Imperial . . . the heavenly court with Dowager and eunuchs. Guess what he returned with?

A haw-hawing King George!' Mr Kavasji's laugh surprised the crows which gathered on the balconies.

For the first time he saw her cheerful, the tea seemed to have warmed her delicate lips. Lilian motioned to her maid. She disappeared, then returned with Hiran's milk.

'I'd prefer a whole set, a tea set really, one made for pirates . . . the skull and cross bones on a black shield,' Mr Crabbe announced with a smile. 'Perhaps Harinbaboo would like one with a story!' They smiled at him. 'I remember a story, a rather funny one.' Mr Kavasji sipped from his cup, and cleared his throat. 'My father had taken me to see a show at the Opera House to celebrate Muktad – before the Zoroastrian New Year. We knew there'd be two plays – *Leila and Mejnoon* in Urdu, and *The Taming of the Shrew*. I was very excited. My sisters told me I'd see *real* Parsee girls on stage, not men dressed up. Of course, I understood neither English nor Urdu. Throughout the show, I kept looking at my father's face. When he laughed, I laughed. When he frowned, I frowned. He seemed to follow the actors' lines, clapping at the end and shouting, "Encore, encore," like everybody else. When I returned my sisters asked me: "So, wouldn't you die for your Leila, too?" Die? I'd tame her with a whip!'

Hiran saw the shadow return to Lilian's eyes. She still held the cup, her face reflected in its bone white. She seemed to infect it, by her golden hair and drooping mouth, with a touch of her sadness.

Soon it would be time – her hour for chills and shiver. She glanced restlessly at the clock, hands beginning to shake like the soft flutter of a dying snipe. She picked up an armorial plaque or a chestnut bowl, aimlessly sifting through Mr Kavasji's recent collection. Yawn – first, barely through parted lips, then violently. 'Ayah!' she called, plunging a hand recklessly into the boiling teapot. Her eyes filled with tears, but not for her scalded skin.

Sneezing would be heard along the long corridor, muffled under blankets, or pillows. Suddenly a hot flash released every pore, draining her – mucus, sweat, urine – arms flailing at the punkah's cord. Her breath blended with moans that would finally wake her ayah from her afternoon nap.

By the time she came up the stairs, Lilian would be in her yen sleep.

Only particular sounds woke her – like the esraj. She thought she was hearing the whir of looms, and a thousand babies crying for milk. A knot at the back of her throat made her stain her pillow with bile. Then, there were cramps, a sickness that penetrated everywhere – even her twitching sex contracting in pleasure and pain.

'Ayah!' This time Ayah would be ready, holding the beaker to her lips. She would fight her sleep, remain in a state of drowsiness broken by moments of supreme clarity watching the seductive coalescence of a colourless drop on the tip of colourless glass.

Gradually she had spread her pleasure among the servants. One day the ayah came to her with a running stomach. She gave a medicine that relieved her, but after a while the trouble returned. On a day of thunderstorms the gardener slipped in the kitchen yard and broke his arm. Before the durwan could sling him over his shoulder and run to the Civil Lines, she had calmed the howling. She'd press Captain Jacque – a frequent visitor to her dinner parties – to show his trick: how the Chinaman smoked his pipe. He laid down for her on the couch, resting his head on a pillow. With the pipe in one hand, the other dipped a six-inch needle into a jar of opium. Then he warmed the needle over a little lamp till the dark mud softened like clay ready to drop into the bowl. He pulled on his pipe, made faces that made everyone laugh. 'As he sucks and swallows, the veins in his forehead get thicker, till he looks like a satisfied pig! The more he sucks, the finer his nostrils become, like an enraptured hog! He lies on one hip all the time. Has a crooked walk, poor chap!'

For her, the drops ruled – 'deluxe doses' made to tingle and itch. She felt brittle, not the fear of falling to pieces, but as in an ecstasy of rupture. Her breath was easier, the bed seemed soft. She recognized each vase and picture, knew the precise occasion of their giving. Sometimes she appeared on the balcony in a chemise soiled by her secretions, the ayah following her through dark corridors with a wet sponge. She'd complain of a heaviness in her stomach. 'I can feel the baby drop . . .' She'd wink, feign labour. Ayah would play her part, massage the belly, raise her knees to her chin.

She and Ayah would spend a whole afternoon in the dark, stop playing suddenly when they heard Mr Crabbe's steps on the stairs. She'd push her ayah away and start a different game, whimpering, lugging, wrapping herself around his camel jacket, flailing at the cords of his silk robe. She would speak in the voice of the Fens – a deep gurgle of marshes and fetid air.

He would look alarmed when she came sliding naked down the mahogany rails of the stairs to meet him – attempt to steer her into a room. She would escape his hold, hide behind the settee, make a lewd gesture with the esraj.

'I hate those stupid crows . . . stop them, Jonathan.' He closed the shutters, tried to read to her. 'Hate stories . . . stupid crows, stupid dogs, stupid death.'

'We're at Scott's tonight. It's his farewell. You remember, don't you?' She made a face. Her ash burnt a hole on the wicker.

'Shall I ask Kavasji to join us?'

'Stupid, stupid, stupid,' she whispered.

At the party in the Scott mansion, Mrs Fay was describing her chef – a Mong Khansama from Burma, with 'heavenly looks'. A couple of native gentlemen hovered around, stained with the odour of brandy. Lilian heard Captain Jacque's laugh, as he entertained the company with his jokes and lies about everything and everybody. 'Once I knew a Frenchman who loved turkey . . .' She knew that story. She returned to Mrs Fay and her stories about thieving servants: 'Ramsingh is a barber's son and a barber himself, but he pretends to be a carpenter. He managed to remain in our employment for ten years undetected. You should see his atrocious creations!' She told stories about Janoose, a Malabar girl who had stolen her pencil bracelet, Calloo, the cook who tried to pass off a stolen typewriter as a musical box. Mrs Fay ruled supreme over the whist table. Her husband, the Magistrate, was soon to be knighted.

Like a wind on the river Lilian blew from one table to another. She felt like a cloud dissolving through skin and bones, circulating in the veins, unresisted. Restless feet ached for a touch of the lawn. Before the gong could sound and assemble everyone under the royal portraits, she had escaped to the pantry. The servants seemed to have disappeared, like well-fed rats into their holes. She passed the cellar full of boxes: Martell, Hennessey, V.H.D., Moët, Bass, cunningly shaped bottles suggestive of schnapps and cocktails, barley ham and sweet-smelling English bacon in cloth-wraps. She came upon a short black boy wearing a red velvet skull-cap sitting on an empty shelf. 'Good evening, Mrs Crabbe,' said Vinny.

When she woke during the night, the thought tempted her, and if she lay awake she was likely to yield. 'Ayah . . .' she would call in a feeble voice. 'Ayah . . .' Each time raising her voice a little till she woke the woman and spread her temptation. Then all would be equal: a white lady and her black ayah holding the beaker to each other's lips. She'd feel a cosy arm in the silence of the lace-loom.

Hiran grew accustomed to sitting on the balcony with Mr Crabbe after their readings. Mr Kavasji would often be there too, and the three of them talked about ships and wars. Hiran found Mr Kavasji as knowledgeable as Vinny, but more cautious. Their chat shifted like smoke from an open fire. Mr Crabbe would tell them of the woes of the Chinese. He'd recite one imperial edict after another, pretending to be a pig-tailed Mandarin: 'Keepers of opium shops must be strangled, their assistants given a hundred strokes of bamboo and three months of prison followed by banishment to a distance of one thousand miles. Boatmen will be similarly dealt with; customs officers will be fined, even for carelessness. Only the addict will go free . . .' Hiran looked at him amazed.

'How do you punish the dead?' Mr Crabbe asked by way of explanation.

Hiran shivered in the breeze.

'Didn't you learn Ayurvedic medicine at the tole?' Mr Crabbe asked.

'All brahmins are required to know the basics, I'm told.' Mr Kavasji looked at Hiran encouragingly.

'Maybe you can help Lilian. She's been suffering lately,' Mr Crabbe said.

Later, returning home on the tram, Hiran felt confused by the request. He hadn't said yes or no, but somehow his agreement was assumed. Would they believe him if he said he knew nothing of Ayurveda? That his mother probably knew more about foul-smelling, evil-tasting mixtures than him? That his teacher at the tole was keener on palms than herbs?

Hiran resisted the urge to consult his mother. Not only would he betray too great a familiarity with his pupil, but she might resent even more his patient – a memsahib. Her suspicions had already been roused: 'What do you teach that takes so long?' 'You mustn't allow his wife to touch your feet. Bless her, if you must, from a distance.' 'Don't be a fool and teach him everything you know.' He suspected his mother smelt the cheroots on his shirt. Probably she saw through his other lie as well – a full stomach from a brahmin's meal at Madan Mohun Jiu's temple on his way back.

He also dismissed Annada as a possible helper. She could not be trusted. Hiran feared her mischief, feared she might mix up the herbs for her own purposes.

In the end, he could only think of Nabinbaboo. Perhaps he could give him something too to calm his heart when he stood next to Lilian on the balcony.

'Hahneman was a white brahmin,' Nabinbaboo said cordially

when Hiran approached him with the request for medicine. 'Only the pure in spirit can treat an impure body. That is, once he has mastered the true Materia Medica.' Hiran was careful not to divulge the identity of his patient. He sought an agreement in principle, a contract to treat a disease rather than a living being. Perhaps Nabinbaboo would guess, but he wished to avoid a connection. After all, he'd simply be the messenger – like a court-boy between a hakim and the Queen in purdah.

'It's Lilian, isn't it? She wants your hocus pocus,' Vinny guessed. 'She's gone mad, completely. I saw her the other day, muttering to herself, dark circles under her eyes.' Nabinbaboo looked up from his desk: 'Circles – a dark halo like soot from an oil lamp, or a wound full of pus?' He waved Vinny away impatiently, then spoke in his usual measured tone. 'Look, Hiran, a doctor doesn't need rumours, but facts. You must bring me what I ask for – pulse, tone of the skin and tongue, any abnormal signs like swelling or faltering breath. You must check if she is deaf, weak in eyesight, if she is given to fits. If she complains of pain, you must verify its duration. If she looks pale you should enquire of her bleeding.'

'What if she is only pretending?'

'Then pretend to be her doctor.'

'What if the Military Brahmin is lying, passing her off as sick and mad?'

Hiran worried at his failure to hide his patient's identity from Nabinbaboo and Vinny. Could he be infected by her disease? 'Not if you stay far enough away!' Vinny gave him a knowing smile. What if he made a mistake reading the signs, poisoned her by accident? Nabinbaboo laughed out loud. 'Then you'll be hanged!'

Hiran felt tense on his next visit to number 15. The familiar glass of milk failed to soothe his nerves. More than once he glanced over his shoulder expecting to see her shadow. He could hear her pulse through the wall, and a small dry cough – like women threshing rice. Her yawns floated through the open window.

After Lilian had entered the room, he hastened to note her symptoms as advised by Nabinbaboo. He remembered his careful instructions: 'Start with the face – always. It's the lamp that lights up the darkness. Folds and wrinkles on her skin, hair, teeth, tongue – never overlook the eyes.'

It had seemed as natural as reading her pulse. Her sickness suited her, somehow the darkness of the room desired her ghostly white.

Hiran followed Mr Crabbe and Lilian across a strip of mud to board the dinghy. It would be his first ride on a budgerow. The invitation had come at the end of the monsoon season when the river was calm. A forest of masts darkened the horizon. He smelt tea-clippers, heard the hum of a steamer's engine. Flags swirled from masts: a blue cross on white, a yellow anchor, a swallow's tail, a red and white fork flapping like a kite, pennants circling like a dragon.

He looked for Mr Crabbe's 'Jolly Roger'.

The head boatman motioned Hiran to enter the cabin once their dinghy arrived at the budgerow. But he wanted to remain by the bridge near the stern, to see the flags. He saw the Yankee boat from Boston filled with Wenham Lake ice packed in sawdust. It had caught fire last year – and melting ice had floated on the Ganga, as if from the frozen Himalayas.

His eye was drawn too to the native rafts – like dancing beggars they kept the river alive. A brigful of sailors passed, waving their arms. The Harbour Master's siren slowed them while search parties scanned the holds for smuggled ore or raw opium. A ship carrying pilgrims went by. Lamps flickered on peasant faces, eyes needlessly scanning the shore. They were bound, he knew, for Sagar Island at the confluence of river and sea. A few joined their palms in greeting to Hiran, taking him for a wealthy zamindaar. He knew of his mother's wish, to take her petition to Sagar Island, to Shiva. He alone could find a bride for her errant son. Each year her wish seemed just within reach. Perhaps her daughter-in-law would come along too, she thought, after the wedding – to pray for a grandson.

He saw restless pansees ferrying captains and leadsmen to their ships. A drunken bunch circled them a few times, singing. A bride and groom made their way towards a dark grove of thatched huts. From the lighthouse a voice rang over the churning . . . *jahaj malum hota sahib* . . .

The river was full of bodies, he was told. Strong tides would bring them from as far as Patna. These were the cursed – the poisoned and trampled, burnt or drowned, those condemned never to ascend a pyre. Wild dogs dragged them through the mud, losing their catch to the river. They would get caught in anchors' lines, get tangled up in nets, scaring the fishermen. A lamb would have to be sacrificed to break the evil omen.

Would *he* come up too someday, in a net darkened by mud?

The head boatman again nudged him to follow. Inside the cabin Mr Crabbe sat with Lilian motionless on his arm.

Silently, Hiran reached for Lilian's limp arm. Then he closed his eyes and heard her white vein pulse beneath her white skin.

Her palm appeared in his dream. Rosy and thin, Conic like his. Her delicate fingers picked up a gold-trimmed cup.

'Hmm . . . She complained of the light but her forehead was free of perspiration.' Holding his glasses in both hands, Nabinbaboo seemed to balance the evidence.

'It's nothing but a simple sunstroke.' Vinny was emphatic.

'Then why didn't the brandy bring her to her feet?'

'They were drinking on the budgerow! What else were you up to, Hiran?' Three heads crowded over Nabinbaboo's volume of *The Gentleman's Guide to Domestic Practice.*

He knew his hour had arrived. Waking her with a splash of water and gentle rubbing behind the ears, they had taken her off the budgerow. In the carriage on the way home, Mr Crabbe sat holding Lilian's head, her legs propped on Hiran's lap. At 15 Alipore Road she left Mr Crabbe's arm and slid into her ayah's.

'Didn't she speak to you even once? Perhaps she'd forgotten

your face. Hysterical women sometimes mistake their dogs for their husbands!' Vinny smirked. No, she hadn't spoken, just smiled shyly before going in.

'Did she show her teeth? Her gums?' Hiran remembered her smile – a set of white buds on a bed of pink rose, with a line of blue just visible.

'Blue!' Nabinbaboo brought his fist down on the table. Shutting the volume, he seemed firm in his conclusion: '*Camomilia* – two drops in a tumbler of water, and opium.'

'You'd give opium to an addict?' Vinny was dumbfounded.

'*Similia similibus curantur.* Like is cured by like.'

Concealing their essence, Hiran handed over two glass bottles to Mr Crabbe.

'What is it, dear?' Lilian asked over the teapot. 'I didn't know brahmins practised homeopathy.' Turning the bottles upside down she counted each bubble. They seemed small for her pains. She made a face. 'What is it? Should I put it in my tea?'

'It's Jacque's brain.' Mr Crabbe winked, prompting one of her rare laughs.

From autumn till winter, they pored over her symptoms, arriving early to hear Hiran's report. He would begin at the right place, flooding Nabinbaboo and Vinny with details. Unknown to himself he had found a way of describing her, learned to read her sadness – from pain, lack of sleep, or mood. From her footsteps, he knew if she felt heavy or light, did not need to ask if she was hot or cold, sleepy or awake, if her stomach growled for everything but food. She would come down to the library while they worked. Mr Crabbe would stop reading, rustle the pages of his book to draw Hiran's attention. She would sit by her husband, like a pupil ready to recite.

valibhir mukham akrantam
palitair ankitam sirah
gatrani sithalayante
trsnaika tarunayate

Behold my face, ugly. Behold my dead hair . . . limbs rotting and weak. Behold my desire – my sapping flower.

She received her medicine shyly and waited for a few moments before going back to her room.

'My people use *Agar Agar* for colds.' Vinny had heard of the magic seaweed from his half-Portuguese grandmother. The Malays boiled it to a succulent jelly, the Chinese spread it over bird's-nest soup. In the heat of Malacca, his sailing ancestors would squeeze a handful of the weed then rub it over their skin. 'In seconds they'd feel a mountain breeze!'

'Perhaps she is carrying.' Vinny frowned.

'Carrying what?'

'An Anglo-Parsee-Hindoo son!' Vinny danced around the table then whispered into Hiran's ear. 'Maybe it's Nabinbaboo's, the trick of his medicine!'

After a while, Hiran began to be called by the maid. Instead of bringing him his milk, she would lead him upstairs. Following her along a dimly lit corridor, he would see Lilian everywhere – sleeping under a mosquito-net, looking out towards the river with her back to him. He saw her on restless days, pacing the hallway, wiping her feverish face in an imaginary towel. When he was with her he felt alone, the maid disappearing back along the dark corridor.

By the time he had heard her shy or absent-minded replies and descended the stairs, the esraj would have stopped.

Between the three of them they chased her troubles. In a month's time the blue line on the gums had disappeared, but then both knees started to swell. They turned pages in a frenzy. From her knees, the genie travelled up till it knotted her belly in violent starts. She felt her abdomen rising, wavered between thirst and nausea.

With three globules of *Arsenic* they brought her sleep after nights of terror.

Then, a malignant fever covered her body with blotches, turning it black. This worried Nabinbaboo more than anything else. 'It could be *mort de chien*, frequently fatal.'

'Cholera,' Vinny whispered.

In Annada's village they called it The Curse of the Snake Goddess. Like a snake it was all around them, yet chose to strike when one was least aware. Ugly scabs made the victim resemble the predator. In her village, they would tie the sufferer up like a snake and apply a hot iron to his feet.

Her fever rose on the day of the eclipse. Moon and tide had a remarkable influence on her breathing. Then, it slipped mysteriously into harmless vertigo.

Hiran noticed an increase in the amount of mohors he received each month.

Hiran, Vinny and Nabinbaboo were no longer concerned by the normal course of business. Even news of a disaster at Ass's Point sinking two hundred chests worried them less than the lady's fever at number 15. Normally, Vinny would have brought gossip from the ships and the sinking would have kept him occupied with fantastic theories: 'The Captain, disappointed in love, committed suicide by drowning with his ship.' Or, 'There were ghosts, like on the *Imogene* . . . a murdered deck-hand, you know.'

She had become their mystery, their mud: adding spice to the crude and measuring the oily skin, correcting its course, stroking with graceful kash, hoping to return the glow to a withered bud.

A ray from her Line of Life passed over the Heart to the Mount of Saturn. It was a hand of unrelenting memory. Spears and triangles marked a jealous love. Love was its goodly estate. It longed to feel and stroke . . . kneading, tempting. Its pleasure as much a matter of the soul as ardent passions. Longed to merge, to feel the invisible. It was a dream of union.

To Hiran, she was like a book. Her secret entranced him. She became the story he could read without end, surprising by its unevenness. He delved into her wounds, smears on her milk-white lace. Nothing was lost on his passion: a dismissive reply, a nervous flicker at the temple. Yet, like an arresting tale, she took him beyond the verse into the unwritten. He had become her creator.

'Your mother must worry about you, an unwed brahmin.' Hiran was surprised by Nabinbaboo's comment. Usually they avoided the personal, except for disease and wages. He had not considered the effect his bachelorhood might have on the gossip mongers at the Auction House. Did his visits to number 15 stoke their fantasies? Would the gentoos now bestow on him the knowing look they reserved for Mr Kavasji? Did they see him, too, flourishing on Lilian's bed?

In Saraladebi's mind, fate was the chief culprit – robbing her of a husband, and turning Hiran's mind away from slokas. With the patience of a would-be mother-in-law she waited for her wish – a daughter to finally erase all her failures. Saraladebi was willing to wait for the right one.

Annada had advised: 'Get him married before he's too old, before they start laughing behind his back.' She was better than his mother at reading the matchmaker's hints. She heard the questions behind the questions. 'How *old* is he? *Didn't* he find a priest's job in some temple? What does he do at the *sahibs'* office? He's *still* a brahmin, isn't he?'

In her dreams Saraladebi would leave their decrepit attic in Jaanbazaar and enter a mansion. She would be received as the groom's mother, women in finery would fuss over her, and an exquisite, pious and auspicious girl would gently fan a breeze of young palm. She could almost see her face. Settling for anything else would be like marrying her Hira to Annada.

'If you wait any longer, he'll find his own bride in the alleys of Boubazaar!'

'Shhh . . .'

As they sat on the balcony, he would be drawn to her arms, freely open, her breasts visible through a negligent chemise. He studied them for a sign of turmoil within. He could smell the water from her aromatic bath, her sweat a thin bead spreading over her lips like a spider's web. Her breath kept him guessing.

But as much as he was touched by her frailty, she invoked less than desire, seemed an obsession without hunger. Lying awake at night he would go over her in minute detail, naturally excluding his own presence. He felt like the breeze – touching without being touched, the unreflecting mirror.

He would hold up his palms to the light of an oil-lamp: a narrow channel between the lines of the Head and the Heart. The Head was the more robust, proud and angry, casting a shadow over the meek Heart. He knew the Head would dominate, rein in feelings with an iron hand. Yet, a secret branch reaching upward suggested a deep wound. He wondered about that for a while. Who could hurt the unfeeling?

From his voice, Hiran knew who it was. He had stood up at his desk, anticipating Vinny's 'human tiger', imagining scruffy side-burns and flaming red whiskers. He expected a pair of sunburnt cheeks and a red nose.

It took him a while to get used to Captain Jacque sitting across from him, looking not at all as he had imagined him, except for the sunburnt cheeks and nose. He sat with his eyes on Hiran, and his ears everywhere, turning his head slightly from time to time.

'Ah! A brahmin,' Captain Jacque said as he noticed the white thread peeking through Hiran's vest. 'Tell me, Hiranbaboo, how long have you known Vinny?' Surprised, Hiran stumbled over the years. 'Did you know he has a twin brother? Bartholomew. Works for the Constabulary in Madras. A gun inspector. A jolly fellow, a shorty like Vinny. A real joker.' Captain Jacque rolled up a sheet of foolscap like a telescope: 'There!' He pointed through the window to his ship berthed on the river. 'Now, Batty is coming over to help his brother for his wedding. You know about that, yes? Our friend wants a grand reception at the pier – trumpets, bouquets, the whole thing. And, he wants all his friends to come. You are invited, Hiranbaboo!'

'Who are his friends, Captain?' Nabinbaboo's voice was full of laughter.

'Anyone who has an ear for his chatter, I suppose.' Captain Jacque laughed too, then fixed his eyes on Hiran.

'And who will arrange for the trumpets and bouquets?' Nabinbaboo asked.

'I shall, of course,' Captain Jacque said.

Hiran was intrigued by Vinny's sudden reticence. He had often spoken of brothers and sisters as the two of them strolled by the Strand: 'We lay on the same sleeping-cloth, used the same little room.' The boys had all grown up keranees. His sisters had married well – 'All officers, my jewel, *pucca*-sahibs.' His father had worked his way through the ranks, a coolie boy, managing somehow to escape the filthy docks to a small house in Kidderpore.

Now Hiran felt guilty for not having shown more interest in Vinny's wedding. Somehow, number 15 seemed to intrude into every moment of his time. He was kept busy by his patient, and by his pupil. He had doubted that Marie even existed. How would Vinny get to Macao anyway, or wherever she was? The news of Vinny's brother's imminent arrival made Hiran ashamed of his doubts. After all, his friend might truly be on the way to his wedding. He resolved to catch up with Vinny.

'Identical twins,' continued the Captain. 'One could replace the other. Once I painted his brother at Cochin on my way to Malacca and sent Vinny the picture. I'm told he claims it's him!'

His eyes came to rest on Hiran again. 'You'll come, won't you? Brother Bartholomew will arrive by the *Flying Cloud* at noon by Chandpal Ghaut.'

The next day, Hiran searched everywhere for Vinny. The gentoos hadn't seen him for a few days. But that was normal, he was given to disappearing, on 'special duties'. A junior clerk called Hiran aside. 'He's getting ready for his marriage. A foreign girl . . .'

Alone during tiffin-break, watching ships preparing to sail, Hiran wondered who would arrive to help for *his* wedding. Would Mahim return on a ship, to trumpets and bouquets?

Nabinbaboo was his usual sceptical self. 'If you believe a sailor, you'll believe anyone. Always lie is their motto . . . must keep their patrons salivating.' But he asked Hiran to check the precise hour of the ship's arrival.

The *Flying Cloud* belonged to Dicky Knight, a familiar bidder at the Auction House. A 600-ton clipper barque born at the Brunswick Dock, she had first crossed the Atlantic with whale-oil in her hold. She was on her way, Hiran was told – her mast was sighted at Melancholy Point.

He blurted out the whole story to the Crabbes as they sat on the balcony of number 15. They seemed amused.

'Twin grooms for a single bride!' Kavasji's cup shook. 'Is he old enough to marry?' Even Mr Crabbe appeared touched by the arrangements: 'It's a pity we can't fire the guns in salute, but it's a merchant ship not a man-of-war.'

'Maybe you *should* fire the guns, dear, our merchants are our best warriors, aren't they?' Hiran detected irony in Lilian's comment.

'Come, Lilian, let's not scare poor Batty!'

'When will *you* get married, Hiranbaboo?' He felt Lilian's eyes on him. 'The older a brahmin is, the more he is in demand, I'm told. Like a prize stud.' Mr Kavasji smiled. Hiran lowered his eyes.

Their talk turned to the races – to the Victoria Cup. Mr Kavasji, as usual, served up the details of horses and owners. There were worries, he said, in certain quarters, that the Governor would fix limits on betting, like in Lord Wellesley's time. Too many people were said to be going bankrupt, the moneylenders benefiting from miserable Europeans.

'That'll unite us all – English, French, and Dutch – against the Viceroy!' Lilian sniggered.

When he returned to his desk next day, Hiran found a note – from Vinny: 'Tomorrow at noon to meet the *Flying Cloud*. URGENT!'

Hiran wore Mahim's jacket, and a pair of cricket flannels bought with his extra mohors. He carried a garland of marigolds. Under the shade of a tamarind he saw Nabinbaboo with his own garland.

A line of black heads reached to the very end of the pier like a snake writhing on the river. A roar went up as the *Flying Cloud* crested, offering her broadside as if saluting the crowd. Hiran counted faces that he knew. Europeans, squeaking from well-pressed suits, sat fanning themselves under giant kittesaws. Servants ran back and forth from a tent with pitchers of iced water. Women and their ayahs, firmly clasping the children, had marked out a lawn under the flagstaff. The servants were busy there as well, balancing trays, spraying the lawn with water. From behind a pair of binoculars, as they reflected the sunlight back from the lawn to the jetty, came a gasp of disbelief.

Hiran heard the trumpets and gongs of a Regimental Band. *All this for Vinny's brother!* He read the same disbelief on Nabinbaboo's face. Hiran saw a line of dinghies on the river. A horde of policemen descended from nowhere, urging the crowd to clear a passage for the new arrivals. He heard a curse or two.

Would he be able to spot Vinny and his brother in the crowd? He felt an urge to move forward, to join the men on the jetty, but he was afraid of being trampled. Perhaps he'd be better off climbing a tree like an urchin. A group of missionaries under black umbrellas appeared then disappeared quickly with tonga-wallahs who had cleverly hidden their carriages under the tamarind tree. Surely, it was time for the brothers to make their appearance. Hiran searched for Vinny. Perhaps he had made arrangements, meeting the ship before it reached the moorings. Would they alight together – the twins? Perhaps Captain Jacque was with them, shepherding his favourites.

He was reminded of the donkey in the cucumber field. Fast asleep, the farmer heard him singing, his ears trained for the single note that mattered. The crowd would recognize the brother of a half-Portuguese. He felt relieved, resting under the shade with an ear open for the call of the boy who greeted each new arrival. What would he call Vinny . . . *kala sahib . . . kintali* . . . Hiran felt embarrassed for his friend.

As he would later recall, a bum-boat twice the size of a budgerow had set the crowd in a roar. Moving gracefully from the *Flying Cloud* to the jetty, it seemed like a floating tent, like a demure bride. Policemen shouted orders, lifted their batons to push men back along the jetty. Horns rose above the clamour, neighs from tongawallahs' horses sent a shiver down Hiran's spine. The handlers were ready with hooks to drag the boat ashore like a giant whale. Silence followed gasps as the muslin unfurled. Hiran heard shrill blasts from a conch-shell, and Nabinbaboo's racking laugh.

'A tiger! A live one.'

The crowd danced, some openly wept. Some, regaining composure, spoke glowingly of the Maharajah of Oudh and his gift to the people of Calcutta, soon to take up residence in the Zoological Gardens.

Inside a breaking crowd Hiran saw Vinny with a bouquet of roses. 'Did you see her?'

'Who?'

'Marie . . . *my* Marie. Captain Jacque said she might arrive by the *Flying Cloud*.'

'I've heard your father was killed by English horses.' Lilian smiled at Hiran. 'It was an accident, wasn't it?'

'Yes.' Perhaps all deaths were accidents, he thought. Without vicious forks and sudden stops the Life-line could go on for ever.

They talked about new arrivals to the port. Lilian shared his love of names, added her own: St Helena and Cape Town, Funchal and Madeira – stops on her way to India. She told him about Madeira wine, of evening balls on the deck. He told her of Vinny's Macao. She warned him not to believe Captain Jacque's stories. 'He's been going around with one about a tiger arriving by Captain Hawthorn's *Flying Cloud.* A lie I'd say . . .'

When Mr Crabbe and Mr Kavasji joined them, the talk would turn to war. Lilian was skilful – siding always with the winners. One day, Mr Crabbe described recent scraps between the British and the Chinese. 'The Chinese Viceroy in Canton has been forced to make concessions,' he declared triumphantly. Lilian wasn't impressed. 'Who cares if the Chinese do or don't allow foreign women into Canton. I wouldn't dream of living with pig-tailed monsters!'

'It's a strategic gain, not a practical one.' Mr Crabbe's response addressed a pouting Lilian and a silent Hiran.

'A friend of mine calls it "a necessary indulgence, an entail not a possession",' Mr Kavasji declared. Mr Crabbe seemed impressed: 'Who is this friend?'

'Mahim Chakraborti of Jaanbazaar. We were at college

together. A gifted boy, rich and rash like all wealthy Bengalees. He's in England now, in some trouble I hear.' Mr Kavasji stopped suddenly, looked at Hiran. 'Why, of course! He's Hiran's uncle, the one who taught him English, isn't he?' They all looked at Hiran curiously.

He felt tongue-tied. What could he tell them about his uncle? His mind drew a blank.

'Mahim's double' he was known as among the residents of the Jaanbazaar house. Yet he felt shy about going into shops and walked past the windows at Cossitola, studiously avoiding the best: Phelps & Co., Civil & Military Tailors, By Special Appointment to His Royal Highness The Duke of Connaught. Or Ramsay Wakefield – Mahim's favourite. Hiran felt awkward, asking to be measured for a diagonal morning coat, didn't know if they would consider him a pauper. From the advertisement in the *Englishman* it had seemed well within reach – twenty-one rupees. He toyed with the idea of asking Vinny to come with him, but feared his curiosity. *They're overpaying you . . . what do you have to do for her, jewel?*

Finally he went with his mochtar cousin to Old China Bazaar Street, to Girish Chunder Dey & Co. Hiran smiled at the sign on the entrance: Our Tailoring Department is under the management of a first-class European cutter.

'A first-class chillicracker imported from an orphanage!' his mochtar cousin laughed. Hiran felt relieved. An old Muslim wearing a lace cap measured him for a long shirt with an extra collar. He felt the soft cashmere, fancy angoras, serge and flannel. He handed over his mohors with great relief.

The rumble at Jaanbazaar started soon after the visit to Girish Chunder Dey & Co.

'They've paid him to convert.' As he climbed the wooden stairs he'd hear the hissing, collected and fermented on their roof by Annada like her favourite pickles.

They feared he was one of those who had fallen by the soul rather than the flesh. They knew that his steps did not pause in the nearby alleys of Boubazaar and that his breath did not reek. But perhaps he had gone further. 'Does he still recite the *Gayatri*?' Annada asked Saraladebi. 'Why?' Annada kept silent for a while, then it spilled out: 'They say he goes where no brahmin should go. To the races, on a big boat all by himself, inside a phaeton. Where does he get the money for his special clothes? Have you asked him?'

Saraladebi growled at her, 'Ask them to keep their eyes to themselves, and throw their rotten minds to the dogs.'

'There will be trouble marrying him to a decent Hindoo girl. What if he marries –' but Saraladebi would not let her utter any more blasphemies.

'Tell me, what were you doing at the races?' she asked Hiran.

Gradually, she came to yet another painful conclusion. Her Hira was but a simple liar.

Even after six years, he felt sheltered at the Auction House. In Nabinbaboo's eyes he was still the apprentice, still perfecting his role as office-clerk. As on his first day, he sat facing the river lost in thought over a sheaf of blue-lined Manila. 'Hmm . . .' Nabinbaboo would wake him from his trance. 'Another poet of the waves?' Embarrassed, he'd read aloud. 'I call upon the mercantile and manufacturing classes to consider how their own welfare and prosperity are concerned in this question; and to ask themselves whether this dishonourable traffic in a poisonous drug shall be permitted, any longer, to deprive every other class of merchants an open, unrestricted, and honourable trade with China?'

'Missionaries?' Nabinbaboo asked. Hiran nodded his head. Then there was a longer silence, as Hiran tried to slip an envelope unseen into the wicker basket. 'What was that, Hiran?' He felt caught. His ears turned red. Retrieving the envelope, Nabinbaboo grimaced at the crude sketch of a brahmin straddling a mem.

Maybe he should stop going, he thought. In his mind he composed a letter of regret. *Dear Mr Crabbe, Owing to circumstances I shall henceforth be unable to provide assistance to your esteemed self in the noble endeavour of translations. I hope . . .*

He wondered about the 'circumstances'.

'It's the Mutiny, jewel. The children are angry with their mother. They are suspicious of us. If you go with an Englishman, you must be his servant or his spy. You can't imagine what I face . . .'

He could easily see himself as a servant – supplying stories, and white drops for Lilian. *Remember, these people value everything by silver . . .* Hiran recalled Nabinbaboo saying. He felt near, but not close. Friendly, without friendship.

One day Mr Crabbe returned to the story of the crow and the owl. 'Tell me, Hiranbaboo, who is more powerful – the fighting birds, their callous ruler, or the greedy jackal?' Lilian looked up from her crochet. 'Let me guess . . .'

'No. There must be one unquestionably. Mustn't have to guess or think too hard.'

Hiran felt his tension returning. What did he want him to say? That they were one and inseparable. Was it in him, the Military Brahmin, to seek 'one' when there were many? 'You make it seem simple, Jonathan, simple as your stupid wars with stupid guns and stupid . . .'

'But isn't it? Simpler than you think?'

'Nothing is simple here. Nothing.' She had resumed her pout. 'You'd think the darned English here would be simpler than back home, or the Indians simpler than the darned English . . .'

Hiran felt Mr Crabbe's eyes on his broad forehead. 'Who would you rather be? The dying fool, or the cunning survivor?'

'That's unfair.' Lilian wasn't willing to give up. 'Ask him if he cares to know. They don't have a choice in the matter, do they?'

'They?'

'The Indians, of course.'

'They're the ones who wrote the story, dear.'

'Well, then he knows the answer, doesn't he? Why don't *you* tell him who's the more powerful. Tell him why we're here.'

For the first time he saw Mr Crabbe disconcerted. He sipped his cold tea, face flushed. Mr Kavasji sat silently, staring at an unusually busy nest of crows. His face showed just the right mix of attention and withdrawal.

'I didn't mean to invoke the English and the Indians.'

'Who *did* you wish to invoke?'

'I meant *us* . . . you, me, our friends.'

'Why Jonathan, that's simple. You and I are the birds.' Mr Kavasji had moved quickly, inserting his calm voice between the two. 'Why don't we go then, all of us together, to a Hindoo Charak puja. They dress up as birds and animals, enact amazing tales, I'm told.'

Most evenings he returned by the eight o'clock tram. Hoofs echoed over a silent river. Nearing Jaanbazaar, Hiran would wake to a singing drunk, or the shrill whistle of a policeman. Only once had he failed to wake on time, winced at the baton jabbed under his ribs at Chitpur Yards. Must have smelt a foreign scent on his clothes. A harbour-clerk, they must have thought, late home from his inspections.

He knew Saraladebi would wait for him. By ten o'clock her shadow paced their roof, pausing every now and then to pray before the shrine. Her worries kept Annada awake. Saraladebi turned her face away from Boubazaar and its narrow alleys teeming with rickshaws. Her Hira wouldn't be on one of those, stumbling like a one-eyed drunk. She wasn't distracted by quarrels. Even a policeman's stick ringing on the pavement wouldn't deter her from her vigil.

On a night of rumours, she had left their roof to wait by the arched entrance. Annada had brought word of looting, peasants raiding the rice-barges at Kumartooli. She spoke of arson, of floating bodies on the river, sergeants gone mad . . .

Saraladebi rued the day they left Patna. Her mind, caught for ever in the violence of men and horses, searched for an exit. Who could she turn to? The family would smirk at her loss – *a fallen brahmin deserves his fate.*

By the time Hiran returned, she was like a trapped animal.

'When will you finish with your lessons?' she asked him. 'We should return to Patna. Your father's senior will help us. You must marry and live like a simple priest.'

'My friends want me to go with them to see Charak.'

'Your friends?'

'Mr Crabbe and the lady . . . and –'

'Tell your friends your mother will not allow her son to go anywhere.'

That night he remembered Kavasji's words. *He's now in England, in some trouble I hear.* It seemed natural – for Mahim to be in trouble. Hiran tried to see him in a room full of books, or in a theatre. Did he still keep his unusual hours – sleeping and waking late? Who polished his boots? Called a ticca-gari to his door? Annada carried around the usual rumours: 'He's under the spell of a mem – a vicious one . . . makes him do terrible things.' 'He has lost a fortune on horses and wine . . . the son of an honourable father forced to live like a common thief!' She predicted that he'd never return to Jaanbazaar.

Hiran imagined Mahim's trouble in different terms. Perhaps he'd been imprisoned for penning blasphemy . . . or gone mad.

He felt anxious. What would the Crabbes think if he declined their invitation to Charak? His mother, he knew, would not change her mind. He wished he had lied to her. Or used one of Annada's stories.

He was saved by an early spell of rains. A pair of moist lungs kept him confined, invited Saraladebi's pick of foul-tasting herbs. Every day she watched over him as Annada warmed a bowl of mustard oil to rub on his chest, till the stinging vapour made him sneeze and cough in fits.

The peon came a few days later with a letter from Lilian, in Mr Kavasji's measured hand: *Dear Hiran, we shall leave for the Charak puja by the Outram jetty* . . . He felt relieved that his illness excused him from the trip.

*

In a few weeks he felt ready to play his part once again on the balcony of number 15. Waiting alone, before the others arrived, he wondered how the visit to the Charak puja had gone. He expected each of the three to have a story: Mr Kavasji would most likely dwell on details. Perhaps he would express regret . . . *seemed a different affair altogether, didn't it?* A gentle Mr Crabbe would have something strange to report. He was unsure about Lilian, perhaps . . .

He found himself alone with Mr Crabbe. A touch distracted but concerned, he asked if Hiran practised his own medicine on his lungs.

Then Mr Crabbe leant forward and spoke quietly. 'I need your help. Can you think of a way of acquiring a child – a newborn, an orphan perhaps – for us? Of course, I'd be ready . . .'

He saw a shadow fall over the teapot, heard a whisper behind him like the flutter of wings in a net.

'Yes, Hiranbaboo, get me a child. A blackie-white boy.'

Instinct brought him to Mr Kavasji. As he crossed the neat lawn, Hiran looked up at the windows of the west wing. The shutters were drawn over the Superintendent's window – like a closed hand in a deck of cards. He hesitated over filling in a visitor's slip, wondered if 'personal matter' would qualify for entrance. The Pathan doorkeeper looked at him with suspicion.

He had hesitated earlier – wondered if it would be wise to discuss the Crabbes' request with their dear friend. But he had no one to turn to. Sitting before Mr Kavasji in his office, Hiran tried imagining him on the balcony of number 15. His face was still the same – pleasing and ready, willing to expand or digress, delicate as a portrait, blue under a coat of wax. He heard him exclaim over a rare find, the Saldanha de Albuquerque – the arms of the famous Portuguese merchant – on a platter stolen by Jacque's servants from the Governor of Malacca's collection.

Mr Kavasji asked him about Mahim and about Hiran's letters to him in England. Did he write about his work, or the Royal Commission? He skirted the Superintendent's trial, and talked cheerfully about the surprise winner of the Victoria Cup. After a while, it seemed Hiran had come to discuss Mr Kavasji's 'personal matter' rather than his own.

'Your uncle used to speak highly of your mother. What strength and resolve! he used to say, don't dismiss the Hindoo, their power lies in their women.'

It felt strange to hear Mahim speak in the voice of Mr Kavasji.

'Who can replace a dead father . . .' Mr Kavasji sighed.

Hiran saw his opening, waited just long enough for his mentor to clear his throat.

'Who would willingly give up a son?'

Mr Kavasji looked at him with kindness. 'Only the wretched, Hiran, those forced to devour their own souls. There are so many, living like animals among men.' He appeared to read Hiran's mind: 'Tell me, don't you wonder why the ocean drowns so many?'

Hiran was used to the tone – distant yet kind. 'But what if there was one still breathing?'

'Then you must save him, Hiran. Bring him to shore. There are more sons than fathers. You have to find him a father.'

It seemed unnatural – *who must belong to whom?*

Once again Mr Kavasji seemed to read his mind. 'It's futile, Hiran. You can't find Him. Easier to find him a father.'

It was the beginning of his sleeplessness. The more he thought about his talk with Mr Kavasji, the more he felt he had found the answer but not the solution. He had expected a clever excuse, one he could offer himself: *But adoption is forbidden in your faith, isn't it?* Or, *Who'd trust a brahmin with a fair exchange!* But Mr Kavasji was relaxed. He seemed to speak in the voice of number 15. Was it his wish too? Hiran returned to his earlier suspicion. A way to stop the crow and the owl killing each other?

Growing up in Jaanbazaar, Hiran had heard of women unable to bear sons and of women willing to sacrifice. The exchange seemed fair to most. Mothers became aunts, after a few years even the nurse would forget. He had seen a family tree in a rusted trunk under his mother's bed. Saraladebi had whisked it away before he could climb down to its roots.

It was common, he knew, among rajahs to exchange sons for power. Annada would whisper about priests supplying heirs to barren zamindars. 'They do more than simply chant slokas,' she would say. But to raise a native child among foreigners? What if the child had brahmin's blood? Who'd teach him the rites of prayer and fasting?

Hiran felt trapped. A pair of eyes stared at his forehead whichever way he looked. Leaving for tiffin-break, he would pass quickly under the portico hoping to avoid Mr Crabbe's glance over the lawn. He went less frequently to Cossitola lest he should meet Lilian entering or leaving a shop. He refused an invitation to the Royal Horticultural Garden's annual flower-show – offered one excuse after another as summer drew them inexorably towards operettas, hot-air balloons, dog-shows by the tank of Lal Dighee.

But there was nothing to stop him on Sunday mornings. Leaving as usual by the horse-drawn tram he would be snared among throngs of devotees at Madan Mohon Jiu's temple. Eyes smarting from the cloud of incense, he would feel an urge to escape.

Back on the balcony of number 15, Lilian's voice floated over a cushion of still air: 'Wouldn't you have missed your father more had you seen him alive?' Hiran smiled.

'It isn't about missing, but *knowing* what one must endure,' Mr Kavasji's voice had a tinge of regret, 'losing and never having . . .'

'You mean the deaths, don't you? How we killed your fathers . . .' She seemed fretful. Mr Kavasji smiled kindly. 'The violence of death is no more than the violence of birth.'

They had settled under a cloudy evening to share the balcony with a stream of flying ants drawn to the blue and white teapot.

'What if the end was uncertain,' Mr Crabbe followed quickly. 'One never knows who does what and to whom . . .'

'But why should one care?' Mr Kavasji turned to face Mr Crabbe, holding up a delicate cup in his delicate fingers. 'It *is* after all a matter of force and yielding, isn't it? Like this cup . . .' He dropped it without warning from the balcony and the crash blended with the call of a fledgling for its mother.

Hiran saw tears well in Lilian's eyes.

*

'It's our mistress's wish.' Vinny was concerned but confident. 'Both the Military Brahmin and the snake have failed, it's your turn now. You *have* to do it, jewel.' After the initial shock his mind was busy, discovering hidden meanings in a mountain of facts. 'It's clear as pani! Crabbe has planned everything. He knows Lilian can't give him a boy – she has too much mud in her belly. So, he thinks of buying one. But what will he tell friends back home? That's why he got rid of Mr Scott, so none will know that their little chimp is a chilli-cracker not a real sahib!' He looked triumphant. 'She has fooled everyone with her sickness. It's nothing but a simple trick. She wants to hide so no one will notice her flat belly and wonder where the baby came from!' His words came faster than ever. 'You mustn't tell anyone, not even Nabinbaboo. Top secret!'

Vinny was worried for Hiran. The Auction House was full of spies, he said, lowering his voice. Hiran must beware of his own shadow. There were peons and gentoos, guards noting down everything in secret ledgers. 'He'll have you whipped if you fail.'

'Who would give up a son?'

Vinny stared ahead at a gang of wreckers stripping a grounded ship. 'Your neighbours, jewel. Your friendly sisters in Boubazaar!' Hiran looked perplexed. 'You mean?' 'Yes! Who else would willingly part with their own flesh and blood? You must pretend to be a wealthy baboo. The whores mustn't know who you really are. You must make them greedy for mohors, make them believe your story.'

'Tell them I am looking for an heir?'

'Ssh . . . no, my jewel,' Vinny hushed. 'Why would a baboo look for an heir in a brothel when there are widows in his household? Tell them you're looking for an albino for your private zoo, or a blackie-white to train as a jockey.'

Hiran thought of asking if Captain Jacque might help. Maybe he could fool some coolie-mother. That, of course, could present other dangers.

What would he tell Saraladebi? Where would he hide the

baby? Suddenly the track from Jaanbazaar to Alipore seemed endless. What if he was seen?

'We can hide him in my sister's house in Lalbazaar. What's one more chillicracker in the home of a chillicracker!' Vinny suggested. But he would not come with Hiran to roam the dark alleys.

'No, my jewel. You must go alone. It's better that way. Otherwise I'd have to dress up as your servant!'

Lying awake, he thought of dressing up himself. He might disguise himself as a missionary, a zealot on the prowl converting Hindoos. But he feared the women. He knew of some who threw dung on natives dressed as Europeans. He had heard of some who tied sons to trees for days hoping for a return to senses. A sudden gust on the roof made him shiver.

How would he convince a mother to give up her child? Then he thought of Annada snoring in her afim-sleep.

Growing up, he had learned always to trust Annada. Ever-ready with solutions, she cared neither for problems nor answers. Hiran felt he could rely on her. Perhaps she'd find a story to pave his way. People would believe Annada.

Next evening he waited for Annada to finish sweeping the kitchen, turn out a tray of Saraladebi's herbs to moisten under the night's dew, and stir her afim.

'Strange, I had thought too of a child. A grandson for your mother.'

'It's for someone else,' Hiran stumbled, 'I'd like to help . . .'

Annada smiled. She had her own explanation. 'It'll free you of a burden.' She gave him a knowing look. 'I'll keep an eye open.'

Vinny came in excited. 'We're being Shanghaied! He's at it again!'

'Who?'

He pointed across the lawn towards the Deputy Superintendent's window. 'He wants us all to move closer to the yellow devil . . . to China. "To be effective we must be close to the customer." ' Vinny imitated Mr Crabbe's voice with a tinge of disgust. 'He'll drive us mad.' His eyes darted from Hiran to Nabinbaboo. 'Can you imagine what it'll be like? Drinking monkey-brain soup, wearing pig-tails like their coolie-king.'

'You'll be closer to home though, won't you?' Nabinbaboo teased.

'Home? They hate us down there. Call us Black-Barbarians!'

Surely they won't send everyone, Hiran thought.

'He is going there himself after Christmas to break the news to the Chinese traders,' Vinny announced.

Who will he take with him? Hiran thought.

Nabinbaboo looked at Hiran with a question in his eye. Had Hiran known and hidden it from him? Would he go if asked?

Normally they would have grieved over Mr Scott's absence, lamented the unusual pace with which orders flowed back and forth across the lawn. But Hiran was still brooding. He worried about the extra 'charges' he had received since Mr Crabbe's request. He wondered how many gold coins – each with the head of a dead Emperor – equalled a half-sahib. A sudden revulsion made him choke over Annada's tiffin.

That night, he dreamt he was a beggar wandering with his son from one village to another in search of alms. Women and children crowded on the roofs to hear them sing, threw a copper anna or two. They slept in temples, praying every day to be released from their misery. Then they came upon the home of a wealthy merchant. Father and son settled before the iron gate and tuned the esraj.

They were warned to leave. The merchant was known for his evil temper – not even his wife or children could bear to spend more than a few days in his company. In his dream, Hiran played on – two voices following the esraj.

Then the merchant appeared before the gate, face flushed in anger. He had dreamt that a beggar would come and bestow him with riches. But he would need to punish, show his cruelty to extract. The merchant asked the beggar to hand over his son

– his only child. Hiran pleaded with him, his voice choking with tears. He told the merchant they were in a different story then handed him a stick and demanded to be struck over the head so that he might turn into gold. He screamed, *Go on . . . kill me!*

He felt Annada's palm on his burning face.

In the end he decided on his disguise – a simple aachkan and dhoti. He didn't want to arouse Saraladebi's suspicion. Dressed as a baboo he would blend in easily with the men who circled the alleys.

The flower-seller gave Hiran a knowing smile. He bought jasmine – two strands of six each. The mohors wrapped in a soft bag around his waist felt heavier than the swagger-stick slung over his arm at Annada's advice.

'You must be prepared. The man frying oil by the corner will know where to take you.'

It seemed a reasonable plan – find an infant and bring it in a ticca-gari that night to Vinny's sister's house in Lalbazaar. She was expecting him. Vinny had spun her some amazing tale – a Company man hiding his offspring from a jealous wife. They'd play their usual roles merrily by day, wait until sunset, then leave for the Jockey's Club. Vinny's sister would arrive by the tram, with the baby, using her fan to soothe and cheer. From there it would be simple – another carriage ride for the three of them to number 15. Vinny said he would wait at the gate, distract the doorman with his gossip while Hiran made off to fill Lilian's lap. 'Be sure to tell her about me . . . maybe she'll invite me to her tea parties too.'

Hiran tripped over a sleeping dog. It gave him a pitying look. Soon, his eyes adjusted to the light. He saw more than he expected. He saw mottoes and prayers above doorways, ugly faces to ward off evil. There was more to the houses than the windows he had seen from their roof in Jaanbazaar.

Eyes peered at each door. He was greeted with smiles. Come! Whores tugged playfully at his jasmine.

Like a beggar stopping for alms, he went from door to door.

A song wafted by from a nearby window like a fresh breeze. He knew the tune. Annada humming in the kitchen. He felt like singing too.

The man frying oil at the stall was expecting him. Hiran hesitated, then, following Annada's instructions, asked him about the baby that he had promised her. The man offered him a mixture of puffed rice and greasy onion, then looked for a companion. 'Where's your maid? You'll need someone to hold the child. Should we fetch a girl for you?'

'No, no.' He felt uneasy. *How would he quieten a crying baby?* The shopkeeper read his doubt. 'These ones don't cry!' The man smiled.

Hiran followed him from one narrow lane to another. Someone coughed, asked for a light, then offered a full bottle of spirits. Hiran smelt the country brew. Suddenly afraid, he counted the mohors by habit, sweating from the heat. His walk became cautious. Looking over his shoulder he caught sight of his own shadow, stooped like an old man.

He thought of Mahim. What would he have said of his favourite nephew's mission?

The man stopped before a curtained door, a finger to his lips. Inside the room, Hiran heard the *Hermione* playing on a music-box, just as on Lilian's balcony. A waltz! A dark lady sat on a recliner wearing a gown and a topi, surrounded by empty bottles. She motioned Hiran to sit.

A shadow fluttered with the breeze on the wall. She reminded him of someone, he tried to remember Annada's advice. Should he speak, offer his mohors . . .

A man standing behind him started to speak. He seemed humble, offering excuses for a less than ideal situation. It was a pity, he said, that they didn't have much time to prepare for Hiran's request. The woman nodded kindly. There was trouble with policemen and the hakim, he said.

Hiran eyed an empty bottle.

The man continued, as if providing a long explanation to his master: 'Everyone relies on our black memsahib.' He looked at the woman. '*Great Indian Circus*, Badur Bagan's *National Circus*, tantrics, wealthy zamindars. She knows how to find a good one – you won't be disappointed, Sir.'

A faint drizzle blew in through the open window. The smell of friendly manure filled the room. The man offered him tea, then went on.

'Our black mem knows how to fool the judge! She wears a burkha and pleads before him. *They're mine, huzoor . . . stolen from my lap!* A real mother would believe her story. She's better than the whores at the theatre.' It seemed impossible to Hiran that a mother could be taken in by the guile of an actress and give up her child. Hiran glanced at the woman quickly. She gave him a serious look, then started cleaning one boot with the tip of the other.

'Sometimes the policemen are unkind, they disbelieve everything, order rattans – like the trouble at Coolie Bazaar.'

After a while it was difficult to follow. Hiran wondered about Annada's advice.

The lady was drinking from an open bottle, her eye on the man.

'You may be disappointed, or you may not . . . depending . . .' Then the man left by the curtained door to return with two wrapped bundles. He laid them over the worn settee, muttering, 'Both the same. Twins.'

The bundles twitched. In one, a boy, bald, with his arms twisted back by the force of iron clippers behind his shoulders, and his brother in the other – feet turned inward like a flapping gull.

'They'll be ready within weeks. Look! Won't they have them laughing at the circus! Little devils! They'll be a big hit, you can count on them . . .'

As he fled through the curtained door, Hiran saw two pairs of eyes staring at him, without tears.

*

He let the trams come and go, and started to walk steadily towards the docks.

'Where have you been, jewel?' Vinny was astonished to see a brahmin enter their colony. Under a colourful maze of laundry he listened to Hiran's story.

'You should never have trusted Annada!' He took Hiran into his room – taken up by a bed and a dresser hung with pictures – then fell silent when he saw Hiran's face, pale after a night of fear. They sat facing the river and a line of gulls solemnly holding court over a bare mast.

'At least they let you escape with your mohors. Fancy paying in gold for cripples!'

They resumed scheming during tiffin-break. Toyed with the idea of a 'miracle cure' for Lilian's womb. Prised open Nabin-baboo's books, frowning over lengthy passages. But Nabin-baboo's glass bottles seemed woefully unequal to their task.

'She needs a tantric, jewel. Who knows what they might do with their mumbo jumbo.'

Hiran recalled overhearing Annada's tales of the tantric's cure for barren women. A cloud passed over his face.

'Wait! We may still live!' Vinny jumped up and down on the pier with excitement. 'We can go to Viper Island. I should've thought of that before!'

'Viper Island?'

'Yes, to the prison island. In the orphanage there we can surely find Lilian's boy!'

Hiran felt unsure. Was it yet one more of Vinny's fantastic stories? Why would a prison house an orphanage? He gave Vinny that half-believing look.

'You don't believe me?' Then Vinny told him about the penal colony not far from Calcutta, where hardened criminals were sent. 'Murderers, armed robbers, those planning to overthrow the Raj.' A Scotsman, he said, Reverend Martyn, was the chapel's priest at Viper Island. Vinny made the mark of the cross. 'Reverend Martyn is more dangerous than all the prisoners put together! They call him a bandit!'

Hiran frowned. 'A bandit-priest in charge of an orphanage? Where does he get his babies?'

'Simple. The peasants bring them over – newborns floating on reed rafts, abandoned by their sailor fathers and coolie mothers. Sometimes, the prison guards go on a rampage, female prisoners paying for their fun.' Vinny sighed. 'A priest must do more than pray.'

'To whom do the children belong?'

'They're as good as dead to their real fathers and mothers. Reverend Martyn raises them as his own. They go to school, work at the chapel's printing press, some become priests when they grow up.'

Hiran looked up and saw a rainbow over their heads. 'But why would he give us one?'

Vinny paused, frowning. 'Surely, he won't mind other priests like him taking care of an orphan. We must go to Viper Island dressed as missionaries!'

It seemed like a reasonable plan. But Hiran sensed it would take more than costumes to disguise them. It was a matter of knowing the lines as well, knowing how young missionaries behaved. He had seen them wearing dark coats over white dhotis, distracting passers-by on the streets with songs and speeches. 'Student enquirers' they called themselves.

'Don't tell your mother, jewel! She'll have you thrown out of Jaanbazaar.'

Vinny grew serious. 'But we'll need a letter from Calcutta to be even allowed into the prison. Who can vouch for our character?'

Then Hiran took Vinny to his mission school.

Later, he'd remember little of their visit to Viper Island, except the 'student enquirers'.

They were received kindly. At the hostel, Hiran felt more at ease than Vinny. They shared a room, bare but for two iron cots, with a window facing north.

'Living like sepoys, jewel! Worse, like convicts!'

Between the two they had settled about the beef – spinning an elaborate story around Hiran's obstinate stomach to explain his reluctance to eat Christian food. But the fare was simple, the usual greens served on English plates.

They had to wait for a few days – Reverend Martyn had left Viper Island on one of his rounds through neighbouring villages. Between sharing the daily chores with the young priests of the chapel, and gazing spellbound at the printing press churning out the Bible, the two thought of a plan to convince Reverend Martyn of their need for a baby boy.

'You ask him. He'll believe you.'

'But you are a Christian.'

'But you are a baboo. You look like one, speak like one. You've read books, you can show him what we'd do once the boy is ours.'

'Why don't we tell him the truth?'

'Truth? You mean tell him that the boy is for an opium queen?'

'Just say it is for Mr Crabbe – an honourable officer . . .'

'That's smart, jewel!' Vinny danced around him. 'You could say he's planning to send the boy off to England once he's old enough!'

Vinny returned to the tricky business of getting the boy from Viper Island to Calcutta. 'We couldn't take him with us. There would be trouble.'

'Why?' Hiran said, thinking Vinny was worrying about soothing a crying child. In a flash he saw the cripples from Boubazaar's alley. He shivered.

'Two Christians with a baby on a boat? We'd be taken for kidnappers! We must hire a nurse to bring the baby for us. She can pretend she's a maid to a sickly mother, carrying the baby for her to his maternal home. She mustn't show that she knows us. Until we're in Calcutta. We shall collect the boy once everyone has left the pier.' Vinny laughed. 'The Military Brahmin will be proud of us!'

Over a row of bowed heads – convicts praying in a long cabin – Hiran saw Reverend Martyn. Unlike the Portuguese priests at the mission school, he spoke good Bengalee. His face seemed oddly familiar too. 'Now we know where Mr Scott's been hiding!' Vinny exclaimed. They sat behind a whitewashed pillar, black coats in an assembly of white. The student priests blended in easily with the convicts.

Vinny had made arrangements – met the orphanage's warden, showed him the certificate from the mission school.

'It's up to you now! See if you can convince the bandit-priest. He likes stories, I'm told. You must tell him one.'

They seemed to know each other already when they met in his bare-walled room. Reverend Martyn read Hiran's letter from the mission school and asked if the boys still played blindfold games – daring each other to find the Bible in a pile of books, while covered from ear to ear in a cloth! Hiran explained how he had played and lost several times before discovering the trick – an embossed cross on the hard cover. Reverend Martyn laughed. Hiran was tempted to tell the story of the two merchants.

Reverend Martyn led them to the open courtyard. They walked absent-mindedly from one building to another, ending at a cabin where men stood in line with enamel plates.

'Who is the boy for?'

'An English couple, most honourable . . .'

'For ever yours.'

For ever yours? Hiran wondered if Reverend Martyn had listened before accepting his request.

They returned on a boat full of clay. A dark woman – head covered by a saree – held a moaning sack against her breast. Vinny had hired the woman, explained her duties. Hiran watched her from the corner of his eyes. She reminded him of Annada. He tried imagining the boy on the balcony of number 15. What will they name him? He felt proud of his success. Will Lilian stop now . . . give up her opium for her little boy? The boatmen cleared a space around Hiran and Vinny, the young preachers. A mother drew her son away with sharp words.

Hiran saw ghauts lining the river: Pathuriaghaut, paved with stones, Armenian Ghaut, Rusomji Ghaut named after a wealthy Parsee, Baboo Ghaut, Clive Ghaut. Vinny whispered in his ear, 'Watch for the Burning Ghaut, jewel . . . see if you can spot a floating skull or two!'

Hiran heard a call to prayer. The boatmen knelt over bamboo strips. The barge drifted over the Ganga, facing west.

They were safe, except till the very end, almost in sight of the pontoon bridge at Calcutta's harbour. In the receding light Hiran saw a swarm of dinghies, cavorting like porpoise. The boatmen appeared nervous, told Vinny and Hiran to cover their heads. Within moments the dinghies were close, and they were surrounded like prey. 'Jack-tars,' Vinny murmured. Cries rose from the women in the boat. The boatmen howled. 'What do they want?' Hiran asked. 'It's their fun. Scaring the natives,' Vinny replied.

The boatmen crouched like convicts, covering their heads with straw mats. A rock landed near Hiran's feet, struck a boy on his temple. A spray of blood sparkled on Hiran's dhoti. One of the sailors jumped into their boat, swiped at a frightened peasant. Others boarded, screaming and making lewd gestures at the boatmen. Hiran heard splashes – peasants diving into the river to escape. The nurse seemed frightened, she looked towards the shore as if planning to abandon the child and jump into the water. Would he have to jump too? Who would protect the child? He felt tension clawing at his throat. He saw Vinny rise, then dash over the rocking boards towards the woman at the back with the child in her arms. Snatching the bundle from her, he held it firmly, covering the small head with his chin. Then, in the blink of an eye, he dived into the Ganga, splashing wildly ahead.

Hiran lost them in the darkness. Paralysed on the boat, he scanned the night for a sight of them. Then he saw his friend's triumphant face, a hand clutching the jetty at the river's edge, and a pair of fair limbs clinging to his dark 'preacher's coat'.

The darker subjects stood at the back, behind the horses. They had come to see the inauguration of the new Viceroy. A full hour before the arrival of the cortège, cavalry lined the streets.

Great pains had been taken to decorate the station. The platforms were carpeted in crimson, archways prettily decked with folds of red and white cloth, a marquis' coronet over the main exit. On rows of raised seats on either side of the main platform sat the ladies, their finery matching the flags draped from Venetian masts.

Chowringhee was brilliantly lit, from the Europe Hotel to the Bengal Club. Thousands of gas-jets covered the Museum from the base to its tuillerie roof. The Octerlony Monument beamed like a lighthouse.

The Police Commissioner distributed cloth to the poor. Prisoners were released to mark the occasion. The Great Eastern Hotel hosted a luncheon. By the time the vice-regal cortège passed the bandstand, the National Anthem had been sung.

About a hundred men with their families sat at the guest-of-honour enclosure: Secretaries and Magistrates, Commissioners and Aides-de-Camp, Justices of the Peace, men of ships and trade, cadets, members of the rugby shield. Among them was the newly appointed Superintendent of the Auction House, Mr Jonathan Crabbe, with his wife, and their newborn son, Douglas.

At nine the fireworks started. First, the Royal Portraits, then set-pieces streaked over: horses, locos, ships, lions, stars, the cross . . .

By midnight they were ready for the finale – an eighteen-gun salute by the *Eugenia*, blasting off over the ramparts of the fort.

To Hiran, the Ganga seemed to be on fire.

Canton

Midnight: Barometer falling. Lightning on the horizon and a steady drizzle of rain. The thunder has ceased and in its place, silence.

1 a.m.: Dense, lurid sky. The barometer has fallen an inch since four bells. Sea rising. Unearthly moan heard away to the N.N.E. Captain summoned. All hands called at once to shorten sail. The moan becomes a deep groan. After a few seconds, it becomes a mighty roar.

Squalls now of intense violence, and the noise deafening. Impossible to raise head over the weather rail for the spray and rain. Whilst the topgallant was being taken in, the gaff topsail flew away like a giant bird. Lee boats and davits also torn away. Weather boats smashed to pieces.

2 a.m.: Sea now a mass of seething foam. Solid columns of rain pour over the ship, her hatches in the water. Ship scuddying. Four lee guns chafed through the breeching.

3 a.m.: Squalls every quarter of an hour.

4 a.m.: Squalls every ten minutes.

5 a.m.: Squalls every five minutes. Barometer 27°30. Carpenter and hands stationed at masts and weather rigging with axes ready to cut away at command. Square foresail threatens to take the foremast. Cut away from the yard with great difficulty.

Brig rolling heavily as well as plunging.

Cooks and stewards lying about in the wreckage of the saloon. Impossible to go aloft. The noise – like heavy guns.

6 a.m.: Brig's nose buried in foam, some water-fiend beneath

dragging her stern foremost. Cots slung to beams in tweendecks banging. A bos'n's mate and eight men dispatched to secure the brails with extra lashings. The third officer and two quartermasters manage to serve a stiff grog.

7 a.m.: Stars on the horizon, both rising and setting. Ship becalmed in a curious turmoil, sea running in every direction. Not a breath of air. The eye of the storm.

8 a.m.: Watch relieved. Wind south on starboard quarter; ship going 12 knots.

9 a.m.: Set course N.W. Set topsail, new fore trysail, staysail and jibs.

10 a.m.: Land sighted.

The *Warrior Queen* was in disarray, reeking of brandy and sickness. Among the first to recover, besides a dozen or so officers, were the grinning New Caledonians – hired deckhands from the South Seas – fine strapping fellows, already washing down the decks, or busy with the rigging. By the time the *Queen* had drawn close to the Malay coast, the rest of the crew were about too. In the aftermath of the storm, ears and tongues seemed sharper. Manilamen and Indians, Coffrees and dark Madrasees worked together easily.

As the third officer doled out fresh water, hammocks were piled up, and at eight o'clock all hands ate breakfast. There were repairs to do, new sails to be stitched, logs to be carried back and forth at the carpenter's order. It took all afternoon to sort the muskets, laying out the powder to dry in the sun, greasing the barrels that had shone like silver on the night of lightnings.

The first mate brought out a chess-board of carved ivory. The quartermaster joined him, and the two of them played and smoked cheroots. The planters spun yarns over the din of hammers, and the civil servants resumed worrying about transfers from one posting to the next. Company men, whisky pegs at their elbow, shared stories. There was much talk of live birds and dead animals, of polo games and tiger-shoots.

The third officer wrote the ship's log, and kept a diary in his spare time. For him, a voyage usually began with a list of names, any that caught his roving eye.

Mrs Jones – Fat
Miss Jones – *Whene'er I view those lips of thine*
Their hue invites my fervent kiss
Rev Fowler – Dresses like a Chinaman without a pig-tail
Mr and Mrs Holmes – Fanatical. God bless their servants!
Baby Holmes – Holy terror!
Bully Waterman – Dandy
Mrs Culver – Reminds of Aunt Beatrice
A brahmin and a black Christian – Opium-wallahs from Calcutta; seem harmless

Hiran found Captain Jacque on the spardeck with a baffled deckhand sitting for him. He had placed his easel to catch the best of the afternoon's light.

'Looking for your friend? He's with the pirate.'

But Hiran knew where Vinny was, in the carpenter's workshop, chatting with Fokie Tom. At first he thought it was Fokie's pretty Malay girl that fanned Vinny's daily urge for a chat.

'Are you mad? He'd chop me into a thousand bits! Do you know what his name means?'

He would return with soft candy made in Calcutta, in red wrappers marked with strange characters. Usually there would be a story as well – told over a whole afternoon, and recounted in minutes.

'Remember the ghost on the *Imogene*? Fokie was on that ship, saw it with his own eyes!'

Vinny and Hiran shared a cabin with a door between them and the boatswain's. Hiran's trunk barely fitted in.

'What are you carrying, jewel? Is it *you* getting married or is it me?' Vinny had a sambhar-skin bag . . . *presented by none other than the port's Commissioner to my father when he retired from service.* In it was concealed his wedding gift for Marie. 'Top secret! You'll find out at the right time.'

Hiran was worried about the trunk. On Saraladebi's order, Annada had packed a small urn filled with Ganga mud. 'It'll remind you of home, keep your mind pure as the Ganga!' 'Take it, Hira . . . bring it back full of sea water to quench my ashes.' Saraladebi was certain that Hiran would return only after her death. She reminded him of the last rites of a Hindoo son for his dead mother. Hiran worried in case the mud spilled and ruined his serge and cashmere.

Saraladebi's nightmares had started early, on the day a letter landed on Hiran's desk with the stamp of China and the signature of his old pupil.

> Dear Hiranbaboo,
>
> Over the past few months I have felt the need of an experienced hand to sort out office matters. Everything in Canton is so much more difficult. It would be a great convenience to me if you were to visit, albeit for a short while in light of your current responsibilities. If you agree, I will issue . . .

He had gone to number 15 with the letter, hoping to meet Mr Kavasji and Lilian.

The durwan led him to the balcony. It was empty but for a boy who stood on the settee, reading aloud to the smiling maid, his glass of goat's milk beside her on the floor. Hiran sat facing the trees, while the boy tried to draw his attention, running around the settee with the maid in laughing pursuit. The milk spilled. He waited to hear a voice behind his shoulder. But from the floor, the maid looked up and scolded Hiran. He was too late, she said, memsahib had left for the races.

'There's somebody on the ship who loves you, jewel!'

'Who?'

'Fokie's girl – Alaya. She asked me about the Brahman. Were you homesick . . . missing your wife!'

'What did you say?'

'I said, maybe, maybe not. I suggested she find a bride for you, then we could get married together! She said, but he's different, not like us . . . so tall, so quiet. Maybe he fancies a mem.'

On the Strand during tiffin-break, Vinny had read Mr Crabbe's letter in silence, then flashed his smile. 'Great! Now you can come to my marriage.' He had seemed more than eager, flooding Hiran with urgency. 'No, it isn't a lie. Captain Jacque wasn't kidding. She was to have come, but she fell ill at the last moment, missed the *Flying Cloud*. She's waiting for me now – in Macao. I'll have to go over, bring her back with me. Mr Crabbe wouldn't mind an extra hand with his *sorting out*, would he? You could convince him, jewel, to take me along?'

Nabinbaboo's reaction had been different: 'How will your mother explain to the mother of your bride that her son has sinned the sin of passage? It'll be hard to find willing parents.'

As always, Hiran had consulted his palms. Spreading them out like leaves, he had looked for the sign of passage which ran from the Life-line to the Mount of Luna. It was there – a ray under a cloud waiting to emerge. A small cross at its end showed disappointment; a square meant danger; an island indicated loss. Shooting towards Jupiter it promised a long voyage – a fateful journey.

He had thought of going back again to number 15. Perhaps Lilian would ask him to carry a letter for Mr Crabbe, pretend she was anxious? They'd end up, probably, chatting about the boy. 'Douglas!' she'd call to him below in the garden. 'Bring me my flowers . . .' The gardener would smile, hand a bunch to the boy. 'He misses his father. Why does it take so long?' She'd talk of typhoons, of pirates who stole Europeans for ransom. Her eyes always on the boy. 'Douglas!'

He knew what Mr Kavasji would say, even before he called him to his west wing office. 'Congratulations! Mahim will be very proud of you.'

Only the problem of Vinny remained.

Then Captain Jacque solved it. Vinny, he said, could share a berth with Hiran on his next run to Canton – 'free'.

'Not even a copper anna with Queen Victoria on top!'

'What if you show up and find he's sold your berth to a leopard?' Nabinbaboo smiled.

'Then he'll have to have me as bait.'

Almost two weeks after leaving Calcutta, the *Queen* crossed the Bay of Bengal and sailed close to the Malay coast preparing to arrive in Malacca, her first port of call. As they entered the estuary at dawn, they passed clumps of acacia and bamboo. A pilot's ridge light alerted them to the false mouth of the river – a broad sheet of shallow water full of mud and sandbanks. They could see limestone quarries burrowed into gentle hills.

Thousands of birds, as large as ravens and as small as magpies, swirled in the air. Wild swan, geese, duck, waterfowl, curlew, snipes, teal, rice-birds – pure white, like young crane. Flying round and round, unwilling to leave, until the rising tide shifted them.

Low over the reed, their wings brushed the water, sending giant ripples to shore.

From the deck of the *Queen*, a loaded double-barrel stirred a different trajectory, rising higher than the infant sun.

'Silly . . . we're far too far away,' Holmes sneered at Bully Waterman.

'Why do they call him a pirate?'

'To the English all Chinamen are pirates.'

In their Sunday best, pockets full of silver coins, the passengers waited for the river pilot to lead them into harbour, behind a white-paddle P&O steamer. Already, children were climbing rope ladders with baskets carefully balanced on their heads – like monkeys hanging by their tails – offering cool coconut and spicy shark fin.

They waited for Captain Jacque to order the unloading of the cargo chests before they could go ashore. He had few words of caution for the eager passengers, except, 'Watch out for your cousins!'

Vinny explained. In Malacca – the great colonial flower-bed – everyone was related to everyone else. 'Portuguese with Chinese, Dutch and Malay, flowery lips on fair skin, Coffrees with blue eyes.'

They went to the big red and white church at the city's centre, smelling of pleasant gummy oil, where Vinny bought a rosary of shells with a cross. 'It's for my brother. The one in Madras who makes guns at the factory.' Vinny cocked his arm. 'He knows the Bible by heart.'

On their way back from their stroll around the church and the bazaar, they saw Reverend Fowler from their ship haggling over a bag of oranges. He smiled at them.

'He's the one the pirates fear.'

'The Padre?'

'Speaks Chinese like a Chinaman. They think he's only disguised as a white man. He's a friend of our mud, speaks to dealers and boatmen in their tongue . . . scolds the Emperor's sons if they get too greedy. Knows pirates from peasants.'

'A missionary saving our opium?'

'It's not like that. We need his help – in exchange we give him money to buy bibles and crosses for the poor Chinese. He'll convert them all, jewel – Reverend Fowler will be the Pope of China!'

Hiran watched the squat man disappear inside a narrow bazaar.

'Once, the pirates kidnapped his wife – a rich English heiress. They sent word to the Reverend, asked for a big ransom. She was ugly but rich, and he needed her. So, he dressed as a Chinaman and went to meet them. He went alone, on an old wreck, with the Royal Navy right behind him. He went where no one goes and hopes to return alive. The pirates were anchored in the mouth of the river with their fleet – sixty-four junks with two hundred and forty guns, each the size of ours on the *Warrior Queen* . . .'

'They let him go alone?'

'That's the power of the Reverend.' Vinny's face was flushed. 'The pirates took him for another pirate . . . threw stinkpots, waved their mighty banners, cursed through bullhorns. He kept going, not left or right, but straight to the biggest junk of all. Stunned them when he came on board and introduced himself as an emissary of the Chinese Viceroy of Canton. The pirates were friendly to the Viceroy. They received him well.'

Hiran saw Reverend Fowler leave, followed by a small boy carrying a basket full of fruit: papaws, mangoes, melon, pitanga, prickly durian.

'He scolded the pirates, told them they were foolish, that the foreign devils would pray to the Emperor to send troops down. He said they'd better let the woman go . . .'

Hiran looked in amazement at the short retreating figure of the churchman, still dressed in a seafarer's loose trousers and long jacket, a straw hat on his head.

'He said mass on deck next morning, then left with his wife.'

'Did he convert the pirates?'

'That would have been a mistake, jewel. How can Christians rob other Christians?'

In the evening they saw the Reverend Fowler again, on the deck, watching a cock-fight with the sailors. He sat silently among the cheering crowd, covered with feathers.

'He likes betting.'

'Padre's cock first class!' Fokie Tom had joined them.

'Wait for the monkey-fight. Chinese monkeys are better than Malay monkeys.' Vinny pretended to be an expert.

'Not true,' Fokie was vehement, loyal, as Vinny explained later, to his Malay mother over his Fukkien Chinese father who had disappeared in the sea before Fokie was old enough to know monkeys from men.

Fokie dropped his voice: 'Padre very clever . . . without him no chance. Canton – no chance.'

Vinny explained, deftly translating for Hiran. Canton, the final destination of the *Warrior Queen* was now under siege.

There were rebels everywhere in China, Vinny said. Canton's Viceroy – the Mandarin who ruled in the name of the Emperor – was their favourite target. The rebels had encircled Canton's port, no one was allowed to land or leave. 'The Europeans are trapped there – in their factories . . . nothing to do but play cards, drink claret . . . miserable!' Ships arriving stood moored at Lintin, a small island, three days' sail down the Pearl river to Canton's port. Only the smugglers were making a profit, sometimes dying under bullets from both sides in the attempt.

Hiran was alarmed. What was Captain Jacque going to do?

'The *Warrior Queen* isn't afraid of war! But Captain Jacque plans to be quiet, smart like the Padre, land the mud himself and keep the silver rather than be robbed by damned smugglers.'

Reverend Fowler's bird came up winner. He smiled. Then he passed around a bag of oranges.

'You're one of Mr Crabbe's men, I suppose,' he said, stopping in front of Hiran.

'Yes, Sir.'

'You've heard what's happening in Canton. Yes? Will your owners now be convinced that it's better to be safe than profitable?'

Unprepared, Hiran offered a stock reply. 'Soon it won't pay to trade in opium, Sir. The Chinese are growing their own . . .'

'Yes, yes.' Reverend Fowler frowned. 'But who'll count the Emperor's share, keep him happy? Who'll account for the chests?'

'The Chinese themselves, I suppose, Sir.'

'They've been known to cheat honestly.'

There was more talk that evening. From their table apart in the dining-room, Hiran and Vinny listened to the European passengers. The surgeon, Mr Waterman – Bully – held court among the ladies: 'Take opium, mandragora and henbane, equal parts, pound and mix with water. Dip a rag in the mix when you want to saw a man's leg off, then hold it to his nose. He'll sleep so deep that you may do what you wish.'

Mrs Culver – an elderly widow, a teacher on her way to the Governor's school in Hong Kong – was curious. 'What *is* it, exactly? Something to bring on sleep, or to keep you on your toes. Is it *hot* or *cold*, surgeon?'

Mr Waterman frowned, unwilling to enter into a long explanation. 'Could be both, Bettie. Depends on what you want.' Which prompted a sniggering Mrs Holmes to ask, 'But it must cure *some* disease, mustn't it?'

'What is disease but a deficiency or excess of excitement?'

'How long does it take one to be hooked?' Mrs Culver persisted. Mr Robinson – the tea planter from India – had come to join them and offered what seemed a reasonable scope: 'Could be one pipe smoked daily for a week or ten days. Could be higher – four pipes, ten pipes – a dozen certainly if he lives till eighty! Coolies die faster from spirits.'

Bully Waterman smiled. Would the ladies like to observe them – the 'addicts'? They could see them just down in the crew-hold: thirty men smoking on two tiers of plank. 'Like vegetables. A bunch of sweating skeletons.'

He paused, then added with a chuckle, 'There's always an old addict celebrating his *last pipe*. Of course, they'll return to smoke tomorrow, celebrating someone else's *last pipe*!'

'Is there then no way to stop?' Mrs Culver seemed truly sad. 'What a curse. Destroying everything, destroyed by nothing . . .'

'Not a curse, dear.' The Reverend Fowler had joined their table, unnoticed: 'Small imperfections in a magnificent whole.'

'The smugglers must be stopped then,' said Mrs Culver, unsoothed.

'And who'll stop Her Majesty's men? The fathers of all smugglers!' Few laughed at Mr Robinson's words.

The surgeon was more rigorous: 'It's helpful, actually, to some of them – the poorer ones. Slows the rate of digestion in their long intestines. Then consider its effect on the lungs, those bronchial tubes filled with the sludge of the marshes. It's an antiseptic, as well as an anaesthetic. Do you know how many

Chinese coolies die of consumption? Remove opium and you've got death.'

'Better to die *of* opium then?'

It was getting late. Mrs Culver was holding up their post-dinner stroll on the flushdecked promenade. Mrs Holmes – the sniggering wife of Canton's Postmaster General – left with her husband. Only Mr Robinson and Mr Waterman were left chatting over a most complex logic of numbers. 'Three thousand, four hundred chests of opium imported annually would yield thirty-three million, three hundred and twenty thousand taels of smokeable extract, and this, divided by three hundred and sixty-five, yields nine hundred and twelve thousand regular victims, allowing to each one tael per day. Amounts to only one three hundred and twenty-sixth of the whole population, even less if one were to allow for those to whom it was simply casual indulgence.'

'Is it true misfortune haunts those dealing in opium?'

'The spite of the dead, jewel, and the living.'

Sitting on the forecastle with a globe lamp, Vinny told Hiran the story of the haunted ship *Imogene* that had left the London docks on the ninth day of September, 18—, bound for Bombay. 'No one knows what it was they saw on that ship, a dead sailor, or a spirit that had caught in their sails at the Cape of Good Hope.' He imitated the voice of the Irish boatswain, 'Why d'ye see, Sir, I saw its face first. It turned round an' looked at me as it was runnin' away. Yes, by Saint Patrick! I'll swear t' that. His tail was three fathom long, an' th' end ov it was coiled round an' round his neck. All ov a sudden he vanished in th' middle ov a flash of flamin' lightnin . . .' And then, a whimpering black cook, 'Fetish! Fetish! Obi man! Dat's him!' Hiran shivered.

'"Put the helm down," the captain sang out as they approached shore. But the ghost took his voice . . . *Put it up again.* "Mainsail haul!" the captain called. The ghost said, *Stay.* The sailors were confused and ran around the deck dazed, each swearing he heard a different command. The officers stared at the captain, watched for his lips to move, then shook in horror. "*Die! Die!*" the captain screamed into their faces. The spirit had entered him!'

A thin mist blew out the Chinese candles one by one.

Lying awake later, Hiran thought of Vinny's story. Who would be the perfect ghost on the *Warrior Queen*? The doctor – cursed by a man who had died in his arms? Fokie – a drowned father's revenge? The Reverend? He remembered the words of his old teacher at the tole: 'Even ghosts must beware of mischievous men.'

A distant chorus blew in with the breeze from the shore. The air seemed alive with ghosts. Only a soft lapping of the water on the buoys reminded him where he was. Otherwise he could have been on their roof in Jaanbazaar, listening to the beat of baijis in the alleys below.

'Is it true what they say about you, jewel?'

Hiran turned his face towards Vinny in the dark. 'You've read your palm, and strictly follow its lines. That you're waiting for your uncle to die. That you've never loved, not even your poor mother. That all we see is a disguise . . .'

Hiran was silent.

'They say you can't be angry, can't suffer . . .'

Hiran heard a restless ocean, saw a moon reflected over waves, then a thousand of them – unclouded.

'Ever thought of going back to Viper Island?'

Hiran thought of the Reverend Martyn, dead of snake bite not cholera, plague, or ague. O God, when Thou hadst created India, what object was there in conceiving hell?

'They say you want more than the crow waiting to steal his wife . . . that you're the owl – the one who guards and kills at the same time. True?'

They left at dawn, Vinny, Hiran, Captain Jacque, a Malay boy and a crew of Chinese boatmen. The boy carried the musket. Mr Robinson, Mr Waterman, and Miss Jones followed in a sampan, Bully Waterman in his umbrella hat and rush waterproof, Mr

Robinson in green from the chin down, Miss Jones dressed in hunter's khaki, 'a college-girl' with 'a suitor on board'.

They fastened their boats on a sandbank, sat on wooden planks over the treacherous mud. Captain Jacque urged them to stay close, to keep their gumboots tangled – an officer had been lost not long ago in these marshy banks off the coast of Malacca. He hushed them with his finger as Bully Waterman splashed over a crater of sand.

Robinson, the planter, was first, spraying his musket, loaded with grape cartridge. Others quickly followed, pumping more wire into the stationary surf, till it came alive with a roar. Captain Jacque passed his gun back and forth to his Malay boy, loading and firing, loading and firing. The cries of wounded birds turned their heads. A boatman came towards them, carrying a wild swan, its head over his shoulder, feet dragging on the ground.

Rice-birds were the prize – too lazy to fly away, too tame to fear the muzzles. A roar of applause from a neighbouring ship greeted their success.

Miss Jones, still on the sampan, circled the bank and dodged fire. She collected the prizes, pointing with an oar towards fluttering eddies on the water.

From the wicker awning of their junk, some Chinese fishermen watched Hiran and Vinny, pointing at Hiran's foot, smiling. He smiled back. Then Vinny slapped their tangled knees and screamed. Hiran saw a green snake wrapped round his ankle like dead seaweed, leapt to his feet and tumbled into the mud and water.

For a moment he thought of his poor mother, then lost fear and hope.

Underwater, Hiran felt he was being dragged along by a friendly ghost, almost a kind one, merely offering to show what lay beneath the dark shining mud. His naked feet hugged molten rocks, felt no pain. He saw coral – like a bed of white nails – shallow flats with catted anchors, as he slipped under the *Warrior Queen*.

With the eyes of a ghost, Hiran examined the pride of the Thames. He saw her surging before a fair gale – a bone-white lady prancing on a white horse. Noted her gilded tops, carved balconies, curtalls inlaid with the royal coat-of-arms and motto: *Deo ducente nil nocet.* Cannons and demi-cannons poked their grinning heads through gunports. From a porthole, Ramah the cook waved at him as he laid the breakfast table. He closed his eyes as he passed Miss Jones' cabin, heard a bucket emptying over the washstand.

The ghost took Hiran to galleys stacked with chests. He recognized Mr Eliot's seal. What did the *Warrior Queen* carry, he wondered . . . *what is it, exactly, surgeon? Is it hot or cold?*

They laid Hiran down on a mat with Vinny dancing around him, chattering at a high pitch. The Reverend Fowler calmed them both with brandy. 'Drink up, young man, it'll chase away the snakes!'

For hours Hiran slept on his roll in the dark cabin. Vinny came in from time to time, placed a finger under his nose to check for breathing. 'What would I have told your mother?' He nodded his head wisely. 'She'd have blamed it on me – a chillicracker drowning a brahmin. Mr Crabbe would've called for the whip.'

Miss Jones sent to enquire after him. So did Bettie Culver. Fokie nicked his finger when he heard, his girl let out a gasp.

In the evening everyone left the *Queen* for Malacca to a concert.

Hiran didn't mind staying back. The Reverend Fowler's brandy brought on bouts of dreamless naps. Propped up on his bed, he looked out towards the town of boat-houses, thought of beginning a letter to his mother. He could hear dogs barking over a hum of voices. Temple bells ringing around the edges of a native horn.

He thought he heard Saraladebi crying. His mind skipped over a pool on their roof, coming to a stop before her door. Then he woke to the sound of the tide lapping. The crying seemed close, stretched from one end of the ship to the other, clotting in short bursts below the wooden floor. The darkness blinded him as he passed empty cabins, the wind trapped within. A giant candlestick at the quartermaster's table swayed gently. He heard the cry of the wounded swan, mixed with heaving boatmen. And creaking, almost like masts in full sail. He stumbled in the dark, picked up a wooden mallet. The moaning seemed to rise, darting from one secret corner to another. His hand grazed hard wood and metal – sharp. Nails scattered from his step. A shaft of light gleamed on the spiral stairs. He saw the Goddess – brown, naked, breasts heaving – squashing a helpless Fokie, like a bee clinging to ripe blossom. Her face turned towards Hiran, cries pierced his forehead.

Before arriving in Hong Kong – the Island of Sweet Waters – the *Warrior Queen* sailed into the teeth of a different storm. They had left the Strait of Malacca and were heading north on the South China Sea, when deckhands, officers, passengers and crew threatened revolt, with Mrs Holmes leading the charge against 'infractions on modesty'.

The sailors were blamed, for an 'unauthorized feast' their last night on shore in Malacca. Cheating cooks had fed them dogs, it was claimed – howling syphilitic creatures that kept them awake at night. 'They're lucky to be alive . . . could've been the poisonous flesh of a komodo dragon!' Vinny had seen them parading to their feast, near the ramshackle whore-house, drunk already, sick in the stomach at the thought of yet another journey. A few of them had hooted at Vinny, calling him a *fart from a whore's arse.*

It must have been the dogs, and dragons, or whatever they had managed to land in their bloated bellies, plus the ripe durian – sweet but fatal. Some started to vomit before they got back, almost falling into the sea from the dinghies. They sprayed the burnished deck of the *Warrior Queen* with whitish jelly.

'But how did the sleeping Englishmen catch it?' Hiran asked.

'Dirty hands, drooling mouths . . . from hand to belly.'

Mr Waterman had a different explanation for the sudden attack: 'Check the water tanks.' Inside rum-puncheons and casks, the water had turned thick as treacle, blue as indigo, with a smell that would make a pirate faint.

They were all sick – with or without dogs – except Captain Jacque. He stuck to gin and biscuits, seemed in high spirits, sailing almost single-handed, never turning in but dozing with an eye open in a deck chair on the poop.

'Hundreds died in the Mexican campaign. Nearly five thousand in Spain. Some returned home only to die among their own.' He'd go around the cabins, telling stories of disease and battle.

Mrs Jones was his favourite. Holding the thermometer to his nose, he'd make a face. 'Did you know the Chinese put up prize money in the first opium war? Twenty thousand dollars for sinking HMS *Alligator*, five thousand dollars for her captain, alive – dead he'd fetch only a third. One hundred dollars for a soldier, twenty dollars per head for sepoys.' Still heaving, her eyes fluttered. 'And what would they offer for a woman, Captain?'

'A she-devil would command no less than the Emperor's sword!'

Mrs Jones had been the first to wake on the night of the sailors' feast, hearing the revelry of their return. Thinking they were pirates, she had dragged her sweating body over to whisper into her daughter's ear. 'They're after my jewellery,' Emily said, trying to slip a gold chain off her neck. It caught in her red hair, and she bit her mother's palm, fearing a thief. Mrs Jones had it bandaged next morning by Mr Waterman. She had tried to pass it off as a scratch, but the surgeon had frowned at the mark.

'Field-pieces loaded with grape were planted along Canton's crowded narrow streets, to mow men, women and children down like grass till the gutters flowed with blood.'

'Horrible, Captain!'

He'd have a better reaction from Mr Robinson. He showed a healthy respect for the captain's tales, groaning with cramps. 'Hold on a minute, Captain . . . these damned . . .'

For Mr Robinson, Captain Jacque embarked on the grand opium wars – salvos and truces, burning forts and treaties signed in cities with unpronounceable names, ending with the Chinese Prince Kung's plea to Sir Rutherford Alcock. *Take away your opium and your missionaries and you will be welcome.*

Hiran, when it was his turn to listen, was impressed, although he had already heard most of the tales on the balcony at number 15. He knew of the Arrow Incident, the Opium-Bonfire, Commissioner Lin and Captain Eliot – of concessions, Hong Kong and the four other treaty ports.

Did he know of Indians fighting alongside Scots and Irish in China? 'From Madras and Bengal, arriving in twenty-seven transports. There was a near mutiny – the sepoys were more afraid of the sea than of battle!' Captain Jacque eyed Hiran who groaned in his cabin bed.

'And there is one – a gunner – from that campaign, still here.'

'Here?'

'On the *Warrior Queen*.'

Only Bettie Culver, the lady teacher, was resistant to the captain's stories. She had suffered the most – a ruptured tube threatening to block the flood – bearing her pain with soft whimpers and occasional sighs. They were worried for her. 'Should we turn back, Sir?' the first officer had asked. Mr Waterman, barely conscious himself, pointed at a clear liquid in his valise. Captain Jacque warmed it, held it to her nose as she gurgled it down like a little girl. That night she broke out in sweats, moaned and howled, barely able to crawl to the toilet, soiling everything then cursing herself for the mess. The Joneses, mother and daughter, came to her aid, holding a warm cloth to her face when she wanted cold, and cold when she shivered from the breeze. Miss Jones and the third officer mopped the reeking cabin. Captain Jacque teased, 'He doesn't mind the mess, Emily, as long as you're near!' Even Mrs Holmes offered her ginger biscuits to Mrs Culver. Mr Robinson ate them, standing outside the door in his nightgown. By morning, she had recovered enough to insist on her deck chair and Bible. Captain Jacque greeted her with a tropical rose.

'Why are you going round scaring sick people with war stories?'

'Because disaster is better than death.'

Only Nabinbaboo could have shown greater zeal. For a whole week – the time it took to sail from Malacca to Hong Kong – Hiran went over the copious notes he had made while observing his superior's homeopathy at the Auction House. He tried out his learned skills first on Vinny and himself, then on a steady stream of miserable sailors. They would stand before the first mate's desk to collect a thin tube with a rubber stopper – opium mixed with camphor, nitric acid and calomel under Mr Waterman's supervision. Then, they would come directly in ones and twos to stand outside Hiran's cabin.

Fokie, he found later, had spread the word. A brahmin's miracle.

'Hindoo-pani good for tummy,' Fokie had trumpeted. He had been the first to join Captain Jacque on deck, once more walking steady on his feet.

Hiran read his scribbled notes by the light of a globe lamp. He heard Nabinbaboo's even drone: 'The suffering is similar to a mother's at childbirth. There is a painful burning, insatiable thirst, anxious breathing. With excessive discharge, a coldness spreads from the lower limbs; the face and lips become blue, the tongue presents a shrivelled appearance, eyes turn bloodshot, voice feeble and hollow like a dying fowl.' And he remembered the simple path to a cure. 'Each particle of matter obeys a principle it cannot transgress, and combines in beautiful proportion with the element necessary to complete the plan.' The trick, he knew, was to find the alluring partner that would carry the hideous colic away like an angel on its wings.

'Are you sure just a few drops will do it? You're sure Nabinbaboo didn't only have memsahibs in mind?'

'The Creator made this world from the invisible and the infinitesimal,' Hiran replied in the voice of Nabinbaboo.

Fokie's girl Alaya came one evening, alone. Unlike the others, she stepped in lightly, then waited as if Hiran had asked for a meeting. She stood with her body facing him, face turned: a sickness looking for its beautiful partner. He heard her laboured breathing, saw dark nipples straining against wet cotton in effort, delicate feet set apart.

hotaram api juhvantam
sprsto dahati pavakah

. . . it burns even the priest
who stokes her fire

Hiran sat facing her.

He had begun to walk the echoing corridors of the ship at night. Some nights he heard the sea, other times he'd forget they were on a ship. He'd pass Mr Holmes, still looking for the WC: 'Ah yes, whoever designed the ship must've . . .'

His feet took him always in one direction. He tiptoed past the stewards' mess, taking care not to startle the animals in their pens. He heard Captain Jacque whistling. It was rare for the captain to come down to his cabin. Must've been a damp night. Hiran heard his cough – slow but regular, keeping his neighbour Mrs Jones awake. He steered towards the dark, waited for a flickering candle to restore an even cone of dimness.

As he entered the carpenter's workshop he stepped carefully over the shavings, to avoid deadly nails. A cabinet of Jack-planes and chisels greeted him like a belt of tinkling bells. Stepping cautiously, he would hold a creaking door steady and look. Slowly, his eyes would adjust to darkness.

On some nights she wandered in a *Kadamba* forest, drinking the flower's wine, mingling laughter and dance, binding and unbinding her hair – each movement stirring and generous – like twigs twining, or rising bubbles. She was *Prakriti* – a void filling spirits, arm around her stem of lotus – her nectar. He smelled saffron and sandalwood, musk. A delicate body lay crouched in a corner, a soft belly rising and falling. Some nights he saw her red as the rising sun – *Sodasi* – with a crescent moon and crown on her head, in the embrace of *Makakala*: like a *Yantra* – splitting into two, both dead; the whole alive.

Amorous Goddesses – night after night she would reveal herself: *Tara* – shining blue with a swollen belly; *Bhuvaneshwari* – for ever in union; *Bhairavi* and *Chinnamasta* in tableaus of intercourse; a frenzied *Matangi.* Sweat dropped in beads from Hiran's forehead, he heard the crash of a million hammers, the gnashing chisel, the swish of naked blades; her cry would enter each instrument, give it life. He would forget the journey, immersed in her rhythm.

In darkness, her face would turn towards Hiran. Always.

He looked like the butcher in Boubazaar's market: grim eyes under deep brows, thin lips surrounded by an island of beard. Hiran saw him first at Malacca, although Vinny swore the man had boarded in Calcutta. The second officer had found him snoring over his bedroll when the captain called for all hands on deck. He was punished with no ration for three days, but few of the officers believed he went hungry – 'the sailors would happily starve for him'. The storm seemed to have little effect on him. He sat cross-legged, as usual, shifting position every so often, to face west. 'How can he know which way is west without a compass?' Hiran asked. 'That's why they call him a pir, jewel!'

Hiran knew of pirs from Annada. They were holy men, born to see the future.

'Fetch the pump-hose,' the senior mate ordered, and the sailors would run and fetch it for the bearded pir. 'Scrub the deck!' the quartermaster shouted, as they prepared to arrive in Hong Kong, but the sailors did not let the pir kneel over the planks, except to pray. The purser refused to pay him at first for he had done no work, but Captain Jacque calmed him. 'Think of him as their pet, like Ramah's cat. Would you take away its bowl of milk?' Mrs Jones found him spooky, and wouldn't go to the WC alone at night. 'He makes me think, dear, of those terrible things – sepoys hunting innocent English people.'

To Hiran, the pir seemed innocent.

'Why don't we both have our faces read by the pir . . . so we'll know if there is a girl waiting for you.' Vinny stopped half-way. 'Why, jewel, I had completely forgotten. Maybe we could have a cock-fight between the two of you!'

'Cock-fight?'

'You can read palms, he can read faces. We'll see who wins!'

Hiran and Vinny sat watching a strange invasion. Boats full of laundry-girls had the *Warrior Queen* encircled within moments of arriving in Hong Kong. Sculling with a large oar over the stern, they shouted for attention and gestured with their hands and wicked smiles. They reminded Hiran of a swirl of birds on a sandbar.

'They live all their life on a boat. Some of them are pirates' sisters, they make greenhorns pay six times the proper fee. Little witches!'

An older washerwoman came up the ladder with her young ones amidst the cheers of the sailors. In a moment they were all over the ship – from the captain's cabin to the cook's galley. They lined up their baskets on deck, marking each pile with a small red chop. Captain Jacque watched them with a smile on his lips. 'They never lose anything. Once a seaman left his dirty shirt behind. When the fleet sailed home twelve months later he found it waiting for him, pressed and cleaned!'

It was an occasion for scrubbing and grooming as Hong Kong welcomed them with a flotilla of clippers and steamers. The signs of New Year festivities were all around them. Fokie – smiling broadly – pointed through the port window at the paper figures lined up by the docks: 'Chaou-Foo – kind lady; monkey-god . . .' A camel dressed like a leopard, a tiger holding an umbrella over its head. Lucky charms for children, Fokie explained.

A veteran of Hong Kong, Bully Waterman dressed himself carefully in a velvet coat with lace collars. 'We ought to visit the *devil-dwarfs* at the circus, they'll make you laugh and cry at the same time.'

'I wouldn't venture within an inch of the devil's shamiana.' Mrs Holmes screwed up her nose.

'No, I wouldn't if I were you . . .'

'Who'd want to sit next to smelly sailors, dirty Chinamen . . .'

'They have special seats for *Fan-Kweis*,' Bully protested. 'Foreign Devils, you know. Really, they're quite all right. You shouldn't miss the costumes . . . quite lovely.'

They had planned a farewell dinner for Mrs Culver who was leaving the ship at Hong Kong, then perhaps they could go ashore to visit the circus.

The plan changed. A cutter came in the afternoon with a note from the Governor's ADC for Mrs Culver. A teacher, it read, was urgently needed at the recently opened mission school in Canton. It promised excellent facilities and ended with a touch of humour . . . 'I'd send my peon's boy there if I could, except that his father plans to have him become a woman . . . at the opera!'

Holding her bible open on her lap, she had said yes, even before finishing the note. Then she looked at the others. 'I guess dinner will be off then.' 'No!' they shouted in chorus.

'Fokie will take us to the circus. We'll sit with the sahibs,' Vinny said.

Hiran had seen yellow-devils before – shoemakers, dentists, thieves, crowding the narrow alleys of Old China Bazaar in Calcutta, smelling of dried fish and pig's intestines. Worse than low-castes, Saraladebi would say – even whores wouldn't look at their faces.

'Fokie's girl would like to come too, except he won't let her,' Vinny confided.

'Why not?'

'He thinks they'll steal her. Make her a laundry-girl.'

'Where did Fokie find her?'

'Top secret! Girls like her don't grow in trees. He's afraid for her sisters too.'

'Who protects her on the *Warrior Queen*?'

'She has a weapon of her own. Don't go near her, jewel!'

They left for shore after dinner in a fleet of sampans. Captain Jacque allowed one revolver to each boat. 'Pirates!' Vinny whispered.

For a whole evening they walked from stall to stall inside the giant circus tent, watching jugglers, fortune-tellers, men in costumes enacting strange tales, quacks displaying rows of bottles with human organs painted on them.

'Wake up, jewel!' For a moment Hiran thought he was still dreaming of the circus. Vinny led him down the staircase, past creaking doors, Ramah's cat prancing in front of them.

'The cock-fight is about to start – it's you against the pir! Everyone is waiting.'

Fokie was sitting in the middle of the stewards' mess – bare-chested, eyes swimming in shamshoo – surrounded by an eager crowd of sailors. All faces turned as Hiran entered.

Ramah offered Hiran a stool, then set out the rules. Fokie was to be the subject of their inspection. Each was to pronounce his verdict on a past that only Fokie could know. By a nod of his head the carpenter would score them, two sahibs would proclaim the winner. And the prize? Two hundred rupees, a brown and red prized cock, and a night with Fokie's girl. Everyone laughed, even Fokie.

'I'm all for you, jewel,' Vinny exclaimed. 'The pir's just a fake!'

A strange veil seemed to descend upon Hiran, to cover him like a tent, its dark lining glittering with known faces and stories. As on the night of the storm, he thought he saw his mother, saw her sitting on their roof with her embroidery. He heard her sigh. Beneath the veil a voice whispered, 'It is time, Hira . . .' He felt his old teacher wipe the blood from his lips.

'He has two or three children,' the pir announced, barely casting a glance at Fokie.

'*Or?*' Ramah frowned.

'He means, one could be dead from cholera.' A young sailor interpreted for the pir. Smiling, Fokie nodded his head, then held out his hands, palms upward, to Hiran.

Hiran saw a square box on a faint line, running down from the index finger. Was it a box or a star? Box for a living subject, star for a dead one. Then he relaxed. Of course, the smiling subject was still alive. He told a story to the crowd.

One day a boy was playing with his brother in front of their house. A sadhu appeared by the door and asked for alms. One of them ran for his mother, but the other stopped him. Let the old fool wait, he said. Hearing this, the sadhu became angry. He disguised himself as a crow and flew away. He came back with two stones in his beak, and dropped them on the boys' heads. One died instantly, the other lived, but the injury made him forget the face of his mother. He has been searching ever since . . .

'His brother died young,' he said, his eye on Fokie.

The carpenter's eyes filled with tears and he sighed deeply.

The crowd's excitement grew. Someone ran to the kitchen and returned with a bottle of ginger ale for Hiran. The pir's face glistened. He grimaced, pointed at Fokie's arm and neck, then whispered to a sailor.

'He says his bones are bad . . . brittle, aching . . .' Fokie nodded grimly.

'He's deaf in one ear,' Hiran announced in turn.

'How do you know that, jewel?' Vinny whispered.

He pointed to two clear dots, like dead flies, under the mount of Jupiter. Fokie smiled agreement.

Hiran wondered where Alaya was. Vinny was leaping around Hiran, spurring him on incoherently.

'Ask them if he's married,' Hiran heard someone say.

'No, ask how many girls he's had, how many virgins.'

'Ask if his girl has a baby in her belly.'

'Ask if he's his father's son.'

'Ask . . .'

The pir fixed his piercing eyes on Fokie's head. He started to sing, a song full of sadness like a graveyard lament. The sailors knelt down. Hiran was amazed. Where had he learned that song? Like the morning breeze it was both sad and full of hope. Fokie had fallen into a trance, head rolling over his shoulder, mouth open. Then, Vinny interrupted.

'It's unfair! He's hypnotizing the subject, Sir.' The pir kept on singing, almost under his breath, but his song had changed. Now it was a sea shanty, imbued with the rhythm of oars, heaving and pulling. Someone screamed from the back, 'Catch the half-caste. Feed him to the sharks!'

'Has his Jisu given him eyes like the pir?'

'How can a drunk decide what's true and what's a lie?'

'Ask if he remembers his name.'

At that point, as the men came alive with angry words, the boatswains stepped in. From now on there'd be no singing, no cursing, no betting. From now on, the rules would be followed.

Someone tried to bring them back to where they were before. 'Where is his mother?'

Fokie woke with a start and inched closer to the pir.

'This is your chance!' Vinny muttered into Hiran's ear.

The pir frowned.

'Well . . .'

'*Shud.*'

'*Shud?*' Fokie muttered, confused.

'He means she is dead.' The pir nodded wisely.

Suddenly he looked like a little child, lost in a crowd. *Shud . . . shud . . .* Fokie kept muttering to himself.

'Your turn, baboo,' Hiran heard the officer say.

'Kill him now!' Vinny squealed.

Hiran looked at Fokie's open palm. He saw a star, a simple mark – like a solitary bloom in a garden. It sat on the Line of Fate, not far from rising arcs and sloping mounts. It seemed to invite, to seek a meaning. Silently, he started counting its distance from other marks. The carpenter's life fleeted before his eyes – early tragedies, battles, pride and affection, journeys, passions and greed – then met at a simple star: death, by a fatal accident only a few moons in waiting.

'Speak, jewel . . .' He heard the hum grow. Even the pir was looking at him. Fokie seemed to have fallen asleep.

'Two hundred rupees . . .'

Hiran felt the veil lifting, bringing him back to a room full of drunks and a silent pir. He felt a strange calm.

'She's alive . . . another man's wife.'

Like a shot Fokie was awake, lifting Hiran off his seat with powerful hands. *Alive!* he muttered, eyes shining, a child's grin on his face.

'You are too much, jewel. Is my Marie alive too?'

A letter bearing the seal of the Queen came on a steamer from Canton. The *Warrior Queen* had just left Hong Kong, travelling up towards Portuguese Macao – their last stop before Canton. Captain Jacque waved, then floated the envelope over the deck like a low-flying gull. It landed at Hiran's feet. Mrs Jones and her daughter stopped chatting and glanced over, intrigued. 'They're sending you back, aren't they! For misbehaving!' Captain Jacque roared, distracting Hiran momentarily from Mr Crabbe's letter . . .

> Dear Hiranbaboo,
>
> You may have heard already of the trouble in Canton. Given the siege of the city, I am afraid it might not be possible for us to meet at the harbour. You are advised to seek the captain's help in contacting Mr Guo, an eminent Chinese merchant, who has been our friend for a very long time. With his help you should have no trouble reaching –

'They've arranged to transfer you to a convicts' ship, haven't they?'

> You may ask Captain Jacque to furnish you with a signed bond, vouching for your berth on his vessel. Your visit then may be seen merely as a transit.

'What is it, jewel?'

Hiran told Vinny about Mr Guo. 'The camel,' Vinny smiled. 'He had crossed the Gobi desert like a camel a dozen times before discovering our mud was more valuable than silk or tea. He's our protector in China, keeps everyone happy. The Chinese Hong merchants and their leader – the Hoppo, the Emperor's Viceroy, pirates, even Jacks.'

Vinny smiled at Hiran's ignorance, 'You'll learn, jewel.'

The deck was abuzz with speculation. Mail steamers returning to Hong Kong from Canton passed messages to the *Warrior Queen.* Every morning they heard of the rebels' advance against the Viceroy, of new waves of beheadings, and of the plight of the trapped Europeans. Opium ships were rumoured to be turning back for fear of pirates. 'Perhaps we should not go on to China either.' Bully Waterman had his telescope out, eyed a constellation as if it held a solution. 'I wouldn't take the rumours too seriously. The Chinese have been known to float trial balloons,' Mr Holmes suggested. He, after all, was returning home with his wife and young son after a family visit to Calcutta, unlike the surgeon who could afford to return without having set foot in Canton. 'But we should be cautious, dear.' Mrs Holmes was unusually mellow. 'I'd rather be on a smelly ship than a deathly shore.'

Mr Robinson was curious, asking the captain all sorts of exasperating questions. 'The Hoppo', he was informed, was short for hippopotamus, meaning he lived in the mud between land and water – between the Emperor and the foreign barbarians. He was the celestial's eyes and ears, representing the Chinese merchants on shore and the foreign ones on their ships. Miss Jones let out a squeal. 'A hippo! Really, Captain!'

'We bribe the Hongs, they bribe the Hoppo, he bribes the Viceroy, who bribes the Emperor,' the Captain continued. 'Somewhere along the way, the pirates get bribed too, but the Reverend knows more about that than I do, doesn't he?'

Reverend Fowler smiled. 'You made just one error, Captain. The Emperor bribes the barbarians too, doesn't he? Think of our treaty ports, and Hong Kong.'

'They are hanged first, aren't they?' Mrs Jones asked quietly.

'The Hoppo?'

'The Hongs. Our dear friends. Once in a while the Emperor wakes up, doesn't he, hears his concubines moaning with opium, and lets loose his rage on some poor Viceroy, who lets loose on some poor Hong, who . . .' Mr Holmes nodded approvingly at Mrs Jones.

'I wouldn't call them poor, dear. You have surely seen their palaces towering over the pagodas behind Canton's wall!' Mrs Culver sounded less than generous.

'Yes yes, but how many of them have friends like us to protect them? The French, the Dutch, even the Americans don't really care whether or not they live or die – real vultures!' Bully Waterman was ready to inject a dose of precision into the discussion: 'Our seal has always been the proof of quality, the only reliable source in a thugs' business. We're the ones who have stood by the Hongs, not just those who are our friends but all honest Chinese merchants threatened during the wars.'

Reverend Fowler beamed from his deck chair. 'Don't forget the church, surgeon. We were the first to bring the gospel.'

'The Jesuits got there before you, Reverend,' Mrs Culver observed dryly from her perch.

'Yes, but we were the first to give Him a Chinese name. *Shang Ti* – The Emperor Above the Emperor.'

'And did you replace bread and wine too, with rice and tea?'

'In any case,' the surgeon returned to his cogent assertion, 'if you leave out a few well-meaning explorers, we can justly claim to have ushered in a civilization unseen before in these parts! We and the Parsees are the only honest ones.'

'I wouldn't call it honesty, Mr Waterman. Good practical sense, perhaps.' Once more they despaired of Mrs Culver.

Mr Robinson seemed impatient to come to the point. 'Tell me, gentlemen and ladies, if it really is the way it seems then why should we worry about landing in Canton?' That brought forth all of Mrs Holmes's sneer. 'Because some of us must bear the burden of European commerce by living with the half-witted barbarians!'

'Floods, bandits, bribes, and a weak Son of Heaven,' Captain Jacque summarized. 'The only ones you can trust are the whores.'

Mr Robinson seemed assured. 'I was told they were all thieves . . .'

'They are, dear friend,' Reverend Fowler reassured him. 'But some may have already been redeemed.'

'Is it true they prefer beheading to hanging?' The tea-planter took another chance.

Once more, Captain Jacque relished the details. 'To hang is to honour. It's what they would do to a proud General at the end of a battle. They'd dress him in finery, feed him royally, even offer him a night with a beauty. If they want to punish, however, a sizzling blade rules over a simple noose. There are other options . . . tying the prisoner to a slab of stone and throwing him into the Pearl river, crushing a man's bones one after the other with an ingenious . . .'

'Horrible, Captain!'

'Why go to shore then?' Miss Jones seemed distraught. She cast a furtive glance at the third officer standing watch above the stern.

'My dear . . .' said her mother, thinking of home, the Assistant Commissioner of Trade's mansion in Canton.

'Maybe our young Indian friend knows why,' said Captain Jacque. All eyes turned on Hiran. In his confusion he tried repeating Mr Crabbe's words.

'Madness asking him to go there at all!' Mrs Culver declared. 'It's India's opium that's behind all the trouble.'

'Why should the rest of us suffer because of him?' Mrs Holmes drew her boy close to her heaving breasts. 'Shouldn't they be responsible for their own opium?'

'It's the folly of the India trade, really.' Mr Holmes grew with each assertion. 'Left to silk and tea, we'd hardly attract attention. Do we have to fight a war for loading our hold every tea season and racing back to England?'

'Your tea had us almost bankrupt. How do you suppose we

paid for it? With silver – plain and simple. The Chinese weren't buying anything. Not our clocks or sparkling cutlery, our whisky or cotton. Opium saved us, didn't it?' Bully Waterman poured cold water on Holmes's pride.

'But it's *they* who benefit,' Mrs Holmes said, pointing at Hiran. 'While we suffer the wrath of the Emperor.'

'It's true, Daddy says India is an utter loss without her opium and saltpetre.' Miss Jones glanced impatiently at her watch. They'd retreat soon to the dining hall, joined by the ship's officers.

Hiran felt embarrassed. The idea that his gain was threatening those around him hadn't occurred to him. *The British are fighting for us . . .* Vinny's words rang in his ear.

Captain Jacque came up smiling. 'So, they're not sending you back to Calcutta after all.' Hiran outlined Mr Crabbe's suggestions. Captain Jacque frowned at the mention of Mr Guo. 'Mr Crabbe would like you to be accompanied by a Chinaman, armed with *my* words?' He kept on frowning throughout the evening. Hiran wondered if he should mention Mr Crabbe's other suggestion. *You may offer your assistance to the captain in landing the chests, and employ Mr Guo's craft for such purposes . . .*

'What are you hiding from me?' Vinny asked.

The next day the mood on board was sullen. Passing boats carried large boards with dark news: *36 beheaded; Englishmen on hungerstrike; Pirates rule Canton harbour.*

At dinner that night the talk turned from the chaos in Canton to pirates.

This time, Mr Robinson was more cautious with his questions. 'Why did we abolish the Head Money Act? I thought . . .'

'Call it the foolishness of men living under the shade of Westminster,' Bully Waterman said profoundly. 'Remember Shap Tsai. Remember Chin Po. Who do you think tamed these rascals? Twenty dollars was a paltry reward for going after those scoundrels.'

'Twenty dollars to catch a pirate?' A wide-eyed Miss Jones brought on another snigger from Mrs Holmes. 'No, dear, for a dead one.' Once again Captain Jacque had to intervene: 'The act made a trial unnecessary. Spot a pirate and kill him, that was its motto. Till it drove out everyone – laundry-girls, fishermen. Then our Hong friends started to complain. Even honest smugglers – those who took our mud ashore – were being felled. It was a catastrophe.'

'How can you tell if someone is a pirate or not?'

'You look at their teeth, dear, see if they've enough left to chew.'

Mr Robinson tried one last time. 'I mean how would *we* know?'

'In the same way the Chinese know if we are going to attack them, I suppose.' Then Mrs Culver addressed Hiran directly: 'You have instructions to go ashore at Canton, don't you? What do you think will happen to us once the rebels find out?'

Before Hiran could answer, Captain Jacque raised his voice. 'Leave that to me, Bettie. A captain's job isn't complete till he has landed his cargo.'

Hiran found Vinny in Fokie's workshop discussing his wedding plans. They were only a few days away from Macao – their last stop before Canton. Captain Jacque, he learned, would meet with Marie's brothers on Vinny's behalf and finalize everything. 'Macao has twelve churches, jewel. We must fix on one.' He would also take Vinny to the best tailor, and help him buy a pair of rings from the jewellers on Praya Grande. Pirates and rebels did not distract Vinny. 'She knows I'm coming. Captain Jacque has sent word through the mail-steamer. She'll be waiting on the sand with a bouquet!'

'Tell me, is it legal or illegal?' Hiran asked Vinny.

'What?'

'Our mud. Opium. You know . . .' The two of them lay on

their berth in the tiny cabin, musing over their imminent arrival in Macao.

'You know how it is, jewel. The Chinese lost the opium wars, they had to accept our opium, just as they had to accept Reverend Fowler's church. But they don't like it. As soon as you go beyond the treaty ports it becomes illegal to sell opium. Then, the Chinese Viceroy's boats are upon you, demanding a bribe. That's why the ships need the Reverend – to bargain with the smugglers, find out secret routes to go further inland. It's legal in Canton, Macao, Lintin, Hong Kong, but legal doesn't mean safe, jewel. Where there's mud there are crocodiles too, no?'

Could they arrest Hiran then, if he went ashore with all these chests as Mr Crabbe suggested?

Vinny laughed. 'Mr Crabbe wouldn't let you get into that. Would he?'

He reached over and slapped Hiran on the back. 'You worry too much. Canton is still far off. Forget what the Europeans say. Think about what you'll be wearing to my wedding instead. Blue for the best man, jewel,' Vinny said. Hiran was surprised. He would have thought black or white, a simple choice, happy or sad?

'Hindoos wear white, Muslims black, Chinese yellow, Malays red. It's blue for us, like the sea that brought us here.'

In his trunk, Hiran had a blue serge suit with a high collar.

'Don't worry about food, Fokie has solved it.' Hiran looked at Vinny, puzzled. Who'd cook a brahmin's meal in Macao?

'Alaya has offered to cook for you. How can a brahman eat pigs and cows? she said. She'll stay with Marie's family and cook.'

He felt a wonder spread over him. 'That's not all. Fokie knows a place for you to stay, a decent place. You'll see.'

'Are you sure Captain Jacque will let you return on board with Marie?'

'Return? Who'll return? Just Fokie and you. I'll stay on shore. Her brothers would be offended if we escaped too soon. They're *solid*, jewel. I'll see you on your way back, Marie and I shall have our own cabin, just like the Holmeses. You'll be proud of us.'

'Does Captain Jacque know that you'll board the *Warrior Queen* on her way back?'

'On the *Warrior Queen* with my queen!'

'It's the Island of Women, mistresses, wives, and hopefuls more numerous than the men. On the day of the Feast of Corpus Christi, they line up along the crescent at the edge of the sea, or bunch like wildflower on the church steps. In full evening dress, with hats, passing back and forth, waving and bowing. When the Company boats come back from Canton at the end of the tea-season, there's a celebration on shore – men meet their babies for the first time, go straight to the church of St Catherine of Sienna, St Francis Xavier, Our Lady of the Conception. There are duels – shipboard friends become bitter enemies ashore.' Captain Jacque stared wistfully across the last remaining stretch of sea to Macao as they waited for the pilot to come on board.

'Looks remarkably like the Bay of Naples, doesn't it?' Captain Jacque said. To Hiran it looked solemn, white houses like widows kneeling with their faces turned to the sea.

Captain Jacque chuckled: 'Here mems lose their men to slave-girls, or to warm graves under the swaying palms.'

'And this is where women come to capture men too, isn't it?' Mrs Jones held her knitting close to her chest to ward off the morning mist. Captain Jacque roared with laughter. 'Tell them the story, Captain. Men make it sound so romantic!'

'This was before the war,' the Captain began. 'Foreign women were still barred from Canton. So they waited for their husbands in Macao. Except Newby Kendall's. Poor soul, Kendall was in dreadful fear of his wife. She spent her winters in Calcutta and came to Macao every summer, and each year Newby would feign *official duties* and escape to Canton in the nick of time. I was carrying her over once, when she saw an out-of-season boat leaving Macao harbour travelling north. We set chase and boarded her just as she was ready to sail. Poor Newby saw her coming on the deck, and in a mad rush he jumped over the gangway and fell into the water.'

'Tell them what he said when they revived him!'

'They pulled him up, of course, and laid him out on the deck. His wife thought he was dead, started wailing, poor thing. Seeing her so, Newby whispered to the mate, "Do you suppose you could confirm my death, young fellow. I promise I won't disappoint you next time you set foot on Macao!"'

'Is it true you can see Golden Lilies on the promenade?' Mrs Jones looked at Vinny in surprise. 'I mean, Chinese girls with tiny feet,' he muttered.

'Won't have time to look at their feet, my friends!' Captain Jacque roared.

Vinny was the first to notice the schooner, pointing it out to the others as they stood around Captain Jacque's easel. It had drifted silently alongside them and lay like a barren rock or island. They would have taken no notice of it had Vinny not pointed out the white board lashed to its railing. The light was poor now but it was still easy to read the warning. Captain Jacque left them immediately to confer with his officers. Even Mr Robinson knew the meaning of the white board. He grimaced over at Bully Waterman.

They watched from the deck as the small boat containing the third officer, the surgeon and the quartermaster approached the ship, but the evening mist seemed to have thrown a veil over them all. Miss Jones went up to the stern to catch a better view. There was silence, broken only by a few hushed murmurs. Coming up on the deck, the cook started on a lengthy explanation, helped by Fokie Tom. They seemed to recall a similar sign on a ship. The frowning pir had joined them.

'Might be a boatful of rebels, put out to sea without food or water.' Mr Holmes spoke with an assurance they had grown familiar with.

'How awful!'

'Might've beheaded them before setting sail. As a warning,' Mrs Holmes added. Mr Robinson tried another angle. 'Pirates, perhaps. A trap . . .' Miss Jones, still searching for a sight of the cutter against the black hull, whispered urgently, 'Come on, Harry!'

But the Reverend was certain. He had recognized the ship, knew it was none other than the *Citizen*, owned by Captain Keen. 'Yankee Keen, he's called. A keen hunter. Shot his fingers off in an accident.'

All at once, they saw the third officer and the others emerge from the mist and appear on the deck of the silent boat. For a moment they paused, then the quartermaster bent over and vomited.

'Cholera.' Vinny was the first to say it.

They could see Bully Waterman drawing on his cheroot, waving his arm at the captain's coop. Through the mist they saw vultures turning circles under the clouds.

It was a long wait, a whole hour of hovering between fear and revulsion. Mr Holmes had the most reasonable theory. 'Wretched bumboats. Obviously must've traded cast-off garments for milk – diluted with infected water.'

'What if the port itself is sick? What if there's an epidemic in Macao?' Vinny asked.

All eyes turned on Mrs Culver, who was staring at the bible on her lap. They knew of her twin tragedies – a husband and a son, lost to an epidemic. Who could forget those terrible years – a quarter of the army decimated in Madras, 18,000 victims on the Persian Gulf – *Asiatic Cholera* galloping ahead of all disasters. In Calcutta, she had seen it through the latticed windows of the Bhabanipore Church where her husband was pastor. Surely its smell – rising over the vapours of malodorous canals, must have filled her with a sort of wonder. Her husband had locked the gates of the compound. There were six of them inside – the couple and their son visiting from Devonshire, the maid, the jamadar and the coachman. They scrubbed and boiled, burnt away leftovers, sprinkled sulphur-salt around the drain. 'Cleanliness, pure air, a healthy diet, and above all, a calm and even mind are essential in warding off an attack,' her husband would repeat. 'Giving way to fear is fatal. Open the gates and all the disease has to do is enter and take possession.' They survived a month on the meagre stores she had saved for quite another purpose – a siege by dacoits lured by the chapel's donation-box. Day by day their spirits rose, till they heard no more cries. The first person they let in was the dhobi, with a neat stack of starched and pressed uniforms for their Devonshire cadet. She was relieved to see him, spent an hour asking news of the neighbourhood, then sought his help in replenishing their depleted larder. Even her husband, normally suspicious, was sanguine. The boy was clean. As they feasted on fresh melon brought by the boy, she asked her husband, 'Why do they call it *Asiastic Cholera* when people die from it back home?'

'Because here it reaps its richest harvest.'

Only the coachman and Mrs Culver were spared. She was found almost lifeless on her bed, wearing nothing but a flannel bandage over her bowels.

They were roused by Mr Waterman's voice through a bullhorn, craned over banisters to see the cutter approaching the *Warrior Queen*. 'First-degree infection . . . captain dead . . . unsafe port . . .' The sailors lowered a hose to spray sulphur-salt over the cutter. The third officer waved at Miss Jones as he clutched a ship's log under his arm. The quartermaster was first to take off his jacket and fling it overboard. Then all three started casting off – Bully Waterman reluctantly parting with his breeches, his hat floating like a baby whale's snout.

'Shut your eyes, ladies.' Captain Jacque's voice was drowned by the gush of golden crystals which almost tipped the cutter over. The three men danced over a mountain stream, screaming like porpoises, eagerly seeking the lashings. Before they climbed up, one by one, and were wrapped in ship's blankets, Miss Jones had sat down by her mother and started to weep silent tears.

'Whisky,' Bully Waterman's voice sounded hoarse, 'and not too much soda, please.' He was the one who had entered the *Citizen*'s hatch and found the captain sprawled over his bed with a gun in his fingerless right fist. The ship had been carrying few passengers, loaded rather with iron and quicksilver. Bully had stepped carefully over a soiled staircase, listened for a moan or the sound of breathing. They had heard calls for help, but went no further for fear of infection. In the saloon they had seen evidence of a vain struggle – empty bottles of calomel and arsenic scattered around. They saw empty drums of chlorine too, and wondered whether there had been a warning of impending disaster from shore perhaps. Then, on the verge of returning to their own ship, the quartermaster had heard a voice – not a whisper or a drone, but the strong clear voice of a woman, a voice that betrayed neither fear nor emotion – from the small chamber next to the captain's. She had asked the quartermaster to look for a bottle of spirits hidden under her bed. A sick Rosalind Keen had received the bottle in her exquisite white palm which peeked from beyond the red curtain.

Huddled in corridors between cabins they discussed Captain Keen's tragic end and the fate of the stricken *Citizen*. No one disagreed with Bully Waterman this time. 'It's better to die of a bullet than like a shrunken vegetable.' It helped bring to focus Mrs Holmes's resentment at being sent back to Canton against her dearest wish. 'Back to pestilence and a thankless service.' Mrs Jones joined her, stung by her daughter's sudden fragility. 'Only the English may be counted upon to die stupidly!' For a whole day they avoided the deck, shunning the stricken ship as if a mere glance could spread the virus. Captain Jacque rode the cutter busily, alerting the captains of arriving vessels, which lined up like an armada facing the lonely *Citizen*. They heard his crisp orders – to check the scullery, to drain the water from casks. The quartermaster shouted at the sailors to bring their sacks over to his office for inspection, going through them like a prison-guard, searching for a ripe durian or a bag of sala bought from the laundry-girls in Hong Kong harbour. With an ebony walker, its head carved like a dragon, he lifted dubious items. A string of Malacca pearls brought a smile, and cheap silk vests, bamboo flutes, deep-sea shells, cure-all oils bought from Cheeny-hakims. A deckhand displayed a tiny Buddha made of mother-of-pearl. 'Fat man give him fat boy.' Fokie led a round of laughter. Even Alaya laid out her treasure, reaching inside a varnished wooden trunk to bring out a coconut shell shaped like a monkey's claw. 'To stroke her back!' Hiran heard Vinny laugh. And a silver lime-box. The quartermaster opened its lid, drew it close to his face, then smiled. Hiran saw a streak of dark mud on his red nose.

'*Afim.*'

Puffing on his cheroot, eyes still bloodshot from the soaking, Bully Waterman paced the deck, checked his watch frequently.

'If it comes, it'll come soon,' he explained to an agitated Mr Robinson: 'Within four hours the bowels will begin to rumble, discharge flowing in rapid succession becoming more and more watery. A painful burning in the stomach –' A frantic Miss Jones stumbled into their conversation. 'Shouldn't you check his pulse. Should he be sleeping this long?'

'Trust in whisky, my dear.'

'Remember the three Cs,' Hiran could hear Nabinbaboo saying. 'Chlorine, calomel, cuprum.' He knew speed was essential, yet did not offer his vials out of shyness. Fear of the mysterious ship played on his mind too, he remembered the story of the haunted *Imogene.* Reverend Fowler's eyes were on him, his smile serene.

There were rumours circulating, about sailors going over to the *Citizen* at night to loot, or to find their brothers. Mrs Holmes almost fainted at the thought.

'Given half a chance they'd strip Captain Keen of his bloomers!' Captain Jacque laughed, but he gave orders for an extra watch on deck.

'How would anyone know if they smuggled someone back?' Mrs Holmes choked.

'From the howling, I suppose.'

'Harry said they looked like black skeletons with grins on their faces.'

'Rigor mortis.'

'Perhaps we should go hunting on deck tonight.' Mr Robinson mimed lifting a barrel to his eye.

'Won't stop the greedy ones.'

They all looked at Reverend Fowler. Would he pull one of his miracles now? 'Tell them, padre. Perhaps they'll listen to you,' Mrs Holmes pleaded. Even Mr Holmes was concerned. 'Perhaps you could say a mass after dinner.'

'A mass for Moslems and devil-worshippers?' Bully Waterman was sceptical.

Reverend Fowler smiled, but made no reply.

It was getting dark. Distracted and fretful, they delayed going over to the saloon till the quartermaster announced supper, then turned cold at the sight of food. They shrank from the bubbling soup tinged with delicate herbs as if it were a pond of bacteria. A salad appeared ominous. Emily choked on a leaf, starting a round of coughing and choking and dropping of spoons. Mrs Holmes gave a start as the mess-boy – his nails blackened – lowered the fowl curry on her table. She whispered to her husband. Soon, they were all whispering and following the waiters with suspicious eyes. Mrs Jones made a mental note to urge the captain to start a hygiene-drill each morning. The tension was not broken until someone fished a dead fly from their dish of curry. Then they vented their anger on Ramah the cook, the waiters, the boatswains, even Captain Jacque himself. A bottle of claret smashed to the floor. Only Reverend Fowler was quiet, turning an empty glass in his hand, smiling at Hiran who sat alone at his table. He had looked all day for Vinny without success.

Captain Jacque's voice boomed over the din as he entered the saloon. 'Alas, we must skip Macao. We leave at dawn, full steam ahead for Canton. Now, if you'll pardon my interruption, I'd like to offer a toast to our visitor, a happily recovered Madame

Keen.' They raised empty glasses in silence to Captain Keen's wife, exquisite in her red velvet gown.

Later Mrs Culver could be heard to murmur, 'And who will care for those dying on the *Citizen*?'

'He who wears the crown of wild olives, dear.'

Hiran passed an empty scullery, pausing to check for snoring from the boatswain's cabin. The ship was silent.

Tiptoeing past the Europeans' cabins, he stopped at the door of the sailors' hall. Vinny wouldn't be there, he knew, but he waited, hoping to hear him. He heard voices and, curious, lifted the curtain of gunny-sack and entered. A powerful smell rose from two tiers of planks lit by dim oil lamps. He saw a sea of dark heads, heard a moaning like the breeze caught in sails. As he waited for his eyes to focus, he rested on a sack by the door, his legs raised above the dark swamp of the floor. About a dozen sailors lay on the planks, arms and legs entwined, wedged against each other, nestled in the hollows of each other's dark skin. A glowing bowl passed from one set of outstretched lips to another, an invisible arm guiding it, following a crafted path over the bodies. At each stop it would sputter for a moment, never missing a beat, like one of Mr Pinchback's spring toys.

Hiran felt a head brush against his lap. A mess-boy, one who courteously bowed on deck, held his arm. His eyes were closed, and sweat covered his face up to the roots of his hair, flowing into a drooling mouth. Hiran tried to free his arm.

Naked except for their loin-cloths, they spoke in a dozen tongues fused into an even all-comprehending drone, nodded and gestured, tugged playfully at each other. A willowy Hakka man – face like raw flesh – held a make-belief pipe to his mouth in imitation of the ship's surgeon. They all laughed.

He could sense the breath of euphoria exciting the veins to madness, saw the union of so many desires, realized the futility of so many lines on so many palms – crests, loops, and stormy ridges – that meant little to kneeling forms whose lips moved and eyes misted for a separate destiny, one differently scarred.

*

He found them lying on the carpenter's bench – Fokie and Alaya – covered in a sea of golden shavings, and a pair of eyes glowing in the dark devouring their flesh like raw poppy.

Once again, it was Vinny who was first to spot it: a Mandarin boat cruising towards them flying a yellow flag emblazoned with a red dragon. It seemed to be coming from Canton, only a few days upstream from Lintin island where they lay moored with other opium ships. Under a silk umbrella, fanned by attendants dressed in red and white, sat a large bearded man smoking a long pipe. As he came aboard with his retinue, Captain Jacque went over to the gangway to receive him, then introduced him to his awed and silent passengers. Only a smiling Reverend Fowler stepped forward.

They spoke briefly together in some unpronounceable tongue, and conferred over the scroll an assistant hurriedly presented, then Reverend Fowler looked over his shoulder, raised his voice. 'Baboo Hiranyagarbha Chakraborti. He's looking for you, Sir.'

'Him?'

'He carries a document from Hiran's employer, requesting he be granted safe passage to Canton.'

The man in the silk gown stared at Hiran, frowned, checked his scroll again, tried in vain to pronounce the name. He kept looking at the Reverend, drawing his finger under the word, till he was reassured. Then he sighed and rose to leave. In a whirl, Hiran's trunk was dragged over the deck and lowered by wooden attendants on to the Mandarin's boat. Vinny danced around him. 'You must wait for me . . .' Fokie offered a toothless smile. Hiran strained to look behind him, at the opening to the winding stairs. He felt Captain Jacque's strong hand on his shoulder. 'Farewell, friend. I hope they don't serve you up with other delicacies!' Turning to the stunned passengers, he winked. 'The Maharajah of Jaanbazaar!'

Hiran sat beside the Chinaman, an umbrella over his head. As they pulled away, he could see heads peering over the railings of the *Warrior Queen*, slowly returning to life.

'Maharajah! Did you know we had one on board all this time?'

Alone at Mr Guo's house, Hiran sat by the rock-garden, examining a kingdom of flawlessly carved pets. He felt like a Maharajah, left to his whims. He could hear attendants watering the magnolias, adding tiny worms to a feeding pool swarming with goldfish, hiding like stone animals behind the shrubs. Brooms rustling over wooden floors made him look up, expecting to see the short men in green trousers who had led him into the pavilion on his first day. Then they had disappeared quickly, blending like chameleons with the weeping willow.

For the next few days Hiran wondered if he was a guest or a prisoner at Mr Guo's house. His mind went over Mr Crabbe's letter, searching for a hidden signal. Did he wish Hiran to outwit the Chinaman, and land the chests himself? Was he even aware of Hiran's presence in Canton? Hiran was worried. Used to the regime of sahibs, his tongue had retracted at the sight of the unknown. The *Warrior Queen* had given him a taste for the unfamiliar: spicy fowl laced with Malabar peppers, snipes dipped in a nectar of honey. His mouth would water at the ship's table over mutton and lamb, roasted pork, even the forbidden. 'You've become a Military Brahmin!' Vinny had been amazed at his gluttony. The remnants of beef on his plate had resolved the confusion over his identity: he was a 'fallen brahmin', the mess-boys whispered in the kitchen, one who read palms but didn't care if his own touched the unchaste.

On the first evening at Mr Guo's house, he had followed his

nose to a steaming bowl of rice. Invisible hands placed his meal behind a partition at the precise moment. But he was afraid to lift the bowl's lid for fear of what he might find. Even the sweet-smelling rice appeared strange, crowned with white petals. He had woken and found the dish replaced by a plate of warm gruel that smelled of wheat-flour and honey. Still he resisted, pacing the garden, weak with hunger. A fresh breeze did little to revive him. His mind fleeted back to feasts at Jaanbazaar.

Then he discovered sweet red potatoes, ripe melon disguised as a sticky paste, dark and ugly balls filled with delicious spinach, fresh and warm. Cautiously nudging green slimy creatures with the edge of a stick he was relieved to find them dead, and tasting surprisingly like pickled cucumber. He ignored dubious exteriors, biting into yams and pumpkins, dipping everything into a dark sauce floating like refuse over blue and white bowls. He smiled at the trick – scaring by look but pleasing by taste.

After a week, just as he had given up any hope of meeting with his host, Mr Guo came. Suddenly, like buds blossoming all at once, the garden was full of attendants in green trousers, bowing and smiling at Hiran as if they had known him for years. He seemed to know them too – had seen these faces pruning shrubs or fishing dead leaves from the pond.

His host apologized for the delay. Hiran, he had thought, must be weary after his long trip, and Canton's moist air was sapping. Mr Guo pointed to his own slender bones. Speaking softly, almost under his breath, he congratulated Hiran for visiting at such an auspicious time – the wedding of his only daughter. Mr Guo smiled, asked Hiran of his own children. 'Not even one?' Mr Guo looked a touch deflated.

He was a Hong, and a 'linguist', he said, licensed by the Hoppo to interpret for foreigners. Mr Guo did not once mention his business, distracted by the men in green trousers, who called out in a friendly tone from the shade of the pavilion. Nor did he show any interest in Hiran's mission. Canton was recovering from an early spell of cold, he said, it was safe once more to test the morning air. Then he rose to leave, finishing his tea and setting down a fine porcelain cup.

Hiran dreamt of two birds feasting on carrion. The bigger one sat on the head of the dead beast and picked at its eye. The younger perched over the soft belly and sipped the blood trickling from a wound. 'Beware!' the younger bird said. 'It can see you with its dead eye, might return for revenge in its next life.' The older one ignored his warning. 'The dead cannot see,' he said. 'Also, why would it spare the hunter and seek revenge on a poor scavenger?' He kept on with his feast while the younger bird flew away fearing an unknown danger. Suddenly, the bird saw its own beak reflected in the large crystal eye of the beast, like a vast lake. Saw itself being dragged into the water by an invisible force. Fluttering its wings it fought to lift itself, but the more it tried the greater was the pull. It struggled in vain to break free. Moments before drowning in the beast's eye it whispered to its younger sibling, 'You must take my place . . .'

Hiran woke in despair.

Mr Crabbe was either hiding from him or had been killed by the rebels. Hiran recalled Mr Kavasji's last words, spoken under the shade of a tree in the lawn of the Auction House, a cold anxiety filling him now like the morning mist. 'I hear you've been chosen for our trouble at Canton . . .'

He remembered the look in his mother's eyes just before his departure. As if she was looking at her husband on the morning of 14 June – a final glance.

He missed the buzz of the *Warrior Queen*, the voices of his shipmates, Mr Robinson coming up after lunch offering a game of chess: 'You want to crush me again, don't you, little devil?' The casual flow of conversation among the ladies: 'Oh, those dhobies. Fancy receiving your neighbour's delicate garments, and they yours!' He even missed the strident Mrs Culver, as he examined the sailors' outstretched palms: 'Don't you have anything better to do, young man?'

From the rock garden in Mr Guo's house he could see the *Warrior Queen* docked in the harbour. He knew they were all there in Canton – Vinny and Captain Jacque, Bully and Mr Robinson, the Joneses, the Holmeses, Fokie and Alaya . . . He felt a sorrow of parting. Did they miss him, he wondered, or was a week in China enough to erase the memory of a month on deck?

One afternoon, while sitting alone again in the garden, he drew an Englishman's face on the sand with the edge of a stick. Gave him a long nose, like Mr Scott, a hard look, sideburns and a hat. He drew a starched collar around the neck, and a steaming pipe at his lips.

And then, quite suddenly, Hiran was surrounded by the bustle of the wedding. He watched the preparation, fascinated, from the window of his pavilion.

By the time the bride left her house, riding a red chair carried by six men, Hiran had seen the many faces of Canton without even stepping out of the door. He'd seen the guests lining up in the courtyard, waiting patiently to bless the bride with bolts of silk, jewellery, large urns of wine, and knew the power of a Hong. He'd seen the poor kinsmen too, carrying their gifts of live geese and steamed dumplings. And bridal furniture, the gift of the Viceroy, carried in on a mule-cart. Hiran had seen Mr Guo kowtowing before a man with a shaven head, saw the monk's gift of yellow and white flowers.

From his garden he heard English voices mixed with Chinese. Curious, he left his pavilion, following the neatly laid garden path, coming up to a small chamber surrounded by trees. Inside, Bully Waterman was holding court, while other Europeans lounged around a table laden with decanters. Mr Guo was there. Afraid to linger, Hiran looked quickly around the company, searching for Mr Crabbe.

Vinny came next morning.

'Are you all right, jewel?' He seemed scared, kept a distance, looked at Hiran only out of the corner of his eyes.

'The people here thought I was an escaped convict. I swear, they almost sent me upstairs!' He pointed towards the sky. Then, he broke out laughing. 'I told them I was the prince's barber. You'd better get me a pair of scissors!'

'Prince?'

'That's what they think you are. A prince exiled from Hindoostan, under the protection of the English.' Vinny rattled off one story after another. 'That's why the Mandarin came personally to the *Warrior Queen* to fetch you, made everyone else look foolish. They were envious, Mrs Holmes kept charging up and down, *why do they favour an Indian over the English*, till Captain Jacque reminded her of your riches! She understood then. Miss Jones said you looked truly like a Maharajah, and what a pity it would have been if you had drowned during our shoot.'

Hiran felt relieved to be among friends once more. 'Who started the rumours?'

'Mr Crabbe, of course. You mean you didn't know?'

They eagerly discussed their theories about the invisible Mr Crabbe. Vinny thought he was hiding in the Viceroy's mansion, advising him on ways to quell the mutiny. The beheadings of the rebels by Canton's guards were *his* idea, not the Chinese Viceroy's. Vinny knew all about the Guo wedding too, an act of kinship, he explained, after the tragic death of Mr Guo's son and daughter-in-law in a fire last year. 'They share each other's riches here. Not like your stingy uncles.' And Mr Crabbe was a friend to the Hongs, he was their 'snake', both friendly and vicious. 'He wants to own all the smugglers, rival them for profit from our mud. He's smarter than Scott. There's nobody to catch him here – so far from the Auction House – no ledgers, no hammer. Nothing.' Listening, Hiran felt the comfort of the familiar. He was once again at the Strand with the river before him, in the company of a master storyteller.

'Sometimes he's with the English. Sometimes with the

Cheenys. And sometimes just himself. That's why he wants you.' Hiran struggled to follow Vinny's subtle thread.

Two bowls of tea sat on a tray inside his room. And a wooden barber's bench. Making a face with his first gulp, Vinny waved aside Hiran's doubts.

'What matters, jewel, is that here he's free. Striking deals without anyone looking over his shoulder. The long arm of the India Office doesn't stretch this far. This isn't their colony. Only the most vicious win here.'

The rest of the morning was spent going over the mystery. Vinny offered one revelation after another, spinning a spider's web around Mr Crabbe, the Hongs, the smugglers and the Mandarins. Hiran did not ask him about Marie.

Casting a look over his shoulder, Vinny lowered his voice. 'You must tell me about Cheeny girls, jewel. Do they really bark at night if they're unhappy?' Brushing aside Hiran's denials, he went on . . . 'Don't worry. I won't tell your holy relatives, or Nabinbaboo. A prince without a princess is like mud without addicts. What's her name, jewel?'

Then, staring at the neat row of houses on Ass's Point, he came to his own conclusion: 'In Canton, who needs a wife? What's the use of one when there are so many? They fight among each other to spend a night with a barbarian. They follow you from street to street, say strange things, like, *come chin-chin with me.* You can go *chin-chin* with them any time you want, and if you're Fokie, stay as long as you wish.' Hiran looked at him surprised.

'Alaya will kill him. Finish off the scoundrel if he doesn't bring it upon himself. One wrong step and he'll float face down in the river.'

Hiran felt jealous of Vinny, living over Fokie's uncle's grogshop on Hog Lane, next door to Fokie and Alaya. 'You can hear him climbing the stairs late at night, stumbling and cursing.'

Hiran worried about Alaya. He worried about Vinny too. Had he abandoned his Marie?

'Fokie's uncle is a real gentleman, treats Alaya like his daughter. You must meet him, he's a poet, spends his time drawing lines with a big brush. He's rich too, his shop has the best rum in Hog Lane, always full of Jacks. But he lives simply, never drinks, never fights, doesn't go chin-chin. Fokie's uncle will find a boat to take me over to Macao.'

As always, Hiran was amazed at Vinny's luck. First, a free berth on the *Warrior Queen*, and now Fokie's uncle.

'If I don't go to Macao soon, her brothers will marry her off to some Chinaman. Then I'll have to fight a duel!' He saw a frown appear on Hiran's forehead. 'It's all luck, jewel. If you don't try, you never win.'

Just as he had got used to the quiet regime, a chair arrived for him along with six bearers. Even without a word, he knew where it would take him. Hiran sat on the cushioned seat in his blue serge suit, riding like a Maharajah through the giant doors of Mr Guo's house. As he looked down, he saw dark heads swirling around like shoals of fish in a narrow and winding stream. Up ahead, two conical hats led them deftly through the crowd. From an open square, he caught a glimpse of ships' masts in the harbour.

When they arrived finally at the Council House, another giant doorway led them into a courtyard with adjoining gardens, crowded with waiting chairs and bearers. Hiran was lowered to the ground and led up to a balcony. He heard voices – sharp and brief, ringing like silver. Through open doors he could see occasional glimpses of a pair of polished boots, or the trailing edge of a grand coat; attendants wearing white socks silently shuffled in and out bearing trays. And he smelt the familiar waft of cheroots.

Hiran hesitated near the head of a flight of stairs. A passing attendant stopped to pick up an empty tray then smiled at him, pointing towards an open door.

Inside, Hiran found a library with a large table set in its centre. Men in formal robes sat around it, with a Chinese servant behind each chair. Portraits stared down from the walls, like dead ancestors.

He heard Mr Crabbe's voice before he saw him. Measured and even, it appeared to have gained in irony. His face was shaded by a hanging punkah, but Hiran could see the fine veins even from a distance. He was staring ahead over the stooping men, into the garden.

'Once there lived a merchant, an old man, with a beautiful young bride.' Hiran crept closer to the table. 'He was unhappy because she loved his riches rather than him. Neither his frail body, nor his wise mind drew her affection. They lived together like strangers. One night, as the young bride was lying in bed, her face turned away from him, a thief crept into the house. She saw the villain going through her box of jewellery with a knife in his hand. Frightened, she clasped her husband, and hid her face in his chest. The old man was delighted, wondered at his sudden good fortune. Then, he too saw the thief and knew it was fear that caused his wife to embrace him. He went over the options in his mind. Raise the alarm, or allow the thief to steal. Keep his riches, or keep his wife . . .'

Laughter rippled around the table.

'Better be a bit afraid than lose your wife!'

'Maybe he should pay the thief a salary!'

'What if the thief kills them both? Takes over the mansion?'

'But thieves are scared too. A little money makes them happy.'

'Why doesn't the wife run away with the thief?'

Mr Crabbe sat glowing. All around him, Hongs seemed bent on discovering the secret of his story. 'If she knew of the merchant's pact with the thief, then she'd be afraid no more.' Mr Guo nodded his head. A frown marred his smile. 'If the thief finds out, he may become bolder too . . .'

'The merchant must worry a lot.' A senior Hong sighed.

They sat sipping from fresh bowls of tea proffered by kneeling attendants. Mr Crabbe glanced at a scroll held open on the table by four carved rabbits. The sun, casting one long beam through the window, cut the table in half.

Mr Crabbe spoke slowly: 'The Viceroy must know that his security is threatened by weaknesses.' There was silence – the silence of a cold night in the merchant's mansion.

'Does he know? Do the rebels?' He addressed the punkah.

Silence turned to nervous twitter.

'Would the rebels win if they knew? Encircle the Viceroy in his mansion rather than charge about stupidly at the harbour?'

A senior Hong cleared his throat. 'Perhaps he knows. Perhaps that's why he's raised the scare of beheadings.' The others mulled this over and an air of confusion filled the room. 'Three hundred beheaded in a single night!' said one. 'He kills fewer than he claims,' said another. 'It'd take many arms to remove so many heads.' Some disagreed. 'He must have killed more not fewer. Half the river is the blood of innocent men.' A few ignored the Viceroy and talked about a danger closer to home.

'At this rate, he'll drive everyone from Canton. The shops will be empty.'

'Perhaps that's what he wants.' They looked at Mr Guo, who spoke slowly, as if suffering from a hidden wound. 'I mean, to drive away our foreign friends.'

'The wife wants to be free of her husband!' The man sitting next to Mr Crabbe tried to lighten the air. But Mr Guo persisted. 'Some say it isn't the rebels who are his enemy, but the merchants. This way he can get rid of both.'

'By destroying Canton?'

'Precisely. Which is why he must know who his *real* enemies are.' Pointing at the Viceroy's fort on the roll of paper, Mr Crabbe was more emphatic than before. 'Who will tell the rebels where he hides his jewels?'

Hiran was proud of his pupil. He knew him to be a good translator. Now he saw him using a story to win over his audience.

Finally they met, at the door of the reception room. Mr

Crabbe patted the sleeve of Hiran's blue serge suit. 'Welcome, Hiranbaboo. I thought the Captain had smuggled you off to Shanghai!'

'No one's told you about the bird?' Vinny made a gesture with his palms. 'It's a strange one, never seen before. From far away it looks like a looming typhoon, with dark wings many miles across. A bird with a human face, they say it looks like the barbarians who bring mud and take their silk and tea.'

They sat together in an empty grogshop, Vinny flapping his arms, and rolling his tongue for effect.

'Fokie thinks it's the Emperor in disguise. Keeping an eye on foreigners. Some say, it's come to taste the blood of the innocent convicts beheaded in the harbour. The sahibs tried to shoot it, but it flew from the gun's range.'

Hiran wondered what the pir would have said if he had looked into the bird's face.

'You must come on your chair, like a sahib,' Vinny had said when Hiran told him he planned to meet him at the shop in Hog Lane. 'Everyone will bow before you! And the girls will go crazy! You can chin-chin with them all if you wish!' His eyes danced. 'Do you think it might be possible for me to have a ride?'

Hiran had surprised his bearers by going out to meet them at the gate of Mr Guo's house with his request. They had looked at each other, then brought him by their usual route to the Council House.

He had tried again, asking them again to take him to Hog Lane. This time, they took a circuitous route, ending up once more in the empty courtyard of the Council House, via an unfamiliar passage.

After that, Hiran accepted that his chair could travel only to one destination, and travelled by foot following Vinny's directions.

'It's a graveyard by day,' Vinny said, as they went into Fokie's uncle's grogshop through the back. It was still too early for real drinkers to have recovered from last night's brawls. Hiran knew now how Hog Lane had won its reputation.

He returned to his pavilion at dusk. His tray was waiting behind the partition, the bowl of tea still warm. He ate quietly under the watchful eyes of invisible attendants.

Over the next two weeks, Hiran dreamt repeatedly of the bird with a human face. It sat on a branch in the garden, like a white owl, and observed his prayers. He recognized Reverend Fowler's smile. Hiran wished it would fly, so he might see its fabled wings. In his dream he'd try to scare it with a stick, shower a stream of pebbles. But it didn't move from its perch, like a stone bird in the garden. He asked Vinny for a trick . . . he was sure Vinny would know one. But even his friend was puzzled, asking, *Are you sure . . . it isn't dead already . . .*

He thought the bird was waiting for him – like Saraladebi. *Tell me, Hira, when will I become a grandmother?* He felt weak. Its sharp beak reminded him of Mr Crabbe. The bird was daring him to kill – to become like his pupil.

A sampan was waiting at sunset, bound for Macao. Fokie's uncle had planned it all from his bed, between spurts of coughing. Vinny had a scroll sealed with a red chop – a proof of kinship – that would allow him to board. 'He's calling me a merchant in it, jewel. Just like you're a prince!' The voyage would take a long time so Alaya had prepared a small basket for him. As they sat together earlier in Vinny's room next to the sambhar-skinned suitcase, Vinny had seemed strangely calm.

'Mustn't open my big mouth, jewel. No need to say how friendly I am with sahibs.'

'If they're rebels, I'll act like one too. If they're pirates –'

'I'll read their palms, jewel, talk your mumbo jumbo if they try their mischief.'

'If they steal my suitcase, I'll be back! Can't go empty-handed to my wedding.'

'Mustn't fall into the river.'

They had spent two whole days going over the ceremony. Vinny must be prepared, Alaya said, to be married as a 'Chinese, a Christian, and a Hindoostani'.

'Why Hindoostani?'

Because the priest might be one, from the Malwa coast. His Hakka in-laws, Alaya explained, would expect the bride to return to Macao in a year.

'Great, jewel! Then you can come back with me and marry her sister.'

Alaya seemed different. Sitting with them in Vinny's room, she behaved more like an elder sister, mixing advice with caution, scolding Vinny like a brother. She made Hiran her accomplice, deferring to him frequently.

'Brahman baba comes ready. Always neat and clean.' She pointed to his shaven face. Vinny's in-laws might take him for a convict fleeing Canton, she warned. Cheeny girls were scared of men with stubble – they reminded them of devils.

Hiran was amused. Despite Saraladebi's urgings, it hadn't occurred to him that he was indeed 'ready' for his own wedding. What if he were to return to Calcutta with Marie's sister? 'Then your mother will send you off to Viper Island, and your bride to Boubazaar!'

Alaya reminded Vinny to take the medicine Brahman baba had given him for his stomach, and waited patiently as Hiran repeated Nabinbaboo's routine, checking the tongue for patina. Vinny teased her for her seriousness, chided her for wasting her time with Fokie when she could have chosen a powerful Hong, been his concubine. Maybe Mr Guo's son-in-law would be willing. Perhaps even a 'red-barbarian' – they were known to fancy native girls. Alaya smiled. Try as he might, Hiran couldn't detect his Goddess in the soft glow that filled Vinny's room.

'You should be here at night, jewel.' Vinny smacked his lips.

As they walked back to Mr Guo's house together, their talk turned to Mr Crabbe and his stock of stories. Hiran started to tell Vinny the story of Nachiketas and his three wishes. He felt he knew what Vinny's three wishes would be: *A wife like Marie, a kothi like a sahib's, and a gentoo's job . . . thank you, Jesus!*

But Vinny surprised Hiran: 'I'd ask for every orphan to have a father, jewel.'

Suddenly, Hiran remembered his friend clutching a child in the river.

Now they waited together for the promised sampan on a bamboo bridge over the creek within sight of the joss-house. Hiran glanced around from time to time, but they saw none. Alaya's wicker basket smelled of jasmine-rice.

A boat would come with its back to the setting sun, laden with mulberry like an ordinary sampan. Vinny was instructed to show his letter, than at last they would bid each other farewell.

Vinny's anxiety was growing. 'What if Fokie's uncle made a mistake, asked him to wait for me at the pier?'

'What if he's taken us for two monkeys, and passed by?'

'What if he's been beheaded on his way?'

'What if he's scared seeing two of us? Thinks we're robbers?'

They decided Hiran should leave, to allay the boatman's fears.

'Wait for us in Macao. Tell Captain Jacque to keep a cabin ready!'

Hiran entered a narrow lane as a dog started barking behind him. Walking along cobbled pavements he passed houses with closed doors. He was struck by the silence from the crowded homes normally buzzing as beehives. He felt sad leaving Vinny, worried for his safety. He heard a distant gong, and cries echoing through empty streets.

It sounded like a wedding procession – clashing cymbals,

banging drums, shrill flutes, and firecrackers. He hoped to see the bridal-chair, and the band of musicians.

He heard the call of a voice through a bullhorn, followed by bangings and strange howls. A swish cutting through air like a whip.

Suddenly, he heard someone calling out to him – a voice choking for breath.

'Hiran!'

He saw Vinny running towards him through the empty market, dragging his sambhar-skin suitcase and Alaya's basket.

'He's gone mad, jewel! He's beheading everybody . . . hundreds killed already. He'll burn the city when he's finished.'

Vinny's head was bare. He tugged on Hiran's arm, his words shooting out in spurts. 'That bastard Fokie knew what was happening. That's why the boatman never came. The soldiers are going round from house to house, pulling out those they suspect, anyone with a face they don't like, they don't need a reason to kill.'

They lost themselves in the middle of the street, reassured by each other's presence, oblivious to the steadily growing bang of a gong in the distance. Suddenly, Vinny shrieked, 'Look, Hiran!'

The musicians were upon them: dressed in white, carrying their instruments like bearers in a funeral. A short man in a red coat shouted orders, turning his face from left to right to address the silent homes. Behind them, a mandarin sat on his chair looking impassively at the empty street. Hiran felt Vinny grab him and pull him, like a sudden breeze, towards the folding door of a shuttered shop. They pushed the door open, and Vinny threw his suitcase inside. 'Quick!' They pulled the door shut behind them. Hiran sensed the presence of others, but kept his eyes firmly on the crack of the partly opened door.

Soldiers carrying whips and chains ran beside the Mandarin, dragging along prisoners with wooden collars around their necks, bare hands holding up signs declaring their crimes. Behind them, the convicts walked in rows, heads drooping over rags, some struggling to keep pace with the soldiers.

He felt Vinny's frightened breath on his back. 'Tell me what you see.'

One of the prisoners stopped just in front of the shop, his face dark and glistening with oil.

'Makes it easy to chop off the head.' Vinny shuddered. 'Can you see any girls? He's vowed to kill off the whores.' Hiran saw men dressed as beggars, saw a few who looked like the attendants at Mr Guo's, saw one man dressed much like the Mandarin himself.

Boots ground to a halt outside the door. Hiran shut his eyes. A shadow, darker than the room, seemed to surround them. His ears rang with the heavy breathing of the prisoners, picked up subtle strains – a stifled sob, prayers. He heard Vinny's lips whispering, *Jesus, Jesus, Jesus, Jesus.* He heard a firecracker explode like a cannon in the distance.

It was a long time before they realized that the procession had come and gone. The echoes of the prisoners' feet, clanging with iron, remained even as the gong grew faint. Hiran felt Vinny tugging on his arm. 'We have company.' In the glow of a street lantern, Hiran saw the interior of the shop, crowded with old glass bottles, and the faces nesting among them. They gazed at Hiran and Vinny without expression – some old – hardly breathing, like stone animals. One woman – wrinkled and ghoulish – sat crouched behind a vat of dark olives. She made a gesture with her eyes, signalling them to go.

They were lost. The empty streets made navigation impossible. It was hard to tell a market without hawkers, a joss-house without devotees. They saw white streamers hung in doorways.

'Marks a recent death,' Vinny said. *So many deaths . . .*

'They aren't allowed funeral processions, the streets would be crammed. They just dump the bodies in the river.' Hiran thought of the Ganga. *All rivers were full of bodies.*

'The mad Viceroy is emptying gaols, killing convicts to gain honour from the Emperor, dragging men from their homes, anyone who might aid the rebels. Gunsmiths, carpenters, cobblers. All horses to be slaughtered.'

They were close to the river. An erratic breeze caught and spiralled them. Hiran felt cold beneath his Scotch wool. The smell of jasmine rice seeping from Alaya's basket blended with pickles, revived their appetites. They stopped among the stilt-houses facing the pier, and lunged into the neat compartments of the basket.

'I am worried for the *Warrior Queen*, jewel. What if it's the sahibs' turn next? Where would they hide?'

Both turned instinctively towards the harbour, scanning the horizon for masts. A row of burning torches lit up the field like a circus tent. With a shock, they realized how close they were to the execution ground.

At the centre of the field, men crowded around three giant platforms, each with a wooden cross and a butcher's block. Prisoners were being herded to the platforms, chains around their waists. A calm-faced gaoler was tying a rope around a convict's neck, twisting it neatly behind the head. 'The ones with fewer crimes are strangled. The rest are simply beheaded.' Vinny shuddered. Some of the prisoners sat around in circles, like men at the end of a hard day, a small cloud of blue smoke rising above them. Hiran peered closer. 'It's opium, isn't it?'

The prisoners took turns to climb on to the platforms, like obedient animals under the loving gaze of the gaoler. Those at the bottom never looked up, simply passed the pipe from one to another.

Hiran lowered his eyes.

With a roar a man was led up, a 'real' convict – taller, naked but for his loincloth. The man in the red coat climbed on to the platform, read something out before the kneeling prisoner.

'Don't look, jewel.'

Hiran heard the soldiers cheering. One of them chased after the Mandarin's servants, made a mock gesture with his sword.

'Don't look, jewel.'

The prisoner had his neck on the block. The torches burned brightly.

'Don't!'

Nearer to them, smaller fires lit lines of bodies on the ground. The soldiers were busy, carrying bodies over from the platforms, placing a white paper over each.

Splashes echoed over the river – bodies tipped over to float for a few moments before sinking, like clay images into the Ganga.

They started to run. Vinny dragged the suitcase behind him by its broken handle, tripping over it as he ran. A barking dog caught up with them, sniping at their heels if they showed signs of slowing. Hiran took off his coat.

'Don't go back to your pavilion. Maybe Mr Guo has joined the Viceroy. Handed over his household to the madman! If the soldiers come, who will save you?'

They stopped for a moment before a giant arch. 'The Gate of Heavenly Peace. This is Cheeny heaven, jewel.'

Hog Lane calmed them. Friendly banners stood over an empty street. Vinny knocked on the door at the top of a winding staircase. There was no answer. They were scared of knocking again, of soldiers hiding close by, perhaps, waiting for them to return. Had the procession come this way too? Suddenly, they felt exposed. Then Vinny said, 'I'm such a fool. Who'd open his front door on a day like this!' They went around the back, to the grogshop. The door was open. Relief rushed over them. Dropping his suitcase, Vinny ran to the back of the counter. 'Let's have a drink. I can make a *first-chop rum* for you,' imitating Fokie's clumsy tongue. Then both were struck by the silence.

Hiran followed Vinny up the stairs. Fokie and Alaya's room was empty. A small shrine at the corner stood crowded with knick-knacks. Among the crosses and joss-sticks, he saw a blue *Kali* wearing a string of fresh hibiscus.

Then they heard a sob. In Fokie's uncle's room, they found an old man cradling Alaya, who lay on the bed, her face swollen with tears. Fokie's uncle nodded his head at their questioning look, then pointed towards the harbour – towards the execution ground.

*

When he returned to Mr Guo's pavilion next morning, the cold wind had resumed, blowing dry leaves from the peach tree to the garden's pond. Hiran wondered if he had been missed, if breakfast had replaced supper on the tray. From the rock garden the river seemed far away – a shimmering curtain behind manicured borders. He saw a shadow on the marble porch of his room. Mr Crabbe sat on a chair with his back to the garden, facing the river.

'The Chinaman is rude and wild. But it isn't reason enough to condemn or despise him. On the contrary, his character deserves our attention. He is at once civilized and uncivilized, kind and cruel. His savagery stems from his heart. It is abundant. We are troubled not by his strength, honesty, swiftness, or beauty, no, although he's remarkable in all that and more, but by the unevenness of his judgement.'

He took Hiran's silence for doubt.

'Look at his honour. An accuracy of purpose and action. Dealing with him over the years we've never had occasion to doubt. His chop is dipped in gold, not ink. Your host had many a reason to waver, reasons that would scare our friends at the Auction House. There were times when he'd be *us*, while we were away. One needn't be perfect to claim respect.'

Mr Crabbe continued speaking in his low and even voice, looking not at Hiran but towards the river. Sipping his tea from time to time, he cast a sideways glance at the gravel path as if expecting Mr Guo to appear.

'Our friends are worried, Hiranbaboo. It's more than the fear of an earthquake or a typhoon. This is the fear of human destruction, the result of a folly preventable if dared.'

Hiran wondered why Mr Crabbe hadn't simply summoned him to the Council House. Why had he come himself?

Mr Crabbe made a gesture with both hands. 'It would be unwise to wait for that destruction, don't you think?'

Hiran's mind returned for a moment to the execution ground. He shuddered.

'Precisely. And it still might be prevented.'

Hiran wanted to ask him about the beheadings, about the rebels and the Viceroy, where they – the English and the other merchants – stood. He wanted to know why Mr Guo was in danger. What had happened to Fokie. And what would he do with the mud, now that it was his. Why had he asked Hiran to come so far simply to live in a garden? Most of all, he wanted to ask Mr Crabbe if he had news of his mother.

Mr Crabbe seemed momentarily distracted, his eyes following the mast of a departing clipper. Then he resumed.

'He needs our help, not our derision. Think of him as a prisoner in his fort. Who does he see as his friend? Not a vain Emperor thousands of miles away. Not his subjects, meek and powerless.'

Hiran was surprised. He had observed Mr Crabbe at the Council House, frowning each time the Hongs reported more beheadings. The numbers seemed to worry him less than the very occurrence. While Mr Guo and the others argued, Mr Crabbe would be silent, eyes on the roll of paper before him on the table.

'What would *you* do, Hiranbaboo? A servant's work isn't always beneficial to his master. He can give obedience and service, or simply cunning and revenge. How would you treat your servant? With indulgence or cruelty? Treat the servant kindly, and you lose his gratitude. Treat him ruthlessly and you find him dead.'

'Then why is he beheading them all?' Hiran protested.

'Because he doesn't know how to keep them without losing them. That's why *we* must help him. Help him to be just – the single imperfection that plagues the Chinaman.'

His pupil was kind. He knew he had been right, whatever Vinny said. *He is hiding in the Viceroy's mansion. The beheadings are his idea.* What would the Military Brahmin do? Order men-of-war to fire at the platforms. He remembered Bully Waterman's words, 'What can bows and arrows and pikes and shields do against a handful of British veterans?' Hiran felt proud of the British.

'You must help us, Hiranbaboo. Help us to help him. He must know who his real friends are. He must listen to us.'

Did Mr Crabbe mean *him*? A Hindoo prince exiled from Hindoostan, the gentoo, the black-barbarian, convincing the Viceroy of Canton that the British were his true and sanguine friends?

'You must help him by making him more afraid than he is till he loses confidence in his allies and comes to us for help. You must invoke love through fear.'

'Why would he listen to me?'

Mr Crabbe smiled. 'You will speak to the rebels. Tell them his secrets.' He held up the scroll Hiran had seen him reading at the Council House. 'Secrets that none but us know. Then the rebels will train their weapons on the right target. The Viceroy will have no choice but to defend himself. With our friendship.'

Hiran thought of the headless bodies at the execution ground. Fokie's lazy smile flashed across his mind. He closed his eyes.

'When the rebels encircle him, he'll truly become mad. His insanity will bring Canton to the verge of catastrophe. Hiranbaboo, he'll turn the entire city into an execution ground, crosses will replace trees.'

Hiran raised both arms, as if to protect himself. Mr Crabbe smiled. 'Then you'll hear death approaching. The hissing of the *kundalini* . . .'

'He could destroy everything. Destroy us all.'

'He could. But before that, we'll come to his side, help him to save himself, save Canton.'

'Who is there to trust but you?' Vinny shot back. 'Why would they listen to a Chinaman? He could be the Viceroy's spy. Or a sahib? They aren't known for their kindness, jewel! There is only you. Truly alien, weak like themselves, with nothing to lose.'

'Trust?'

'If the Military Brahmin can trust you, why not the rebels? After all, they can behead you quite easily if you try to fool them. The weak can be trusted.'

Hiran felt even more uneasy.

What if the Hongs didn't trust him? Took it upon themselves to betray him to the Viceroy? He felt watched. He peered through Vinny's window at a sleepy hawker polishing pears on a dirty sleeve.

'It's easy to win and easy to lose. That's the beauty of it, jewel.'

As he rose to leave, Mr Crabbe had said, 'You've heard about the bird with giant wings that circles Canton, haven't you? It's a myth, of course. Just a myth, born of troubled times. But *you* could be that bird, Hiranbaboo, sheltering the city beneath your wings.'

Vinny and Hiran walked around the market. The hawkers were quiet. Even their goods seemed stale, faded.

Only the opium stalls were busy. Hiran was struck by the variety on offer. 'All mud is not the same,' Vinny explained. 'Look how many rivals we have! The soft yellow stuff is from Camby. The British don't like that. The red is from Constantinople, the dirty-green from Thebes.'

'That's ours!'

Hiran recognized the mango-wood chests. He had seen similar ones on the deck of the *Warrior Queen*. The shopkeeper caught him staring and opened one of the lids. Hiran saw two trays, each with twenty compartments, each compartment filled with a shiny black ball the size of a double fist.

'Cannonball, jewel!'

'Muchoo good.' The shopkeeper nodded his head. He held one ball in his palm where it shone like a giant black pearl. Hiran's mind went back to Mr Eliot's factory – the Boiling room, the Drying and Balling rooms. He could see the men, dark as opium, climbing ladders with chests on their back.

'Indu ya-pien muchoo good.'

He felt proud.

The shopkeeper weighed an empty clay jar first, then filled it with black Bengal mud and weighed it again. His customer thanked him and left.

Hiran saw sacks of dust, golden pills, a gummy plaster that looked like raw tobacco leaves, *K'uai Shang K'uai* – the infamous Quick-Quick. 'They'll have the needle here too. Morphine. Deadly!' Vinny said men from Japan brought the mud from Calcutta, then did God-knows-what to make it like water. 'Water to make your blood boil!'

'They prick your arm and in moments your skin changes colour. A Coffree looks like a sahib, a sahib like a Cheeny. It's worse than a snakebite. This is for rich men – Hongs and Hoppos, their wives and concubines . . . sahibs too. You see them in the dens. Decent *real* sahibs – merchants, commissioners, captains.'

How did Vinny know? What made him both visible and invisible?

'A blackie-white has no choice. He must know everything, see everything.' With a leap, Vinny cleared the wooden chests and tugged on Hiran's arm. 'Let's go see the needle-wallahs.'

Vinny knew a boy, who let them in *just to see.* 'It's not for everyone. Only those the owner knows personally.' Hiran heard a soft rush of strings, like the sound of children playing. In doorways curtains swayed gently, tempting a look. 'Women come with their lovers, lie down next to each other, to sleep.' A lady smiled at them, her hair rolled like the wings of a butterfly.

Hiran watched the play of light on downcast faces. Sculpted foreheads, bone-ivory teeth through parted lips, quivering nostrils. They seemed to be both awake and asleep – drooping like a poppy, pouting and sweet. An eyelid might lift showing a sparkling star, temples rise and fall like a bird about to lay her egg. On some, veins glowed like old silver.

All this from mud. He saw buds bursting through the walls, swollen with sap, erect, dancing in the breeze like ballerinas in chiffon. A blue sky and a rich dark soil replaced the sphere of light and darkness. Echoes seemed to go around, enter and search each room, then return. He saw an old man with the face of a child. A woman with a glittering diamond.

aghratam maranena janma
janmena maranam

Birth is scented with death
Death with birth

Later, dipping their fingers into Alaya's pickle-jar, Vinny told Hiran about his one and only dose of mud. 'Fokie made me a pipe the day Captain Jacque fled from Macao.'

They were curious about his age. *A prince yet childless.* Mr Guo beamed, then offered his own explanation: a life spent at sea, fleeing from one kingdom to another. He was sympathetic. Mr Crabbe wore an indulgent smile.

Who'd have thought young Hiran would be so well versed in maps! They studied the roll of paper, looking puzzled as Mr Crabbe introduced Hiran. It seemed truly exceptional for an Indian prince to be fluent in the art of warfare. A young Hong traced his finger along the cannon turrets of the Viceroy's fort. He looked questioningly at Hiran.

'Our friend from India has a plan.' A hush followed Mr Crabbe's announcement.

Standing behind Hiran's shoulder, he continued, revealing the mystery of arrows and broken lines, sudden shifts in slopes, half-circles lined up like pigeon eggs. Hiran was as amazed as their silent audience. At the end of a monologue, as servants filled empty bowls with tea, the Hongs spoke, one after the other, like respectful Mandarins before their lord.

'The fort is protected on three sides by walls and a canal. Why is the fourth left open?'

'Does he think the rebels can climb the wall faster than the steep hill on his open flank?'

'Are his guns wedged into stone blocks, or free to move?'

'Which way do they point – towards the harbour, or the hill?'
'Does he know he might have rebels in his own rank?'
'Why's the parapet thicker in some parts than in others?'
Did Hiran know?

Before Hiran could feel alarmed, Mr Crabbe stepped in. 'Let's leave warfare to the Generals.' It was most important to see that the strength of one lay in the other's weakness. 'What is weakness,' he asked, like a teacher at the tole, 'but the absence of a wise friend?' The Hongs nodded, then resumed their scrutiny of Hiran.

'They're puzzled by your willingness to help us tame the Viceroy,' Mr Crabbe said next time they met in the reception room. 'The rebels, even the Viceroy would be less suspicious. They are of a different kind, Hiranbaboo, driven by inspiration, less inclined to look for intentions.'

'Remember the story of the merchant and the beggar? What if the beggar hadn't appeared in his dreams, if he had simply stopped at the merchant's door and asked to be struck down? The merchant would've doubted, would've wondered about the beggar's motive. It was a dream, Hiranbaboo, that made him kill. Not gold.'

They walked from one end of the corridor to the other, before the Hongs arrived. Like conspirators, they planned their moves. Hiran was to remain silent, except in the beginning. He would announce his intention to return to Calcutta, make as if to question Mr Crabbe's elaborate scheme to trap the Viceroy. Like actors they were to play their parts before their audience, examining each other closely.

'Perhaps the Hongs aren't ready. Perhaps we're going too fast . . .'

'Yes. Perhaps we might make it seem even faster.' Mr Crabbe sounded thoughtful. 'Might we talk about the International Treaty on Opium? Make them read the writing on the wall, realize they must all act quickly before our mud, and theirs too, becomes history.'

'An International Treaty,' Hiran remembered Nabinbaboo

saying. 'It's in the addicts' best interest, not the merchants.' Have you seen a jackal act in the best interests of a deer?'

'Perhaps you could tell them about the Royal Commission.'

Later, when he was alone, Hiran thought of his own motives. What made him agree to take part in Mr Crabbe's plan? Again he heard Nabinbaboo, *Remember, your employer is simply your employer.* He had expected to be asked to sit with a ledger – like the one at the Auction House – offer his assistance in guiding a stream of harmless letters. And yet, he felt far from trapped in Mr Crabbe's net. It seemed like an adventure – like the trip to Viper Island – a journey, open and uncertain. He was not tempted to explore Mr Crabbe's motive, *He's the one, jewel . . . the thief.*

Mr Guo made a sign with his arm – clashing water on a steep face. He smiled at Hiran. The Banyan Tree Village stood at the top of a cliff, ever at risk of slipping over the perilous edge. Speaking slowly, relying as much on his linguist's art as on gestures, he described Hiran's destination. It was a beautiful spot, he said. The monks had been given it centuries ago – a gift from a rich warlord. A man goes to the Banyan Tree Village to be blessed, also to taste the cormorant's catch. Mr Guo smacked his tongue. It was the closest one could get to heaven – so quiet – unlike Canton. Those who went never returned. The monks were hospitable, the nunnery full of kind souls. Hiran would be tempted to stay. Mr Guo had thought of going himself after the terrible events of last year. Mr Guo fell silent, then sighed.

Would Hiran meet the rebels in the Banyan Tree Village? Mr Guo nodded his head. There were rebels everywhere, even in Canton. Hiran frowned. *Then why not meet them here?* To whom should he give the maps Mr Crabbe had so carefully prepared? Mr Guo's face lit up. He made a gesture, shutting both ears with his palms. A deaf man? Mr Guo beamed. A monk?

Who would help him return to Canton?

Mr Guo pointed to a horse swishing its tail by the peach tree, and to a young man who stood nearby. 'Tomorrow.' Mr Guo smiled, and left Hiran's pavilion.

Suddenly, Hiran felt alarmed. Tomorrow. Why had he agreed

to this? Vinny's words rang in his ear, *He'll trap you, jewel, just see. A sahib is more dangerous than a tiger, he makes his victims love their death!* From words overheard at the Council House, he knew the Banyan Tree Village to be the rebels' nerve centre. It lay near the sea, not far from Canton, but to reach it one needed to ride over inhospitable terrain. The Hongs had spoken of its natural defences, the steep face of a cliff that rose like a phantom over flat soil. Hiran had heard them speak of the monastery itself – where rebels in the guise of monks enacted the daily task of plotting to overthrow Canton's Viceroy. He had heard them speak of the rebel leader, the Deaf Monk, their voices falling to whispers at the mention of his name.

That night he thought of his mother. Her warnings, neglected over the years, returned to haunt him. First the typhoon, then cholera, then the beheadings . . . had she seen them all from her roof in Jaanbazaar? Did she know too of her son's fear of horses? He lay awake all night trying in vain to erase the image of a horse swishing its tail by the peach tree.

Riding in front of the young warrior on the same saddle, Hiran felt the beating of two hearts. Fear made him lose sight of the terrain, ignore other riders. He lowered his eyes to a blur of gravel and mud. Shallow puddles reflected a dark sky. Hiran shuddered. A thousand hoofs thundered inside his head.

Even when they had left Canton behind, Hiran's mind was in turmoil. He understood the fine web of Mr Crabbe's plan better than he understood this journey on a dusty road. He wished they could stop for a while to quench his thirst. The journey would be short, Mr Guo had said. But it would seem long.

They flew past crowds, through sharp and narrow corners, scattering fruit from market-stalls. Men squeezed themselves flat against walls to let them pass. They seemed different – darker, beaten, like prisoners. Women, faces aged with dust and grime, carried children in baskets slung over their shoulders. Some wore gaudy jewellery and covered their heads. More women than men, Hiran noticed, more babies, forlorn, ugly.

For the first time in months, his nostrils were free of the river's clay and algae. They passed quarries and towns full of stone-cutters. Hiran saw clusters of men sitting around slatey homes burning an acrid pit of logs with billowing smoke.

After a while, Hiran stopped being aware of his companion, as if he had become part of the animal that was carrying him.

They spent that night in a clearing set apart from the villages they had passed. The young man built a tent for Hiran, placed a basket smelling of jasmine-rice inside, then left.

The next day they mounted again, still in silence. By the end of the hot day, they were beginning to skirt small hills, sitting like islands in the middle of a flat valley. The villages nestled at their feet seemed deserted and melancholy, like the drooping bamboo surrounding them.

By sunset they faced a huge overhanging rock, black, like the hood of a snake, resting among smaller rocks as on a bed of nails. A set of steps appeared from nowhere, carved with pain out of the hard rock. The horse came to a stop, and Hiran started to disembark. He felt a strong arm on his shoulder, and a volley of orders. Hiran clasped the mane again, feeling a surge, rising steeply, then a drop. He swayed and clashed against his co-rider. The man held his neck, hissing commands under his breath. He heard the splash of water on rock. The air seemed lighter. Through closed eyes, Hiran knew he was staring straight at the sky.

The animal struggled on, a spray of foam wetting Hiran's forearms. Finally, when they arrived at the Banyan Tree Village, the young man fell silent again.

The cool air stung Hiran's eyes, his ears still ringing with sharp orders. His companion pointed. A temple floated, suspended from the clouds, over a thick shrub rapidly darkening. Hiran heard gongs and bells ringing. Lanterns lit up the huge rock. He felt truly in Mr Guo's heaven.

*

Exhausted, Hiran fell asleep instantly. It would take him a whole day to breathe easily in the strange mountain air, a whole week to find his way through the maze of pavilions and hovels that housed the monks. As in Mr Guo's house, his meals arrived silently. A young monk with a shaven head would pass him a steaming bowl of tea. He smelled sweet oranges and cloves. A swarm of fan-tailed pigeons watched him finish his tray, then joined the pet mice to squabble over the remains. From his very first morning, Hiran grew accustomed to the sound of chanting.

From his window, he could see young monks memorizing their prayers. The sun shone on their shaven heads, on a string of ripe lotus buds. He saw their teacher stare absent-mindedly beyond them to a white tower half-hidden behind the temple.

As he waited for his afternoon meal, Hiran recalled Mr Guo's description of the monastery at the Banyan Tree Village. 'Paradise admits everyone . . . the poor, even orphans. Only the unjust are not allowed.' Mr Guo had recited the names of the many pavilions that made up the monastery: the Hall of Great Lotus, the Hall of Obedience, the Hall of Prosperity, but Hiran had forgotten what they stood for. The Deaf Monk was seldom to be seen, Mr Guo had warned, but it was to him, and to him alone, that Hiran had to hand over the secret documents from Mr Crabbe.

He learned that his riding companion of a few days before was called Tai-ma, and that he spoke English. He had studied under English missionaries in Soochow. Tai-ma took him for a walk, pointing out fine old trees, the groves of mandarin oranges. Pyramids of flowers stood at the crossing of gravel-walks, lending colour to the dark moss. Setting out on a different path each day, they passed the same landmarks. Tai-ma never failed to name them each time, till Hiran could recite their names with ease.

'To be born in Soochow, to live in Kwang-tung, and to die in

Liaow-chou.' As he learned more about him, Tai-ma seemed more a monk than a horseman. He was born, he said, only when he joined this secret society of rebels, 'entered Paradise'. He had his secret book, and wore a string around his *five-claws.*

'Five claws?'

The rebels' secret language, Tai-ma explained. '*Claws* for fingers, a *lion* for a warrior, a *wild wind* for the enemy. Words aren't simply words,' he said, staring into Hiran's eyes, 'but the fragrance of Paradise!'

The rebel monks had saved Tai-ma from the life of a beggar. Sitting next to lepers, he had shared their water. Sometimes, he had pretended to be a leper himself. For sixteen years he bore the curse of a leper, till the monks bought him out of poverty. They taught him how to flick a sharp dagger, to feed the *black dog* – the fort's cannon – and ride the steep slope up to the Banyan Tree Village on a horse.

Lying awake at night, Hiran wondered about the secret language. Why *sand* for rice, *slave girl* for fish, why was a woman a *long grass blowing in the breeze*?

Hiran watched monks practising with bows and arrows, not for aim, but for strength. Several sheets of soft leather hung from a beam – the arrow simply throwing the leather back, then falling. One had a bow-string drawn to his ear, with the bow outstretched in the other hand. Most could only bring it up to their shoulder. They strengthened their arms by lifting heavy beams weighed down by stones.

Wherever Hiran and Tai-ma went in the Banyan Tree Village, Hiran saw men huddled together, sharpening spears, cleaning muskets, rolling barrows heaped with cannon-balls. Young monks played around a cache of matchlock; incense from the temple crept into a cloud of gunpowder. Hiran was as drawn to the archers as to the thousand candles in the temple.

He saw nuns too – lighting the temple's lamps, sweeping its entrance, fanning the huge wooden image of a female Buddha. At sunset, gongs sounded the call to evening's prayer.

'Widows, scorned wives, spinsters, virgins, even whores,' Tai-ma said with a serious face.

As they sat together, watching cormorants chase fish underwater, he pointed out white figures: 'Look for the one with a mole on her cheek, she's both a widow and a spinster, and two monks have drowned in the great sky for her.'

Hiran's eyes widened. 'She was given in marriage to a dead man. He was a secret messenger for the Deaf Monk, and died in a heroic battle before his marriage. She came to live in her dead husband's home, but his mother hated her. She needed her mother-in-law's permission to remarry, but she wouldn't give it. For years she lived as a slave, till the monks learned of her suffering and brought her to the temple.'

A ring around the cormorant's neck prevented it from swallowing its catch.

'In the Society's eye she was married. But the monks argued among themselves. There were two claimants. One claimed her as his wife. Another announced he was the father of her child to be. She was blamed. *Only a newborn doesn't know what's hidden under her robe.* A meeting was called, everybody came.'

People go to the Banyan Tree Village to taste the cormorants' catch. Hiran thought of Mr Guo.

'Who had her finally?'

'The trial was long. Some monks argued that it was a case of wife robbery – the two-legged disgrace must be divorced instantly. But who would speak for a dead man? There was no way of knowing his wish. And she refused to speak. Not even the shaman, who had given her medicines for her swollen belly, could force her. Some were in favour of a *ch'ih* – light blows with a bamboo cane, eighteen or twenty-one depending on the hour of punishment. Then, she ought to be sent back to her mother-in-law, or to Canton to become a whore. The Deaf Monk let a whole stick of incense burn to ash before speaking. He said, the whole universe came from one womb. We men are born to have one mind, one will, be faithful and loyal. The

Paradise was in our soul – a fish hiding under a rock waiting to be devoured by greedy cormorants. He said, if a man seduces the wife of another who is dead or has gone abroad, if he gives her his child to bear, if he steals her to sell her in another place, then he must be slain under a shower of blows.'

'Did they kill the two men?' Hiran asked. Then he fell silent.

'She's the one with the mole, keeps her eyes open during prayers. The monks say she can see her three dead husbands clearly.'

'Did she have a child?'

Tai-ma pointed towards the white tower behind the temple: 'She had made up her mind.' Hiran shuddered. *Is that what they mean by the Baby Tower?* he thought. *A place to murder the unwanted, the impure?* Tai-ma looked at him defiantly. 'Better than a life spent begging in the streets.'

An initiation ceremony was being planned for a group of fifty-one horsemen from the north. Tai-ma took Hiran to see The Hall of Great Assembly where the ceremony would take place. The stage was to resemble a great ship. It would remind the recruits of their impending journey over the neighbouring sea to Canton. The columns needed repainting, Tai-ma said. The monks had abandoned other work to join hands. It would be foolish to rely on carpenters and artists.

Even at his pavilion in Canton Hiran had been reassured by the sight of masts in the harbour. They reminded him of the *Warrior Queen*, of his friends from the deck. Now he felt truly alone. The make-belief ship joined him to his past, as if he was still at his desk in the Auction House, gazing out through the window.

'Hello, Maharajah!'

Reverend Fowler beamed under his silk cap, clasping Hiran's hands like an old friend. He was still in his loose trousers and Chinese vest, but now he carried a stick.

'Canton was not to your royal taste, I suppose!' He winked at Hiran, then led him to a small fountain under an old tree.

'There's trouble I hear . . . not everyone will play by the same rules. Do you suppose the Hong merchants might go along with us, or give in to the Viceroy's whims?'

Hiran smiled politely. For a moment he wondered if Reverend Fowler was a fellow conspirator. Did his words bear a secret message? They stood in silence for a while.

'Why don't we meet in my quarters, in the afternoon after your friend has left?'

When Hiran met Reverend Fowler again, he was sitting under a tree in front of his room. Hiran had come prepared with questions – those that kept him awake at night. Reverend Fowler offered him an orange.

'The Chinese are a curious puzzle. One sees a mix of cowardice and courage, pride and servility, clannishness and ego.'

Hiran kept his eyes lowered. 'Do you know how they discovered their religion, Mr Chakraborti?'

'Some taoists heard of the birth of the Messiah, sent their wise men over Tibet. But the emissaries never reached Jerusalem. Lost on the mountains, they found the Buddha in India and returned.' Reverend Fowler spat orange pips on the ground.

A group of young monks who had been playing in the garden came over to them. They displayed hollow bamboo boxes filled with a great variety of insects. Reverend Fowler chose a few, deposited them in a small cage by his feet. He handed the monks some copper coins and an orange each.

'Superstition has replaced piety. Think of . . .'

Hiran remembered seeing feasts left before shrines of ancestors. 'Do they believe that the dead have to eat?'

'How can you possibly suppose that?' Reverend Fowler looked astonished. 'But they aren't the determined pagans that one might think. There's virtue in their lies.'

Hiran felt confused. Like Mr Crabbe, Reverend Fowler seemed skilful in avoiding the most pressing issue.

'You are safe here,' the Reverend nodded smugly, 'away from the executioner and the executed.'

Hiran wanted to ask Reverend Fowler about the beheadings. Why was he here collecting insects, when he could be saving souls at the execution ground? Was he waiting too, like the Deaf Monk, for Hiran's secrets?

'You think all this trouble is a result of your mud, don't you? It's more than that, I'm afraid. Remove the pipe and you'd still have Mandarins and soldiers, gaolers and convicts. No, it isn't simply due to the success of your Auction House.'

Hiran frowned. He thought it customary for priests to condemn opium, rather than to absolve it of its sins. Nabin-baboo had convinced him that missionaries were behind the Royal Commission. *Quakers, drawn to the soul of the Chinaman, not his pocket.*

Reverend Fowler scoffed at the idea. 'The alien has become intrinsic, indispensable in its union with cells, with blood, and marrow – become an element of nutrition. It's no longer pleasant or unpleasant, just like the air we breathe. You understand, don't you? You think only China has taken to opium? It's everywhere – Singapore, Malaya, Burma, even England has been infected.' He paused to spit out the orange seeds. 'We'd be here, mud or not. Mr Crabbe and his men would be here too, even if not one ounce of opium was raised in the Ganges valley.'

They were both after something else. *What?* Who called the merchant, the soldier, the priest . . .

He dreamt of the same two birds. But now they were alive, chasing fish over a stream. The older one was more skilful, diving under rocks, swimming far ahead of the other. What do you see? the younger one asked. I see an ocean of fish waiting to be swallowed. Who do you think has filled the ocean? One who has given us hunger, and the strength to kill. The younger one seemed distressed. Does he know that with each success we reduce his creation, does he care? The older bird returned with a fish caught in its beak. Does he see that you have ruined his perfection? Dropping the fish back into the water, the older one said, *Perhaps he knows not why.*

Word came that the Viceroy's soldiers were on their way. The monks prepared to fortify the stone steps leading up to the village. Tai-ma asked if Hiran would join them, become a *horse.* Hiran thought he was joking.

'How can a foreigner enter the womb?' he said.

'They know you are different, not a red-barbarian or black, but . . .'

Hiran was curious. Where did he think Hiran came from? He thought of Vinny. *The Cheenys don't know where we are from. They've never heard of Hindoostan. They think we've come from the southern forest.*

'The land of clouds.' Tai-ma made a motion with his fingers, as if drawing on an opium pipe.

Long after the attack had been repulsed, he sat in his room and thought of Tai-ma's words. He thought too of Saraladebi, and of Annada packing his trunk in the light of an oil lamp. 'Beware of devils and friends!' Why friends? he had asked. 'Because they'll lead you to the devil, and stay till you've become one.' What would Vinny say? *Look what the Cheenys have done to the Maharajah of Jaanbazaar!* He felt strangely happy.

A closed envelope rested on his pillow. He held it up to the lamp, excited. This could be his call, the spark to begin his mission. With the skill of a letter-reader, Hiran peeled along the edges and took out the contents, releasing the fragrance of a rare flower. Then, he read.

My dear one

My house on the mountain-top has lost its soul. Every day it waits to cast its eye on one who'll return it to its bosom. I sit with my embroidery on the terrace, pass hours gazing at the valley. It's beautiful. Hills are in autumn bloom, and red leaves drift slowly down to the river. A blue haze rises from the valley. I hear peasants in their fields, the duck-man herding his flock with a long bamboo. I smell the rich earth. Sometimes I see a bride travelling to her new home. Her servants sing and dance, scatter golden dust along their path. I imagine what lies ahead of her. What lies ahead? I wonder. My heart lingers after her, like a moon throwing its face on a lake. I see myself on her bridal-chair. Hear the sweet rustle of silk, the tinkle of gems and jade.

A deep fear darkens my days. Will you disappear like dancing specks on a burning sun? Without you there's none that I care to see – not even my favourite Tai-shan peeking above the clouds. No sunset will enflame my heart, unless I am able to share it with you. Like a solitary pine tree I shall remain in mourning, a convict's chain will bind my soul to an empty room. As a blossom withers unseen . . .

Which one of them? he wondered, puzzled. From their shaven heads they had all looked the same, the young nuns sweeping the temple's altar. This message must be for Tai-ma, he concluded, from a secret lover. The letter must have fallen out of his overflowing bag when he came to meet Hiran that morning for their walk.

The next time Tai-ma came to visit, Hiran placed the envelope where he could see it, as if it had fallen from his sack of odds and ends. Tai-ma saw it, then looked away.

Hiran was still puzzled. He tried to catch Tai-ma's attention again, feigned wonder at spotting the envelope. Holding it up to his nose, he offered Tai-ma a share of its perfume. But Tai-ma was unmoved.

He seemed keener to talk about Hiran's initiation. Hiran tried explaining that a brahmin couldn't be anything but a brahmin, that he had already transgressed once – become a gentoo. Tai-ma listened with his ear but not his heart.

'They are planning to visit you. They want you to answer their questions. You must be prepared.'

Hiran began to worry.

He began to see the letter as a secret message, not of love, but of war. He mulled over every word, determined to hear the inner voice. Who was waiting in *a house on the mountain-top*? Didn't they all? The bridal chair seemed an awkward metaphor for the throne of a ruler. Perhaps the Viceroy's? Who would want to climb down the mountain and ascend the throne at Canton? The Deaf Monk, Reverend Fowler . . .

Some nights he couldn't sleep at all. 'Owls keeping you awake, are they?' Reverend Fowler asked. 'Roll up your bed for bed-bugs,' he'd warn. He made Hiran restless with his probing.

'You're a brahmin, aren't you? What brings you among the dog eaters?'

Hiran was certain the Reverend knew. He felt sure that he too was part of Mr Crabbe's plan, sent to keep an eye on Hiran, remind him if he neglected his duty, trick him into submission should he betray his superior's confidence. Reverend Fowler, he was sure, was as much a part of his secret visit to the rebels as was Mr Guo.

But he hesitated over sharing his other secret – the secret of the letter.

My dear one

How fortunate of me to see you once more. Like a mist you have cast a veil around me, I see nothing else; when I woke this morning, I was sad, not knowing if I would see you again. Days of waiting had me restless. I didn't care any more if I saw the sun rise or set, the river gush over rocky banks, if I heard a single bird sing, or a child call for his friend. I would exchange all the birds in the world for you; give away the magic of twilight just to feel your darkness around me.

Then you came. Looking so serious, lost in your thoughts. Your companion – the red-barbarian – seemed eager and happy. Were you listening to him? Were you thinking of one to whom your sight is the greatest fortune of all? What did you think of my last letter? Such silly things I write . . .

My friends say you may leave soon, or you may stay for ever. They too know you're different – a forehead like the Buddha, eyes like a budding lotus . . . did you come from your land just to find me? Tai-ma respects you like an elder brother. You are wise and kind, he says, you recite mantras each day like the monks; you too could become a powerful horse, feared by all. He says you are thinking, preparing to meet with the Elders. Are you thinking of me, your dear loved one . . .

Before I saw you my nights were wrapped in harsh memories . . . fear and loathing kept me awake. I heard gongs and screams, or the false laugh of baby-buyers visiting famined villages. Stars were like my mother's eyes – weeping their rays; how many more nights remained? I wondered.

Now I stay awake for you, dreaming of a sun that'll never set from my eyes. I stay awake just to think of you.

With every stroke of my brush I send you a bit of my heart . . .

Awake, his mind covered all possibilities. The monk bringing him his tray would linger, strike up a conversation through signs and gestures. Pointing towards Hiran's watch, he'd smile with curiosity.

Hiran started to take his tray inside himself, shutting the door behind him. The monk waited outside.

When he took his morning walk, he saw faces hiding behind the trunks of old trees, peering through the dragon's eye at the Hall of Obedience. Among the monks, he searched for the one who recorded his moves. The nunnery haunted him.

Hiran kept his eyes lowered, passing shaven heads and white robes. They would fall silent as usual but now he felt they were examining his forehead and eyes. Those sweeping the temple's floor seemed to take longer, flicking a broom casually near his feet. At prayers he felt the hush of a scandal. What were they whispering under their breath?

*

His head had caught in the long-cloth shirt with stitched front and cuffs as he pulled it on. As usual, he put on the blue serge suit as if he were visiting the Council House. Tai-ma bowed to Hiran, motioned him to sit on a stool facing the monks.

The story of the Warrior and the King crossed his mind. He couldn't help but sense an irony: warriors commanding a king's emissary. Did they know of his link with the red-barbarians?

A man with the face of a convict started to speak. Hiran sat quietly, listening to the questions, and Tai-ma's halting translation.

For whom was he named? Hiran struggled for a moment, then pointed towards the temple – the Creator.

Had his parents died in war or sickness?

'I said your mother was alive, but sick,' Tai-ma explained. Hiran knew one needed to be an orphan to become a member of the rebels' society.

A young man with a sharp face smiled at him. Did he chew clouds?

'Chew clouds?'

'He means, do you smoke opium?' They laughed at his denial. One made a mock gesture, cutting an imaginary pipe in two with his sheathed knife.

Who was his enemy, the one responsible for the death of his father? Hiran smiled. *He wasn't killed by horses, nor men . . . nor even by Gods.* Tai-ma looked at his face. Hiran said his father had been killed by the unknown.

Did he feel a danger around him – a threat more powerful than death?

What could he tell them? Surely they had heard of the headless bodies. Who was he to tell them about danger? He spoke softly about the terror of pirates on high seas, forcing Tai-ma to strain his ears.

Did he favour women?

Did they know of the letters? Hiran started sweating under his serge coat. The front row smiled encouragingly.

Did he meet the padre last night?

Would he have woken if he had heard a cry in the night?

Hiran felt suffocated in his suit. *They have resolved to make you one like them.* Perhaps they were simply testing his loyalty, closing all paths of escape.

Tai-ma cleared his throat.

Was he married?

'Yes.' Hiran answered instantly, then started to loosen his tie.

As the meeting ended in confusion, Tai-ma looked at Hiran sadly. He'd have to wait till his wife learned of Paradise, and gave him permission to enter. She'd have to come too. Then Hiran could move into a room closer to the temple, one large enough for the two of them, and their young warriors.

Hiran kept the questioning a secret from Reverend Fowler. But he probably knew anyway. It might even have been his idea in the first place.

Reverend Fowler dismissed the monks' coded language as a fruitless obsession with secret messages. They should be worrying about their future. Before the butcher of Canton turns the river into a floating morgue, they must find a way to his fort. The tables were turning, he said – the Viceroy was no longer the invisible ghost ordering hangings. His bald head could be seen everywhere – at the port as ships were unloaded, lighting joss at the Temple of Longevity, visiting foreigners at the Council House. 'He's a friendly man, I hear. Not friendly enough, I'm afraid.'

Reverend Fowler seemed well informed. 'One by one the Viceroy has won the merchants' favours – through fear. He has two heads. One thinks while the other sleeps. He is faster than the rebels. The barbarians – the English included – are anxious, ready to settle for peace. He has started to raise the heat, clearing land for more execution grounds.' Hiran remembered Mr Crabbe's words, *He'll turn the entire city into an execution ground, crosses will replace trees.*

He tried to imagine the Viceroy at the Council House,

surrounded by Hongs. Would Mr Crabbe tell him the story of the merchant and his young wife? Perhaps they were looking together at a map.

Reverend Fowler seemed a touch distracted. A heap of orange skin lay at his feet.

Hiran decided to ask him about the Deaf Monk.

Reverend Fowler cleared his throat. 'He was once a Mandarin, a powerful one, married to the daughter of Canton's Viceroy. Like the others, he dealt in silk, tea, opium, convicts. He was well respected and poets found favour in his court. Then he fought with his father-in-law, the Viceroy. Simply greed, or power, I'd say. The Viceroy struck first. Even his wife couldn't protect him from her father's wrath. They arrested him, cut off his ears. He and his wife fled Canton, came here, started a secret society to overthrow the Viceroy. He's your Deaf Monk, your invisible host.'

He read Hiran's question in his look. 'Yes, she is here as well. She's the only one who's not a nun.'

And Mr Guo – what was his link?

'Oh yes. Most gruesome, I'm afraid. Mr Guo's son was married to the Deaf Monk's only daughter. In anger when his daughter fled, the Viceroy had his own granddaughter and her husband burned to death.'

Reverend Fowler fell silent.

'Why do you suppose anybody kills?'

It seemed an irresolvable puzzle. Hiran's mind darted from the Viceroy to the rebels to the English merchants. Could you drive an enemy until he became your friend?

'Who will win this struggle?'

'Everybody is afraid of losing.' The padre spoke carefully. 'Here the Deaf Monk rules absolutely, like a Rajah. But in his heart he is a boy. Why do you suppose he sends his men down the cliff to die by the river? Why does he fill empty homes with presents? Why does he wait to strike?'

Hiran waited.

'You want to know? The fact of the matter is they are all

paralysed, frightened and suspicious. Now the Viceroy has taken the lead, killing three hundred in a single night.'

Hiran saw the torches of the execution ground, and Fokie's smile.

'You know about the Hongs and the English, don't you? How might the same plan work in the hand of the Viceroy?'

Hiran felt confused.

'What if the Viceroy knew of the merchants' plans? What if –' He stopped, smiling at Hiran's look of consternation.

You must invoke his love through fear. Hiran knew the aim behind his mission – to tempt the rebel monks down to Canton with his secret maps. *He* was the instrument of fear. They were to be the sacrifice, leading to a union between the Viceroy and the merchants.

'What if the two are friends now, engaged in another plan? Together against the rebels?' Reverend Fowler asked.

Why hadn't Mr Crabbe sent for him? Hiran wondered. Did he plan to treat his servant with cruelty or indulgence?

Tai-ma brought more news. The rebellion was spreading. The Mandarins were fleeing, leaving the province in the hands of the warlords. It would soon be time to leave the Banyan Tree Village. Tai-ma smiled fondly at Hiran. Perhaps Hiran's wife would come to join him in Canton – the City of Rams.

'The Deaf Monk has asked to meet you. It'll be after the initiation ceremony. You are invited.'

This then was the dawn of release. He would hand over the maps and his mission would end. He'd be free to chase other streams of paper. He knew Vinny would be waiting for him in Canton.

The next letter amused him at first. Almost cheerful, it sounded shy.

> For a week I searched in my closet to find gowns fitting for a woman who is alone. You have a wife, my dear one, you have a wife . . . I wept for seven days, and at the end of the fountain of

tears, I found love. It was as if you were waiting for me to wake, and listen to your breath echo on my door.

Do you forgive me, for my harsh words? I know you have come far, like a bird that has left its nest. You are alone. Tai-ma says you spend hours staring at the river, or watching young monks study under a tree. Do they remind you of those you've left behind? Are you sad, my love?

From now, it'll be my duty to protect you. A heart that is busy can't mourn; I shall help you return to your own kind. Yes . . . even though I shall certainly die without you, my hand will guide you safely . . . you will smile again. You will live with the memory of one who died for you.

Hiran frowned.

I know I shall see you soon . . . at the Great Hall. My heart races. Will you recognize me? Shall I give you a hint, my dear one . . .

Breathless, he read on.

But you must promise not to speak to me. I have resolved never to disturb you . . . never to be touched. Only my eyes shall embrace you. You mustn't look too long, promise never to tell anyone – not even your barbarian friend. In one glance I shall be yours.

You will find me with the lion.

Could Reverend Fowler be writing the letters? Was it his way of 'saving' him, did he wish a share of Hiran's soul too, to keep like a pet insect? Hiran quickly dismissed the idea.

Alone at night in his room, he sat before the maps. *Tell him everything at once . . .* . Hiran started to trace the boundary of the Viceroy's fort with his finger. The maps were unnecessary, a ruse he understood, a mere excuse for his journey here. If Mr Guo knew that, others here must know too, why would they wait for an exiled prince from Hindoostan to set fire to Canton? Hiran felt like an actor bereft of lines – a stranger on the stage.

Why feed the brahmin then? he wondered, as he sat before his morning tray. Was *he* the offering, a sacrifice for the Gods? Had Mr Crabbe brought him so far just to make him the bait of love?

Hiran prepared to meet the Deaf Monk at last. Sitting next to Reverend Fowler at the initiation ceremony, he saw the recruits enter in pairs. They had already pledged their lives solemnly to the Society. Now their wives sat in mourning robes. 'They must pretend their husbands are dead.' Reverend Fowler nudged him as the recruits passed under a bridge of swords. At the end of the line a barber waited to chop off their tresses.

Hiran was impressed by the stage, set up as a giant ship. Monks marched the recruits up the gangway into the hold, then up on to the deck. They seemed frightened, like chained prisoners. A low hum rose from the nuns. Hiran saw everyone around him close their eyes. A deep voice spoke.

'I see them going on a voyage. Roaming the world without a home. I see white herons flying over their heads. A black mountain sits at the mouth of the river. There are three paths – two around it, and one through its heart. It's a stream, a gentle one. They journey on a stream to enter the gates of Paradise.'

A recruit was led to the edge of the hull.

'Nothing will stop him now, he must fly to reach his home.' The recruit bowed before a friendly-looking man whose head was bandaged from ear to ear.

'The Deaf Monk,' Reverend Fowler whispered to Hiran. 'He has asked to see you too, I hear.' He smiled conspiratorially at Hiran.

He wanted to ask the Reverend about the lion, but hugged close the valise with the maps inside.

'Be careful . . .'

A procession of paper animals and birds burst into the Hall. The residents of the Banyan Tree Village followed in groups behind each figure: young monks and their teacher behind a fluttering cock, warriors with horses, artists flanked by lambs, barbers led by mice, nuns surrounded by a ring of pigeons. The old monks stood grimly behind a black ox.

Hiran saw a green lizard, an elephant with tusks, a monkey with a long tail, and a lion. A woman wearing a white dress stood holding a flower basket beside it.

He leaned closer. A delicate face hid beneath a bamboo hat. *You must promise not to speak to me . . . only my eyes shall embrace you . . .* He stood up from his seat. She might spot his suit in the sea of flowing robes. Surely, she'd notice the black-barbarian.

He felt an arm on his shoulder. Reverend Fowler watched him gazing at the lady by the lion. 'The Viceroy's daughter,' he whispered.

Hiran would remember less of his meeting with the Deaf Monk after the ceremony than of that moment in the Hall – a pair of eyes staring at him beside the lion.

Hiran stood silently, holding the valise in both hands. The Deaf Monk seemed calm; unwinding the cloth from his head, he wiped the sweat off his forehead. His eyes were kind, his head bald like an old monk's. In place of ears, two holes dipped gently from banks of his smooth skin.

His eyes were close to Reverend Fowler's face, reading his lips as he translated. He nodded from time to time. Then, he whispered into the Reverend's ear.

'Hiran, he wants to know who you would like to meet at this very moment.'

'My mother, Sir.'

The Deaf Monk smiled.

'He says, may you live ten thousand years, ten thousand times ten thousand years . . .'

Hiran dreamt of Mr Crabbe's story. A merchant, his wife, and a thief were standing on a ship's hull. Each whispered a secret into

Hiran's ear. The merchant stepped in first, bringing close his old face. He took a long time fumbling with words. The young wife was proud, her face held high. Hiran smelt her fragrance. She spoke in a determined voice, blowing a rush of hot breath on his cheek. The thief was last. He limped and moaned, took a long time to climb the planks. He said but one word into Hiran's ear.

Like the Deaf Monk, Hiran heard nothing.

Hiran saw a row of battleships lined up facing the Banyan Tree Village.

Between the first sighting of the 'devil ships', and the opening of fire, Hiran searched for the face he had seen the night before, in empty pavilions and deserted courtyards. He ran against the tide of fleeing monks, wandered aimlessly from one set of closed doors to the next.

The broadsides would continue until the rebels' guns fell silent. Even from a distance, the captains of the warships could judge the number of dead, moving leisurely into a siege. Hiran remembered the stories of war he had heard on the deck of the *Warrior Queen*, knew the invaders were waiting to land soldiers on the deserted shore. They had come prepared to destroy, not to ransom. Was Mr Crabbe among them? Hiran wondered.

He saw children huddled together in dark corners. They would take him for a barbarian and scream. He heard screams from all directions, but he was afraid to investigate. *They kill their women before surrendering to the enemy.* He remembered Captain Jacque's words. *They kill their own for fear of our killing . . .*

Where were the rebels? They seemed to have disappeared without trace, deserting the village almost as swiftly as it had been encircled. Where were the new recruits?

A dead horse sprawled over the neat lawn of the nunnery.

Hiran searched for the Deaf Monk. Where would he escape to

now? To Canton? In Mr Guo's pavilion, resting in the rock garden? He saw a monk he knew, heard him call from the ruin of the Baby Tower. Hiran ran towards the nunnery. They held each other. The monk's hands shook too.

In the nunnery, sobs drew them along empty corridors. Hiran feared less for his own safety than for the source of the pitiful wails, till they stumbled in the dark over heaps of bodies, slipped in pools of dark blood.

They were everywhere, dead and dying by their own hand, vomiting poison, veins flooding, hanging from hooks in the ceiling.

Tai-ma was dead, curled up like a child by his horse.

Hiran stood paralysed before the nunnery. The cannons had stopped, and in the silence he heard the voice of Reverend Fowler and saw him perched high on a horse, looking much like a rebel himself. He seemed surprised to see Hiran, and pulled him up on to the saddle without a word.

As he left the Banyan Tree Village, Hiran felt only relief.

'Tell me you aren't a ghost, jewel!'

Vinny leapt from his bed.

'You aren't dead? Not killed by a deaf monk on some godforsaken mountain?' Excitement made him lose his voice, but only for a moment. 'Now they'll make you a real Maharajah. You are a hero! You've stopped the beheadings. You can have a seat in the west wing now!'

Afraid of losing Vinny, Hiran had come straight to Hog Lane on his return to Canton. Now he felt happy, but exhausted.

'You're safe now. Free of that bastard Guo – a rebel disguised as a Hong, holding you in his clutches!'

'Mr Guo?'

'He was the one who spied on Mr Crabbe and the Viceroy. Serves him right. He was the last to be beheaded. After him, no more.'

Hiran looked at him dumbfounded.

'How did you convince the devils to let you go? Oh! what would I have told your mother, jewel!'

'How did you know I was in danger?'

'Mr Crabbe complained to the Viceroy that the rebels had captured his friend from Calcutta. He said you were special, a jewel of jewels! He offered the Viceroy a choice. To go with him on the man-of-war to your rescue, or to stay behind without the protection of English guns.'

So he was there, Hiran thought. 'And the Reverend? Did you know about him?'

'Of course. It was he who sent word that you were there.' Vinny frowned at Hiran's silence.

'You mean you didn't know?'

Hiran thought of the Banyan Tree Village, of Tai-ma's dead face. He saw the monks sitting before him, staring at his forehead. And the kind smile on the face of the Deaf Monk. Why had he waited so long to see him? Why was he dismissed so easily, with scant interest in his 'secrets'?

Gradually, he began to understand, to see the pattern. Perhaps the Deaf Monk had suspected the motive behind Hiran's visit, refused to play into Mr Crabbe's trap. He must have known that once cornered, the Viceroy was bound to seek the shelter of superior English guns. The Reverend must have sent messages back to the Council House. And so the Military Brahmin had resorted to his final trick – offering to fight the rebels in exchange for the Viceroy's friendship. Perhaps he cared little for Hiran, his gentoo assistant, sure to perish in the siege of the rebels' village. Poor Mr Guo, Hiran thought, only he was true to the plan, only he had believed in the secret of the maps. But, of course, he wasn't interested in friendship, only in revenge for the murder of his son. Hiran felt more proud than ever of his pupil – not simply a translator, but a true creator of tales.

Only a single mystery eluded him. *Even though I shall certainly die without you, my hand will guide you safely* . . . Hiran felt a pang of inescapable loss.

In his excitement, Vinny had forgotten his biggest news.

'The *Warrior Queen* is leaving! Passengers are asked to assemble at Ass's Point. The Viceroy himself will flag her off, accompanied by the Hoppo's band. Captain Jacque is thrilled. Mr Crabbe had recovered your trunk from Mr Guo's house and planned to deliver it personally to your mother. Now he'll deliver her son to her too!'

'You'll have a cabin all to yourself, jewel. Marie and I will have one too. I'm going to wait for her here, we'll travel together to Calcutta on an English boat later.'

He opened his sambhar-skin suitcase and took out the box wrapped in gilded paper from Mr Pinchback's shop.

'Think you can take it for me, jewel? It's my wedding present for Marie.'

Hiran smelled the jasmine-rice bubbling in Alaya's kitchen. He raised an eyebrow.

'She wants to come to Calcutta, as Marie's chaperone till we're married. Think you could convince Lilian to take Alaya as her maid?'

Hiran's mouth watered for pickles.

'Which one are you waiting for, Marie or Alaya?' he teased Vinny.

'Call me a leper if I've lied!'

The return was slow – a ceaseless watching of wind and course. After a languid start, the *Warrior Queen* shifted between steady runs and forced idleness, steering just ahead of a junk convoy. She shied away from the open sea, preferring to cling to the shore. There were fewer passengers on the way back, and no ladies. The evenings were quiet. The men sat together, exchanging stories like hushed secrets. These old hands cared less for the journey, passed their time playing cards and drinking whisky. Hiran sat by himself.

After a while Hiran ceased to pay them any attention, searching instead for familiar faces among the crew. He recognized only a few of the waiters in the dining-room, some of the deckhands too. But Canton, he found, had been disastrous for the *Warrior Queen.* She had lost most of her European seamen to other ships, lured away with the promise of higher pay. Captain Jacque was forced to settle for a Manila quartermaster, and a couple of dark boatswains. 'But I'd be damned,' Captain Jacque said, 'if I waited for Chinamen to turn white!'

Only the gunner remained, the black Madrasee with his golden cross. He dined occasionally at Hiran's table.

Even Mr Crabbe seemed remote. Hiran was struck by his silence when they met on the deck of the *Warrior Queen* for the first time since their parting. Though he had seen him behind a thin veil of mist, standing alone at the stern, staring at the flotilla of junks behind him.

Now they only spoke in the company of others. Did not even acknowledge a past acquaintance. He imagined a letter on his desk: *Dear Hiranbaboo, In the light of present circumstances it might be wise to hold our Sunday meetings in abeyance till further notice.* And one in Mr Kavasji's tidy hand: *Dear Hiran, I would like you to help my nephew's son. He is only seven, but clever, and needs help to improve his spelling. If you agree, I shall inform Mr Crabbe. I am sure he wouldn't mind . . .*

He wondered what Lilian would say. Would she look for him? But she had her living medicine, one surprisingly white. A little sahib.

At least the gossip would stop, Hiran thought, but still he felt wistful.

He lost his appetite, fainted one morning on deck during his daily stroll. His body shook violently with fever, feet swelling up to his thighs. For three nights he suffered from acute cramps, unable to crawl to the ship's toilet. His groans attracted complaints to the captain. Almost by chance, they discovered a doctor on board – a Dutchman who had been appointed Consul for Sardinia and was travelling back to Europe. He examined Hiran's box of glass bottles, smiled, and offered to take blood, 'Blood and rosy port!' Hiran was bled twice, then left to recover in the cabin with the gunner offering to keep watch.

Over a week later Hiran woke to find the black Madrasee smiling down at him. He laced his wound with bark, brought him water and, just as he showed signs of diarrhoea, C&O pills from the Dutch doctor. When he slept, strange dreams lifted Hiran's spirits, only to bring him crashing down again in agony. He needed more pills. Camphor and opium.

He heard himself speaking in the voice of the donkey in the cucumber field. His throat filled with ragas. A clear sky stared back at him like a mirror. He saw himself, and a thousand others, the naked blades of their knives reflecting the moon. He kept on singing.

He saw a face close to his. A golden cross danced before his eyes. Then he felt breathing burn his naked skin. He longed to turn his face and behold his goddess. She was there – covered with golden sawdust – waiting to dance with her consort. He longed to see her radiant flames burning them both, as they locked in embrace.

Then he would fly like the bird whose wings were many thousand li in breadth. Rising with a mighty effort above the sea, like a cloud. He saw the ocean far below like a celestial lake, yet at the same time felt the eyes of fish staring at him in wonder.

The Madrasee held him down with strong arms, throttling his groans with a pillow. His skin felt both hot and cold. He was a butterfly, fluttering hither and thither, a body with no substance entering where there was no crevice.

He dreamt of Lilian, the nun with the shaven head, hanging from a beam, a sack over her head. Vinny and Reverend Martyn stood arm in arm, a snake coiled around their necks. They called him.

The doctor stopped the blood-letting, fed him dried fish and pickles. The other passengers laughed to themselves over the opium-wallah's plight. 'Now he knows the taste of his own medicine!'

By the time they arrived in Malacca, Hiran's fever had gone. He remained mostly awake, weak, uncomprehendingly sad. His nurse shared his cabin when the gun-deck spared him. Hiran didn't know what to say. *Did you know of Indians fighting alongside Scots and Irish in China? There is one – a gunner – from that campaign, still here.*

He saw himself in their courtyard in Patna, running around his mother, memorizing slokas. It was morning, she had lit a wood and dung fire to boil water for his bath. Smoke filled his eyes, and he started to cry. His mother wiped his tears with the edge of her aanchal. She was crying too – remembering the morning Hira's father had left her to worship his patron's god. He tried to soothe his mother, but his words only upset her more.

On the deck he saw a sunless sea – womblike, still. His

thoughts dispersed in the wind, floated over the surf and sank. He gazed at the heavenly embryo – churning, tongues of a million gods lashing endlessly, a deep navel in its elixir of immortality. The Creation Hymn was on his lips, *Rig Veda* – the first.

> There was neither non-existence nor existence then; when the realm of light was immersed in the realm of darkness. What stirred? Where? In whose care? Was there water, fathomless, deep?
>
> There was neither death nor immortality then. The One breathed by its own desire. Desire came upon that one in the beginning. All this was water; there was a seed. There was desire beneath, and power. Order and truth were born from the heat. From that was born night; from heat was born a billowy ocean.
>
> Moon was born from his mind; from his eyes the sun. And from his breath wind was born.
>
> Who really knows? Whence this creation? Gods came afterwards – drew forth a sun hidden in the ocean. Who then knows?
>
> One who desired – or perhaps he does not know.

Alone, Hiran felt the eternal rhythm: the breath of desire – from spirit to life – and then the other, the returning breath.

At Munikhali, barely a day's sail from Calcutta, they weighed anchor. A familiar night, buzzing mangroves and uncanny jackals, kept him awake. Captain Jacque called for an all-night ramble on deck with burning torches. 'That'll keep the tigers away.' He winked at Hiran. 'Might even be a present from the Maharajah of Oudh!'

As Hiran sat on deck listening to the first mate playing the banjo, a cutter flying the Jack drew alongside and a burly man beamed up at the *Warrior Queen*, blowing smoke from his cheroot. Then he and the captain disappeared into the coop.

They left almost as quickly as they came. 'A small but delicate business,' Captain Jacque explained. The passengers nodded gravely, then gazed at the departing cutter, speeding away with Mr Crabbe on board. 'Charges of defalcation, I'm afraid. Must answer for unlawful profits from opium.' Sitting on the cutter, Mr Crabbe's face was half-turned towards the buzzing mangroves.

'It'll be livelier in gaol, I suppose,' the first mate quipped.

The sin of passage took a further toll on Hiran. Heads leaned over balconies to catch a glimpse of the man who waited in a phaeton below. Saraladebi looked worried. A visit from sahibs and policemen could only mean trouble.

Mr Kavasji smiled at him, then led him to where his phaeton stood waiting. He made the usual enquiries, then cleared his throat. 'Listen, Hiran,' he said, 'I have come to you about something important. Our friends, you know, have fallen into special circumstances. Quite unfortunate, of course. They are required to return to England, at least for a short while, so that matters can be sorted out. It's all so sudden. So sad,' he went on, smiling through his pince-nez.

'Of course, there's nothing to worry us. We'll miss them though, won't we? They have left everything behind at number fifteen. Douglas too, not quite the right moment to introduce him, I suppose. Our friends, Hiran, have asked for Douglas to be placed in your care. They hate to trouble you, but you've been such a loyal friend. Perhaps it is for the best. For all.'

He pointed at the phaeton where Lilian's maid sat with the boy in her lap.

'If you agree, I shall inform them that Douglas has found a home in India.'

Throughout that morning, and for days afterwards, a steady procession passed by their attic room, scattering his mother's herbs. They came to see the boy, as he slept on Hiran's bed. Like a strange animal, he seemed to charm and repel at the same time.

'He's an orphan, sold by gypsies . . .'

'No. He's Hiroo's Christian brother, born of a priest and a whore . . .'

'He's their new tenant!'

'He has the same forehead . . .'

Saraladebi barred her door. 'I asked for a grandson, not a serpent.'

Only Annada didn't seem to mind the boy, displayed an affection in keeping with her character. She followed him with a glass of milk, listened patiently to his chatter and escorted him to Madan Mohon Jiu's temple for an evening's aarati. A deep layer of kajal made him look almost 'natural'. Some who saw him took him for an albino. As they returned through the alleys, she'd cover his ears lest his young mind took note of sharp words.

In the beginning, Hiran hoped for a letter from England. *Dear*

Hiranbaboo, We wish to express our deep gratitude to you for caring for Douglas. You'll be glad to learn that our period of difficulty is over, and that we shall return soon to number 15. We wish you'd communicate to Douglas . . .

He wished he could have Nabinbaboo's advice. But Nabinbaboo wasn't to be seen at the Auction House any more. 'Banished to Kashi by his brothers,' the peon confided in hushed tones. 'Squandered fortunes, sank the family's name. Bankrupted by debtors. Them too.' The peon motioned towards the west wing.

'Yes. Nabinbaboo was Crabbe's favourite moneylender – borrowing lavishly for his parties, her china, everything! How do you think they lived the way they did? Not on an officer's salary! He promised to pay it all back, and Nabinbaboo believed him. This is how it always ends,' he sighed. 'Between lender and borrower – one bankrupt, the other disappeared.'

'He hoped for a big catch. They both did. Mr Crabbe was confident our mud would make him rich. Nabinbaboo had a fit when he heard of the corruption charges. Flew into a rage, smashed up all his glass bottles.'

Hiran longed for Vinny.

Gradually, the 'unnatural' began to seem 'natural'. Hiran gave up his bed to the boy, slept himself on the terrace under the open sky. He bought him cricket bats, flannel pants, a pair of whistling maynahs. They went together to the kennel on Alipore Road, passing the boundary wall of number 15 on the way. Hiran watched the boy closely. Did he remember and long for his missing parents?

They became a familiar sight – the two of them winding their way through the narrow alleys, engrossed in stories. Sitting on their roof, gazing up at battling kites. Donkeys and birds, fools and snakes seemed as inextricable to their daily regime as the mission school which Douglas now attended. Whenever he was free, Douglas would look for his Baboo, flood him with endless curiosity.

'One day the farmer appealed to the donkey for help. A swarm of pigeons devouring seeds was turning his field barren. *Uddhata* agreed to guard his crop and bray to scare away the birds. In return he asked for an organ, one played with the mouth . . . just like the one belonging to the boy who sits with his father at the kite shop.' His eyes gleamed.

'Why would he need an organ, when he himself is a master of ragas?' Hiran asked.

'Because birds may be drawn by his braying, in the hope of fresh cucumber!'

Hiran laughed. 'And who would *you* scare away with your mouth organ?'

Douglas pointed towards Mahim's window, made a frightful face. 'Ghosts!'

Despite Saraladebi's anger, and the curiosity of strangers, both seemed to have crossed the bridge between the 'white' town and the 'black' – from number 15 to century-old Jaanbazaar. Soon the family tree would entwine another among its numerous shoots. One without a holy thread over his shoulder.

His schoolfriends called him by many names. To the teachers, he was simply Douglas Arthur Crabbe, the ward of Baboo Hiranyagarbha Chakraborti.

Hiran lost count of the seasons, of the years since his return on the *Warrior Queen*, and Douglas's arrival on Mr Kavasji's phaeton. The boy was his, truly.

Then, when he was twenty, he returned home at midnight – drunk, mouthing obscenities, strewing their attic and Saraladebi's altar with filth – just like the half-caste blackie-white beef-eating chillicracker that he was.

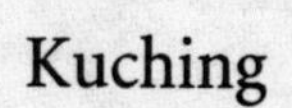

Kuching

It would take nothing short of a miracle to save them. By 1914, war had broken out in Europe. Almost a miracle. It brought smiles to the faces of the workers at the Patna factory, and to the gentoos at the Auction House, hungry for a daily feed of paper.

The twentieth century had started disastrously for all those involved with opium. International treaties threatened to ban the trade. From Europe to Asia, men gathered to pass laws that would make it illegal to grow or sell the poppy, except for medicinal purposes. Everyone seemed to be infected by the zeal: the British and the French, the Dutch, Portuguese, Americans, even the Chinese.

Yet the times had never been better for the mud. It had spread rapidly throughout the Americas, scattered by railroad labourers from China. In England, it spread among the sailors and shipbuilders, among miners in Australia, and plantation workers in Borneo. The bans threatened to ruin everything, spoil the fortunes of traders and growers alike.

War changed all that. Turned attention away from treaties, spurring on further demand – among soldiers and their victims. But it would be different now. Morphine, delicate and flowing, interested a different breed of suitors. Some came from as far away as the Danube, some from Edinburgh and London. Men of science and skill, they dutifully followed the armies, bringing succour to the battlefields with a needle.

But the orderly flow was disrupted – Calcutta to Malacca,

Hong Kong, Macao, and Canton. Now, the mud needed concealment and diversion. From Calcutta, it travelled in the false bottoms of crates and trunks, under false labels, hidden inside canvas bags, wrapped under blankets. Who would smell it among a case of dried shrimp, or soap? Who would suspect it nested inside eggshells, or fancy it snug in Bologna sausage!

A good decade after the removal of the infamous Crabbe for profiteering, the Auction House persisted with files and ledgers – registering the flow precisely. Letters still arrived and equal care was taken to reply. Gentoos mulled over fine distinctions, treating petitions and appeals with due attention. Even Lord Kydd could not have spotted the difference.

Sitting under an electric punkah and an electric bulb, but still facing the river, Hiran heard a new rhythm: Kobe and Basel, Chicago, Yokohama . . .

Rarely seen at the Auction House since his retirement, Mr Kavasji aroused curiosity: a man in a white muslin sudra asking his way around the east wing. The new peon took him for a Christian Father. His cane tapping up the wooden stairs, he came to a halt at Hiran's door, waited long for a pause, then gently cleared his throat.

Both the visitor and the visited were cautious at first. Mr Kavasji, smiling as always, reached inside his kisseh-i-kerfeh, the pocket of good deeds, and showed Hiran a white envelope with an embossed red crown. A telegram. Inside, Hiran found Mr Jonathan Crabbe's announcement of his wife's sad demise in London, for the notice of their friends in Calcutta.

Hiran would have grieved for Lilian if he could have remembered her face at the balcony of number fifteen. By the end of their acquaintance, she had appeared less herself, resembling other memsahibs he had known, tending a fleet of ayahs and gardeners. Did they cure her in the end? he wondered.

Even after her departure, he would spot her by mistake in a crowd, a fair face would distract him from the scent of bread-baking in Signor Peliti's shop in Cossitola. He'd fancy he saw her at the flower show, clutch Douglas in alarm.

He had heard gossip of her for a while. Captains and boatswains had fed the flow, reporting talk overheard at whist tables. An Armenian visitor to the Auction House swore he had seen her at a private club in London, holding court among a handful of startled ladies, 'tipsy, positively'.

Usually the talk depicted her in less exalted circles – banished to a lunatic asylum in chains, in the brothels that lined London's docks, or returned to the Fens.

He remembered her searching for Douglas who had hidden under an enormous fern in the lawn.

As he returned that evening from the Auction House, Hiran tried to recall the precise words of the telegram. *Lilian has departed, sadly* . . . Memories of number fifteen flooded back, like memories of a distant childhood. He tried to remember her as Vinny's 'sleepy memsahib', as Nabinbaboo's 'patient'. Then he remembered that they had all left together, like a fleet of clippers, leaving him alone with Douglas.

He had waited for years for a postcard from Macao – one with a picture of European homes facing the promenade, and a tall pagoda. When Vinny did not return, he had gone over to the west wing and asked Mr Kavasji. Even Mr Kavasji didn't know.

Over the years he had checked the lists of arriving vessels, hoping for news of the *Warrior Queen.* But of Captain Jacque he heard nothing. Some claimed the captain had joined the gold rush in America. Others had him dead in a typhoon, or kidnapped by pirates off the coast of Sandakan.

Vinny would have approved, he felt, of his raising Douglas as his own in Jaanbazaar. But his approval would have been mixed with caution: *You must raise him as a black, or a white. Not both. He must have one heart, jewel.* He would have laughed at Douglas's stories. *He's growing up to be a Military Brahmin!* Advised Hiran to vanish with the boy. *Take him to Patna, to the land of his ancestors.* With a serious face he would have described the senior priest's disbelief: a tiny white boy laying claim to the home of Jyotirmoy Chakraborti!

Where was Vinny now? Dead or alive? In a bandit's lair? Who would pay his ransom . . . or the one for Marie?

Hiran imagined them together on the *Warrior Queen*, huddled over the forecastle. Vinny, as usual, would be the first to probe. *They say you don't care for the living or the dead . . . not even your poor mother. They say you can't be angry, can't suffer . . . true?*

But Hiran's suffering had begun. Fear clutched at his throat when he thought of losing Douglas. Every morning, he repeated a list of instructions for Annada: escort the boy to the mission school, stopping on the way to buy his favourite sweets, make him bathe and gulp a mouthful of bitter herb from Saraladebi's store. She should mark his forehead with a spot of black to ward off evil, keep an eye out for him as he swam in the neighbourhood pond. On days of minor celebration, she was to help him fast with glasses of lime water mixed with sugar. 'What if he asks for a thread like his cousins?' 'Tell him he's too young for one.' They took turns staying up at night when the damp air of their attic threatened his young lungs.

What if the snake wants him back?

What if he grows up a Jack-tar, or a 'Student Enquirer'?

He suffered for the orphan as he had never done for his dead father. Like his mother, he worried over how to protect the boy from their neighbours. Gradually, he was drawn into Annada's stories of malice and hate. He fought with everyone – his aunts and cousins, the maids, even the little boys who chased Douglas over the roof with words their parents taught them. Jaanbazaar whispered behind his back – their Hiroo, gone mad over a little white devil.

You'd choose a chillicracker over your mother!

When he looked at the boy, he heard the pounding of hoofs. His father's heart beating in him.

One more time, Vinny seemed to urge him on. *You have become his father, jewel!*

Who can replace a dead father?

It sat on his teak almirah, facing a travelling clock from Messrs Cooke & Kelvey. The wrapper from Mr Pinchback's shop had lost its brilliant gloss, mould adding a patina in keeping with the texture of a century-old house. Perhaps Vinny would return to claim it; until then Marie's wedding present sat unnoticed, except during bouts of cleaning, when Annada would take it on to the roof to dry out in the sun.

Then Douglas discovered it. He showed it to Saroma – the mochtar cousin's daughter – and together they unwrapped it by the light of an oil-lamp. They found a handsome box, and in that, a golden butterfly, its spread wings set with gems. There was a key as well – about the size of a thumb. Saroma held up the butterfly in her delicate fingers, while Douglas wound the lock concealed beneath a set of shapely feelers. It started to hum and whir, shaking its wings as if to fly away from her palm. In surprise, Saroma dropped it, but it kept on whirring for a long while.

On quiet afternoons, they would open the box again. Saroma, more than Douglas, was drawn to it. She asked for it to be wound every time it stopped, never venturing with the key herself. Then, one day they lost the key in a pile of knick-knacks. Afterwards, they would just open the box and sit before the butterfly, imagining its whir.

'Once *Vishnu* disguised himself as a dwarf and came before the court of *Bali* – the demon king. This was after the great battle between gods and demons. Bali had defeated the gods, and ruled over the universe. Surrounded by cruel generals, he received the dwarf. *Vishnu* asked him for a boon. "O King, ruler of rulers, give me the space covered in three strides." *Bali* was flattered. How far could a dwarf walk? he thought, then he agreed. Neither he nor his consorts recognized the danger. Then the dwarf – the Lord – stepped over the heaven, the sky, the earth, and the universe in three strides.'

Clapping his hands, Douglas pressed Hiran for more stories of disguise: *Vishnu* as a boar saving the earth, as a fish rescuing *Manu* from the great floods, as a tortoise, a lion . . . 'Even demons know the trick of disguise, don't they?' Hiran frowned at Douglas. 'You mustn't make up stories about gods and demons.'

'It's the *Mahishasura*, the buffalo-demon, have you forgotten? He attacked the Goddess after she destroyed his army. She hurled a noose over him, he escaped and became a lion. She cut off his head, he appeared as a man. She pierced him with arrows, he became a giant elephant.' Hiran looked at the boy amazed.

Demons were Douglas's favourites: *Picasa* the flesh-eater, *Susna* the scorcher, *Ghatotkaca* the headless monster. Even *Saroma* was a demon, wasn't she – *Indra*'s messenger, seduced by rotten *Panis*? Douglas would tease Saroma, until Hiran came to her rescue.

To the residents of Jaanbazaar, Douglas was a demon. He was *Kaliya* the snake. They blamed the half-caste boy for corrupting their sons, for their failure at the tole, breaking a fast, or hiding passion cards under books of slokas.

Annada usually offered the protection of her tongue. Like a thunderbolt, her fury would streak from the attic to the door of the offender. The boy was pure, she'd declare, 'Purer than pimps and brahmins!'

Some days, Saraladebi herself would leave her room and join the stream of accusers, shouting at Douglas as he hid under Hiran's bed. Grown frail over the years, she'd clutch her maid's arm and demand to speak with Hira. Annada would try calming her with lies, *The boy will be sent away soon to a hostel.* Unconvinced, Saraladebi would scream at the boy. *It's a monster!* she'd shout, then she'd lunge at him. When Hiran returned, she'd make a face at him too.

'Kill me, Hira. That's what you want. Then you can marry your mem and live with your little boy.'

Douglas's best moments were reserved for his Baboo, and his for Douglas. Returning home from the Auction House, Hiran would find Douglas on their roof, ready with his kites, or glass marbles. From early evening till late, an ageing man still in his office coat and a little white boy ran around the jars of drying herbs, shouting to other boys on neighbouring rooftops. Annada would warn them not to topple the jars, urge them to finish their afternoon's glasses of goat's milk. They would ignore her, pulling impatiently on the line of a sagging kite.

Late evening was reserved for stories. From Hiran's *Panchatantra*, they had moved on to those they made up themselves. Pointing at Mahim's closed window, Douglas said he had seen a ghost sitting inside, scolding the portraits that hung on the walls. 'He was beating them with a stick, shattering the glass!' Hiran laughed.

'Did the ghost punish his Byron too?'

'Byron?'

*

In the space of a summer, their relationship changed. It started with a scream from the well of the dark courtyard. Heads rushed to the balcony, stuck out from between gunnysack curtains. Perhaps Annada had seen a ghost inside the well . . . the dead coachman, of course . . . pulling her down by her hair, like a demon . . .

Annada screamed again. Then they saw what she saw – Mahim, paying the coachman at the gate.

By the time he had collected his belongings and climbed the stairs, their neighbours were agog with speculation.

'He's ill. Blind in one eye. The sahibs have robbed him of his health.'

'He has lost everything. Didn't you see him beg the coachman to be let off. Pity a brahmin's son forced to return a beggar.'

'His mem will follow soon. She's coming by the next boat.'

'That'll make two of them on the roof. It's time to get out of Jaanbazaar!'

Saraladebi wasn't spared either. 'Now she'll have a full circus. God knows how many white monkeys Mahim will bring home.'

In his haste, Hiran stepped in a vat of drying herb, spreading a cloud over the roof. When the dust cleared, he saw a man in a dhoti and aachkan, dragging behind him a portmanteau. For a moment, Hiran was uncertain. The man appeared too thin, with a sharp Adam's apple. His hair, usually tumbling and unruly over his forehead, was plastered back. And he seemed reserved, but determined in an oddly childish way.

Mahim smiled at Hiran, then bowed to touch Saraladebi's feet. She raised her right palm, and wiped his face gently with her aanchal. Brother and sister stood facing each other for a moment. Then Saraladebi sighed and took out her keys to open the tall shutters that barred Mahim's window.

Over the next month, Hiran hesitated to renew his acquaintance with his uncle. In part it was his own regret at failing to fulfil his uncle's prophecy that held him back. *I shall return and find you an Editor, no less than Derozio, teaching these stupids a lesson!* Had he become a *stupid* in Mahim's eye – a simple keranee minding the flow of mud from his table by the river?

But it was also that Mahim seemed strangely quiet – almost sad. Even Saraladebi noticed it. One morning, she found him standing before her shrine. At first she thought it was Hiran, early for his puja. She felt the usual sting of betrayal, for what use was a prayer when the heart was impure? Then she realized it was Mahim – barefoot, still in his dhoti and aachkan – eyes fixed somewhere between the deity and the rising sun. She saw his shoulders quiver in the morning breeze. He seemed frail, almost transparent.

Hiran felt worried too, but about Douglas. What would Mahim make of him? Would he believe the gossip? The boy, he knew, was curious to meet his 'ghost'. Then one day he found Mahim and Douglas together. Through the tall windows, Hiran saw Douglas pacing before Mahim's desk. Mahim wore an amused smile. He seemed to stop the boy every now and again, appearing to disagree, then let him go on. He'd nod his head vigorously, or frown. Douglas too seemed more animated than usual, charged like an actor.

Hiran felt a pang of loss.

One evening Annada came to Hiran with a red face, motioned him to follow her to the dark stairwell. Mahim, she said, had been seen entering a house – a 'known house' – in Boubazaar's alleys. The man frying oil at the corner had seen him: an umbrella covering his face, a string of jasmine coiled around his arm. 'He's been trapped by a tigress! Spends all his money on her. You must save him.'

'What if he has some other business?' Hiran felt ashamed of his own foolishness.

'There's only one business in a whorehouse.'

Gradually, Hiran plucked up enough courage to re-enter Mahim's quarters. He came to sit on his bed on Sunday mornings and listen to his uncle read aloud from newspapers, as he had used to do before he left for England. Only now, in place of the *Calcutta Gazette* and the *Calcutta Chronicle*, he read from the *Sanjibani* and the *Bangadarshan*. Hiran saw new portraits on the walls of his untidy room. 'Freedom fighters,' his uncle called them, some dressed as college students, some looking like prisoners. And a white woman, hair tied up in a golden bun.

'Annie Besant,' Mahim said. 'She's one of us. Three quarters of her blood and all her heart are Irish!'

Hiran waited for an explanation. Instead, Mahim threw down a copy of the newspaper. Hiran read:

> The English have taken all which the Natives possessed; their lives, liberty, and property. We are made to feel as helots, hewers of wood and drawers of water in our land of birth. Men are pervaded with a sense of helplessness, they are convinced that they would starve and die; they want to do something. We have become weak, lifeless; anyone may lord over us. Our shouting has no more effect than the sound of a gnat. But, the future belongs not to those who rule the lesser breeds without the law, Manchester manufacturers, or those within Congress who profess a policy of prayer and petition. The future belongs to the imagination of young men.

And yet, in Hiran's mind, Mahim hardly fitted the image of a revolutionary. He had seen then picketing Lalbazaar's Police Station, singing songs, shouting slogans. He'd seen bonfires too, burning English cloth, tobacco, jewellery, gramophone records, a grand organ set ablaze before a zamindar's house on Old Court House Street. At the Auction House there was talk of 'Home Rule'. 'The British have learned a lesson. After the war is over, India will be free.'

The war was on everyone's mind. Indian soldiers were dying for Britain in Mesopotamia, in the Channel Ports, Sudan and Egypt, China, Palestine, and Aden.

'England's adversity is India's opportunity,' Mahim said. Hiran had come prepared with arguments.

'But surely the British are better than Bismark.'

'We are in no way accountable to an alien people.' His uncle seemed unwilling to concede. 'Don't you think it's hypocritical to pray for victory over autocracy in Europe, and to maintain it in India?'

Hiran had seen men-of-war lined up before the Banyan Tree Village. Surely, Mahim had seen them too – the instruments of maximum inequality.

'Not much muscle is required to shoot Europeans, Hiroo.' His uncle described how black Abyssinians were lynching Italians in Adow, spoke of Japan's victory over Russia. 'Look what the newspaper says: "The native soldier has accepted the service of the Government for the sake of his stomach. They too are men of flesh and blood; they know how to think. When the time comes, the revolutionaries will have the support of native soldiers, and their English arms." '

Hiran worried for Douglas. The boy spent his evenings with Mahim now. The terrace rang with laughter and singing. Douglas had grown taller, seeming taller than other boys of his age. A pair of grey eyes blended into lighter hair, broad lips seemed perpetually open – about to speak, to sing, or smile. When not in Mahim's study, he could be found on a mat facing the sun – his limbs bent into incredible positions. Hiran wasn't exactly sure who had taught him the yogic postures. The parents of the other boys began to admire him for unslovenliness, while to their sons he was the undisputed leader. Annada pressed Hiran, 'Purify him from his unholy parents. Make him a brahmin.'

'What good would that do?' Hiran frowned.

'Then he can marry a brahmin's daughter, not some half-caste.'

Saroma came to look for him, to play with their boxed butterfly. But she rarely found Douglas now. Hiran offered her the box and promised to return to Mr Pinchback's shop to buy her a new key. But she declined, hoping to return again, to find Douglas.

Hiran worried about more than half-caste girls. He had heard stories of young boys drawn into dangerous games: throwing bombs at Englishmen, robbing trains, boycotting English goods, burning the Royal Portrait, courting gaol.

He would glance over the terrace at Mahim's window – at a head stooped over books.

Then Douglas disappeared. When he returned one evening from the Auction House, Hiran found Annada waiting for him before the arched gate of Jaanbazaar.

'He has returned to his mother. Go find him,' she wept. He was last seen, it seemed, before a fireworks shop. He had gone with the other boys to buy crackers, had bought himself a dozen rockets. Then, he had asked the others to go back, staying himself for a further look.

Panic gripped Hiran. His first instinct was to barge into Mahim's study, but Annada told him Mahim was ill, sleeping under a dose of Saraladebi's herbs. He thought of his mochtar cousin. A man from the Courts must know where to find a missing boy. The mochtar had already warned him: 'Control your Douglas, or there may be trouble,' he had said. 'The Lieutenant Governor is a hard man, he won't think twice about sending a boy to gaol, or having him flogged. Tell him to stop these games.'

Annada and Hiran hovered between hope and despair. Hiran asked her to go over secretly to Saroma. Maybe the girl would know. But she returned with a glum face. Saroma didn't know where Douglas was. She had found, though, a handbill printed on coarse paper among his books. Hiran read an announcement for a play – *Anandamath* – he knew of that play, had seen a copy of it among Douglas's books, a gift from Mahim.

The man frying oil in Boubazaar's alley pointed towards a vacant field behind an abandoned temple. He told Hiran that the play was to be staged there by the boys of the Boys' Association. Didn't Hiran know of the Boys' Association? The man seemed surprised at Hiran's ignorance. They were the best, he said, best in everything. One after another, the man rattled off their merits: masters of yoga, masters of books, first to help the poor and starving. 'They never wear anything but a white dhoti and a white aachkan.' The man stared disapprovingly at Hiran's coat. Their plays too were different, unlike the frolic of baboos at the Emerald or the Star. He looked at Hiran sternly. The boys were interested in freedom.

Hiran knew about the abandoned temple, a den for trouble-makers.

For the best part of the night he sat in Douglas's room reading the *Anandamath*. He read about unjust rulers and bandits, dying peasants, and an army of monks. He felt a knot in his stomach, going over passages sparkling with the blood of sacrifice. He could imagine the boys chasing each other in costumes armed with crackers and rockets. The temple erupting in mock gunfire. He sat reading long after Annada had fallen asleep. Then, when Douglas returned, he dragged the boy out of the room on to the open roof, and for the first time and the last, dealt a blow to his fair face, promising all the while to never, *never* let him dwell again in the dangerous world of stories.

Next morning Hiran visited Mahim in his study. He had come prepared with the mochtar's warning: 'They're watching Jaanbazaar. One wrong move and we'll all end up hanging like terrorists.'

With a white bust between them, he had started angrily, then spelt out his arguments in a measured tone, like the teachers at the mission school.

Just like his old self, Mahim had shot back:

Sparta, Sparta why in slumbers
Lethargic dost thou lie?
Awake, and join thy numbers
With Athens, old ally!

None knew where their mud went any more. Even without a Superintendent, the west wing carried on its monthly auction, with scrambling gentoos filling up ledgers almost as quickly as the chests emptied.

Occasionally there were disquieting reports – men agitating against opium, blaming the British for drugging a nation. Indians returning from England – those joining up with the likes of Gandhi – were particularly strident. There was trouble in Assam – followers of Gandhi had dumped a boat's supply into the Brahmaputra.

Saraladebi knocked on Hiran's door after her evening puja. He was surprised to see her. She rarely came from her room, and was hardly on speaking terms with him any more.

'Give me your medicine, Hira.'

He was puzzled.

'The one you make with your white friends.' She pointed towards the river.

He decided to ask Annada about his mother.

'Your mother is happy, she doesn't remember your father any more, or the horses. She is like a little girl, yet to be married. Ask her about Patna, she'd say it was a fish!' Hiran wished to ask her about afim, but Annada dodged with a clever lie, 'Who knows what they sell in shops these days – beans painted black, or afim.'

Hiran saw his mother again, at midnight, strolling over the roof. A soft moan floated around her white saree – like a spirit from the temple's ruin.

'Why don't you take him with you to the Auction House?' Annada said, pointing towards Douglas. Hiran was surprised. It hadn't occurred to him that there was a simple solution to Douglas's problem. He stayed awake that night, scheming. What would he tell the boy, and Mahim? What would he tell the gentoos in the east wing? How could he get the boy a job at the Auction House?

His Section Head feigned seriousness. 'Whose son is he?' Hiran said he didn't know. 'Tch-tch.' The Head nodded sympathetically.

'Then who'll vouch for his character and conduct?' Hiran said *he* would. Was he, then, a relative, the son of a friend perhaps?

Hiran told him the boy was a half-caste, raised by priests.

The Head lowered his voice. 'Try the captains, Hiranbaboo. They are known to be looking for smugglers.'

Finally, Hiran gathered the courage to write a letter to Mr Brown the senior officer: *Dear Sir, I am writing on behalf of a needy boy, most obedient, and appearing for his matriculate examination. I hereby beg you to consider him.* It was returned to his desk by the peon, bearing Blinkey Brown's scribble in the margin. *Yes, send him over.* He was relieved by Mr Brown's assurance that he would find a place for Douglas in the Auction House.

What would he say to Mahim? Better a humble keranee than a *dirty nigger*? He feared Mahim's influence with Douglas. In the end he decided to approach the boy himself with his proposal.

He made several false starts. 'Once there was a vain lion . . .' 'Once *Indra* spurned the poor brahmin . . .' 'Once a lioness raised a half-caste – a cross between a lion and a jackal . . .' Douglas smiled at him. Annada had already told him all about the office frequented by sailors. The boy knew a great deal more about the trade and auctions than Hiran had imagined. 'Is it true there are special guards to protect the chests of mohors collected each month from the bidders?' He seemed excited and

Hiran was astonished. Once again, Annada's 'solution' surprised him.

And once again Saraladebi cried, but these weren't tears of loss. Once, there had been hope in her despair, whereas now it was final. Her Hira was a keranee simply breeding another. She watched from her room as Annada marked Douglas's white forehead with whiter chandan. As he left to catch the tram to the Auction House with his Baboo, he left with a maid's blessing.

For a long while Mahim's silence puzzled Hiran. His uncle had made no attempt to interfere. Hiran had rehearsed his lines well, taking his cue from Annada. 'Tell him, times have changed. Baboos can no longer afford to play. Ask him where the phaeton went. Ask him how this palace came to resemble a slum. Ask him what he's done with his motor-car. If he tries to stop him, ask him to hand over his hidden mohors.'

But Mahim didn't stop Douglas. Their lives seemed to go on as before – telling stories to each other in the evening, after the boy returned from his job at the Auction House. If anything, Mahim allowed Douglas to complete his stories now with fewer interruptions. They'd leave his study to stroll over the roof, looking down towards the lights of Boubazaar, an ageing native in a dhoti and aachkan, and a European in his recently tailored pea-jacket, like a sahib and his assistant surveying the spoils of battle. Hiran longed to join them. But somehow, the two seemed beyond the need of other company.

At night, he'd try to catch up with Douglas's stories, then share his own. But the boy would fall asleep before Hiran had time to finish.

Hiran had new fears now. To onlookers, Douglas appeared fully European. The Pathan stood up from his seat to salute him when he entered, gentoos stopped to let him pass in the corridor. He sat in a room at the entrance to the west wing, with his own desk. His voice too was like a sahib's: 'Good morning, Mr Brown. Good morning, Sher Alam, leave the durwaja open, will you?'

Hiran's ears were finely tuned for gossip, but for the first month he heard nothing but rumours. Several times he was tempted to stamp on them, and to tell them what the boy wasn't – *not* a whore's son, *not* from a poor one raped by drunken sailors, *not* bought or sold by gypsies. He wanted to tell them the 'real' story about Douglas, but did not. What was the real story? he wondered.

He dreamed of returning to Viper Island. Perhaps they kept records. He remembered the long barracks that surrounded the house. The hospital. He had seen convicts entering and leaving, smocks covering their arms and faces.

Born in a barrack, delivered by a half-caste nurse and a black-Christian doctor, surrounded by convicts dying of snake-bites and plague?

For the first time he felt a real resentment towards his friends from number 15. Why had they not taken the boy with them to England? English gaols were better than Indian palaces, he had heard. He saw Lilian's arm around the boy. Was her love flawed too, like her body? How could she have left him? Was she drugged by her husband, locked into their cabin?

Returning home on the tram, he would hear Reverend Martyn. *For ever yours . . .*

The boy was kind, corrected mistakes in chits in sky-blue ink, rather than vicious red. His head was full of numbers. He could count chests and reckon their value in seconds. The peasants trusted him. Even cheats felt less anxious turning chits over to him. He would ask them to wait, smiling through his grey eyes. They learned the meaning of 'waiting' – a kind refusal in place of the whip.

The boy had a smart head, they said. If only the other sahibs were like him.

Hiran felt he should tell him more – about their mud, the Royal Commission, Mr Crabbe and Scott. Douglas listened patiently as they sat together on the tram, then pointed towards a convoy of boats on the river.

'Look! The Viceroy is sending relief to famined villages. What would happen if he sent our mud instead of rice!' Hiran was confused. 'Why not feed them what they grow?'

Hiran smiled. 'Opium is for profit. Feed afim to peasants and you'll have cripples. Who'd tend the poppy then?'

'What if they took it secretly?'

'They?'

'They. We. All of us. I mean natives. What would the sahibs do with a nation of cripples!'

'That would be suicide.'

Douglas smiled.

He told Hiran the exact number of acres under poppy, in Bengal, in the north, and west. 'It's worse than indigo,' he said.

'But they were growing poppy before the Raj. The Moghuls and Rajahs were their patrons then. Why blame the British?'

Douglas fell silent.

He doesn't yet know the dangers, Hiran thought. A gentoo shouldn't talk like a rich boy returned from England. Much less a blackie-white who looked like a European. Douglas seemed too open, too willing to embrace all.

Gradually, men of the east wing came to accept him, as a Mr Kavasji, somewhere between their own stock and sahibs. Except that fondness replaced derision. The fact that he was a half-caste sometimes came up among the older Section Heads, but they'd simply point it out like a past illness – frightening, but hardly expected to recur. Gentoos felt free in his presence – forgetting to lower their voice, or stand up the moment he entered the room. He would return the Pathan's salute with one of his own, making the old face break into a grin. He went frequently to Socials – open to all – but not to the Governor's Ball. Few spoke of him as a half-caste, fewer still mentioned Lilian or Jonathan Crabbe. Among the officers it was still a touchy subject.

Hiran was relieved. He did not want his boy mixing with British officers. God knew how they would treat him.

'You must get him married,' Annada said, straining herbs for her sherbet. 'Otherwise, he'll end up just like you.'

For once, Hiran agreed. It was time, indeed, for a brahmin's boy to marry. And a groom with a job in a British company would be in demand. It was time to plan for grandsons, a larger home with a courtyard and trees. There would be a daughter-in-law to take over his duties at the shrine, freeing Hiran for the little ones that would follow.

He was doubtful still. 'Who'd marry his daughter to a half-caste?'

Even the usually agile Annada was silent. She looked up from her sherbet towards the monsoon clouds, hoping to see a 'solution'. There was one, she knew – the outcast *Shiva* living apart from the gods, among half-demons and beasts. *Daksa*, father of *Sati*, was opposed to her marriage with *Shiva*. Fearing to lose his daughter to a stranger, he refused to listen, or to grant his blessing. But the outcast triumphed in the end.

Still, Annada was not sure. *Shiva* was a god, after all!

Hiran woke on *Janmastami*, weak from fasting. He had spent the evening preparing offerings. Annada bathed the dark stone Krishna in rose-scented water, wrapped him in new silk and gold beads. Hiran would fast from midnight to noon, without even a drop of water.

His teacher had taught him the trick: 'Smell the bubbling rice for as long as you can. Saliva will drench your coat, then retract gradually till the stomach feels full – just as if you have been at a grand feast!'

He rose with a headache and nausea, heard Annada pouring water over the terrace, and the rustle of her broom. The familiar sound lulled him to sleep again. He could feel the trickle of a half-century of *Janmastamis* on their roof, and those that would wake him again with an empty stomach. He heard the distant blowing of a conch shell. Then he heard another wave – a rising surf over a restless sea. It seemed to be all around, surrounding his attic like a storm. Then the storm broke, scattering into a million rapids. He woke instantly.

From his window, he looked down on a sea of dark heads. He caught a fleeting glimpse of Annada running towards Douglas's room. A crash broke the silence of the moment. Her earthen pot lay scattered over a thin film of water.

'Bring him out. Bitch!'

He saw a few faces he knew in the heart of the swelling mass, Boubazaar's shopkeepers, servants from Madan Mohon Jiu's temple, the man who fried oil by their alley, pimps, and in among them his mochtar cousin. His cousin seemed the most aggrieved, egging the mob on with a string of curses.

'One half-caste breeds another.'

'Corrupt brahmins, raising a snake in this clean household!'

'Clean as a brothel, you mean!' Annada shot back. 'Blame yourselves for your filth.' More crashes followed. A dazed Hiran, venturing out of his room, faced his cousin.

'Hand him over, Hiroo, before we hunt him down like a dog.'

'Why?' Hiran looked old, standing barechested and weak, with his white thread glowing over pale skin.

'For making you a grandfather.'

Hiran saw more weapons – sticks, iron bars, brooms fitted with needle-sharp thorns. A woman's wail rose like a cloud of smoke from the stairwell. Annada brought her face close to Hiran's, whispered, 'They're claiming our Douglas has given Saroma the belly. She has been raped, they're saying.' The mochtar's wife wailed from the back of the mob.

Someone threw a rock at the figure of Krishna in the shrine. It fell, rolling out of its silk robe.

'Don't wake the monster! Let him sleep his way to hell.'

Hiran saw boys banging on Saraladebi's door. 'Bring the witch out. It's *her* fault.' A burning torch filled their attic roof with smoke.

Where was Mahim? Hiran wondered. His shutters remained drawn, but Hiran was sure his uncle was inside. He knew Mahim could silence them all, and he tried distracting the mochtar.

'But he hardly lives here any more. Out at the Boys' Association –'

'It was his own brother-in-law who did it to the girl,' Annada screamed. 'He's their own kind.' For a moment they were taken aback, then the cursing resumed. 'Now they're pitting brother against brother. The whore's granddaughter!'

'Ask them if it was the priest,' she screamed aloud. 'The poor one was their sacrifice. Ask!'

Hiran wanted to sit down, head spinning from the night's fasting. He had planned to hire a palanquin for his mother, to go for a bath in the Ganga. It was to be his own penance as well – for years of neglect while he was still a gentoo frequenting number 15. The river would be full after the monsoon. He had thought of paying a dinghy-wallah to take him midstream for his ablutions.

What if the boy woke and came out to face the crowd? Hiran thought, panic-stricken. He was smart, but stubborn. He would want to speak to the men wielding sticks. He would step in alone, a young warrior trapped in the enemy's lair.

'Ask them if it's simply envy speaking. The girl isn't pregnant – it's a lie.' Matchmakers, she announced, had chosen Saroma for a rich baboo. She'd become a princess. Mothers were jealous on behalf of their own daughters. 'They've spoiled two innocents with their lies.'

A man with a pock-marked face crept close to Annada, made as if to topple her with a clean swipe. She made a face, threw a jar of herbs at him. The man ducked, the jar missing him by inches, slamming into the side of Hiran's head. He fell, blood streaming down his bare chest, dyeing the sacred thread over his shoulder.

In the moments before he lost consciousness, Hiran felt the surge of feet over the roof – like galloping hoofs – making for the barred door. He heard Annada's scream, and the splintering of wood. And then a man's loud curse, 'The rascal has fled!'

He returned at midnight – drunk, screaming obscenities, strewing the roof with filth. Annada shut his mouth with her palm, dragged him inside. He lay on her bed, cried like an infant cradled in his mother's arms. For a long while he sat by Hiran's bedside – then left. Later, both would wish for a different parting, before each was left to his own darkness.

Annada begged him to take her savings – a small bag of mohors put by for her final years in Kashi. She offered to sell her earrings, but he refused gently. He took the box with the butterfly inside.

On 4 May 1931, an eclipse of the sun was foretold. At the very hour, the *Sultana* arrived in Sarawak from Singapore carrying a regiment of Sikhs.

As the last rim of light disappeared, darkness fell over Kuching, and with it silence. Villagers drove their chickens indoors, dogs slunk under the shadow of stilts. The breeze entered the hollows of empty mines, refusing to draw circles over the river, or rattle coconut groves.

Even the bazaar was empty, the stalls cleared days before. On Khoo Hung Yeang Street, the brothels remained shut. No one knew if the girls were still inside, or if they had escaped to the sampans and praus that floated noiselessly in the harbour. Only a few Europeans on horseback could be seen, on the lookout for a madwoman reportedly running naked through Carpenter Street screaming that the Rajah was dead.

A streak of light appeared, grew, and the day resumed to the sound of prayer. Men emerged into the streets, shaking each other by the hand, and a band of beggars went noisily from door to door, banging on the closed shutters with iron ladles. The river began to flow again.

The Sikhs unwrapped their turbans, letting down great manes of hair to their waists, watched by the *Sultana*'s amazed crew. On the opposite bank, the office of the Borneo Company struck an amiable contrast to the glaring white Fort Margherita with its square gun-ports. A homely-looking house with green and white blinds, it comforted the sea-weary.

Steeples and spires vied for the open sky – St Thomas's Anglican Church, the Roman Catholic Mission to the west, the Mosque Besar, and Moplah temples. Smoke from sago factories blurred crosses and crescents. Astana, the Rajah's palace, stood aloof over closely cropped grass, three long and low bungalows set with squat arches and wooden shingles.

Getting off the *Sultana*, Douglas Crabbe spotted a boy with a beautiful hawk. It was small with bright ruby eyes. The small bird in hood and coloured silk jesse sat on the boy's wrist, red eyes glaring back at the crowd that had gathered around them. The boy seemed only half-awake, startled by the eclipse, one toe of a bare foot missing and the marks of ringworm down his legs.

The bird unfurled its feathers and the crowd shuddered, fearing its claws on their throats. Some threw a coin or two.

For six dollars, Douglas bought the bird from the boy. Then made his way to the Customs House to hand over his papers to his employers. For the next ten years he would take the same curving road until he left, on yet another day of darkness.

To Douglas, it seemed a lost and silent land. For a whole month, travelling from Calcutta to Borneo, stopping all along the coast in Rangoon, Malacca and Singapore, he had heard the symphony of many tongues. In the beginning he had paid attention, tried to decipher natives at the ports from visitors. He was struck by the facility of the captain and his crew, their European mouths filling with strange words and funny sounds. They were passing, he knew, over much-sailed waters – from the Bay of Bengal to the South China Sea through the narrow straits of Malacca – following European ships bound for the Dutch spice islands, the American Philippines, or even Australia. Half-dozing in his cabin, he had tried to remember what he had learned about his destination: Borneo – the big island, floating like a rock a few hundred miles east of Singapore, but infinitely more mysterious. He had learned about the single spot of tranquillity carved out of its wild and primitive jungles – Sarawak, the independent province under friendly British guidance, and its capital, Kuching.

It was a land of many tongues, and as a Customs Inspector at the port, he would need to learn many of these. They would help him forget, he thought, words he no longer wished to remember.

At his lodge by the port, he pulled up the sheets over his head and planned to sleep – deep and dreamless, silent like the hours he spent behind a desk facing the harbour. He wished to hear less, dream nothing, simply keep on like the other officers of the Customs House and their assistants. Like the dozens before him – Heslops, Maddocks, Flemmings – he resolved to hear only the voice of Europe and her subjects speaking in a concert of unsullied harmony.

The Customs House was in perfect order: clean white buildings, and a grass lawn cut close, not even a weed allowed to disfigure the paths. The shapely port windows looked out over the last stretch of green before the river. The rooms felt airy and light despite the paintings which covered very inch of wall. Light reflecting from the glass made the room glow like a prism.

'So, they're sending us children now.' Chief Officer Perkyns stared at Douglas with amusement.

Perkyns wore a blue canvas jacket with an egg stain down the front, white duck trousers creased in naval fashion, flapping untidily over elastic-sided boots. Slightly older than Douglas, in his early forties, he looked more like a public schoolmaster than a man used to the bustle of commerce. His speech too seemed more English than colonial. Also he seemed surprisingly pleased with his visitor.

'I thought they'd send us a regular. You know, the sort that drinks till sixty and lives till eighty then goes home to retire in a Bloomsbury lodging-home, to ride on a tuppenny bus, and occasionally visit the cinema!'

Chuckling, he recited his own résumé. 'Born in Benares, bred in Bradford, back in Borneo. Are you Crabbe?'

Douglas pointed to the file on Perkyns's desk.

'Yes.'

'Made them miserable, did you? That's why they had you exiled from the bosom to the buttocks! Ah, an Auction House man. A head full of numbers, then? Tell me, how many Klings does it take to clean out a cutter?'

He smiled at Douglas's hesitation. 'All in good time, Crabbe.'

Douglas saw a shelf full of books, not ledgers, but real books. There was a wall of sketches and watercolours of the harbour and the mountains. A telescope pointed towards an open window. Perkyns followed his gaze.

'Let me show you your charge, officer.' With a hand on his shoulder, he led Douglas over to the window. 'Tell me when you see something.'

Through the eyepiece, Douglas saw the blue river, the blue horizon, the blue universe. Shimmering, endless, inescapable. Then he began to see forms – dark ants crowding the edge of blue – some dead as flies, others in motion. Gradually, he saw more – the port coming to life, the wharf, the customs-shed. Perkyns looked on with smiling encouragement.

'See the ones in beads and bangles? Dayaks. Head-hunters.'

Douglas frowned.

'Gosh, no. Nothing to worry about. They're quite shy, really. Might kill a stranger in their village, from fear, not out of malice.'

A line of bare-chested men stood by the dock, waiting to hand over small chits to a man in a blue silk jacket and wide black trousers.

'He's the Chinese headman. There's more than one kind of Chinaman, you see.' Perkyns told him about the Hokkiens, the Teochius, the Cantonese, the Hakkas, and the Chaoanns.

'They're into everything. Some say the Rajah is a Chinaman in disguise! Want a good cabinet – ask a Chinaman. Want to sell your watch – ask a Chinaman. Want a good thief – ask a Chinaman!'

'The Rajah?'

'Yes, and a white one at that. An English Rajah.'

'Of course . . .'

'You've heard of James Brooke, I suppose. He was what you'd call a proper gentleman adventurer. Used his inheritance to sail half-way around the world. Came to Borneo, then struck up a friendship with the local chief – saved him from vicious relatives and other enemies. The chief made him a Rajah out of gratitude.' Seeing Douglas frown, Perkyns moved quickly to assure him, 'Oh yes, he became a sovereign in a sovereign land, no less than the King of England.'

'James Brooke?'

'Dead now, I'm afraid. His descendant.'

Before the end of the morning, and shortly before a shot of Perkyns's favourite 'mid-morning fever-curer', Douglas had seen his 'charge', and had learned the essentials from one who seemed keener on the pursuit of ethnology than the art of administration.

'Dayaks, Chinese, Malays, Sikhs, Madrasees, and the English – one hell of a large family.'

Taking one last look through the telescope, Douglas was struck by the sight of a dark man in priest's white, standing by the side of the pier with an open book in his right hand. Men stopped before him, exchanged greetings, then dropped a coin or two into a box. The priest kept on reading.

'Edward Gunaratnam – he's not your usual Kling. Not your typical Indian, I mean, but a Tamil doctor who treats leper patients at Berhala, and preaches revolution.'

As he sat with Perkyns on the lawn of the Customs House after lunch, Douglas reviewed his new employment – wondered if it would involve more than peering through the telescope.

'We inspect cargo?'

'Oh, yes.'

'And propose penalties and fees to the Magistrate?'

'Oh, yes . . . Acquit and punish too, if you will.'

'You don't mean we have to board ships and search them, do you?'

'Oh, yes. Search you must. Here one is Magistrate, Policeman, Postmaster, and Customs Officer rolled into one.'

They'd all belong to him – and he to them. The business of inspection intrigued Douglas. 'Licensed to kill and maim too?'

'Nothing's prohibited by the Rajah, you know. Except for one thing.'

Douglas's mind rehearsed several possibilities at once. Boarding a ship – inspecting every bunker, davit, wooden case and canvas bag, stripping each sailor of his belongings – all to verify and prevent just one article of illegitimate trade. He went through the list of contraband.

'Opium.'

Silence fell over the lawn. A mess-boy removed their glasses. Walking back to his room, Perkyns spoke quietly. 'Not an ounce, not a tael must escape you, Crabbe. It's forbidden to import your *miracle* from Calcutta, or from anywhere else. We grow our own, you know, and the Rajah's government has a monopoly.'

What if he caught a smuggling captain – one from an English ship, say?

Perkyns smiled. 'Oh, yes. Then you must prepare him to meet other Crabbes at other ports. We must teach him to escape detection. No one must find an English ship in violation of anti-opium treaties.'

A customs officer responsible for all those trading from China to Malaya?

'Oh, yes.' Perkyns fixed his dancing eyes on Douglas. 'We are not a trading company. We are a government.'

He called the boy Angel. From the moment he saw him at Kuching's harbour, sitting with the bird, he knew he would have to hire the boy. The bird was his pet after all. For six dollars, he had bought its keeper too. Angel became the homeboy at Snipe Cottage, Douglas's bungalow, shared the chores with the cook Amma, and the Javanese gardener.

Soon he began to suspect Angel's hand behind the many

mysteries that unfolded at Snipe Cottage. Someone was stealing from the kitchen, Amma complained. Six heads of cabbage became five by the time she returned from a quick visit to the garden. The gardener worried about a curious case of theft – someone was plucking off the white chempaka but sparing the yellow.

Douglas asked Angel about the missing cabbages. The boy frowned. Did he know who had stolen them? 'No, Tuan.' Did he know that Amma suspected him?

'Bluddy pool, Tuan.'

The gardener blamed him too, he told the boy.

'Bluddy pool, Tuan.'

Perkyns applauded his decision to hire the boy. 'Well done, Crabbe! Remember, with natives, the greatest rascal makes the most faithful servant. What will you call him?'

Douglas thought for a while, then bit his lip.

'Angel.'

'Angel!'

'He has to be one, doesn't he, to digest raw cabbages!'

It didn't dampen Amma's suspicion, or the gardener's.

Despite his new position, Angel was rarely seen at Snipe Cottage during the day, following his Tuan home only after the downing of shutters at the Customs House in the evening. Sitting on the lawn, Douglas would hear Angel whistling, bringing him brandypanee and Burmah cheroots with a slow-burning joss stick glowing on a tray. He'd sit for hours with folded hands and a bowed head beside his Tuan, sharing gossip from the bazaar. He would confide in Douglas his fear of ghosts.

'Here, at Snipe Cottage?'

Looking over his shoulder, Angel dropped his voice and spoke about an unhappy spirit.

'Mad Ridley. He came to kill my bird, Tuan.'

Perkyns was amused. 'He means Henry Ridley. Mad Ridley. He made Sarawak famous for rubber. Led a swell life. Lived here before you. Your Snipe Cottage was his dream come true – a real Garden of Eden. He died bankrupt though. His body was found by the river.'

'Why did Mad Ridley come to kill your bird?'

'Because he loves it too much, Tuan.'

'How did you manage to stop him then?'

'I caught him.' Angel showed his bare palms.

The SS *Madison* arrived from Subu, the province to the north of Sarawak, bound for the Indian Ocean. A veteran of the American Navy, she had spent the last few weeks docked in a 'dry' port. Some 'breaking out' was only to be expected.

'They'll make things hum,' Perkyns said. Japanese brothels were their favourites. 'They're dead to the world there!' Last time, a party had started breaking up a 'house', driving the girls out, fighting among themselves without a stitch of clothing on, boatswains and officers nowhere in sight.

'Only one colour can rule over them. They resent the others. You, Crabbe, must control them on shore.'

'Should the captain be charged then?'

'Try!'

'What's in her hold?'

'Trouble.'

'No, really?'

'Yankees. There's no discipline, not like on an English boat. Their captains are no better than the sailors – singing out orders, joining the Bow, just *a good ol man.*'

Douglas asked the Fire Brigade to station its solitary truck facing the brothels. A row of policemen stood guard before every gaming room of the gambling farms. At half past seven he took the salute, then spoke to the commanding officer – a young Sikh whose father had been exiled from India following the Mutiny. He explained that it was their duty to protect the ship's crew from dangers – unscrupulous shopkeepers mixing water with gin, crooked gambling dens. They were to check every complaint of unfair charge, and bring the offender over to the station.

'Do we have to protect them in the smoke houses too?' the Sikh asked.

'Yes. Ask for the number of divans to be increased to accommodate them if necessary.'

'Now we know why they threw you out of Calcutta!' Perkyns laughed when he heard Douglas's arrangements. 'You want to kill them off, I suppose. Drown them in their own soup. Who do you think will take the boat back then?'

'Leave your muskets at the barracks. Batons will do,' Douglas ordered the nervous Sikh.

Perkyns's eyes grew wider as Douglas recited the list of precautions he had prepared to ensure the safety of the American sailors.

'They'll love you in America! They might offer to take you with them. Is that what you want, Crabbe?'

From ten till noon he patrolled the bazaar, stopping off at the Sylvia picture-house to ask the manager to show a new reel in place of the usual gruesome war story.

The Fire Brigade complained about a decrepit pump and the old hose that usually split when filled with water.

'You won't need to pump water into the hose.'

'Then why are we here?'

'To assure our American friends that we are ready in case of fire.' The man stared at Douglas in disbelief.

As he walked back to the Customs House, he was aware of Angel behind him. On the lawn he was met by a delegation of shopkeepers, come, they said, for permission to close all shops by sunset. Douglas pretended to be rudely surprised.

'What, today! On a day of celebration?'

It was the shopkeepers' turn to be surprised. But the Tuan was new to Kuching. Father Gunaratnam was on their side too, they pointed out. He'd have come with them, if it hadn't been for one of his patients.

Perkyns peered down through the telescope at the open window.

The government of Sarawak, Douglas told the shopkeepers, was their true friend. A friend, too, to all seafarers requesting a berth at the harbour. The sailors, he said, would surely reward the shopkeepers for their kindness. 'I would,' he said, getting up to leave, 'if I were on the SS *Madison*.'

Thunder-showers cooled the city and its troubled inhabitants. One by one, the shopkeepers laid their goods over the pavements to entice customers. Among the customs officers, starched collars wilted in the damp air, shining buckles moulding over. None complained about the longer shift. They knew Mr Crabbe would be kind, give them an extra hour to doze the next day.

From his window, Perkyns could see the distant mast of the SS *Madison* fluttering the Stars and Stripes. Still a few hours before she arrived. Perkyns raised his gin. 'To a hospitable Kuching, and her Customs Officer!' His face clouded. 'Your parents must've left you awfully long in the tropics. How do you speak such good Hindoostani? Surprised the Sikh, I'm sure!'

An hour after sunset, Douglas boarded a cutter and rowed out to the *Madison*, followed by his men in sampans hired from the local fishermen. He could hear the sounds of revelry from the shore, could see a cloud drifting over the bazaar. He knew the sailors were already ashore; were they burning old clothes before invading shops – or something more sinister? Music floated over the brothels, mixed with loud cheers.

Douglas boarded a silent ship. In silence they made their way across the deck to the first row of cabins reserved for the carpenter and the third officer. A light burned at the head of the stairwell. He held a warning finger to his lips and crept down. He heard even breathing from behind the doors, whispers, an occasional cough. Through the crack of a door he saw the captain dressed only in a bathrobe and sprawled over a settee, with a man in a blue silk jacket and wide black trousers. Douglas faintly remembered his name, Ibrahim, a Chinese trader from

Kuching. He told his men to wait along the corridor, then he entered alone.

The captain sprang up with a profusion of apologies, offered a seat to Douglas, eyeing his starched uniform. A sickness following a mystery fever in the outer islands, he explained, had him confined to his cabin. A wound suffered at the hands of pirates refused to heal. It was his age – this 'positively' was his last, his final visit to Kuching. He raised his glass – empty.

By then, Douglas had circled the settee twice, and had picked up the square medicine box from a side table, marked with a doctor's slant: *Three times daily after meals.* Inside he saw rows of gleaming black pearls – Bengal Mud.

By midnight, Douglas was back on dry land with his men, their search of the SS *Madison* exhausted. A solitary prisoner sat silently beside him in his bathrobe. Before returning to Snipe Cottage, Douglas presented the American captain to an astounded Vyner Charles Brooke, the third honourable white Rajah of Sarawak.

'The devil, trying to fool us with his trick!' Sitting over drinks with Douglas in the garden of Snipe Cottage, Perkyns seemed a touch deflated by his own credulity.

'Keeping a whole town busy looking out for his sailors while he finishes his deal.' He called out to Angel for a refill.

'He would be sick, wouldn't he, if he'd followed the doctor's advice. Three times daily after meals!' Inching close to Douglas, Perkyns confided, 'I was worried for you for a moment there, Crabbe. The Rajah hates a fuss, has to pretend he's ruling, you see. I thought he might see your actions as mutiny – conquering his kingdom with a bunch of Yankee drunks!'

In a deep cane chair, a tall glass tinkling at his elbow, Douglas was content to let Perkyns talk.

'First, James the Brave, then Charles the Wise, and now Vyner – positively the Last White Rajah of Sarawak! Now, James was my sort, you see. The first one – born in Benares, bred in Bath, then back in Borneo in 1839.'

Pinkie glowed with pride. 'It took charm to conquer the savage. But he had to fight too. And he won everyone over. The Malays said he had a beautiful mouth. Didn't stop the Chinese from plotting though. They rose in mutiny in 1857, the same year as the sepoys did in India, tried murdering James.'

'Was he the one who brought opium to Sarawak?' Douglas asked.

'Oh, no. The Dutch were at it before us. The Customs House was built on the ruins of the first opium warehouse in Sarawak. No, James was too busy fighting pirates.'

'And who was his Ranee?'

'He didn't have one. An injury, I'm afraid, took him out of the succession business. The second rajah, Charles, was his nephew. They called him the "Pope".'

'Pope?'

'Anyone who questioned his authority landed in gaol. Chinese, Malay, Indian, or British – he didn't care.'

With another refill, Perkyns continued. 'Charles got his nose into everything, from the bazaar to the church – even zoology! Never sat in an armchair, disliked luxuries. That's why his Ranee fled back to England, spent her life writing books, throwing parties, dreaming about Sarawak, while Charles grew old and deaf. He was loved and feared, cajoled and flattered. Like an Indian Maharajah. Only a wise one.'

Douglas looked doubtful.

'Oh, yes. Wise he was. He had a passion for planting – rubber, spices, gambiar, paddy. Rubber fuelled the boom. He went on a building spree in the 1890s. Built everything, from churches to prisons to schools. Then the idea struck! Opium, arrack, and gambling. All three were declared monopolies and auctioned off to the highest bidders. Golden rain started to fall!'

'Who smoked?'

'The Chinese, of course – lured by Charles. They came to work in the farms and mines, then spent the rest of their lives paying back their headman.'

As the evening light faded, Perkyns talked on. 'The first thing the Germans do when they occupy a country, you know, is build a barrack. The French build a railway. The English build a Customs House! Sarawak grew rich. Even made a contribution to her big sister fighting the Germans in Europe. Raffles and bazaars, balls, all raising funds for the defence of the Empire. It's not like India. Sarawak isn't part of the Empire, you see. Our Rajah is both the King's subject and his cousin. They're fellow monarchs. Sarawak is the dream of a few Englishmen, but not quite a part of Britain.'

He took Douglas's silence for more doubt.

'Oh, no. They're all friends – India's Viceroy, Malaya's Governors, Sarawak's Rajah. That's why we protect each other's interests. Take opium for instance.'

'I thought we had all banned it now.'

'Banned opium!' Pinkie laughed. 'Oh, no. Just signatures on a piece of paper. Statements, Crabbe, are one thing. The curtailment of a profitable industry is another.'

Cigarettes glowed in the dark.

'Ban opium, and you have rebellion. A few years ago, a Dutch captain prohibited smoking on his ship. The crew poisoned him.'

'Then why do we prosecute smugglers?'

'Because they are but mere mortals. Driven by greed. Adventurers must be replaced by government monopolies.'

'What if the government is an adventurer?'

'Indeed! The use of opium as medicine is permitted. But now ask, what's medicinal? What happens when one man's medicine becomes another's pleasure? Meanwhile, everyone is after profit, and the home market is not enough. That's why you are here, Crabbe.'

Douglas repeated the question he had asked Perkyns on his first day. 'What if the *Madison* had been flying the Union Flag – what then?'

'Then you would have helped the Rajah's friends. Helped them to conceal their *medicine* from the observation of customs men in other ports. Opium is the real story. The others are mere distractions.'

*

They called him Black Crabbe – for his black moods. Mr Awdry, secretary of the Officers' Club, described it best: 'It was as if his drink was poisoned.' Others noticed it too. Wrapped from ankle to waist in mosquito nets, they made quick work of their brandy and sodas, wishing the ladies could join them from the Ranee's Club nearby. Normally, the evening would not be far advanced before someone came up with a ghost story. Tonight it was Mr Awdry's turn. Passing the drinks around, he had taken his cue from a visiting naturalist.

'Once, Subu the Rajah's hangman executed a mad Dayak woman. You've seen his knife, his kris, haven't you? They both went down to the far end of the prison's cemetery where the men had cleared a shallow grave. They were chatting and laughing – the woman didn't seem afraid at all.'

Dr Hose, the naturalist, nodded his head. 'Asiatics as a rule have little fear of death.'

'He asked her why she had murdered her small child. For pleasure, the mad woman replied – just as it would please you to kill me. Both nodded their heads. Then, sitting by the edge of her grave, she asked if she could smoke a Rajah's cheroot. Subu gave her one, stolen from the Astana, let her have a few drags, then plunged his kris into her shoulder and thrust it through the heart.'

There was silence. One of the officers twittered nervously.

'Next day, as he was about to cross the prison yard, he heard a call from the fresh grave at the far end . . .'

In a flash, he was gone – Doug Crabbe, the customs man.

'Poor boy! You scared him away, Awdry!' Dr Hose led the chorus.

'Now he'll need Subu to drive away his nightmares!'

'Perhaps he's heard the call of the madwoman!'

'Must've had cockroaches in his brandy!'

Douglas ran. Jumping over the hedge of the port officer's garden, he ran the length of the pier and splashed into the river in full uniform. With every stroke he fought the waves, smashing the skull of an invisible monster. He swam following his ear, upriver, past the hum of the bazaar, and the howling circus of pariahs.

Then, at the boundary of the sago factory, he strode out of the river like a demon, and joined the Dayaks gathered around a fire. No one noticed him. Slurping rice beer from a passing cup, he stared at the glistening faces then closed his eyes.

For a whole night he heard the drums. First, they seemed like a pair of feet, a boy running from one end of a marble balcony to the other, chasing a string of glass marbles, which dropped one by one over the steps of a winding staircase. He heard the voice of the maid chase the boy around a settee, then the crash of a vase. Someone handed him a long pipe. He heard the drums more clearly now, like animals chanting in human voices, repeating a phrase over and over – familiar, but hurtful. He felt like shutting his ears. For a long time he rolled and growled on the sand, till he became one with the drums – a rush of feet over a barren roof, the smashing of glass bottles.

At daybreak he rode back to Snipe Cottage on a buffalo, like a Mahisasura – King of Demons – with a streak of red betel juice trickling down his lips.

The noise of church-bells got on his nerves. On St Peter's day, unable to sit still in his room, he called the Commander of the Sarawak Rangers and set out for Ulu Ai where the villagers were holding a barque hostage against claims of looting and rape by the crew.

It was an easy battle. The villagers submitted quite meekly. But the Sikh Commander of the Rangers returned almost in tears. Mr Crabbe, he said, 'most brave and noble', had had the headman and his brothers kneel with their necks resting on felled tree trunks. He had paraded up and down before them, shouting out charges, making as if to chop off their heads with a parang.

'I was afraid, Sir. It would have been punishment without trial,' the young Sikh told Perkyns. The Rajah had strict rules. Violating the native without just cause was a serious offence.

He had raised the parang, then brought it down on the shiny pigtail of the headman, cleanly severing it. With successive gasps, he robbed each of the offenders of their valued tresses, then returned to Kuching on the liberated barque.

They hung on his wall now: pirate trophies – tufts of black hair suspended from nails.

There were nights when, trying to escape his black moods, he would set out on his bicycle for Jalan Tiga. He would stop at a small house between the second and third crossings and drink plum wine till the Chinaman showed him into a room filled with smoke. Men and women, memsahibs and native men, sat smoking through long pipes, or reclining on divans with rich silk coverings. Newcomers like himself would glance around nervously as the pipe was brought to their lips, then take a small drag, letting out a cloud of smoke through the nostrils. Dolls in kimonos went in and out of the room, filling cups – smiling at Douglas as he sat on the edge of a divan. The newcomer would make as if to get up. 'Have a whiff,' her consort would offer. Then another . . . 'Have a whiff.' Dolls started leaving the room with native men, or memsahibs.

Douglas would look into a pair of closed eyes. Bones peeking through a frail body. A door would slam and he would hear the maid again – running over a marble balcony to her memsahib, and the crash of broken china.

She would speak through her closed lips. 'Bring me my flowers, Douglas.'

For the most part the other officers at the Customs House thought him pitifully British – aloof, unable to express himself. His past would come under frequent scrutiny.

'He was a lieutenant in the Hussars, I'm told,' Mr Awdry said, 'court-martialled for his behaviour.'

'I heard he spent ten years on the Indian railways. Must've held different jobs, our Crabbe.'

The curator of the Rajah's museum had known someone from Calcutta's Auction House. 'Crabbe has a habit of disappearing, I'm told. Left his job there ten years ago, went into some kind of business.'

He would sit primly at his desk going over warehouse ledgers, occasionally straightening to receive a delegation of port agents. He was thoughtful and quick, a man of few words. A well-chosen phrase usually ended without further invitation to dialogue. To superiors, he was always ready. 'Likes facts, our Douglas, doesn't he!' They learned to trust him. Their man on the spot, inspecting cargo, arresting defaulters, but above all keeping immaculate records. 'Nothing matters as long as the records are kept straight.' And so, within a few years of arriving in Kuching, he became the master. Quick to spot the illicit, he was the scourge of 'hostile' vessels, the upholder of justice, applying fines to the erring, and stiffer penalties to those who showed skill in 'artful deception'.

To the 'friendly', he became the ultimate tutor, correcting oversights, solving dilemmas. From Canton to Calcutta, they spoke of the young tiger of Sarawak.

His superiors saw virtue in his other side too – Black Crabbe given to bouts of 'limited indiscretion'. Before long, he was assigned tasks according to his mood.

'Are you sending Crabbe to . . . ?'

'Yes.'

'He won't do any good there.'

'There isn't any good to be done.'

The *Sarawak Gazette* proudly carried an account of Mr Crabbe, braving a sudden outbreak of plague at the harbour. 'It was good to see,' the article ran, 'a Rajah's officer personally sprinkling petrol around the coal wharves.' Daddy Abrams – owner of the Jesselton Racecourse – presented him with a horse, for saving the lives of many fine beasts who would otherwise have died in the outbreak. But Douglas was rarely to be seen without his bicycle.

'There's one that got away, Crabbe.'

'Who?'

'The Chinaman, the one who was striking the deal with the *Madison*'s captain.'

He remembered the blue silk jacket and wide black trousers. The man had been disguised as the headman, he knew now. He had dissolved into thin air before them.

'Yes.'

'Ibrahim. The most influential Chinese trader in Kuching. Knows everyone. A dear friend too. Now, he has disappeared again, to do his Haj.'

'A Chinaman in Mecca?'

Perkyns could barely conceal his amusement. 'Oh, yes. Now he'll be Haji Ibrahim – purest among the pure!'

Only Angel knew him as he really was – his Tuan, the master of Snipe Cottage. He would hide inside the water-jar in the little room when Douglas showed signs of unrest and the other servants fled, then quietly follow him everywhere. Sometimes, his Tuan would be unable to sleep and he would ask Angel to tell him a story.

He loved the stories of the Manangs, the witch doctors. Manangs could cure illnesses, strike off the spell of an evil spirit. Women Manangs had special powers, they could look into the soul of a sick one. Then catch it and bring it back to the body.

'What if the soul has travelled too far, Angel?'

'She can cross the mountain, Tuan.'

'And if it has gone beyond the mountain?'

'She can swim over the bay, too.'

Groaning from his bruises, Douglas would manage a smile.

'What if it's dark?'

'The birds will help her. The fish, and the trees . . .'

'And if the soul refuses to return? What will she do then?'

Angel fell silent. Then he started whistling again. A new film was playing at the Sylvia. Ladies were fainting on the balcony, he said, laughing hilariously in his sweet baby voice. Douglas asked where he got the money to buy a ticket.

'Easy, Tuan. Chase balls. Bring to officers. Get money. Bluddy good!'

*

Douglas lay with the doors and windows open, absorbing the scent of jasmine. He thought about the witch doctor. Which soul would she set out to catch? The favourite pet of an opium queen? He wondered if chillicrackers had souls.

He saw a woman from his window at the Customs House. A memsahib – slender and willowy with a great mane of coppery-red hair, and pale English colouring. She was talking to the priest he had seen on his first day by the pier. The priest smiled and pointed at Douglas's window. Through the telescope, he saw her walking straight towards the Customs House. The Chinese headman called out to her from the shade of a palm tree. She stepped on to the lawn of the Customs House, lifting her long skirts to save them from the recent watering.

As she answered the headman, her brows knitted for a moment, then she broke into a laugh, looking up again at the Customs House window. She seemed frail, but her voice, which Douglas could hear rising above the din in well-rehearsed bazaar Malay, was confident.

Perkyns joined him at the window.

He saw her approach the Customs House but she did not enter. Later, Perkyns threw a letter across Douglas's desk, left with the doorman by the woman for the attention of Kuching's Customs Officer. 'This is for you, Crabbe. The girl isn't.' When Douglas questioned him, Perkyns seemed unwilling to provide further explanations. 'We're going to Ibrahim's tonight. He's asked to meet you.'

As they drove together in Perkyns's Humber to the mansion of Haji Ibrahim, Douglas asked him again about the woman he had seen.

'Ask me about the Haji. He's more important than a tramp.'

Perkyns spoke as he drove, his voice barely rising over the drone of the engine. 'His father was an immigrant from China, lowest of the low, worked as a coolie in the mines. Ibrahim was born blind in one eye, common among those exposed to the dust of antimony. His father gave him to an influential Malay datu to raise as a homeboy. He learned all the tricks working for the Malay trader in his opium shop. Bought out his benefactor, bribed his way to a lucrative monopoly on arrack. There's no stopping our Ibrahim.'

Douglas asked if the Haji spoke English.

'Oh, yes. The Chinese are hungry for education. Rajah Charles had him sent to St Thomas's. He's what you'd call a learned man.'

'A learned man smuggling opium?'

'Why not?'

'Did our padres convert him to Islam then? Send him to Mecca?'

Perkyns laughed. 'Some say he converted just to show off his wealth. Others say Ibrahim wanted nothing to do with the other Chinese. Of course, there might be another explanation . . .'

Douglas frowned.

'Keep thinking, Crabbe,' Perkyns said, turning into the carriage-porch of Haji Ibrahim's mansion.

Haji Ibrahim sat on his throne in a soiled pink kimono, a pair of wooden clogs on his feet, and his smile reddened by betel juice. He was flat between the eyes and darker than most Chinamen, his protruding upper lip shaded by a bristly moustache. A towchang hung proudly over his shoulder, even though Manchu pigtails had long gone out of vogue. A basin full of carbolic acid and a towel stood close by. After a slap on the arms, the spot was washed and the remains of a mosquito disposed of. Servants flitted in and out of the room supplying fresh towels and tea. In a corner, an old woman sat smearing betel leaves with lime and liquid gambiar, to wrap around a small areca nut. By the Haji's side sat an elderly Dayak.

'Abu Bakar,' Perkyns whispered to Douglas.

Everyone seemed concerned about the war that seemed about to break.

'Kuching is far from England and Germany.' Abu Bakar sounded confident.

'Not so far from Japan though,' Perkyns silenced him. 'Wars, gentlemen, have a habit of surprising the unprepared.'

'May Allah protect us from the fate of China,' Haji Ibrahim said with a grimace.

From Europe they moved to Kuching, following the bazaar gossip about Japanese brothels. Soon, Abu Bakar was telling them the story of a killer crocodile. The Tamil priest Gunaratnam listened attentively.

'It's the number one menace!'

'We mustn't speak ill of the Rajah!' Perkyn's remark brought a round of laughter.

'No, Mr Perkyns. The Rajah is a racoon – sweet to look at but dangerous to have in the house!' Haji Ibrahim thundered.

'Does his Ranee agree?'

'She doesn't even let him into the palace.'

'I hear our Ranee is on the verge again!'

'On the verge of what?' Ibrahim beamed at Perkyns.

'Of adding to the population of Kuching, of course.'

'Maybe she'll finally have a boy. Let Vyner abdicate.'

'How can a child rule over Sarawak?' Abu Bakar asked suspiciously.

'Well, Vyner seems to manage all right, doesn't he? Hiding in the Astana, playing hide and seek with his little girls!' Douglas wondered if the plum wine had loosened Perkyns's tongue.

'It would be a lot easier if Vyner did abdicate in favour of his brother. Bertram would make a far superior Rajah, don't you think?' Perkyns looked at Ibrahim for support.

'But then Ranee Sylvia would have to give up her throne too. How could she surrender to her sister-in-law?'

'You mean Charles should've left his kingdom to the wise daughter-in-law not the pretty one?' Perkyns laughed, lightening the mood.

'Not only pretty but rash too! Have you seen her betting at the Jesselton Racecourse? She'd scare even a Chinaman!'

'There's no denying her love of Sarawak. But Vyner loves her best.' Everyone looked at Father Gunaratnam, surprised.

'He loves Sarawak best, that's why he wants to set her free.'

Perkyns frowned. 'You mean all this talk about abdicating, turning the kingdom into a republic? How do you suppose that'll set her free?'

Gunaratnam kept silent.

Perkyns leant towards Douglas for support.

'Falling asleep, Crabbe? Wait, the fun is yet to begin!'

Douglas wondered what brought such disparate men together.

Ibrahim smiled. 'But who would rule over a republic? Pirates would rule us – smuggling with one hand, and killing with the other.'

'Human life is cheap in Borneo, brass extremely dear,' Abu Bakar added glumly. 'That's why we pay hunters to kill crocodiles. To recover the brass ornaments of their victims.'

With another gulp of wine, Perkyns turned to Douglas. 'It's a gloomy place, Crabbe, even when the sun is shining.'

As they drove back to Snipe Cottage, Perkyns chuckled to himself, unmoved by the drowsiness of his companion.

'It's the old patriarchy, of course. Sylvia, the Ranee, would like it changed though. Given half a chance she'd poison the Rajah and rule herself. You could call it nature's revenge. Vyner wins the throne over his brother Bertram, but loses the line of succession. It's hard for Sylvia, living with the thought of impending loss.'

They stopped briefly for a cloud of mist to roll over.

'A republic would change all that, wouldn't it?'

'I'd say he's suggesting that to spite his brother. *After me the deluge!* Wants to be the last white Rajah.'

'What will we do then?'

Perkyns started the car. He spoke slowly.

'Don't know, Crabbe.'

Before they arrived at Snipe Cottage, Douglas had fallen asleep. As Angel ran towards the car, Perkyns shook Douglas awake and left, his last words disappearing into the night.

'Do what every officer should do, Crabbe. Marry the right girl.'

Douglas left for Berhala next morning. He had first seen the leper colony, a few miles from Kuching's main harbour, from the deck of the *Sultana* on the day he arrived, just before the sky grew dark – a village on stilts nesting precariously over the river. He carried in his pocket the letter from the woman who had come to visit the Customs House a week ago, remembered the invitation at the end: *Awaiting the pleasure of your visit to Berhala.* Angel had wanted to go with him, but Douglas had refused, despite the boy's warning that he wouldn't be able to survive in the colony without him.

'Sick men, Tuan. Everyone is afraid of them.'

'Who takes care of the sick men?'

'Gunaratnam, the Tamil Father, and Ruth.'

'Ruth?'

Angel told him about the English memsahib. 'She's mother to the sick men. Not afraid to touch them. Brings them food and medicine.' Douglas remembered the coppery-red hair and pale skin.

Angel told him too of the Tamil priest. 'He's a famous man, Tuan. He isn't afraid of anyone, not even the police. Fights for coolies, even prisoners.'

Douglas sat on a small boat with a loud engine, watching the boatman use his toes to steer the wheel. He closed his eyes and thought again of Ruth memsahib's letter and of Perkyns's warning, *The letter's for you. The girl isn't.*

Dear Mr Crabbe

We hear of a terrible misfortune. The *Halloween* is on its way to Kuching from China with more than her usual cargo. Infants. Stolen from their mothers, or bought from starving peasants. She's carrying them to be sold to their future masters. We seek your help in stopping the *Halloween* in her evil mission, in saving the babies. You may be the only hope for the hopeless.

Awaiting the pleasure of your visit to Berhala.

He had seen lepers in Calcutta. When he had made his request to the boatman, he had seen the look of horror.

'Berhala, Tuan?'

It was early afternoon by the time they reached the village. It seemed like any other village, shutters drawn sleepily against the sun. As Douglas looked for signs of life, the sound of snorting hogs led him to an intricate garden surrounding a simple bamboo church where he decided to take refuge from the midday glare. As he rested, his mind wandered, and soon he began to doze. The voice of Father Gunaratnam woke him abruptly. 'You're here to meet Miss Ruth, I suppose. I'm afraid you're out of luck. She has just gone to the Customs House to meet you.'

A letter came from Haji Ibrahim, accompanied by a box.

> Greetings, Tuan
>
> If you don't like the jar, please give it back to me, because I do like the jar.
>
> H. Ibrahim

Douglas returned the box, much to Perkyns's horror.

'It's a custom, you know. When you make a gift, an enemy becomes a friend.'

'I am not one or the other.'

'Yes, but . . .'

Perkyns fretted for a while. Then he returned to his telescope, his mood lifting gradually. He showed Douglas an advertisement he had composed for posting in the *Sarawak Gazette.*

> A young English gentleman, respectably connected and holding a good appointment, is desirous of corresponding with an eligible English lady, with a view to matrimony. Apply care of printer.

'It'll be read everywhere, from Singapore to Calcutta. The replies will come on the mail steamer, once a week.'

'But, who is it for?'

'You, Crabbe. And I hope you have better luck than I did. Mine didn't work – only maids and whores.'

'You advertised for a wife? Why didn't you go home for one?'

'Oh, back home, they think everybody out here is a Viceroy. They expect you to live in a mansion. It's better if you live in India. There are more mutinies to quell there, I suppose.'

'Well, what about looking here? There are a number of ladies at the Ranee's Club.'

'No better than tramps, I'm afraid. They flirt, enjoying themselves at a poor man's expense only to dupe him in the end.'

He frowned at Douglas's lack of interest in the advertisement. 'Not dreaming about the letter-writer, I hope.'

Douglas's rejection of Haji Ibrahim's gift produced an unexpected reaction. Angel returned from Ibrahim's house with another letter, an invitation this time, to join a crocodile hunt on the banks of the Saribas. The invitation was for Douglas alone.

The village chief sat under a palm, face moist with tears. He had lost his youngest wife. She had come to the stream as usual, bending over to fill her tin can at the bank. Without the slightest warning the beast had knocked her into the water with its tail, then held her head in its jaws just long enough for her to drown. Like a proud hunter it held up its catch for all to see, swimming up the creek with a scarlet stain trailing behind. It had left the chief's wife there, to rot perhaps, before returning for a feast.

'Welcome, Tuan.' Haji Ibrahim sat down beside Douglas and raised his glass of papaya juice. 'To the crocodile and its catcher!'

'Tell me, Tuan. What do you know about 1857? What do you know about the mutiny?'

The sun through the trees dazzled Douglas and made him blink. His stomach knotted for a moment. He sensed a trick. What did the Chinaman want to know?

'That was another crocodile hunt! Bigger than this one. Much bigger. The river was full of crocodiles – Hakkas, Teochius,

Hailams, Cantonese. And many catchers – all young – Dayaks, Muruts, Ibans. They rounded up men in the bazaar and cooked their heads before their people. What do you know about the Chinese mutiny in Kuching?'

Haji Ibrahim beamed at his guests. The old catcher gave a signal for the hunt to begin. Men stood behind each other – as in a tug-of-war – ready to haul the beast after it had swallowed the bait.

'Rotten monkeys,' Ibrahim confided. 'The crocodile will take nothing else.'

'It has diamonds in its belly,' someone said. 'Brass and gold too.'

'I bet there's nothing more than a string of stones,' Abu Bakar sneered. 'The chief wasted his gold already on older wives.' Out of the corner of his eye, Douglas saw Angel hiding behind a giant paper umbrella.

'Do you know why they rebelled? How little it takes for men to become angry – a fine of hundred and fifty dollars only!' Ibrahim laughed. 'And for what? Smuggling opium! It was the first Rajah's fault. He started to fine all traders spotted smuggling opium. For that, the Chinese nearly killed him in the mutiny!'

There was a stirring, then a ripple. A pair of jaws came from nowhere and snapped over the rotten monkey. The catcher held out his hand to restrain the men.

'It's suffering now. Terribly. Suffering at the bottom of the river from the hook stuck in its throat. It's a strange animal. Knows when it's defeated, doesn't struggle for too long,' Ibrahim went on.

Then, the tugging started, accompanied by cries and chants and the banging of drums. The villagers crowded the bank to catch the first glimpse. As soon as the snout appeared, the old man threw a noose deftly around the jaws and tied it tightly to a tree. A pair of men slammed a bamboo crowbar over the long tail, pinning it down in the slippery mud. Front and hind legs took a while to tie.

Everyone cheered. The catcher bowed, then brought out a

kris. He passed the weapon to Ibrahim. Douglas found the kris thrust into his hand.

'Kill, Tuan.'

'You killed the crocodile, I'm told. What a noble thing for an officer to do!'

Douglas looked away from Ruth's eyes to the river.

'They found a diamond ring in its belly. Now the chief can marry again!'

He did not remember the killing, just the aftermath. The blood spraying his shirt, and a groan from a pair of tightly bound jaws. He had stared into its opaque eyes, then walked away. 'Wait, Tuan,' Abu Bakar had called after him. But he left before they sliced open the monster's belly, with Angel following quickly on his heels.

Still holding the bloody kris, he strode on to the tennis courts at the Club in the middle of a mixed tournament. The ladies shrieked, the men holding their rackets like clubs to ward him off. 'My God! Who has he killed now?' Mr Awdry had steered him towards the bar, for 'a drink perhaps'. For a moment Douglas stood beneath the first Rajah's portrait, then he turned into the Games Room where Perkyns scattered balls over the billiard table. 'Well done, Crabbe. Master of Crocs!' He saw the opaque eyes again, dragged himself into the music room and fainted at the feet of the Ranee who sat at the club piano.

That night he began to shake. The gardener ran to fetch Dr Hose, while the servants bathed his body. Malaria, the doctor whispered. For four nights he lay dreaming of smoked heads hanging from walls. A band of iron seemed to press around his body, becoming tighter and tighter. At times he felt he was already dead – dead and buried. The doctor prescribed brandy and evil-tasting syrup. Angel brought him a broth, full of herbs. This seemed to soothe him, making him fall asleep. Later, he asked the boy what it was.

'Monkey soup, Tuan. He is your friend, he will kill all your enemies inside you.'

Douglas vomited.

Rats overran the room and verandah in their thousands, climbing over the screened door and sprinting across the floor. Black rats. He screamed, 'Don't move!' Huddled over the bed, paralysed. One landed in the bowl of eau-de-cologne and let out a horrible screech, struggling like a beached crocodile before dying. They fell from the bed, the stool, the dresser, landing on the floor with a thud. Then they disappeared leaving only an eerie silence.

'You were dreaming, Tuan.'

'Why didn't you wake me?'

'It's dangerous. Your soul was in another place. It might never have returned.'

They told him of the visitors who had come asking after him during his illness, of the pretty mem who had come more than once.

She sat by the river – knees drawn up to her chin, hands clasped across them. She was pretty, not *pretty* like the ladies at the Club, but tempting. Douglas saw a bangle made of seaweed on her wrist, like the ones sold in the bazaar to ward off lightning and typhus. She spoke with shapely words, cut and polished like precious stones.

'Everyone was worried. Especially the Ranee. She thought it was her playing that made you ill!' Douglas pretended to be busy scanning the horizon.

'And she was worried that the Rajah would hear about her being at the Club.' Ruth's eyes strayed to the horizon too, then she laughed. 'You made them nervous, didn't you?'

Douglas grimaced.

'Why did you write to me about the *Halloween* and the babies?'

'Because you're the Customs Officer. Pinkie said I should.'

'Pinkie?'

'Chief Officer Perkyns.'

Douglas raised an eyebrow.

'My brother.'

This was the beginning. Soon they could be seen together almost everywhere. In the docks, at the bazaar, among officers and lepers, at Snipe Cottage. Jealous brother officers at the Club changed his name to 'Lucky Crabbe', and Pinkie Perkyns, thoroughly disgusted, expressed his disapproval of a respectable English gentleman and an eligible English lady living like the savages of Borneo.

Arriving at the Berhala colony on the morning steamer, Douglas would sit inside the narrow dispensary next to a bench full of bottles and evil-shaped tongs. Ruth would examine her patients in the corner. Without a word, he'd slip through the crowd of sickly babies and mothers. Some noticed his starched uniform, took him for a visiting surgeon. An amputee would thrust a severed leg before him, or a wound rotting with gangrene.

He would sit near her in silence, watch her talking to the lepers. She did not have much to offer: Cough Mixture, Stomach Mixture, Sprain Liniment, Boric Ointment. She would take a few moments to consider. 'Must go easy on the Cough Mixture,' she'd smile at Douglas. 'Otherwise they'll show up every morning for a shot!' One young boy brought her flowers and she bandaged his ankle. A tear rolled down his face as the iodine stung him but he thanked her.

Some of her patients weren't sick at all, Ruth said. They came along just to see the inside of the dispensary. Occasionally, there were drunks. She would say exactly the same thing to each of them, over and over again, then she would send them off to the priest who sat outside under a spreading Banyan tree.

He saw her close to anger when a mother refused to feed a crying baby. She'd point at her own breasts, at the baby's mouth. 'She won't give her milk. She's afraid she'll come to look like an animal.' He saw her close to tears when a commotion filled the dispensary and a small group brought in a man, hands severed at the wrist, and a woman with her lips slit.

They'd drive out silently in the borrowed Humber, she with her hand over her hat to shield her face from the sun.

At the opening of the bay, they sat together under a row of casurinas. Calm spread at sunset, enormous butterflies skimming the surface of the water. They stared at the ripples, then at each other. First Ruth, then Douglas smiled. It was their first embrace.

He lay on his back and saw the sky and the islands. The islands in the sky. Never in all his life, he thought, had there been such a moment, and such a day as this.

As they returned to Snipe Cottage, they came upon a marble slab.

In
Memory
Of
Francis Xavier Witti
Killed near the Sibuco River
May, 1882
Of
Frank Hatton
Accidentally shot at Segamah
March, 1883
Of
Dr D. Manson Fraser
And Jemadar Asa Singh
Mortally wounded at Kopang
May, 1883
Alfred Jones, Adjutant
Murdered at Marak Parak
28 July, 1903
This Monument is erected as a mark of respect
By their Brother Officers

Justice was Done

Douglas and Ruth woke to the sound of angry voices on their first morning together at Snipe Cottage. The cook was blaming the gardener for serious negligence, berating him as he stood with eyes downcast. 'Come, Tuan.' She led Douglas past the kitchen, past the hawk feasting on a red pepper, to Angel's room. He heard snores from inside – one rising, the other falling. 'Look, Tuan,' she said pushing the door open.

He saw a black serpent coiled around a white sandalwood tree.

'Allah has given him a wife before he has given him a brain!'

'A singing voice reaches further than a speaking voice.' Father Gunaratnam guided Douglas around the bamboo chapel filled with the sound of the choir. Outside, under the shade of the Banyan tree, Douglas removed his shoes.

'In Sarawak you can get used to anything, Mr Crabbe. Even slavery. Look at our Dayak brothers. Superstitious about everything. Never see the sun set under a rainbow, never cut your hair if the wife is expecting, never let a guest leave after a single meal. If a woman dies in childbirth during Ramadan, she becomes a holy one.'

Douglas asked him if there were other missionaries like him in Sarawak.

'We have them all: Jesuits, Methodists, Anglicans. But the Lord is yet to save our Dayak friends. It's hard to win their trust. Not all of us can be like Reverend Fowler. He knew the ways of the wild. He had seen trouble in China and didn't care if his feet were over the earth, or under it.'

Douglas had heard of the head-hunters' priest.

'I wonder sometimes, Mr Crabbe, who is the real savage. Us or them.'

Douglas saw Ruth at the window of the dispensary.

Gunaratnam spoke with passion. 'Now *everybody* has an enemy in Sarawak. Sikhs quarrel with Malays, Dayaks with Moslems, British sailors with Chinese traders. Every chief pretends to be the Lord.' He looked at the line of patients and sighed. 'Germs never die, simply pass on from one body to another.'

At the Club, the other officers discussed the growing unrest. War, according to Perkyns, was behind all the excitement. 'War in Europe, in China, on the seas. Can our little Kuching be left behind? And then who will protect us?' The Punjab Regiment from India was a certainty, perhaps a squadron each from Madras and Aden. British help was a more remote possibility. All agreed that the defence of England came before the plight of her far-flung colonies. Someone noticed Douglas at the bar – a rare appearance. What, they demanded to know, would happen to India in the event of war?

'Would we all be moved to smelly Calcutta or rotten Bombay?'

'We'd be safe in the East.'

'I haven't heard anyone mention the Chinese,' Mr Awdry, who was drinking with Douglas, put in. He looked at Perkyns. 'Tell us about your Haji. Is he prepared to betray his kin for the English?'

'I'd be much happier if he was a headache for the Dutch!'

'What if the Japs burn his opium?'

'Oh, no, they wouldn't do that. They'd do what they did in Foochow – make every Chinaman smoke it till he dropped dead!' Dr Hose sounded confident.

'I'd rather see a rope around their necks, wouldn't you?' Ranee Sylvia spoke up from the piano.

'Yes.'

The Rajah came in from a round of golf, tall and florid, in starched tunic and khaki trousers. Talk turned from the war to lighter subjects. More drinks came round.

Once a week Ruth came for Malay lessons to the Home School near the bazaar. She came early, waited for Douglas at the small library, pretending to read Marsden's Malay dictionary. Their feet touched under the table. He watched her reading – counted each line on her face starting with those at the corners of her eyes. 'Six,' he said aloud, breaking her concentration.

'What?'

'Six dollars. That's what Angel paid for his wife.'

'His wife? I thought Dalima was his half-sister.'

'No.'

She thought of Dalima's dark and beautiful eyes, her hair pulled tightly over her forehead to hang in a coil at the nape of the neck.

'Lucky Angel! She's a pearl beyond price.'

Douglas would leave the room when her teacher arrived. From outside, he listened to them talking and reading together. He heard the measured tone of the elderly teacher:

'Look at a word well before you sound it. Don't worry, it'll wait for you. When you've mastered it, you'll hear a singing inside your mouth. It will give your heart relief and comfort.' The teacher spoke well, and softly.

From the Home School they went to the rickshaw stand on Gambiar Road. They would spend the day crisscrossing the town. With her he saw a new Kuching. He smelled acrid joss-sticks burning before a shrine and woodworms roasting over an open fire. He saw a man dressed as a woman, with tattooed arms. He heard the skirl of bagpipes from the Rajah's palace give way to the drum of a dragon dance.

Later, lying in the bath together, he held her face and counted the lines again. There seemed fewer, only three. 'What?' she asked.

'Why wouldn't Perkyns talk to me about you?'

'You'd better ask him.'

'I'm asking you.'

She fell silent. She seemed to be searching for an answer in the dripping stream.

'Because I am a tramp.'

'Where are the hopeless for whom I am the only hope?'

Ruth looked up from her book.

He had kept the letter, read it every now and then, waited for her to reveal 'the terrible misfortune'. The letter had taken him to Berhala.

'The *Halloween* is late. Must've stopped in the Philippines.'

He waited. Ruth frowned, then went on. 'Perhaps the captain has been warned. Maybe he thinks his ship will be searched in Kuching. Taken another route. He knows he's being watched. His own men don't approve.'

'What does he need the children for?'

'To sell as slaves in exchange for guns. There are merchants waiting for the babies in California, in Peru. He'll return with guns to sell to pirates.'

Douglas frowned. 'But trading in coolies has been banned.'

'You mean just as opium has been banned? There will always be slaves and opium,' she said glumly. 'Powerful men on shore help greedy captains. How do you suppose so many Chinese landed in Borneo?'

'But how would he hide them on the ship?'

'In boxes, breathing through small holes – one hole per child. Baby girls are more in demand, fetch more than boys.'

'How do you know about the *Halloween*?'

'Everyone knows. Sailors tell coolies at the docks. Coolies tell their headmen. The *Halloween* is special. Her captain is smart, and he has friends in Kuching. Edward can tell you more about them.'

So, would the priest help her care for the babies after the rescue?

She nodded, then set her eyes on him. 'You are Black Crabbe, aren't you? Save those with a black fate. Stop the *Halloween* before she takes her cargo to America.'

He thought of asking Perkyns, then stopped.

Haji Ibrahim sat on his throne and admired the red hibiscus floating in a celadon bowl.

'Yes . . . Mr Perkyns and his sister. Who can you blame for misunderstandings?' He sighed.

For a moment Douglas regretted raising the matter with Ibrahim. Perhaps Father Gunaratnam would have been safer. He decided not to mention the *Halloween*.

'But why –'

'That's fate.' Ibrahim raised his eyes.

'They are not alike, though, wouldn't you say?' Douglas probed cautiously.

'Yes. Most different. Sometimes I wonder who they really are, Mr Crabbe. No one knows, not even the Rajah and the Ranee.'

'Ruth's the Ranee's friend, I hear.'

'Who do you hear from?'

Douglas looked away. Ibrahim cleared his throat.

'It doesn't really matter that they're brother and sister, does it?'

Douglas decided to try a different approach.

Why did she live in Berhala? What made her friends with Gunaratnam? Why didn't she go to the Club if she was the Ranee's friend? Why did Perkyns call her a tramp?'

'Yes, these are mysteries, Mr Crabbe.'

Then, like the old crocodile catcher, Haji Ibrahim prepared his bait – getting to the root of the problem with meticulous care.

'They were born Indian. Born in India, at least,' he said. 'Of missionary parents who died in a horrible plague. The children were sent back to England, but always loved the East, longed to return. The brother came first. As an apprentice, then started going up to the Dayaks with Rajah Charles. He was like the Rajah's son. The only one who could correct him.'

Douglas knew Perkyns had lived in the Astana some years ago and knew it like the back of his palm.

'He was friendly with the Rajah's son Vyner too. Eventually he brought his sister over from England to join him. They became our friends, Mr Crabbe – just like you.'

'She did what every mem does – married an officer. A pilot. Then . . .' The Haji waited for his older wife to leave the room.

'Then?'

'Tell me, Mr Crabbe, do you know why fate acts as it does? Over a matter of weeks she lost twice. First, her child. Stillborn. Then the pilot vanished over the Sulu Sea. Some say he is dead. Some say he fled. A short time later, she disappeared too. There was a manhunt. They searched everywhere, even the ships leaving the harbour. Ranee Sylvia was most distressed. Suddenly, she started appearing. Like a ghost, among Dayak women at the market, dressed up as one. Floating on a prau all by herself. Nobody knew where she had been or what she had done. Maybe the Ranee knew – but she refused to tell.' There was a glint in Ibrahim's eye.

'First, Mr Perkyns feared she had been kidnapped. He was suspicious of everyone. Even of the Rajah. Then, he thought his sister was hiding from him. He thought Ruth was scared. Of him.'

'What in him could scare her?'

'He is braver than most, Mr Crabbe. But a dreamer. He dreams of setting Sarawak free.'

Douglas thought of the kind grey eyes. Of Perkyns's occasional outbursts.

'As a customs man, he can keep his eye on everything. Having him there is safer too for the Rajah. It kept him away from the

Rajah's loyal officers. Mr Perkyns is lucky. He studied under the wolf but serves under the lamb!' Ibrahim laughed.

Douglas watched an ant peep out over the kernel, then crawl down the stem of the hibiscus almost touching the water in the bowl.

'At last, she was found by Gunaratnam. He refused to say where. She lost all her friends. Officers and wives shunned her at the Club, walked away from the tennis courts when she picked up a racket. Wouldn't invite her to their balls or parties. She learned quickly.'

'And Perkyns?'

Ibrahim sighed. 'Tell me, Mr Crabbe, do you know what happens to orphans when they grow up?'

Douglas dreamt of his mother. She threw a glance at him over her shoulder, and he followed, unable to resist. She was beautiful, fair as a mem, small as a Dayak, dark hair braided like a Manchu princess. When she opened her mouth, a song streamed through her lips. He was afraid of her, and mesmerized.

Ruth's snoring woke him. Holding her head like a child's, he turned her over.

They threw lavish dinner parties at Snipe Cottage – for themselves. They would begin with fireworks on the lawn with the gardener setting off pinwheels and rockets. Angel would trip as he crossed the lawns with a carefully laid tray of brandypanee and joss-sticks. 'Bluddy pool!' he'd curse, and run back to the kitchen. Then there would be dressing-up.

Ruth would disappear with Dalima and Amma, to emerge half an hour later as the Ranee in a golden kain tape which covered her feet and tucked beneath her arm. She would walk cautiously, golden buttons on her jacket jingling as she moved. A brocaded scarf over her head left just enough space for one eye to peep through. When the gardener set off a rocket, she would jump, losing the kain tape in the process.

Sometimes she dressed as a Dayak queen with a straw hat and

long earrings. 'Why don't you kill me a boar? I could make a necklace out of its teeth.'

Amma disapproved.

'Amma wants me to be "Oh, so English. A proper English lady!" You must help me, Mr Crabbe. What's a lady without her gallant escort!'

He sat on the lawn listening to Angel recite one story after another. Entwined, as usual, like dark thread on the golden sarong, they wove serpents with men, birds with spirits.

'There was once a lazy boy who slept all day. His mother sent him out to search for food but he fell asleep under a tree. In his dream he saw a deer. It was searching for food, digging under shrubs with its horn. He saw the deer dig up a small white stone, kick it with its heel. The deer turned white – as white as the stone itself.

'When he woke, the boy looked under bushes and shrubs, in the shade of abandoned huts, and under stumps of dead trees, to find the stone. Finally, he found it. He rubbed it over his arms, legs, belly and face, avoiding the hair. It turned him completely white.'

Angel smacked a mosquito, then looked at Douglas.

'You too could become white, Tuan.'

Douglas stared amazed at his small homeboy.

It started with a fire on Carpenter Street. The driver of the Fire Brigade came running to the docks where Douglas was busy scolding the headman. It was a busy time. The driver grabbed his arm, pointing at the dark sky over the bazaar. By the time they arrived at the mosque, men were running screaming down the alleys nearby. Some dragged sacks full of vegetables, or carried clay ovens on their heads. Rickshaws loaded with chicken and geese clogged the entry to China Street. A solitary policeman blew on his whistle, face white with panic. Douglas snatched his baton and charged into the crowd.

He saw naked flames and sudden bursts, like firecrackers. Men were crowding into shop doorways as shopkeepers threw their wares on to the streets to save them. A heavy chest fell from an upper floor scattering coins and paper money.

Before looting began in earnest, Douglas lodged himself at the top of the clock tower, screaming himself hoarse as he directed the firefighters and volunteers below.

From his perch, he saw Ruth. She was holding up a red scarf, like a flag, and she was alone. Someone tried to clear a path for her but she seemed oblivious, shouting at men who were trying to flee with a stolen clock or lamp. In a moment their eyes met. She waved at him to come down. He shouted. 'Why?' She kept pointing behind her, towards Snipe Cottage, and the docks.

'The *Halloween* is coming in to port,' she shouted up at him.

*

His first instinct was to get the facts – about the ship, its owners, the landing records. Mentally he rehearsed his usual list as Perkyns dozed at his desk. He turned the telescope on the arriving vessel. She was a bona fide tea clipper, heavily sparred and extremely lofty. Even from this distance, he could see solid brass rails shining over panelled deck fittings. The star-spangled banner furled over a solid mast, with a splendidly carved werewolf as figurehead. She was far from a sea-gypsy.

Perkyns had woken by the time the *Halloween* arrived in the port.

'She's as she looks. Better. Captain Dowdy is a character – more of a businessman, really. Might have some Viking blood but he wouldn't admit it. Pure English! Delighted for us to come on board.'

In the evening, Douglas told Ruth what Perkyns had said about Captain Dowdy's *Halloween.*

'I don't care. He might be Prince Charming, but he's hiding helpless little babies. Did Pinkie say he knew the captain?'

'Why would your brother help smuggle babies?'

She frowned.

In Douglas's pocket was an invitation to the Haji's house, to a party to celebrate Captain Dowdy's safe arrival. He wondered if he should mention it to Ruth.

As he waited for the Haji's other guests to arrive, Douglas watched the older wife cut patterns from a piece of green satin. Her eye moved a step ahead of her fingers, and she let out a small sigh of satisfaction each time she completed a shape. Her mind, it seemed, was free to roam although her hands worked with extreme concentration. She reminded him of his Baboo's mother, the madwoman who had shared their roof in Jaan-bazaar.

'Only an unbeliever would deny the good done by the English.' Haji Ibrahim entered the room, still panting from the day's exertions, his Chinese features incongruous beneath a hunter's cap. A triumphant Perkyns was displaying the corpse of a dead otter, and a basket of turtles' eggs. 'You missed something, Crabbe. I've never seen so many together before. We'll be overrun by dark creatures with hard backs!' The Haji's wife took away the eggs before Perkyns could embark on an involved monologue. Douglas looked for Captain Dowdy among the hunters.

'Without them we'd never have known the joy of racing.' The Haji returned to his subject.

'Or regattas,' Abu Bakar added solemnly.

'And tennis!' Perkyns feigned a mock smash.

'Tell me, Mr Crabbe, what would you have missed most?'

Douglas smiled but he felt in no mood to indulge.

'Have you heard about Enright?' Perkyns began. 'He was your usual poor magistrate. Travelled around the estates delivering justice in the name of the Rajah. A pleasant lad, almost humble. Enright kept his job simple, you see. Never veered from his prescription: a simple dose of flogging, whatever the crime!'

Perkyns went on, although no one seemed to be listening. It was time for betel leaves, for tea, and for servants to bring perfumed bowls for each person in the room. Ibrahim resumed his throne with a wife at each side as Gunaratnam arrived, perspiring profusely.

'Poor fellow. He didn't realize he was sentencing a witch doctor. They're vicious, you know, wouldn't think twice about poisoning you.'

'Tell us about poisoning, Mr Crabbe. Who poisoned the Rajah against our friend Mr Dowdy?' Ibrahim's voice cut through Perkyns's meandering narrative. The tea drinkers kept their mouths shut. Not a single slap greeted the buzzing mosquitoes.

'It is not a crime to return to Kuching, is it?'

'No, it's not a crime,' Douglas replied.

'Then why is the captain being treated like a criminal?'

'You mean not being invited to the Astana for gin and bitters?'

Haji Ibrahim remained silent for a moment. 'You know I don't mean that.'

'You should say what you do mean then.'

'Our friends may come and go as they wish, Mr Crabbe. Surely there is no harm in that. Why is he then made to wait for his inspection? Why are his papers still held at the Customs House?'

Perkyns coughed, seemed eager to call for a truce, suddenly flustered. Abu Bakar spoke.

'The Rajah has no friends. Only officers. Who are the officers' friends?'

'I'll tell you who my friends are, but I'm sure you wouldn't want to know.' Douglas stared at him.

'Friends, friends, friends . . .' Haji Ibrahim was conciliatory.

'One can pay back the loan of money, but one remains for ever in debt to an act of kindness. How shall we repay the debt to Mr Crabbe?' Gunaratnam's eyes danced.

'For upholding the laws of Kuching.' Abu Bakar nodded.

'And don't forget the fire. His swift action must have saved a hundred lives.'

The tension was broken. A drum sounded in the courtyard as preparations for the evening's entertainment began.

It wasn't until the entertainment was almost finished that Douglas met Captain Dowdy.

'What if he is in a trance, doesn't know what's real and what's not?' Gunaratnam exclaimed at the end of the whirling dancer's show. Everyone felt more relaxed now, including Perkyns, who chatted with the performers, sharing his smokes.

'What do you make of Mr Perkyns? He doesn't seem his usual self, does he? Is he ill?'

Douglas ignored Abu Bakar's question. But Perkyns had been looking a little frayed, he thought, his features flushed. He wondered if Ruth had noticed anything, or even if she cared. He saw Captain Dowdy walking towards him.

'Ah! Mr Crabbe, isn't it? From Calcutta.' Captain Dowdy handed him a cheroot. 'I heard about you in Macao. Or was it Canton? Sunk the *Madison*, didn't you!'

'How long do you intend staying in Kuching, Captain?'

'We don't waste time, do we!'

'Mr Crabbe likes records,' Ibrahim said, joining them.

'Does he? Plenty of time for that, my dear man.'

The smell of meat cooking in an earthen pot turned them towards the balcony. Ibrahim's younger wife joined them as they sat down to eat, supplying the latest gossip between gulps of tamarind juice.

'You must know Subu, don't you?'

'You mean the Rajah's executioner?'

'He's leaving. He is bored. Sarawak is too tame, he says. Not enough executions to keep him busy.'

'Subu is a fool.' Father Gunaratnam sounded sarcastic.

'His kris is getting rusty. He needs other weapons.' Ibrahim's wife gave Douglas a playful look. 'Maybe you'll show him, Mr Crabbe!'

They are waiting for something to happen. What?

Dayaks sang a farewell chorus then Ibrahim made a short speech praying for everybody's health. Perkyns was to drive Douglas home. As they got ready to leave, Gunaratnam took Douglas aside and slipped him a letter for Ruth.

'What a feast! Let's hope the next one will be at your wedding, Mr Crabbe,' Haji Ibrahim beamed.

The Humber was hot. Douglas loosened his collar. Perkyns seemed more frayed than ever, even a touch depressed.

'So *these* are your friends?'

Perkyns cast him a sideways glance. 'We want to return to our mutton, do we?'

He drove on silently for a while, then started to speak. 'Goodness, Crabbe, were you thinking of friends when you came here? For twenty years I've been their friend, their fool. A friendly fool. A foolish friend!' He cut the engine.

'Friends, yes. It's time to be Kuching's friend, not simply a loyal officer to her rajah. It's time to choose between the Club and the bazaar. Time to stop pretending we are superior to them.'

'We?'

'We, the British. We, the white officers of the white Rajah. We, the master smugglers and empire builders.' Perkyns fell silent, looking troubled under the cloud of smoke.

'But how do you stop what you've started? What happens when there's no desire to rule, simply the routine of governance? What would make Rajah Vyner leave? I mean, *really* leave, after all this talk of abdication.'

Douglas turned to face him in the car.

'You need a play, Crabbe.' His eyes shone in the dark. 'One in which the Emperor finally dies, and his crown passes on to the people. Of course, you need the right actors, capable of friendly cooperation with each other.'

So tonight was a rehearsal for the friendly cooperation, Douglas thought.

'Are your actors ready?'

Perkyns smiled. 'As ready as they'll ever be, I suppose.'

'Are you?'

'Always. From the moment I stepped into the Customs House. It's better to die on that stage than to wait for an officer's funeral.'

They came to a stop before Snipe Cottage. Douglas asked if Perkyns would come in, share a drink with them on the lawn.

'I don't mind you and Ruth, Crabbe. What can a man do when a woman is set on winning him?'

He was tempted to ask Perkyns if he was ill, but didn't.

'Go on, have a nice evening. Gosh, you deserve one, don't you, after all that dancing and singing!'

His voice trailed behind the Humber's engine. 'How beautifully dies the day. Each hue fades faintly out of sight, every change makes heaven look more lovely . . .'

He thought she was brooding, still upset over Angel's eagerness to leave them and return to his brothers in the mountain.

'We really must let him go,' she said. 'He must go back to his family.'

'Don't be silly. What'll become of us if he did that?'

'We mustn't think of just us. What'll happen when we go?'

'And where would you go? Will you disappear again?'

'Disappear?'

'You know. Escape, vanish, abscond – from friends, from brother . . .'

'What else do you know about me?'

'Come to think of it, I know less than most of Kuching.'

He tried to lighten the air.

'Where would we go anyway? Who'd have us? We couldn't go to Australia. Maybe Angel would have us, then you'd be a real Dayak queen. What do you say? Or Ibrahim could adopt us. We could grow opium. Perfect!'

He tried to imagine Pinkie and Ruth, their childhood, alone together. He thought of his own. A solitary boy running over a marble balcony. What would he have done without the maid and his Baboo? At least he had his stories.

He started to yawn, and closed his eyes, felt for a moment that he was back on the roof of Jaanbazaar listening to priests blowing conch-shells at Madan Mohon Jiu's temple. Sleep was overcoming his tired limbs.

Then she began to speak. Before the sun came up over the river, she had told him everything – from the moment she received Pinkie's excited telegram inviting her to join him in Borneo, to her first encounter with Black Crabbe as he stooped over his desk at the Customs House. For the most part she spoke clearly, covering her early days in Kuching with extreme relish, confiding secrets as if to an old friend. She spoke of her friendship with the Ranee, of their pranks, confessed her own negligent manners. They had both fallen in love with the pilot, but Sylvia had let her have him. And she had married him.

She had never returned to England. Not even for a visit, although the Rajah and Sylvia went frequently. There'd be time for that and occasions, she had thought, after the birth of her child. They had plans, she and the pilot. 'He didn't talk much, made a lot of noise with his engines! Flew me like his plane. With minimum repair!' She laughed. The fact was, she didn't remember much about their life together.

They lived on the Astana's grounds and she waited anxiously. She didn't care about doctors. Her husband suggested a hospital in Singapore but she dismissed him. Then the child was born. Her Rimba. Beautiful, heavenly – dead.

'Rimba?'

'My Dayak maid named it. She said it was the child of a spirit mother.'

Then the pilot disappeared. His plane was last seen flying low over the bay on a routine trip to Singapore. She never heard from him again, didn't know what happened, if he was alive or dead. She hid in the Astana till the rest of the world closed behind walls, till she lost every bit of herself. The Rajah and the Ranee sympathized. The Rajah almost more than his wife. She grew close to Vyner, became one of his many fleeting 'interests'. Her nights filled with ecstasy and nightmares. Even opium did not bring sleep.

Her brother suspected. He knew where she was hiding, came to meet her, offered to send her back to England if she wished. He disapproved of her liaison with the Rajah, blamed her, called her a tramp. He threatened Vyner with a public inquiry. He had friends in Westminster.

It was her own indiscretion that betrayed her. Bursting out of her quarters, shivering, she had run to greet the marching bells of the lepers by the river. She thought the bishop had finally agreed to bury her dead child. She was rescued by a priest. 'Yes, Edward Gunaratnam. My kind and trusted friend.'

'Now you know why Pinkie calls me a tramp.'

She sighed, laying her cold palm over Douglas's eyes.

'Is Pinkie up to something?'

She ignored the question.

Still in pyjamas, they strolled over the lawn. A star hung over the mast of the *Halloween* out in the bay.

'Have you seen the spirit mother?' he asked.

'Yes,' she said. 'She comes when it's dark, sleeps beside our bed.'

'Do you speak with her?'

'No. They never answer the living. If I could, I'd ask her.'

'What, Ruth?'

'I'd ask her to show me the road my little girl took.'

The *Halloween* showed no sign of being in a hurry to leave. No one believed the excuse the boatswains offered about repairs. The *Halloween* looked chaste, unravaged, untouched by storm or rumour.

Some said it was waiting for the Rajah, that he was set to abdicate and sail away to Australia on it, a Yankee clipper with an English captain. Some talked of an approaching war, claimed that Captain Dowdy's ship was carrying arms to China for the fight against the Japanese. A few pointed towards the Customs House. Captain Dowdy was angry at the charges levied on his ship, they said, he was waiting to teach a lesson to the vain officers on shore.

Perkyns marched up to Douglas's desk at the Customs House. 'Hell, Crabbe. What do you think you're doing? What business do we have delaying the clearance of his ship yet charging him for blocking the harbour?'

'He hasn't given notice to leave Kuching yet.'

'Captain Dowdy knows what he's doing, believe me. It's just simple sea-sense. He's waiting for a favourable wind before crossing the ocean.'

'He *is* blocking the harbour.'

'So what? Are we expecting someone, Crabbe? The Viceroy from Calcutta, perhaps?'

'He must pay a fee commensurate with his berthing.'

'Tell him, then, will you, when we go on board for dinner?'

'Dinner?'

'I thought you knew. Don't you?' Perkyns smiled. 'The *Halloween* is throwing a party to celebrate her friendship with Kuching. Everyone's invited – datus, important traders from the bazaar, members of the Club. And the Rajah and the Ranee.'

'I thought the Rajah has forbidden dinners for customs men on arriving vessels.'

'Really? If he is coming, then it can't be prohibited, can it? Surely he doesn't mind the *Halloween* spending a few extra days in Kuching either.'

'What if the captain is waiting for something else?' Douglas faced Perkyns over the desk.

'What?'

'Why don't you ask your friends? They would know.'

Perkyns gave him a hard stare. 'You *are* the Indian uncle, aren't you? Ready to disregard the comfort of merchants and subject races.'

Angel came with a new rumour from the bazaar every day. The captain was a pirate fleeing from the Philippines. 'He is your friend, Tuan, waiting to take you and Miss Ruth to England after your wedding.'

Douglas took the steamer to Berhala. He felt he was alone, that everyone in Kuching, except him, knew what was going to happen. He wondered if Father Gunaratnam would be kind to him too, as he had been to Ruth, if he would reveal the secret. What is the essential question? he asked himself, thinking of Mahim. *Is it better to know where to go and not know how, than to know how to go and not where?* The priest would know, he thought, more than Ibrahim or Abu Bakar, even Perkyns.

Father Gunaratnam was arranging flowers in the bamboo church when Douglas arrived, and looked up at him as if he was expecting him.

'An arrow can fly only in one direction, Mr Crabbe. Once released, you can't bring it back. You must be careful.'

Douglas wanted to ask him about Ibrahim and Abu Bakar.

And about Perkyns. *Who stood behind the bow and who was the target?*

'Men aren't important, Mr Crabbe. Only their dreams. Who knows which one will triumph in the end?'

For a whole afternoon he waited for his chance. Maybe the priest would relent, share his secrets with Douglas. Would he take pity on a customs man given to bouts of 'limited indiscretion'? Douglas waited, then left.

For the next day or two his mind kept returning to the priest. He ignored the *Halloween*, and Angel's stories, which were becoming increasingly tame as time passed.

His officers were surprised that he included a mem in the search party. Ruth followed in a cutter as he boarded the *Halloween* a little after sunset. The young Sikh commander of the Sarawak Rangers waited with his men on shore.

The ship seemed empty, only the third officer and a few crewmen left behind, including the cook, who was busy preparing the dinner planned for that evening. Douglas found the captain in his quarters, lying naked on his belly, being massaged by his boy.

'A trifle early, aren't we, Mr Crabbe? Won't be a minute.' The boy brought his bathrobe.

'I am here to search the *Halloween*.'

The search started immediately. The customs men scattered over the *Halloween*, bursting into cabins, scattering luggage, breaking locks. Douglas silenced the third officer with a sharp command but knew the captain would be hard to break. Captain Dowdy stood alone over the poop with two armed officers at his side, staring straight to shore. There was still time before the guests arrived. The Sikh would stop anyone leaving the pier. Except the Rajah. But Douglas gambled that he wouldn't come.

Suddenly, there was a howl of distress. Douglas rushed up to the deck, transformed by the sound of a sobbing child. He could hear a woman's voice, soothing, singing. For a moment he couldn't remember where he was, remembered only a song heard when he wasn't quite awake.

She was the only one, Ruth said, as she clutched the child in her arms. 'He must've sold off the others, or lost them at sea.' The customs men were disappointed. They had expected guns or opium, now it seemed the *Halloween* was a bona fide tea clipper, making an out-of-season run. As they left, Captain Dowdy sat alone in his bathrobe at the table set with sparkling silver.

'We'll call her Polly.' She glanced at him.

'You're sure you want to –'

'Yes,' she said quickly.

'Then, let's call her Polly.' He smiled.

'Who will she look like when she grows up?'

'You, surely.'

'No, you. She has your eyes.'

'They're shut.'

'But she had the Black Crabbe look when she was awake!'

'What will the servants say?'

Angel was waiting for them in front of Snipe Cottage. Even before he could run and grab his Tuan's arm, he was babbling incoherently. Even before Douglas had driven back to the Customs House and seen Pinkie Perkyns's body hanging from a rope above his desk with the telescope pointed towards the river, he had somehow known what the end of the play would be.

The Rajah was late, as usual, arriving at the *Halloween*'s party. Ibrahim and Abu Bakar had come early to the pier, only to find out about the raid on the ship. Thinking their secret had been revealed by someone, they fled to the mountains. And Chief Customs Officer Perkyns, waiting in his office for news of the final act of the play, the news of the Rajah's assassination at the hands of his 'friends', had seen Crabbe and his men run amuck over the *Halloween*. He had known too, then, that the end would have to be different from the one he had planned.

Poor Crabbe, his brother officers said at the Club, he didn't have a clue. Thought he was saving babies, ended up saving the Rajah!

Nineteen forty-one. The news from Europe was depressing. It was clear Sarawak was going to taste the same medicine as China. Their protector needed protection herself, there was no point looking to England for help now. Even before the Japanese started their sweeping charge, before the first enemy aeroplane had flown over Kuching, they knew the end of the dynasty was near. There was a sense of relief – as if the end was about to come not as a result of mutual disaffection, but because of a force larger than the Brookes, than Kuching, than the imagination of the rest. It released everyone from the discomfort of intrigue. For once, there were no grand conspiracies. The Chinese were worried about China, not Sarawak.

The weary battle lines had vanished, there was no more scope for palace rivalries, a sense of nonchalance replacing other ambitions. An unusual calm hung over the villages. Deaths were reported, but only from cholera. It seemed Sarawak had seen her last head-hunter. Yet, there was no resentment or hostility towards the third Rajah. He seemed only to be waiting for one last stroke of luck to settle his burden and leave unscathed.

The clubs were most active in 1941 – officers throwing their might behind the war effort. A Grand Fancy Bazaar at the tennis lawns raised a fantastic sum for the British War Fund. The officers donated a part of their salaries, the bar a part of its income. It was a time for charities.

First Aid absorbed most of the members of the Ranee's Club.

Two local doctors spent entire afternoons going over basics, then trained a special batch to serve as nurses. When not in prim white tunics, mems held air-raid precaution classes among natives in the bazaar.

There was talk among the British of leaving Kuching en masse. They heard stories of horrors in China that shocked everyone, of soldiers going after girls, then cutting their limbs to pieces. They understood some things now. Why the Chinese shopkeepers had refused loans to the owners of Japanese brothels in Kuching. There were plans to send off all wives and daughters to India. Most wished they had gone there in the first place.

The garrison had already received orders to destroy everything possible before withdrawing. Fires were planned at the Borneo Company Yards, the sago factory, and the railway station. Only the locos would be spared, for they wouldn't be much good without the rolling stock. The landing grounds would be scorched. The huge tank holding millions of gallons of water would be left to run dry. The men from the Fire Brigade buried their tattered hose under a pile of refuse. 'Let them put the fires out with their bare hands!'

There was little panic as leaflets rained from the sky. At the Club, the officers read them, making faces as they imitated the 'little Jap pilot' who had dropped them.

'I wouldn't be surprised if they started dropping opium from the air. For their Asian brothers!' said Mr Awdry.

'They wouldn't need the Customs House then, would they?'

When the Punjab Regiment arrived from Singapore it was greeted with cheers. Everybody loved the Sikhs, knew they'd fall before the advancing Japs, but praised them for a fair effort. No time was wasted. Barracks were built around the suspected landing grounds, inviting spontaneous applause and much feasting. The Sikhs remained quite unmoved by the general air of celebration.

The biggest rumours floating in the bazaar concerned the priest. Father Edward Gunaratnam had been taken into custody by the Police Chief himself. He belonged to the Indian Independence League. The Japanese were his friends. They had promised to bring independence to India from the British. He was the leader of a band of conspirators, in touch with followers as far flung as Batavia and Penang.

Nobody knew where he was. The Rajah's cook reported seeing him in the Astana's grounds. He could be on a seaplane, on his way to India to stand trial.

The crowd roared in excitement. An Indian tailor's shop was torched. A jeweller's looted. Before the police could restore order, a street-cart had been overturned scattering spice, four Tamil boys made to walk on their knees on their way back from school.

Everyone had a favourite villain. For some, it was Perkyns.

Crabbe, the customs man, however, was praised. For saving the Rajah from himself.

He had not gained much out of it. 'Poor Crabbe – risked his life to save the Rajah and got stuck with an orphan!'

Sitting with their drinks on the lawn, Douglas and Ruth discussed the departures. The gardener had left the previous week, for Surabaya, casting glances over his shoulder as he went as if expecting the Japanese. Amma had talked about leaving too.

'They are leaving us to die,' Ruth said.

'To die or to starve.'

'What about Polly?'

'I'd better have the two of you sent off to a camp, I suppose.'

'And you?'

'The Rajah's officers will surrender. Peacefully.'

'What about Angel? His wife is expecting.'

'They should leave too.' He smiled, recalling a previous conversation. 'Are you thinking about going to Australia? Like the Rajah and Sylvia?'

'No. I'm thinking about Polly.'

The girl had grown to resemble them both – her face, his temper. Ruth carried her in a sarong like a Malay mother. From a distance they looked like a stalk with two buds. 'There must be somewhere we can go,' Ruth frowned. 'India? You must have relatives there.'

He closed his eyes. Where could he take them? To the roof in Jaanbazaar. A chillicracker with his mem wife and chillicracker girl.

'The English live well in India, I'm told. They get away to the hills in the summer. It's safe there. I'm sure we could . . .'

And Mahim? Was he still alive? And his Baboo?

'Then Polly could go to a convent, learn to speak like a proper English lady!'

'Ruth, I have no family, no relations. I'm an orphan.'

'You too . . .'

What about England? Too risky? They had heard stories of life in Europe. The radio talked about bombs raining over London. They had seen a picture in the *Sarawak Gazette* of a burning dockyard.

From the kitchen, they heard the sound of singing, a child's voice and an older one.

'Amma thinks we should leave.'

They turned back to the lawn, this time facing east. A whole ocean stared back at them.

From Snipe Cottage, they watched clippers arrive and depart. There was no reason to go to the bazaar – it was empty and shuttered for the most part – except to take Polly to the only surviving doctor. Over a week, the doctor changed his mind twice. The girl was perfectly healthy, he said, 'just a touch of diarrhoea'. Then, it was a more serious 'inflammation'. Medicines were short. He suggested the Fort's dispensary. For a month, their lives were ruled by despair. Ruth bathed the child with cold water, held a freshly cut banana leaf to her stomach. They rose and slept with her, Snipe Cottage coming to life only after dark. They feared everything – cholera, plague, yellow fever. But the city was calm. Kuching was unreasonably healthy. Then they suspected mosquitoes and a tent was built on the balcony for Ruth and Polly. Douglas spent his days at the Customs House sending wires to the surgeon in Singapore. But there was more disease in Singapore, more deaths. The surgeon prescribed starving the child.

'She's not yours, is she?' The doctor looked suspiciously at Ruth. Sometimes it wasn't milk or water, germs or poisoned fish that attacked health, but parents. Parents could kill without knowing.

A pirate's blood had no cure. The Chinese doctor seemed resigned. 'Why don't you take her to England?'

Silently, they watched her – a beached gull flapping her young wings. Douglas wired the surgeon again. The line was noisy. He heard waves crashing and a faint voice.

There was nothing to do but sit by Ruth in the tent on the balcony. The child's face changed colour – she looked like her pale mother. Douglas held a warm towel in his hand, should the baby shiver from the breeze. Then she stopped breathing.

They left on a day of darkness, 26 September 1941 – the one hundredth anniversary of Brooke rule in Sarawak. The celebrations started just as the men finished boarding up Snipe Cottage. Douglas sat on the lawn sipping a drink. He saw Angel and his wife wrapping up their meagre belongings. Her belly and breasts seemed to have swollen overnight. 'They don't have to leave,' he had told Ruth. 'Surely we can manage two extra berths.'

'Why would they come with us?'

He didn't know. Why wouldn't they? Could be theirs, for ever . . .

'It's better this way. I couldn't bear to look at another dead child.'

When Angel came to bid goodbye, Douglas couldn't help but notice that he was happy. He seemed eager to set off. He would become a fisherman, he said. 'Angel catch crocodiles, Tuan.'

'Don't be a bluddy pool, Angel.'

'No, Tuan.' He flashed his golden teeth.

Ruth and Douglas did not hear the Rajah read out his Constitution, nor the hushed silence that fell among the inheritors of his throne. 'By voluntarily surrendering these great powers I feel that I shall be making a contribution towards the interests and welfare of the people commensurate with the spirit in which the first Rajah received the government of this country . . .'

A siren sounded just before sunset, and kept on wailing over streets already empty from the afternoon's heat. The sky became dark. The boatman and his wife scampered to a shelter by the wharf. The passengers left too, leaving their belongings on the pier, despite the thieves. As the Sarawak colours were lowered, stones fell silent at the Dhoby's Ghaut, half-washed bundles spread out by the water like coloured crocodiles. Douglas and Ruth sat on the bench at Snipe Cottage and watched the sunset.

They waited till midnight. Then the searchlight of a clipper woke them. Douglas went over on a cutter to greet the captain. He seemed to be gone for hours. When he returned, he nodded up to Ruth. She lifted her suitcase and joined him on the pier.

'Where?'

'Canada.'

'Canada?'

The Returning Breath

The tide rose early over the Lune. From the river's mouth its roar could be heard as far inland as the Merchants' Road. Fishing boats danced over the sudden onrush. The little finger of land jutting into Morecambe Bay seemed remote, cut off from the flooded tidal road. It was a difficult river – flowing past Sunderland Point towards the sea – silting up and changing course. Unexpected islands appeared, new sandbanks vanished almost as soon as they had been formed. Bleak and windswept homes offered little by way of contrast.

It was a moment for daydreaming, and daydreamers could be seen everywhere. They even cast a spell among the newcomers like the elderly man who now lived next to Mrs Burrow and her four daughters.

They thought he had come – like the city-bred – for birds. He looked to them like a painting of a dead man, his face cold and uninviting. He never stayed anywhere long enough to strike up a conversation. It was the year of shortages, but the village grocer had a knack of coming up with miracles. 'Cigarettes, please,' Mrs Burrow's neighbour would say through the window, then he'd come out puffing madly.

Mrs Cuthill from the Second Terrace took him to be her dead husband's nephew. She would come to his small cottage with freshly baked bread, and find him lying on his bed, face turned towards the Lune. She had called him, many times, but his face remained turned. She thought he was asleep, but he kept puffing on his cigarette. She would give up, leaving the loaf on the table.

From his window, Jonathan Crabbe watched the tide, till his very last day. His spirits would rise as water filled the dirt track over the marsh, cutting off escape. The river, of course, was his friend.

And what of Hiran? The chillicracker could have found him, if he had cared to revisit Jaanbazaar. But then, who would have remembered the solitary brahmin and his old mother living on the roof, or remembered the arrival of a small white boy?

The one without desire. He became the faceless man, just like the one he had seen as a young boy in the alleys of Boubazaar, lost the undulations, resembling a shining moon. As he roamed the alleys, he must have scared the women, a ghost, searching for his Douglas, his very own, unlike the father he had never seen. The one who had never desired did so in the end. He discovered the mystery of the two Life-lines on his palms. The one to the left was shorter than the other. For an entire life he had pressed the inequality for an answer. What, he had asked himself, had lengthened his years, and why?

He found his answer. Then wondered why it had taken so long, for desire to come. Why hadn't it seized a different moment? Why? It had clouded his mind for a while, before preparing him for the return. It was the beginning of his journey – to the golden embryo he had hidden for so long in his golden womb.

Tamoso ma Jyotirgamaya
Darkness to light?

There were so many, weren't there? Hearts full of desire, and those poisoned by hate. Dispersed by the wind, hiding in the ocean like flawed seeds: a Reverend wrapped in a shallow grave three feet deep – waiting patiently under a frangipani for the Angel to rise up and fold him in the bosom of the merciful. Or a solitary Parsee praying for recompense from Fravashis descended on earth with thousands, tens of thousands of lamps.

An elderly rebel in a solitary cell waiting to hear the last footstep of a guard over a cold stone floor, believing that until the sound died, the Empire would endure. A blackie-white remembering his days in Hindoostan from the attic of an old shop in Canton's Hog Lane.

Then, the customs man, waiting for the engraver to mark an unmarked grave. Waiting for a fresh dust of snow in a land of so few, for a century of stories to end. Who would have thought? No more vexed by opposing currents, or torn between mothers, belonging to none but himself.

And God's Own Medicine? Pretty and fragile . . . what can be brighter than a field of poppy? Dancing in the breeze like ballerinas in chiffon, swirling like the divine breath itself. Stories, perhaps, were its greatest gift – rising like vapour, filling a grave with minuscule flakes. Evening out the rise and fall. They would still be there, wouldn't they, after the final mark of the chisel?

Acknowledgements

Among several books on opium, those that helped in conjuring a fiction from facts, Margaret Goldsmith's *The Trail of Opium – The Eleventh Plague* and J. M. Scott's *The White Poppy – A History of Opium* were particularly valuable, as was Jack Beeching's *The Chinese Opium Wars*, in following the ancient trade throughout Asia. Tales of the three cities – Calcutta, Canton, and Kuching – have been generously helped by H. E. Busteed's *Echoes from Old Calcutta*, J. Dyer Ball's *The Chinese at Home*, and Elizabeth Pollard's *Kuching Past and Present*, among numerous other books by nineteenth and twentieth century authors. The section on India's freedom movement has benefited from Ramesh Chandra Majumdar's *History of Freedom Movement in India*. Three wonderful books – *The China Clippers* and *The Blackwall Frigates* by Basil Lubbock, and Lindsay Anderson's *A Cruise in an Opium Clipper* – brought alive the clipper ship era. The story of the Imogene comes from A. F. Lindley's *The Log of the Fortuna*. I have been guided in palmistry by Ina Oxenford's *Complete Palmistry*, and in homeopathy by Egbert Guernsey's *Homeopathic Domestic Practice*.